About the Author

Kate McCabe lives in Howth, County Dublin where she enjoys walking along the beach. Her hobbies include travel, cooking, reading and dreaming up plots for her stories. This is her fourth novel.

Acknowledgements

The work is done, the book is finished and now all that remains is to thank the usual suspects.

To my family: Gavin, Caroline and Maura for their encouragement and inspiration.

To Marc Patton who knows everything there is to know about computers.

To the wonderful team at Poolbeg Press: Paula, Niamh, Sarah, Lisa, David and staff.

To the most scrupulous editor in publishing, Gaye Shortland.

To the booksellers for their loyalty and support.

And to you, dear reader, for once more showing excellent taste and discernment in choosing this book.

Enjoy!

For those wonderful Murphy girls, Julia, Maria and Ruth.

Prologue

Maddy wished people would simply forget about her birthday and let it slip by unnoticed. Despite all the upbeat talk about fifty being the start of her golden years and an achievement to be celebrated like winning the Nobel Prize for Literature, Maddy knew what it really meant and she didn't want to be reminded of any of that stuff.

She still felt young and energetic. She jogged every morning before breakfast. She ran her property company with considerable success as the rising profit graph continued to confirm. She was an active member of her local Chamber of Commerce and the Rotary, as well as being a keen gardener and past-President of Sutton Ladies' Golf Society. And on top of all this, she still found the time to be a full-time wife and mother. In fact, she had all the energy and enthusiasm she had possessed all those years ago when she was in her twenties and life had stretched before her filled with abundant promise. So why should she want to celebrate growing old? As her fiftieth birthday approached, Maddy fervently hoped there would be no fuss or fanfare. But she reckoned without her daughter, Emma.

Emma was her eldest child. At seventeen, she was already shaping up to be a younger version of her mother. She had Maddy's tall, elegant bearing, her luxuriant black hair and dark flashing eyes. And she had inherited much of her mother's organisational flare and drive. It was Emma who suggested they have a quiet family dinner in the Ambassador Hotel to celebrate the event and Maddy had jumped at the idea. A quiet dinner would be perfect and then she could put the damned birthday behind her and get on with the rest of her life.

The ballroom should have warned her. Whoever heard of a quiet dinner in a ballroom? But it wasn't till she actually walked through the doors that she realised what was happening. There must have been a hundred people there, neighbours and business colleagues and old friends and relations all sitting round these big tables, their faces aglow with anticipation and goodwill.

And the moment she entered, the band started to play and they all stood up and began to sing 'Happy Birthday to You' while Maddy blinked in amazement and her jaw fell open. That was when she had finally understood she had been outwitted. If there hadn't been so many witnesses she would cheerfully have strangled her daughter on the spot.

When they had finished singing, the guests burst into a round of applause and Emma gave her a great big hug and presented her with a bouquet of flowers and her son Jack pushed a giant card into her hands that had been signed by everyone in the room. Next thing she knew, they were popping champagne corks and people were coming up to congratulate her and tell her that life began at fifty and the best was yet to come. Maddy had no option but to smile and try to pretend that she was thoroughly enjoying herself.

But the birthday celebrations weren't about to end with Emma's party. Just this morning she had received a surprise email from her friend Rosie to say that she had organised further festivities – this time in London. The third participant was to be another old friend – Sophie Kennedy. The three women had known each other since their schooldays and all their birthdays fell within a couple of weeks of each other. So Rosie was proposing a joint fiftieth birthday party, just the three of them. *It's going to be a blast,* she had written. *Looking forward to seeing you again and talking over old times.*

Maddy couldn't wait to go. It had been so long since she had seen them – twenty years in the case of Sophie whom Rosie had managed to track down to Paris where she was living with a young painter half her age. Rosie herself had settled with her family in a cottage in Cornwall where she was growing vegetables and raising chickens and making her own wine while her husband held down a senior accountancy job in a nearby town. It would be lovely to meet and talk once more. Indeed, the more she thought about it, the more she realised that this was one birthday celebration she was definitely going to enjoy.

The odd thing was, when she was younger, Maddy had always looked forward to birthday parties, particularly her own. They gave her the opportunity to be the centre of attention and to wear a pretty dress and boss people around for a few hours. She got birthday cards and presents and, as a bonus, her guests had to invite her to their parties in return. But once she turned twenty-one, her interest began to fade. For one thing, the birthdays seemed to roll round an awful lot faster and they just served to remind her that time was rushing by and she was getting older. For another thing, she was beginning to develop the abhorrence of fuss that would stay with her for the rest of her life. She didn't like it when attention was focussed on her or people singled her out. She preferred to remain in the background and let others hog the limelight. And that was where she might have remained had Greg Delaney not entered her life and changed it so dramatically.

Chapter One

Maddy was twenty-five and Greg was twenty-eight when they met. She was tall and handsome with the type of figure that film critics described as statuesque. She was working for the busy auctioneering firm of Carroll and Shanley whose offices were in Ballsbridge in the heart of Dublin. It was a job she loved even though the hours were long and the pressure was hectic. But there was an adrenalin buzz about her work that compensated for all the drawbacks. Whenever she negotiated a successful property sale, Maddy felt like someone who had just won the jackpot at the roulette tables in Las Vegas.

It was through her job that she first encountered Greg. He was an investment analyst for an up-and-coming stockbroking company and looking to buy his first home. Their initial contact was a simple phone call one Thursday afternoon in May when Greg rang to say he wanted to buy a house and wondered if Carroll and Shanley could help him. Purely by chance, Maddy took the call.

"Do you have anything particular in mind?" she began.

"Not really. I'm wide open to suggestions. I thought perhaps you might be able to advise me."

"What sort of price range?" she continued, hoping for some guidance as to affordability.

"I don't mind splashing out," Greg replied, "provided I get the right place."

Maddy hesitated. Most people knew exactly what they wanted but this Greg person sounded as if he hadn't got a clue. She would need to get more information from him before she could proceed.

"Look, why don't you come in and we can sit down and have a chat? That's probably the best thing. When would suit?"

They agreed on Saturday morning and Greg turned up promptly at ten o'clock, driving a smart black BMW sports coupé. Maddy brought him into her office and asked if he would like some coffee. While she poured, she couldn't help noticing what a handsome man Greg was. He was about six feet tall with fine blond hair, broad shoulders and an infectious smile that spread all over his face whenever he got enthusiastic.

"Do you have *any* idea what you're looking for?" she began.

"Well," he said, stretching his long legs and glancing out the window where the morning sun was sparkling off the forecourt, "I'm single so I don't need an absolutely massive place."

Maddy filed this information away like a good spy.

"However," he continued, "I do a lot of work from home and I have loads of files and stuff so I would need a spare bedroom. And I'd like to be close to the city. Our offices are in Dame Street and it would be handy if I lived within driving distance."

"Plus it would be more convenient for socialising at weekends," Maddy added, just to test his reaction.

"That's right. I do quite a bit of socialising." He gave her a friendly grin.

But Maddy was busy taking notes.

"I'd prefer something new," he went on. "And another thing, I want a property that will hold its value just in case I need to sell it again at short notice."

"That makes very good sense," Maddy replied, "but I think you'll find that property is a rock-solid investment. Let me ask you something." She leaned back and played with her pencil. "Have you ever considered an apartment?"

He stared at her as if she had suddenly sprouted a second head. Apartments were a novelty in Dublin. Most developers were still concentrating on three-and four-bed houses with lawns and garages.

"Er . . . no."

"There are big advantages for someone in your situation," she continued. "You don't have to worry about garden maintenance for one thing. They are mostly owned by single people so you don't have the problem of noisy children. Not that I have anything against families," she hastened to add.

"Nor me. But I hear what you're saying."

"Apartments also tend to be more private. They have guaranteed parking. And they're very secure."

"What if I wanted to sell it again?"

"That wouldn't be a problem. Between ourselves, I think apartment living is the coming thing. And because they are high-rise, many of them have fabulous views." She decided it was time to deliver the *coup de grâce*. "And if you buy now, you would be able to have the pick of the crop."

His eyes brightened immediately and he sat up straight. "So what are we waiting for? Have you anything to show me?"

"I have several," she said, smiling broadly into his face.

The first place was not far from her office. She suggested that she drive and Greg follow in his BMW but he had a better idea.

"Why don't we use my car? No point bringing both."

"Okay," she said, settling into the passenger seat and thinking how nice it must be to own a fancy car like this.

The property was a large three-bed apartment on the second floor of a modern building in Monkstown and it boasted underground parking. It was a resale. Greg looked disapprovingly at the heavy, old-fashioned furniture that cluttered the rooms, tapped the walls once or twice, turned on the taps and flushed the cistern in the bathroom to make sure the plumbing was functioning properly.

"I was thinking you could use one of the bedrooms as an office,"

Maddy suggested. "That would still leave you a spare bedroom if you had guests to stay."

"How old is it?" he wanted to know.

"Only two years."

"So why are they selling?"

She could sense that he wasn't interested. "It was bought by a retired couple and then unfortunately the husband died."

"Oh, dear."

"Yes, it's sad. The widow is going back to live with her daughter."

Greg nodded. "You couldn't persuade her to take the furniture with her?" he said, with just the faintest hint of a smile.

The next apartment was in Ringsend in a large block fronting onto the river. That was its good feature. Its bad feature was that from the outside it looked like a prison, with rows of tiny little windows gazing sadly out on the road.

"This whole area is scheduled for a revamp," she said encouragingly. "It's going to be totally redeveloped. In a few years' time, it will be so chic that everyone will want to live here."

Greg just grunted as she showed him into the master bedroom.

"And it's practically in the city centre," she rattled on. "Yet the postal address is Dublin 4. Best address in the city. Guaranteed to increase in value."

But he didn't seem to care about the address. She could tell by the speed with which he inspected the rooms that he wasn't impressed.

"What else have you got to show me?" he asked, as she followed him out of the flat with a sinking heart.

The final property was a penthouse in Sandymount, down near the sea front. It was in a brand-new gated development called rather grandly The Beeches. When they arrived, the gardeners were busy installing a rose garden in the central courtyard. Maddy opened the front door and took him up in the lift. As soon as they entered, they found themselves in a spacious hallway, the sunlight flooding in from the big wide windows and lighting up the whole apartment.

"Wow," he said and gave a soft whistle of approval.

"Nice, isn't it?" Maddy said.

"It most certainly is."

It was a beautiful apartment – two bedrooms, one en-suite, large lounge, fitted kitchen, pine floors, pastel walls. Everything smelled of fresh paint.

"You could do a lot with this place," she went on. "Put your own stamp on it. With some nice settees, a few cushions, rugs, a couple of striking pictures for the walls, it would look fantastic."

He immediately turned to her. "Do you know about décor?"

"A little," she confessed.

But it was the terrace which took his breath away. It opened off the lounge and was paved with dark red tiles. Greg immediately walked out and peered from the balcony. In one direction, they had spectacular views across Dublin Bay to the gentle slopes of Howth Head. In the other, the teeming city lay stretched out before them, the rooftops gleaming in the bright morning sun.

"Imagine having breakfast out here," Maddy said. "Or a glass of wine in the evening with the sun doing down."

"It's fabulous," Greg said. "It's like something out of a Hollywood movie."

"Apartment living," Maddy replied. "Get the picture?"

They went back inside where Greg examined the appliances in the airy kitchen, inspected the bathroom and went back several times to the bedrooms. He appeared to be making some calculations. Maddy decided it was time to shut up and let the apartment speak for itself. He was clearly impressed. Any further sales talk would run the risk of making him wonder if she was hiding something.

At last, he turned to her. The playful mood was gone and now it was down to serious business.

"How much is it?"

"Eighty-five thousand pounds."

She waited for his reaction. Eighty-five thousand pounds was an awful lot of money to pay for an apartment. But he didn't flinch.

"I assume there are also management fees to pay."

"Yes. Four hundred pounds a year but that takes care of insurance, maintenance and security."

"Have you had any bidders so far?"

"There is one other interested party but no firm offer."

"Hmhhh," he said and ran a hand across his chin. "Let me go away and do my sums."

"Sure. Take your time."

"If you get an offer in the meantime, come straight back to me, okay?"

"Okay, Mr Delaney."

"And one other thing. Stop calling me Mr Delaney. My name is Greg."

By now, Maddy had sufficient experience of the property market to know that Greg was *seriously* interested. Wednesday arrived and she hadn't heard from him. This wasn't unusual. It took time to organise a mortgage and sort out finance. But by the end of the following week when she still hadn't heard, she began to wonder if he had changed his mind. And the other interested party hadn't contacted her either. She began to think that the property might remain on her books for a little while longer.

And then, on the following Monday afternoon, the phone on her desk rang and she heard his voice on the line.

"Hi," he said. "It's me again – Greg Delaney. Sorry it took so long but I had an awkward bank manager to convince."

"Tell me about it," Maddy trilled. "Some of them react as if you were asking for their fingernails."

"Why stop at the nails? This guy sounded as if I wanted his whole hand." He laughed lightly. "Anyway, I'm now in a position to make an offer."

"Be my guest."

"What do you think the developer would say to £79,000?"

"There's only one way to find out," she said. "I'll put it to him right away and get straight back to you."

She put down the phone and smiled to herself. Now the play was about to begin. It was like a game of poker. This was the bit that Maddy really enjoyed although it required skill and steady nerves.

She rang the developer with the offer. She wasn't surprised when he turned it down. The apartment was brand-new and the promotional campaign hadn't even got under way yet. But the developer did give her a base figure that he *would* accept.

Greg sounded disappointed when she called back to tell him.

"I'm on a tight budget," he complained. "You know I've got stamp duty and legal fees to pay on top of the purchase price. And then I've got to furnish it."

"But it's a unique property," she said. "I'll bet my salary it will start appreciating the minute you close the sale."

"All right," he sighed. "Let me see if I can squeeze some more money out of the bank."

He rang again two days later to increase his offer to £82,000.

"You're still £3,000 short of the asking price."

"Yes. But I also have to eat. If I go any higher I'll be living on baked beans for the next few years."

He put the phone down, sounding gruff and annoyed. Maddy could sense that his competitive instinct was now aroused and he wanted to win. But she had a duty to get the best price for her client.

She left Greg to simmer for a few days while she concentrated on other properties in her portfolio. She knew it would increase the pressure on him and it made her feel a little callous. But they were now locked in serious negotiations which left little room for sentiment. On the third day, he rang again. It was a bad mistake. It meant he had blinked first.

"Any news on my offer?" he asked, sounding testy.

"Not good news, I'm afraid."

"You mean they've turned it down again?"

He sounded shocked.

"I'm afraid so."

"Shit," he said, in exasperation. "This developer sounds like he's a real hard bastard."

"Well, he's not St Vincent de Paul."

"Look," Greg said, letting out a long sigh. "Just give it to me straight. What do you think it would take to swing it?"

"Another thousand."

"Are you absolutely sure? I've already invested a lot of time and energy on this venture and I don't like to be given the run-around."

"I'll tell you what," Maddy said. "Make me an offer of £83,000 and I'll personally recommend it."

"It's my final offer," Greg said reluctantly. "If this doesn't work, I'm walking away."

"I understand. Just leave it with me."

She put down the phone and rubbed her hands in triumph. She felt that warm glow that gamblers feel when their bluff has paid off. Half an hour later, she was back on the line to Greg.

"We've got a deal," she purred.

"Well, thank God for that. Now when can we sign the contract?"

She could hear the relief in his voice.

Everybody was pleased with the price Maddy had achieved including the developer and her boss, Tim Lyons, but principally Greg himself who was convinced he'd just pulled off the property coup of the year. But there were a few more weeks to wait while the legal and administrative work was completed. He rang her almost every day to find out how the sale was coming along.

By now all the tension had gone out of their relationship. Whenever they spoke on the phone, the conversation was light and cosy. Maddy began to grow quite fond of Greg and looked forward to the sound of his voice. But she was totally unprepared for the bombshell he dropped in her lap a few weeks later.

It was a bright, sunny afternoon in June. She was getting ready to take some clients to view the apartment in Ringsend which was proving stubbornly difficult to shift, when the phone on her desk began to ring.

"Yes," she said.

"Hi, it's me, Greg."

"Oh, Greg, how are you?"

"On top of the world if you want to know. I've just left my

solicitor's office after signing more pieces of paper than I've ever seen in my life before."

"So the sale has finally gone through?"

"Yes and now I'm the proud owner of a prime piece of Dublin real estate!"

He sounded like a little boy with a new train set. She could hear the enthusiasm bubbling down the phone line.

"I'm absolutely delighted for you."

"Not as delighted as I am," he replied. "I'm going out this evening to celebrate. I've booked for dinner at the Chalet d'Or. And since you helped me to buy the apartment, I'd like to invite you to join me."

Chapter Two

Maddy was delighted to accept. Greg was an interesting man and she welcomed the opportunity of getting to know him better, now that their professional relationship had concluded on such a successful note.

At this time, she was living with her parents, one sister and a brother in the family home at 15, St Margaret's Lane, Raheny. It wasn't an entirely satisfactory arrangement. Apart from the cramped living conditions, there was the question of Maddy's independence. She was twenty-five and felt embarrassed when she had to tell people she was still living with her parents.

Most of her colleagues were renting flats and were always talking about the freedom it gave them and the wonderful parties they had and the boyfriends they were able to entertain. Maddy envied them. She had briefly considered doing something similar with her friend, Sophie Kennedy, who was also living at home and desperate to get out.

But when she thought of the rent she would have to pay to some landlord, she quickly changed her mind. It would be money down the drain. It would make it even harder to afford a place of her own. So, she hung on in St Margaret's Lane while she saved hard for a deposit and kept a sharp eye out for any bargains that might come on the market, although so far nothing had turned up.

Besides, it wasn't all negative. There were some advantages to living at home. For one thing, her mother steadfastly refused to take any money from her.

"Would you get away out of that!" Mrs Pritchard would say any time Maddy attempted to raise the subject. "I wouldn't dream of it. This is your home, for God's sake!"

Her mother even had to be bullied into accepting a contribution for the food bills. She was a superb cook who prided herself on preparing good nourishing dinners every evening and a superb lunch with roast beef and four veg every Sunday afternoon after she returned from Mass. As far as food was concerned, Maddy might as well have been staying at the Shelbourne Hotel.

Mrs Pritchard also did the laundry once a week and tidied Maddy's bedroom which she shared with her younger sister, Helen. And she was always around to take phone messages and act as unofficial courier whenever Maddy wanted something collected or delivered. Really, if it wasn't for the cramped conditions and the lack of independence, she couldn't wish for a better place to live than 15, St Margaret's Lane.

But it was those cramped conditions that weighed heavily on her mind as she put down the phone after speaking with Greg Delaney. Now she had to plan for the evening. And top of her agenda was securing the bathroom for half an hour while she had a shower and washed her hair and got herself ready. She just wished Greg had given her more notice so that she could have squeezed in a proper hairdressing appointment. But he had sprung the invitation on her and now there was absolutely no chance of that.

She glanced at her watch. The couple who were coming to view the Ringsend apartment were due in ten minutes. She would have to hurry. Her big obstacle was her sister, Helen, who was doing a steady line with a car salesman called Joe Fuller and seemed to have taken up permanent residence in the bathroom. Maddy's mind went into overdrive as she thought how she could bribe her.

She lifted the phone and rang Helen.

"Hi, it's me, Maddy."

"Hello, Maddy," Helen said, cautiously. Usually when Maddy rang, it was to ask for something.

"I was wondering if you could do me a favour," Maddy began.

"Like what?"

"I've just been invited out to dinner. Very short notice, I know. But I need the bathroom this evening."

"What time?"

"He's picking me up at eight o'clock."

"Who is it? Anybody I know?"

"Oh, just a guy I sold an apartment to."

"I'm seeing Joe this evening," Helen said bluntly.

Maddy slipped into her best coaxing tone. "I thought maybe you could give me half an hour. My hair's a mess. I have to wash it or I'm going to look like a scarecrow."

"I'm seeing Joe at half eight."

"But you had your hair done at the weekend and it looks beautiful. This is an emergency, Helen. Otherwise I wouldn't ask. I thought maybe we could compromise."

"How do you mean?"

"That red cocktail dress I bought at the Brown Thomas sale. You said you'd like to borrow it."

"And you said no."

"Well, maybe we could do a deal? I'll loan you the dress if you let me have the bathroom."

Helen paused to consider. "I'd want the shoes as well."

"Of course. No problem."

"All right," Helen said grudgingly. "The shoes and the dress in return for the bathroom. But you have to be out of there for a quarter to eight, you hear? Otherwise I'll start banging on the door."

"A quarter to eight is perfect. That will give me loads of time. You're a gem, Helen."

"I know. My problem is, I'm just too accommodating. People are always taking advantage of me."

Maddy put down the phone just in time to see her clients pull into the forecourt in their blue Ford Cortina.

Getting ready was a hectic rush but at least she had the freedom of the bathroom even though Helen stood guard like a sentry outside the door till she was finished. Then, while her mother provided a nice cup of tea, Maddy disappeared into her bedroom where she frantically dried and brushed her long dark hair and hastily applied some make-up. When that was completed, she faced the agonising decision about what to wear.

First dates were pivotal, just like first viewings when selling a property. Maddy was a firm believer that initial impressions were crucial and for this date she wanted to look her best. The Chalet d'Or was a pricey and exclusive restaurant so she had better choose something quite formal. In the end, she selected a taupe dress with a low neckline that showed ample cleavage, with matching taupe heels, gold earrings and a chunky gold chain for her neck.

She examined herself in the wardrobe mirror. She looked good, better in fact than she deserved, given the mad rush to get ready. She was just spraying a touch of Chanel on her wrists when she heard Greg pull up outside.

The Chalet d'Or was across the river in Blackrock. Maddy had never been there although she had heard tales about its eccentric owner and chef, a man called Marco O'Malley. People said he didn't put any prices on his menus and had once chased a customer with a carving knife because he had complained that his steak was underdone. But it had a reputation for exquisite food. Now she was about to find out how much of that was true.

Greg pushed open the passenger door and she settled snugly beside him. She saw him glance at her with admiration.

"You look absolutely stunning," he said.

"Thank you."

"You're going to turn their heads tonight."

Maddy purred. She loved compliments. "You think so?"

"Oh, yes. People won't be able to take their eyes off you."

She laughed with delight. "Do you say this to all your dinner companions?"

"Only the beautiful ones," he said with a charming smile that revealed a perfect line of white teeth.

He started the car and they drove away smoothly up the street. He was in fine form, still excited at getting the keys of the penthouse that afternoon. He said he hoped to move in the following week and was already making plans to throw a house-warming party.

"You've made a very wise decision," Maddy said. "I don't think you'll ever regret it. You do realise you got a bargain?"

He turned to her and gave her a boyish grin. "I'll let you into a secret. I *did* get a bargain. If you had pressed me harder I would have paid the full £85,000."

Maddy said nothing. What Greg didn't know was that if *he* had pressed harder, he could have got the apartment for £81,000. That had been the developer's bottom line.

Greg was proved right. As soon as they entered the restaurant, several diners turned to stare, their eyes transfixed by the handsome young couple who had just walked in. Maddy couldn't help feeling like a celebrity. She had never eaten in such an exclusive place before and now all these people were staring at her with unmistakable admiration. But while she enjoyed the attention, she pretended not to notice. There was nothing more hateful than a woman who was full of herself.

Greg began by ordering champagne while they studied the large leather-bound menus. The rumours were correct! There *were* no prices.

"How are we supposed to know what things cost?" she asked.

He smiled. "That's the whole point. Marco believes if you worry about what things cost then you can't afford to be here."

"Sounds to me like a funny way to run a restaurant."

"Well, it seems to work. I got the last available table," he said, pouring the champagne and proposing a toast. "Here's to my new apartment!"

18

"To your apartment!" Maddy replied and they touched glasses till they made a little tinkling sound. "May you be very happy!"

He looked into her eyes. "It's all down to you, you know."

"Me?" she laughed. "I only sold it to you. You came up with the finance."

"Ah, but it was the way you sold it. You pointed out its best features. You convinced me it would appreciate in value. And the moment I stepped onto the terrace and saw that view, I was totally hooked."

"Well, I'm very glad. We like to keep our clients happy."

"Oh, I'll be happy all right. But now I need to buy furniture and drapes and stuff. I want everything to be in place before I move in. In fact, you might be able to help me."

"Yes?" she said, raising her head from the menu.

"You said you knew about décor."

"I know a little. I know what I like. But I'm not an expert."

"Well, that's perfect because I don't trust experts. They try to bamboozle you and get you to buy things you don't want. I need someone to help me choose. Say you'll do it?"

"Of course, I'd be happy to oblige."

"Excellent," Greg said, flashing his playful grin once more. "Now what are we going to eat?"

The food was superb and Maddy fully understood how Marco O'Malley had earned his reputation. She had Roquefort salad to start and roast duck for her main course. Greg opted for seafood soup and a fillet steak in a succulent béarnaise sauce. With the meal, they drank a bottle of rich dark Burgundy.

"Have you been here before?" she asked.

"A few times with clients. I've never had to pay for it before."

"I hope it's not too expensive," she said, thinking of the menu that didn't have any prices.

But Greg just laughed and squeezed her hand. "Let me worry about that. This is a celebration. Now do you think you could manage a dessert?"

The evening seemed to fly and, before she realised, it was almost midnight and time to go home.

"Thanks for a lovely evening," she said when he finally dropped her outside her house. "I really enjoyed myself."

"Me too."

He paused before planting a quick peck on her cheek.

"I'll be in touch about the décor."

"Okay. You know where to find me."

He waved as he drove away up the street.

Helen was still awake when Maddy entered the bedroom they shared. Maddy suspected she had been waiting up specially.

"Have a good night?" Helen asked in the darkness of the room.

"Brilliant."

"Seeing him again?"

"Possibly."

"What does that mean?"

"He said he'd be in touch."

"Joe and me had a row tonight," Helen groaned. "I think it's all over."

Helen and Joe were always having rows. Maddy had grown used to them by now.

"Don't worry about it. If I know Joe, he'll be on the phone first thing in the morning to apologise."

The following day she had a lunch appointment with her friends Sophie Kennedy and Rosie Blake. Sophie worked as a marketing manager for a small travel company and Rosie was in public relations. They made a point of having lunch together at least once a week.

Maddy left the office at twelve thirty and drove into town. She always enjoyed these lunches. They gave her an opportunity to catch up on the gossip while providing some relief from the hectic pace of work. But this morning, she couldn't keep her mind off Greg Delaney. She had really enjoyed his company last night and was looking forward to helping him choose the furnishings for his apartment. But a little doubt had crept into her mind. She suspected he was the type of man who used his charm to get his way with people. Was this what he was planning to do? Just pick her brains and kiss her goodbye?

The lunch was in a pub off Grafton Street. Maddy found a parking spot and hurried along the crowded pavement, then ducked down a side street. The pub was already packed but she found Sophie and Rosie at a corner table drinking gin and tonics and holding a seat for her.

"Here she is," Rosie announced when she appeared. "Mistress of the Property World. How many houses have you sold this morning?"

"None so far," Maddy said, squeezing carefully into the narrow seat.

"Ah well, the day is young. What are you drinking?"

"Mineral water. I have a viewing at three o'clock."

"A glass of wine wouldn't do you any harm," said Sophie.

"You know my form," Maddy announced. "No booze while I'm working. I have to project a sober impression."

"Well, that doesn't apply to me. I've managed to get the afternoon off. I've got buckets of leave due." Rosie waved to attract a waiter. "Two more G and Ts and a bottle of your best sparkling for our abstemious friend," she barked.

"What did you do to your hair?" Maddy said, staring across the table at the amazing confection that adorned Rosie's head. It looked like an upended bird's nest.

"I got it dyed. Do you like it?"

She fingered the frothy blond locks. Rosie was a small, natural brunette but she changed her hair with the weather.

Sophie however, was wafer-thin and almost as tall as Maddy and unlike Rosie her hair was naturally blond. She had recently had it cut in a pageboy style that gave her face a narrow, youthful look.

"I think it suits her," Sophie put in and quickly finished her drink when she saw the waiter approaching with the fresh ones.

"Yes, it does," Maddy agreed. She knew it didn't matter what they said. Rosie would probably change it again next week when she got bored.

"What are we going to eat?" Sophie asked, eyeing the blackboard where the specials were displayed. "That pasta looks good."

"What's in it?"

21

"Bacon and cream."

"Make that two," Rosie declared.

"I'll just have a sandwich," Maddy said quickly.

Her friends turned to stare at her.

"You're not on a diet, are you?" Rosie asked. "You don't need to diet. Me, now, *I* need to diet."

"I had a big dinner last night," Maddy said quietly. "So I'm not very hungry."

They turned to stare, alerted by her tone of voice.

"Dinner? You mean a dinner date? Like with a man?"

"Well, yes. I do mean a man. He was a client actually. It was to celebrate a sale I negotiated."

Their faces immediately brightened up.

"Well, that certainly sounds exciting," Rosie said, licking her lips and taking another swig from her glass. "Do tell us all about it."

For the next half hour, the two women ate their pasta and drank a few more gin and tonics while they harried Maddy for information about Greg.

"What age did you say he was?" Sophie wanted to know.

"I didn't. But he's older than me. I'd guess he's around twenty-eight."

"That's a good age. Younger guys are a pain in the ass. Either they're such babies or they're so full of themselves that they're insufferable. I find more mature guys are much more attractive."

"What sort of car does he drive?" Rosie asked.

"A BMW sports."

"Wow! That's awesome. And you say he's a stockbroker?"

"He's an investment analyst."

"What's that when it's at home?" Sophie said.

"He does the background on companies. He checks them out to see if they're a good investment, that sort of thing."

"And he's just bought a penthouse apartment in Sandymount?"

"That's right. I sold it to him."

"He must be rolling in it. Where did he take you?"

"The Chalet d'Or."

Their jaws dropped.

"My God, the Chalet d'Or!" Rosie gasped. "You need to take out a mortgage to eat in that place. That's if the mad bastard who owns it will even let you in."

"Well, I wasn't paying so I don't know what it cost. And as you probably know, there are no prices on the menus. But it was a superb meal. That much I *can* tell you."

Sophie sat back in her seat. "This guy sounds like the big *enchilada*. When are we going to meet him?"

But Maddy quickly put her hands up to silence them. "Slow down, everybody. I hardly know him. It was only a celebratory dinner. It doesn't mean anything."

"Baloney," Rosie said. "Guys like him don't waste their money unless they're after something."

"You've got to play him like a fish," Sophie said enthusiastically. "Draw him in slowly and then let him out a little bit."

"That's right," Rosie put in. "The secret is not to let him know that you're keen. Keep him guessing."

"But for God's sake don't lose him!" said Sophie. "It certainly sounds like you've hit the jackpot."

Maddy laughed. "But it was only a thank-you dinner," she protested. "For all I know I might never hear from him again."

"Oh yes, you will," Sophie said. "You take my word for it. And remember, we're always on hand to give guidance, advice and expert analysis. Free of charge because we like you."

"I'll bear it in mind," Maddy said as she called the waiter to settle her bill.

Chapter Three

She left the pub and drove straight to her viewing which was a modest three-bedroomed terrace house in Ranelagh Village. It wasn't one of her properties and she had never shown it before but a young colleague, Jane Morton, who was taking care of it, had called in sick this morning and it had fallen to Maddy to show the prospective clients around. She decided to get there a little bit early in order to familiarise herself.

The house was on a quiet tree-lined avenue called Auburn Grove.

She parked outside and let herself in and was immediately greeted with a pungent smell of mildew. This was high on the list of Nos when selling a property. She guessed that the house must have been empty for some time and the cold and damp had done their work. But by now, it was too late to take any action except to open the windows and allow in some fresh air. After she did that, she made a quick inspection of the premises. The bedrooms were fairly large but very depressing with their dreary old-fashioned wallpaper. The bathroom was in good working order, apart from a dripping tap which had left a large brown stain on the bath. A new washer and a scrubbing brush would soon take care of that. Likewise the kitchen was quite large but she saw at a glance that anyone who bought it would probably have to rip it apart and install new appliances.

The living room ran the whole length of the house and its principal feature was a nice old marble fireplace. But the furniture was grim and looked as if it had come out of a Charles Dickens novel. The front of the room faced onto the street but the back had patio doors which led out to a garden. But here again, the months of neglect had allowed the garden to become overgrown and now it looked like a wilderness. Maddy made a mental note. The house had definitely got some good features and these were what she would highlight. But there was nothing she could do about the furniture and the smell of mildew which seemed to be growing stronger despite opening the windows.

At three o'clock precisely, she heard the doorbell chime. The clients were punctual. Often they were late and sometimes they didn't turn up at all and didn't even bother to ring to cancel the appointment. Maddy quickly ran around the house closing all the windows again. No point in drawing attention to the smell, not that anyone with half a nose could possibly miss it. When she opened the door she found a middle-aged couple standing on the step with looks of apology on their faces.

"We hope we're not disturbing you," the man said. He was in his late forties perhaps and already his hair was turning grey.

"Yes," his wife agreed. "We know you're a busy person so we won't take long."

"Take as long as you like," Maddy insisted. "That's what I'm here for. I'm Madeleine Pritchard by the way. If there's anything you need to know, just ask and I'll try to help you."

"I'm Tommy Reilly, and this is my wife, Annie. I call her my better half."

They laughed and shook hands, then Maddy ushered them into the hall and closed the front door. At once, she saw the man's nose twitch and instinctively he turned to look at his wife although they didn't speak.

"This is the living-room," Maddy said, pushing open the door and walking in. The damp smell grew stronger. It must be in here, she thought, possibly dry rot.

"As you can see, it's a good size and you have these lovely patio doors opening out to the garden. It needs to be tidied up, I'm afraid. But a weekend with a lawnmower would soon lick it into shape."

She laughed nervously but the Reillys didn't appear to see anything funny. They simply nodded and stared at the ceiling where Maddy suddenly noticed a large cobweb hanging like a trapeze across one corner of the room. Next she showed them the kitchen and then she led them upstairs to the bedrooms and the bathroom. They trooped silently in and out of the rooms without saying a word until finally they had inspected the entire house.

"Take a few more minutes to look over it again," she encouraged them.

"I think we've seen enough," Mr Reilly said. "Haven't we, Annie?"

"It's not for us, you see," Mrs Reilly explained. "It's for our son. We're from Clones and he's coming up to Dublin in a few months' time to work. And we thought that rather than go into digs it would be nice if he had his own little place to come home to."

"And you were right," Maddy said, wishing she too had parents who could afford to buy her a whole house to go with the new job.

"But it's too big for one thing," Mrs Reilly went on.

"And it would need a fair bit of work done to it," her husband added. "We're really looking for something that he could just walk into. Something a bit more modern."

"I understand," Maddy said. "We've lots of other properties if you'd like to make another appointment. Why don't you take my card?"

She fished in her bag and produced a small white business card.

"We're sorry to have wasted your time," Mrs Reilly said.

"You didn't waste my time," Maddy said, brightly. "You have to buy what's right for you."

She showed them to the front door again and said goodbye with the certain knowledge that she wouldn't be seeing them again.

She returned to the house to check that everything was in order before locking up. Not for the first time, she marvelled how some vendors couldn't even be bothered to do a few basic things to help sell their properties. Like tidying up the back garden or getting rid of that damned cobweb in the lounge and doing something about the mildew smell. It was little wonder the Reillys weren't interested.

She glanced at the information brochure. The asking price was £20,000. It was a steal. The house had so much potential. Ah well, she thought as she locked the front door and walked back to her car. At that price, somebody was definitely going to get a bargain.

It was after four o'clock when she finally got back to the office.

"Any luck with the Ranelagh property?" her boss, Tim Lyons, inquired as soon as she sat down at her desk. A jovial man of about thirty-five, he didn't look too cheery just now.

"I'm afraid not. The clients couldn't get out of the house fast enough. And I can't say I blame them. The first thing to greet you is this overwhelming smell of damp."

"It's been on our books for ages," Tim sighed.

"I'm not surprised. Couldn't we persuade the vendor to brighten it up a bit? Maybe even cut the grass in the back garden?"

"It's an executor's sale. An old lady owned it. She had been living in it for years. Her family just want to sell it as quickly as possible."

"That explains a lot," Maddy said and examined the list of mail and messages that had accumulated on her desk since lunch-time.

The first thing to catch her attention was a scrawled note from the office secretary:

Greg called and a phone number. There was no time attached.

Maddy lifted the note and walked across to the secretary's desk. She was a smart young woman called Marina with hair cropped tight like a punk rock star.

"Any idea when this came in?" she asked, putting the note down on her desk.

Marina glanced at it. "Oh, that was one o'clock. He said it wasn't urgent."

"Does he want me to ring back?"

"No, he said he was going out to lunch and would ring you again."

"Thank you," Maddy said and returned to her desk where the phone immediately rang and a woman's voice enquired if she could make an appointment to see a property in Booterstown.

The remainder of the afternoon went flying by and when Maddy glanced at her watch again it was twenty past five and almost time to close up for the evening. Greg hadn't rung and she felt slightly disappointed. He hadn't been far from her thoughts all day. But she resisted the impulse to return his call. If he wanted her, he knew where to find her. So she tidied her desk, checked her appointments diary for the following day, said goodnight to the remaining staff and strode out of the office.

She was walking briskly towards her little red Fiat when she heard another car sounding its horn. She looked around and saw Greg's sleek black BMW parked across the road. He was leaning from the window and frantically waving. As soon as he caught her attention, he made a turn and drove alongside her.

"Hi," he said.

"Greg! What are you doing here?"

"I want to buy you a drink. There's something I need to talk about."

She looked into his handsome face, a loop of blond hair falling casually across his forehead.

"Can you follow me to Cassidy's?" he asked. "This won't take long."

"Sure," she said, intrigued by the mystery of it all.

Cassidy's was a pub on the banks of the Grand Canal.

Greg swung into the carpark and she pulled in behind. The pub and its garden was packed with people drinking and chatting in the bright evening sunshine.

"What would you like to drink?" he asked as he locked the car and started towards the pub.

"Could I have a glass of white wine, please?"

"Okay, I'll get it. Would you mind grabbing a table? We might as well take advantage of the good weather. I've been stuck in a clammy office all day."

She found a table and two chairs almost beside the water's edge and soon Greg was back with the drinks. He sat down, loosened the top button of his shirt and let out a contented sigh.

"Isn't this beautiful?" he said, stretching his face to the sun. "This is what I plan to do when I make my fortune and retire. Sit here all day and ruminate on life."

Maddy smiled. "I don't think so. You'd quickly die of boredom."

"But what a way to go — a nice cool drink in my fist, the sun dancing off the canal and a beautiful woman to keep me company. Who could possibly ask for more?"

She sipped her wine. Greg certainly was a flatterer.

"What did you want to talk about?" she asked.

"Furnishing the apartment, what else? I had a stroke of luck today."

"Yes?" she prompted.

"A colleague has put me in touch with a firm of designers who do the whole thing for you. Each room is fully co-ordinated. Everything matches, right down to the television set."

"Oh," Maddy said, feeling disappointed.

"I think it's a wonderful idea. It takes all the hard work out of it."

"Did you engage them?"

"Sort of. I spoke to a woman called Lorna Hamilton and she's coming out on Saturday morning to take a look at the place."

Maddy looked away. She had been looking forward to helping him decorate his apartment. Already, she had several ideas which she had been turning over in her mind.

He glanced at her. "This woman really knows her stuff. Better to leave it with the professionals. What do you think?"

"It's your apartment, Greg, and your decision. But you obviously won't be needing me any more."

"Oh no, that's not true. I'd still want your advice about colour schemes for the walls and so on. Lorna will only be co-ordinating the furniture."

"The walls seem fine," Maddy said coolly and finished her drink. "Besides, it sounds as if Ms Hamilton knows much more about these matters than I do."

She stood up.

Greg's mouth had fallen open. "Where are you going?"

"Home."

She marched back to her car.

The whole way back to Raheny, she seethed with anger. How could she have allowed herself be taken in like that? She had been right about Greg Delaney. He was obviously a spoiled brat – one of those good-looking men who had been fawned on by women since he was fresh out of nappies – and, as she had suspected, was clearly proficient in using his charm to manipulate people for his own advantage. And to think she had almost fallen for his smooth talk! It made her skin crawl with embarrassment.

In the days that followed, Maddy's anger cooled. She was busy at work so her mind was occupied with other things. Then one morning a beautifully embossed envelope arrived in the office post. She knew immediately it was an invitation. She quickly tore it open and withdrew the card.

Greg Delaney warmly invites you to celebrate the official opening of his new abode. Penthouse Apartment, The Beeches, Sandymount, Dublin 4. Drinks from 7pm. Supper at 10 p.m. RSVP.

Scrawled across the bottom in his neat handwriting was a note: *Love to see you again, Maddy. Hope you can make it.*

She stared at the invitation. Part of her was dying to go, if only to see what sort of a job this Lorna Hamilton had done with furnishing the place. But her pride held her back. She put the invitation into a drawer and got on with her work. The autumn sales season was getting under way and she was extremely busy. Everybody in the office was required to muck in designing sales brochures, answering telephone queries, arranging viewings, placing adverts in the national press and closing sales. It was one of the busiest times of the year.

Then one afternoon, her phone gave a sharp ring and she picked it up.

"Hi, Maddy," a deep male voice said.

She felt the breath escape her. "Greg!"

"Yeah, it's me. I don't seem to have received a reply to my house-warming party invitation. I thought since you sold me the apartment, you'd want to be there for the christening. Lorna's done a beautiful job on it. You'll love it. I'm even hoping we might share a glass of champagne together on the terrace as the sun goes down."

She struggled with conflicting emotions. Half of her wanted to go, to see his handsome face again, to share that romantic moment on the terrace that she had thought about ever since the day they had stood there together and looked over Dublin Bay.

"I can't," she said at last.

"Why not?"

She could hear the shock in his voice.

"I've got another engagement. But look, I wish you well. I know you'll like it there. I really hope you have many happy days."

She quickly put down the phone and realised that her heart was beating like a drum. It was over. Now there could never be a reconciliation. Greg Delaney would never contact her again.

Chapter Four

It was October and the property season was drawing to a close. All but a few of the grand houses along Shrewsbury Road had been sold at auction and most of those were now under negotiation for private sales. It had been an excellent season – one of the best that people could remember – and everyone was pleased. Some of the detached houses in the leafier parts of Ballsbridge had fetched prices of £180,000 and £190,000 – sums that were unheard of. Tim Lyons said it just went to prove that the market was on the move again. There was money around and people wanted to spend it. Everybody smiled because it meant bigger bonuses in their pay cheques just in time for Christmas.

But one property still languished unsold despite being on their books for almost a year – the three-bed terraced house in Ranelagh. It came up for discussion once again at the sales conference which was held each month to take stock and review progress.

"Any activity on that house during September?" Tim Lyons asked.

Jane Morton, whose property it was, shook her head.

"Not even a viewing?"

Jane averted her eyes. "Afraid not."

"My God," Tim said, "this is getting beyond a joke. It's becoming like a bloody albatross around our necks!"

A few people round the table giggled. It wasn't their responsibility so they could afford to be light-hearted at Jane's expense.

"I've seen it," Maddy reminded him, coming to her colleague's defence, "and it needs a lot of work. There's a bad smell of mildew the moment you open the front door and that immediately puts people off."

"It's an executor's sale," Jane explained. "So nobody's really taking responsibility."

She looked miserable, as if she would do anything just to get this burden off her hands.

"We'll have to do what we always do in these situations," Tim announced, briskly. "Reduce the price. Put it back on the market at £15,000. And if that doesn't work we'll just have to offer it as a prize in a Christmas cracker."

Everyone laughed and they moved on to the next business.

But something had been stirring in Maddy's mind. As they filed out of the conference room to go back to their desks, she invited Jane to have coffee with her. They went to a new café that had recently opened across the road.

"Thanks for defending me back there," Jane began as soon as they were seated with their coffee. "I feel like a total fool. But they should know that I can't just drag people in off the street and force them to buy."

"Of course, they do," Maddy said, "and they're all secretly praying that it never happens to them. But you know, it's a shame about that house. If it had some work done to it, I'm sure it would sell."

"I've spoken to the solicitor. There are only two surviving relatives, an elderly brother and sister who live in Leitrim. I don't think they've ever been to Dublin in their lives. They couldn't be bothered. They just want the house sold and the money divided up."

Maddy gazed off into space for a moment.

"Do you think you could hold off for a few days?"

"Of course, I could. You heard Tim Lyons back there. I've been holding off for nearly a year."

"I think I know someone who might be interested."

Jane's face immediately brightened up. "Oh! Who is that?"

"Me," Maddy said.

That afternoon during her lunch break she went to see her bank manager. She had been saving steadily and now had almost £6,000 snugly lodged in a deposit account.

"If I wanted to buy a house how much money could I borrow?" she asked.

"Depends on several things," the manager said. "Such as the cost of the house, your salary and future earning capacity and, of course, the condition of the property."

Maddy had already done some rough calculations. The house in Ranelagh would need at least £4,000 spent on it and possibly more if the damp problem proved to be serious. And then there would be stamp duty and legal costs.

"The house I have in mind is on the market for £20,000 but I might be able to get it for less. I have £6,000 saved with you already. I think I would need to borrow around £16,000."

The bank manager took out a calculator and did some sums.

"The repayments on £16,000 would come to almost £180 a month. What is your current salary?"

Maddy told him.

"You could just about manage it," he said. "But remember you'll have insurance payments as well. And before we agree to anything we would have to get a valuation report carried out. You would also pay for that."

"So what do I have to do?"

He fished in his desk for an application form. "First thing is to fill this up and return it with a copy of your annual salary signed by your employer. Then we can start the ball rolling."

Maddy left the bank as if she was walking on air. Granted, £180 a month was a big chunk of her salary. But at least she would have her own house. She would be free at last. No more fighting with Helen to use the bathroom. And Ranelagh was a very good address.

It was close to the city and well served with shops and restaurants. Everything she had learned in the property business told her it was an up-and-coming location and wasn't that the auctioneer's mantra? Location! Location! Location!

Her brother Brian had a pal called Paddy Behan who was a builder. That weekend, she persuaded them to come out to Ranelagh to examine the house.

The builder arrived in his van complete with ladders and tools and equipment.

"The first thing is to find the source of that damp smell," Maddy said, as she let them in.

It didn't take Paddy Behan long to locate it. He used a ladder to climb onto the roof. Twenty minutes later, he climbed back down again.

"Leaking gutter," he explained. "The rainwater is just cascading straight off the roof and penetrating the walls. It looks like it's been going on for years."

"Is it a big job?" Maddy asked, anxiously.

"Fixing the gutter isn't a big job but you'll probably have to insulate the walls."

"What sort of money are we talking about?"

"Twelve hundred pounds should cover it."

Maddy made a mental note. "Okay, would you mind looking at the rest of it?"

Paddy Behan spent another hour examining the house from top to bottom, tapping on walls with a lump hammer and crawling under the sink to examine the pipes.

"The building is structurally sound," he said at last. "It's not going to fall down. But the window frames need fixing. You'll have to replace the plumbing. There are tiles loose in the bathroom. And I would strongly recommend installing central heating. Plus the whole place could do with a fresh coat of paint."

"And the cost?" she asked with beating heart.

He took a notebook from the pocket of his overalls and sucked a pencil stub while he did some calculations. At last, he looked up.

"Six thousand pounds."

He saw her lip quiver.

"But since you're Brian's sister, I'd be prepared to do it for five and half."

"That would cover everything?" she asked anxiously. "Labour and materials? No hidden costs?"

"Everything."

"And how long would it take?"

Paddy Behan laughed. "You women are all the same. You always want everything done immediately. It will take me six weeks – if the weather holds up."

"Okay," Maddy said with a sigh of relief. "I'll get back to you."

Her next move was to talk to Jane Morton again.

"I think this is slightly unorthodox," Maddy said apologetically, "seeing as we both work for the same company."

"Nonsense," Jane replied. "We've been trying to sell that property for ages. And you heard Tim telling me to reduce the price."

"Well, I'd be prepared to offer the £15,000 Tim suggested. Why don't you ring the vendor's solicitor and see how they react?"

Jane came back later in the afternoon with a happy grin on her face.

"They're delighted to accept. They're so keen that they practically suggested I lock you in a room in case you try to escape."

"It would be subject to loan approval," Maddy added cautiously. "I'll have to borrow most of the money."

"Of course. We can put that into the contract."

Despite her nerves, Maddy felt her spirits begin to lift. The prospect of owning her own home was inching ever closer.

"Just let me talk to Tim," Maddy said.

Tim Lyons was in his office. Maddy and he had always got on well together.

"That property in Ranelagh," she began.

"The haunted house? The one we can't even give away?"

"I'm thinking of making an offer for it myself. Have you any problems with that? On ethical grounds, I mean?"

He scratched his chin. "I don't see why not, provided the vendors accept. It's not as if we're attempting to cheat them. We've spent months trying to shift it and nobody is interested."

"So you have no objections?"

"Not at all," he laughed. "Be my guest. Go right ahead."

That evening, Maddy sat at her dressing-table and completed the bank application form. She had already asked Tim Lyons for an income statement and when he gave it to her the following morning she was pleased to note that he had slightly inflated her bonus and commissions.

"It's called creative accounting," he said with a friendly smile. "It won't do your chances any harm. Good luck."

She spent her lunch break returning the form to the bank manager and contacting a young solicitor called Conor Black whom she had got to know through her work.

"I'm putting in a bid for a house," she explained. "So you can expect a contract to arrive one of these days. The agreed price is £15,000 to include contents, not that they're worth very much. But the really important thing is to make sure there's a clause in there making the sale subject to loan approval. I'm relying on the bank to give me the money."

"Don't worry," he said. "I'll see that it goes in."

That night, Maddy went to sleep with dreams of her house foremost in her mind. She had already told her parents what she was planning to do and while her mother looked a little sad at the prospect of losing her eldest daughter, they all knew it was inevitable and certainly for the best.

There was one final thing to do. The bank manager had told her the house would have to be valued and inspected before any decision was taken about giving her a mortgage. And he had said the inspection would take place some day next week. Maddy was determined not to leave anything to chance. That weekend, she borrowed the keys from Jane and the whole family piled into her little Fiat armed with brushes and shovels and clippers and shears.

Her father and brother spent most of the weekend clearing away all the overgrown brambles in the garden and cutting the grass while Mrs Pritchard, Maddy and Helen gave the interior a thorough cleaning till the windows shone and the rooms sparkled, so clean that you could eat your food off the floor. As one last act of insurance, Maddy produced a large canister of air freshener and systematically sprayed each room to mask the mildew smell.

Now all she could do was sit back and wait.

But it wasn't easy. Her nerves were as taut as piano strings as the days slowly ticked away. Now she knew how all those clients must have felt as they waited anxiously for the outcome of offers they had bid for properties. She had set her heart on this house. She had visions of doing so much with it: growing roses in the garden, planting interesting vegetables like courgettes and aubergines, sanding the floors, making new curtains, buying nice modern furniture, redesigning the bathroom and the kitchen, painting the walls beautiful cool pastel shades.

She would never be bored because there would always be so much to do. It would be her home, her refuge to return to each evening after a busy day out in the big wide world. She would own a small part of Ireland Inc. And she knew in her heart that before long Ranelagh would become a very desirable location. People would flock to it and curse themselves that, unlike her, they didn't have the foresight to buy when they had the chance.

But as the weeks slipped by and nothing happened, she began to be tormented by doubts. What if the vendors had changed their minds and decided not to sell? What if the bank turned down her loan application? There were so many things that could go wrong – things over which she had absolutely no control.

Then one morning she got a call from Conor Black.

"The contract has arrived," he said, cheerfully, "and it seems in order. Now I just have to conduct some searches."

"Searches? What does that mean?" Maddy asked, sounding nervous.

"It's routine," Conor explained. "Before we part with your hard-earned cash, I have to satisfy myself that the people who are selling the house actually own it. It's to prevent any messy problems down the line."

"Oh, I see. How long will that take?"

"A couple of days. It's all part of the service."

"And then what happens?"

"If the searches are clear, we sign the first part of the contract and lodge 10% of the sales price. At that stage we have a binding agreement."

"Okay. So there's nothing more I can do?"

"Afraid not," Conor laughed. "Just sit back and enjoy the experience."

Now she had to endure more waiting. But at least the legal side of things appeared to be moving along and she had confidence in Conor.

At last she got the phone call she had been waiting for.

"They've agreed," he said. "The bank has approved your loan."

Maddy let out a squeal of delight and jumped up from her seat so that everyone in the office stopped what they were doing to stare.

"It's a standard bank approval letter," the solicitor went on. "Everything is totally in their favour. They are loaning you £16,000 to be repaid over a term of 20 years. The repayments are £185 per month to include the premium on a life insurance policy. That's in case you pop your clogs in the meantime. Oh, and one other thing. If you fall behind with the payments they retain the right to repossess the house. They've got all the angles covered."

"I don't care," Maddy said, joyously. "When can we close the deal?"

"Friday?"

"Friday is perfect."

"Okay. I'm going to courier this bank letter straight round to your office. Sign it and send it back with the courier. I'll contact you before Friday to arrange a time to complete the sale."

Maddy put down the phone and buried her head in her hands. Suddenly she felt deflated, like the air going out of a burst tyre. All the tension of the past few weeks was oozing away. She was about to become the owner of her own house. When she lifted her head again she could feel her eyes were rimmed with tears so that she had to make her way quickly to the bathroom to wash her face.

She would never forget Friday. She had asked Tim Lyons for permission to leave at four and she drove straight to Conor Black's office in Lower George's Street. Here she sat across a vast old-fashioned desk and signed innumerable documents till her wrist felt sore. Finally, Conor gathered all the papers together, tied them with a red ribbon and handed her a set of keys.

"Congratulations," he said. "You're now a property owner. May I wish you luck?"

In the pub next door, her family was waiting along with Sophie and Rosie and her colleague Jane. Someone had ordered champagne and soon they were clutching flutes of sparkling bubbly and clapping her on the back and shaking her hand and telling her how lucky she was. Plates of sandwiches appeared and before long her father was singing 'Dublin in the Rare Ould Times' and the evening settled down to a party. The last thing Maddy remembered was Rosie, whose hair was now dyed red, dancing with a tall young man in a business suit she had picked up at the bar.

Paddy Behan took longer than he had promised – eight weeks instead of six – but partly this was due to a spell of rain towards the end of November and the intervention of the Christmas holidays. Anyway, people kept assuring her, builders never kept to deadlines and eight weeks was really very good for the work she was getting done.

She had promised herself to stay away because she knew that builders hated people getting under their feet. But she couldn't resist a few secret visits to Auburn Grove to see how the work was coming along. On the first occasion, the front garden looked like a building site with ladders and wheelbarrows and cement mixers littering the lawn but gradually the place began to take shape.

The walls were stripped and insulated. The plumbing was ripped out and replaced. New electric wiring was installed. The kitchen was redesigned and the bathroom retiled. The old, rotting window frames were replaced and modern radiators fitted. At last, in the final week of January, the work was completed. The house had been completely restored. It looked nothing like the dreary dungeon she had first viewed six months earlier. And instead of the overpowering smell of mildew, the first thing to meet her when she opened the front door was the smell of fresh paint from the gentle pinks and yellows and blues that decorated the walls.

She had Paddy Behan's cheque in her purse. She thanked him and paid him his fee and then on impulse, she withdrew a £50 note from her wallet and told him to buy his men a drink. It was insurance in case she ever needed him again. He looked surprised and suitably grateful.

That evening, her brother Brian helped her move a spare bed and a suitcase of clothes into the house. She could ferry across the remainder of her belongings in the days and weeks ahead. Her sister Helen kissed her and said she would miss her but Maddy knew she couldn't wait to get the bedroom all to herself. Mrs Pritchard got emotional and said Maddy was the first of her little chicks to fly the nest and it made her feel sad but Maddy promised to keep in touch and come regularly for her Sunday lunch.

Finally, at eleven o'clock, with the streetlights casting shadows on the front windows, she poured herself a glass of wine and looked around the refurbished house. She had her own home at last. For the first time in her twenty-five years living in Dublin she was going to sleep in her own bed under her own roof.

Even though she didn't know it at the time, she had just completed the wisest investment she would ever make in her life.

Chapter Five

But Maddy didn't get to enjoy her new freedom for long. Within a matter of weeks, Sophie brought up the idea of moving in with her. It didn't come as a total surprise since the two women had previously discussed sharing a flat together. The proposal came one Friday evening in the lounge of the Pink Parrot pub, a week after the house-warming party when Maddy had invited thirty friends to inspect her new home and view her designer handiwork. She had carefully chosen the furniture and the drapes, the rugs for the polished bare-wood floors, even the large porcelain vase with the dried flowers that stood in the empty fireplace.

She put similar care into choosing her guests. She wasn't going to have a crowd of yahoos trampling all over her new house, spilling wine, stamping out cigarettes on the rugs and being sick on the bathroom floor. Those who were invited included Rosie and Sophie, her family, several colleagues from work and some of her neighbours.

Everyone adored the house. At one end of the large living-room she had laid out a cold buffet of meat cuts and salads and a selection of desserts and had splashed out £100, which she could barely afford, on several cases of good quality wines. Her only regret was that it wasn't yet warm enough to set up a barbecue in the garden and hang lanterns from the trees. But that would come. When the weather improved she planned to start work on a patio and turn it into a little oasis of tranquillity.

The evening was a great success. Maddy had opted for subdued lighting from several table lamps strategically placed throughout the house and pleasant background music from the stereo set. The guests brought household gifts – table linen and cutlery sets and ornaments – which she deposited along with their coats in one of the bedrooms. They wandered throughout the house clutching glasses of wine and uttering loud sighs of admiration. But the topic which gave rise to most conversation was the price she had paid. No one could believe that she had secured this lovely house for a mere £15,000.

"You stole it," one guest said in wide-eyed astonishment. "What did you do? Blackmail the vendors?"

"Well, actually, it was the other way round. They were delighted to get it off their hands. And I did have a lot of work to do – it was in a terrible condition when I bought it."

"I can vouch for that," Tim Lyons put in. "At one stage, we seriously considered raffling it."

People laughed but she noticed several friends looking at her with renewed respect while others agreed that what Maddy had done was obviously the clever way to go.

"You buy an old place with potential and you do it up. That's the sensible thing," she heard one young couple say. "Ranelagh is such a lovely area. And it's absolutely bursting with good schools."

It was all music to her ears. It vindicated her judgment and the risk she had taken with the house. She tried to remain cool and unassuming but she couldn't help the warm feeling that swept over her when people congratulated her and said how much they envied her.

By one o'clock the last of her guests had gone home and only Sophie remained. The two women sat in the kitchen and finished off a bottle of wine.

"I hate you," Sophie said, her jaw drooping slightly which Maddy had come to recognise as a clear indication that her friend had had too much to drink.

"Why? What have I done now?"

"You've got this lovely house and I'm stuck at home with my mother who treats me like a fourteen-year-old schoolgirl while you're mistress of all you survey. And you're only twenty-five."

"Twenty-six in a few weeks' time," Maddy corrected her. "The same as you and Rosie. Which reminds me, are we going to have a meal to celebrate?"

"God, I don't know," Sophie groaned. "I'm coming to dread birthdays. Here's twenty-six looming on the horizon and not even the promise of a decent man. By the way, whatever happened to that guy you were seeing? That stock-market genius or whatever he was?"

Maddy had been wondering when the subject of Greg Delaney would surface again.

"I wasn't seeing him," she replied. "He bought me dinner to thank me for helping him with his apartment. I told you it was only business but you wouldn't listen."

"It doesn't matter," Sophie slurred. "It's so unfair. You get to have dinner with these fabulous men and all I get is Chinese takeaways. And now you've got this lovely house."

Maddy laughed. "You could do it too. But first you've got to start saving some money. Once you've scraped a deposit together, the bank will lend you the rest."

"How can I save money on my piddling salary?" Sophie declared. "I can barely keep body and soul together."

"You earn as much as me. There's no big secret. It's just a matter of spending less than you earn."

"That's easy for you to say. I'm already overdrawn at the bank and I'm only halfway through the month."

"We'll talk about it in the morning," Maddy said, suddenly feeling very tired. "Now, why don't you get some sleep? There's no point trying to organise a taxi at this hour. You can spend the night in the spare bedroom. You'll be my very first overnight guest."

"Can I? And use the power shower in the morning?"

"Of course, you can. That's what it's there for. And I'll cook you pancakes with syrup for breakfast and properly brewed coffee. You get premium service in this house."

Sophie threw her arms around her friend in a drunken embrace. "I take back everything I said. You're such a pal. What did I do to deserve a friend like you?"

Maddy gazed into Sophie's cornflower eyes, now befuddled from too much wine. She felt a powerful surge of love and affection for her friend.

"You're my pal too, Sophie. You're loyal and caring and reliable. And that means an awful lot to me. All you've ever got to do to remain my friend is simply be yourself."

But the discussion with Sophie made Maddy aware that some people might be more than just envious. They might actually be jealous of her. She had a lot of things that many women would wish for: she was reasonably good-looking, she had an interesting job and now she had managed to secure a lovely home. There was only one thing she didn't have and Sophie had touched on it in her drunken ramblings. She didn't have a regular boyfriend.

Since her refusal to attend his party, she hadn't heard another word from Greg Delaney. She assumed that by now he was well settled into his penthouse in The Beeches, no doubt with a succession of girlfriends tripping in and out of its well-appointed bedrooms. Greg was the type of man who would have women flocking to him. But not her! She thanked her lucky stars that she had retained enough good sense not to get more closely involved. She had no wish to become another notch on his belt or his bedpost or wherever it was that he kept a tally of his conquests.

But becoming a homeowner did have one serious downside. It meant she now had to curtail her social life. She had a mortgage to maintain and bills to pay and food to buy since she could no longer rely on her mother's hospitality except at weekends when she drove out to Raheny to see her family and eat Sunday lunch with them all.

So instead of pubbing and clubbing several times a week, she was forced to restrict herself to Friday nights, which was how she now came to be sitting in the lounge of the Pink Parrot with Sophie and

Rosie. Later they would hit the dance floor of the Left Bank club in Harcourt Street and let their hair down.

"You know, I've been thinking," Sophie said as she took a large gulp from her gin and tonic. "You've got two spare bedrooms."

"That's right."

"Both lying idle and running up heating costs."

"Go on."

"Would you consider letting one of the rooms to me?"

Maddy thought quickly. The additional income would make a welcome contribution to her household finances and she would certainly welcome Sophie's company.

"I'd pay you a reasonable rent," Sophie continued. "And I'm clean and tidy and I wouldn't make a racket or bring home unruly friends."

"Are you sure you wouldn't miss your mother?"

Sophie snorted. "Are you kidding? It would be like getting out of jail."

Everyone laughed.

"If you rented from me it would make it harder to save for a place of your own."

"Oh, to hell with that," Sophie said, polishing off her gin and tonic. "I'm never going to afford my own place. The way things are going I'll just have to snare myself a rich husband."

"You should be so lucky," Rosie said and they all laughed again.

"Tell you what, give me a few days to think about it," Maddy said.

The following week, she took an early lunch break and met Sophie in the Bits and Bagels delicatessen in Baggot Street. She had spent the intervening period carefully considering her friend's proposal.

"What would you consider a reasonable rent?" she began.

"I'm not sure. We could split the mortgage repayments."

"That would be £90 a month."

"I can afford that."

"But it wouldn't be fair. I own the house. I should pay the lion's share."

"Okay, what do *you* suggest?"

"What would you say to £60 a month and we split the household bills?"

Sophie's face lit up with delight. "I'd say 'Halleluia, Praise the Lord!'"

"There would have to be certain ground rules," Maddy went on. "No mad parties. No loud music. No pets. I've got my neighbours to consider. And we'd need to work out a roster for the bathroom," she added, remembering her experiences with her sister Helen.

"You've got a deal. When can I move in?" Sophie asked excitedly and looked around for a waiter to order another round of drinks.

The move was completed the following weekend. Sophie arrived in a taxi with three large suitcases of clothes, a box of music tapes and two paperback books – *How to Find your Man and Hold Him* and *Lifestyle Tips for the Single Woman*.

Maddy took one look at the luggage and gasped.

"What are you planning to do, explore the source of the Amazon? You've certainly brought enough supplies."

"There's more," Sophie said, sheepishly, "but I can pick it up in the next few days."

"At this rate, I'll need to get an extension built on to the back of the house. Come in. Make yourself at home."

Things worked out like a dream. Sophie was true to her word. She was clean and tidy. She didn't leave dirty dishes piling up in the sink. She did her share of the household chores, emptying the rubbish, vacuuming the floors and dusting the shelves. She did her laundry once a week and ironed and folded everything away in her cupboards. She didn't camp out in the bathroom and she paid her rent and her share of the bills religiously. And she allowed Maddy her own space so that on those occasions when she had office work to do, she was able to retreat to her bedroom and remain there undisturbed. If she had drawn up a CV for the perfect housemate, she couldn't have found a better candidate than Sophie.

Not that they lived separate lives. Far from it! Now that she had finally got out from under her mother's smothering influence, Sophie discovered that she liked to cook. She bought a big book of recipes and every weekend she tried out a new dish – with astonishing results. Her Chicken Korma was a runaway favourite. Every Saturday night they fell into the habit of opening a bottle of wine and dining in front of the television while they watched a movie they had rented from the video store. Maddy soon came to realise that she really enjoyed having Sophie around the house and would miss her if she was gone.

It didn't take Sophie long to gain enough confidence to graduate to dinner parties. The first one was a nerve-wracking experience, even though there were only four of them – Sophie, Maddy, Rosie and Jane from work who had missed the house-warming party and was anxious to see how Maddy had renovated the house she couldn't sell.

Maddy had advised Sophie not to be too ambitious so she opted for a fairly basic menu – smoked salmon and capers on a bed of lettuce for starters and pork casserole in a white wine sauce for the main course. For dessert, they bought a chocolate gateau from the local supermarket. Since it was the first dinner party they had ever given, Maddy decided to use up a couple of bottles of the good wine left over from the house-warming.

The evening went off brilliantly, even though poor Sophie sweated gallons from fear and tension. Maddy set the table with a white linen tablecloth and laid out her best glasses and cutlery – presents that various guests had given her. She turned down the lights, put U2 on the sound system and lit the candles in the middle of the table. The scene looked like something from a five-star restaurant and the meal went down a treat.

"You've really transformed this house," Jane said after she'd been given a tour of inspection. "I wouldn't recognise it. The place I remember looked like that house in *Psycho*."

"It just needed a little touching up," Maddy said.

"Don't be so modest," Jane scolded. "What it really needed was someone like you with lots of vision and imagination."

"And a good builder," Rosie put in.

"Well, of course. But without Maddy's flair it would have remained what it was – a very neglected property that would gradually have fallen apart. Now it's a highly desirable residence. I'd say if we put it on the market again, we'd easily get £50,000 for it."

"Why don't you find one for me? Why don't you find one for all of us?" Rosie laughed.

Maddy shrugged. "I was lucky, that's all."

"No," Jane said and squeezed her hand. "You were far-sighted. And that's not something that grows on trees. That's a gift, my girl."

The party progressed to gossip and inevitably to boyfriends. Rosie's latest beau was a music journalist called Paul who was able to get tickets to all the major concerts. But the drawback was that he worked erratic hours and travelled a lot so that she never knew when she might see him.

"And then I've got all these groupies to contend with."

"Groupies?" Jane said in astonishment. She was going out with a staid civil servant called Clive who worked strictly nine-to-five. "I thought they were only interested in the performers?"

"They're interested in anything in trousers, most of them. And because the music hacks get to mix with the celebs, they become minor celebrities themselves. Anyway, I'm not so sure I fancy him any more. I'm looking for somebody who's a bit more solid and reliable."

It was after two o'clock when the dinner party finally broke up. Everybody agreed it had been a wonderful evening and Sophie's cooking had been superb.

"I had a meal last week in the Terrazo," Jane said. "You know, that fancy place on Stephen's Green that everybody is raving about? Well, I can tell you, hand on heart, the food wasn't a patch on yours. And the bill came to £80. I wasn't paying, I might hasten to add."

Sophie glowed with pleasure.

Maddy rang for a taxi for Rosie and Jane who were travelling in the same direction and when her guests had finally departed she poured two glasses of Bailey's Cream and sat back on the settee.

"Congratulations. That was a great evening," she said to Sophie. "They weren't kidding when they said your food was superb."

"It was nothing."

"It was brilliant, that's what it was. We'll have to do it again."

"I tell you what," Sophie said, suddenly getting all enthusiastic.

"Why don't we draw up a list of people we want to invite and then we'll have great fun matching them together?"

"Yes," Maddy said. "That's a marvellous idea."

"And next time, I'll be a bit more adventurous. That's how you develop, by trying something new every time."

By three o'clock they were ready for bed. Together, they carried the dishes into the kitchen and placed them in the sink. Maddy was about to break one of her golden rules but she was just too tired.

"Let them soak overnight. I'll wash them in the morning. You did all the work tonight."

Five minutes after her head hit the pillow, she was fast asleep.

One morning a few days later, she got a phone call from Rosie at work. It was a call she had been half expecting.

"Hi," Rosie began in her bright, cheery voice.

"Hi, Rose."

"You know, I've been thinking. Ever since the night of that brilliant dinner party . . ."

"Yes?"

"Well, you've still got one spare bedroom."

"And you might be interested?"

"How did you guess?" Rosie asked with astonishment.

"Woman's intuition."

"Well, I would definitely be interested. In fact, I'd be very keen. You and Sophie seemed so warm and cosy in your lovely house and I'm still stuck with my parents. And I'd be no trouble. Honest. I'd be quiet as a mouse and I'd pay my share of everything."

"You don't have to persuade me," Maddy interrupted. "You're one of my best friends. Of course, you can join us."

"You mean it?"

"Sure I do."

"Oh, Maddy, I can't wait! When can I move in?"

"Just as soon as we sort out the details. I'll talk to you in a day or two."

"Whoopee!" Rosie warbled. "I feel like I've just won the Lottery!"

Chapter Six

In February, a senior executive in the auctioneering firm of Carroll and Shanley retired after thirty years. The man, who had been with the firm practically from the beginning, was replaced by Tim Lyons who was popular and well-liked. Then Tim's job as supervisor of the sales staff became the centre of intense speculation. After weeks of deliberation, the directors offered the position to Maddy.

She was as surprised as everyone else. She hadn't lobbied for the promotion. She was by far the youngest candidate and she was a woman, which was possibly her biggest drawback in an era before equal opportunities had arrived. Privately she attributed her good fortune to old Mr Shanley, one of the founders of the firm who had hired her and had always taken a keen interest in her career. Other directors were known to be diehard male chauvinists and there were dark mutterings from some of them about hormonal imbalances and premenstrual tension and what was likely to happen if she ever got pregnant and had to take time off to look after a child.

Maddy was well aware of the criticism because it was a small office and she had loyal supporters who kept her fully informed. But once she decided to accept the promotion she was determined to make a success of it. She knew that not only was her own career at stake but the prospects of lots of other women as well. If she failed, her detractors would be able to shrug their shoulders and say: "There you are. That's what happens when you ask a woman to do a man's job."

The new position carried heavy responsibilities. By now the firm was expanding and Maddy was put in charge of recruiting and supervising a staff of negotiators. These were the front-line troops – the people who took responsibility for individual properties from drawing up the promotional material, organising advertising, conducting viewings, negotiating prices and closing sales. And business was brisk. The promise that had been evident in the autumn campaign had carried through into the spring. In the week after Easter alone, the firm sold fifteen properties – a record in its long history and the cause of a celebratory drinks reception for the staff.

But the rewards were good. Maddy was given a hike in salary, an expense account for entertaining important clients and a company car – a brand-new silver Audi – fully taxed and insured and with a generous petrol allowance. She was able to sell her old red Fiat. For the first time in her life, she had no financial worries. The contributions that Sophie and Rosie made to the rent and the household expenses had greatly reduced the costs of Auburn Grove and Maddy was suddenly able to bank a good slice of her salary.

One of the first things she did was go out and buy a new wardrobe. She was now an executive and she needed to look the part. Besides, her job would call on her to deal with developers and builders, men (and they were *always* men) who thought nothing of spending millions of pounds on a new housing scheme or a block of apartments and who talked in the kind of figures that made her head swim. In addition, a new type of client was now entering the market – the investor who dealt not in one or two dingy inner-city flats but whole swathes of apartments and who wanted to buy off the plans before the units were even built.

Now Maddy began to appear in the office dressed in designer outfits and business suits with padded shoulders. She made a point of a weekly trip to the beauty salon to have her hair and nails treated and avail of a facial.

But it wasn't simply about appearance, important as that was. She also had to master the art of dealing with six problems at once and holding several telephone conversations at the same time while remaining calm and always finding space to listen to problems or offer a friendly word of advice. And she carried it off brilliantly. No wonder her staff loved her and held her in awe. No wonder they started to call her Superwoman.

She loved her new job from the very outset. She loved the challenges and opportunities it brought. And amazingly, no matter how hard she worked, no matter how long her day or how stressful, she never seemed to run out of steam. She put it down to jogging. It was becoming a craze. Everybody seemed to be flying around town in track suits and running shoes. The standard joke in the office was that you were in more danger from joggers in the Phoenix Park than you were from muggers.

Shortly after she took up her promotion, Maddy went out and bought several track suits, a portable radio so she could listen to the news and a cape for those inevitable rainy days. She spent more on running shoes than she would ever have spent on a pair of designer shoes because a coach she consulted had stressed their importance.

"Shoes are the most important piece of equipment you can buy. They'll save you from torn ligaments, damaged cartilages and a host of other injuries. Even if you have to jog naked, make sure you always wear good shoes. And wherever possible, try to run on grass."

Every morning at seven o'clock, her alarm clock went off. By ten past seven she was out on the road, running three or four miles before returning to Auburn Grove, a hot shower, and a breakfast of muesli, toast and coffee. By a quarter past eight she was driving her silver Audi towards Ballsbridge and by a quarter to nine she was sitting behind her desk, perfectly poised, immaculately groomed, half a dozen problems under control and her working day planned to the last second.

It seemed to work. Maddy never got flustered. She never lost her temper. She never felt tired. And there were other benefits too. No matter how many boozy lunches she was forced to endure with builders and developers, no matter how many late-night dinners with investors, she retained her perfect figure, her trim waistline, her firm thighs, her pert breasts and the shining brightness in her face that proclaimed inner health and well-being.

But she did miss one thing – the cut and thrust of negotiating, the adrenalin buzz that she used to experience when she concluded a successful sale. That was why she liked to relax in the pub on a Friday evening with her sales staff while they recounted the week's adventures and Maddy relived the excitement and offered advice or cheered them on with words of encouragement.

"Every soldier needs a little R and R," she would say, implying that they were all engaged in a battle to see which company would win the biggest slice of the profits that were suddenly becoming available in the property market.

Her success with Carroll and Shanley didn't go unnoticed. The Dublin auctioneering world was a small place and word travelled fast. But she was taken aback by a development that occurred a few months later. She got an invitation to lunch from the rival company of O'Leary and Partners.

It was Marina with the punk haircut who took the call. In the reshuffle she had been promoted to be Maddy's personal assistant.

"It's a Mr Peter O'Leary," she said in a hushed voice. "He says you should know him. He says it's highly confidential."

Maddy certainly did know Peter O'Leary. He was the patriarch of the O'Leary auctioneering business which had grown from humble beginnings into a chain of offices which stretched throughout the city. She had a vague memory of being introduced to him once at an industry function but apart from that single occasion they had never met before.

"I'll take it," she said to Marina and reached for the phone.

"Hello, Peter," she said in a confident tone, wondering what on earth this could be about.

"Maddy, good to talk to you. How are you keeping?"

Peter O'Leary sounded as if he had known her all his life.

"I'm fine, thanks. And you?"

"Still breathing in and out," he said with a wheezy laugh. "I'd like to buy you lunch some day. When are you free?"

"When did you have in mind?"

"The sooner the better. I'll clear my diary."

This *must* be important, Maddy thought quickly to herself. Peter O'Leary clearing his diary for her!

"If it's urgent, I could make it tomorrow," she said.

"Tomorrow is fine. Let's say the Shelbourne Hotel. One o'clock. Present yourself at the reception desk. And Maddy…"

"Yes, Peter?"

"I'd prefer if you didn't mention this lunch to anyone."

My God, Maddy thought as she put down the phone. Sounds like something James Bond might get up to. Maybe he's going to give me a gun disguised as a Biro and ask me to assassinate the Soviet ambassador.

The following day, she left her office at twelve thirty and drove the short distance to Stephen's Green and the imposing edifice of the Shelbourne Hotel. At one o'clock she was at the reception desk but when she looked around she could see no sign of Peter O'Leary. She spoke to the duty clerk who immediately stopped what he was doing and said politely: "Would you follow me please, madam?"

Maddy followed him up the stairs and along a narrow corridor till at last he stopped outside a door, knocked politely, then pushed it open and ushered her in.

A thin, frail old man, dressed immaculately in a finely tailored pin-striped suit, grey waistcoat and tie sat alone at the head of a large dining-table which had been set for two people. A smaller table covered in a white cloth stood in a corner. On it were several bottles of spirits, a bucket of ice and glasses. The clerk bowed politely, closed the door and withdrew.

Peter O'Leary rose from his chair, came to meet her and took her hand. He was charm itself, smiling gallantly at his young guest.

"How good to see you, Maddy. You're looking extremely well, if I may say so. I'm so glad you could come."

"Thank you."

"Would you care for something to drink?"

"Mineral water," Maddy replied.

"I think I'll join you. Bit early in the day for the hard stuff. Although there was a time when I could have polished off six Manhattans before midday and then enjoyed a good bottle of Beaujolais at lunch."

He smiled as he poured and handed her a glass.

There were two large menus on the table.

"Would you like to order something to eat before we get down to business?"

Maddy studied the menu in silence as she tried to come to terms with her surroundings – a private room, deliberately chosen so that no one would see them dining together. Whatever Peter O'Leary had to say to her must be terribly important, she thought.

"I'll have the lamb cutlets," she decided at last, putting down the menu.

"Would you care for a little wine with that?"

"No, thanks. I'll stick to water."

"I'll have the same." He lifted a phone on the table beside him to give their order.

"Business brisk?" he then inquired of her, resuming the small talk.

"Hectic," Maddy replied. "I've never known it to be so busy."

"We're coming out of the recession," Peter O'Leary announced. "The country is moving again and the population is growing. There's no big secret about it. It's basic economics."

In what seemed like no time at all, there was a polite knock on the door and two black-suited waiters appeared wheeling a cart with a large silver platter. They silently served the meal, then bowed and departed, leaving Maddy and Peter O'Leary alone again.

"*Bon appétit*," he said, starting to eat.

They continued to talk about industry developments as the meal proceeded while Maddy's curiosity grew. At last, after coffee had been served, Peter O'Leary straightened up.

"You're probably wondering what this is all about."

"Let's say, I'm intrigued."

"I've been watching your career and I have to say I'm very impressed. Carroll and Shanley appear to be making serious progress in the last six months."

"I think everyone is doing well," Maddy countered. "Not just us."

"But some are doing better than others. I believe a shake-out in the industry is overdue. A lot of the smaller agencies will be swallowed up. Some will go to the wall. Call it economies of scale, if you like. But in a few years' time, the property scene will be dominated by a small number of key players. And we intend to be one of them."

He paused while he slowly chewed a piece of meat but he kept his small, gimlet eye firmly fixed on her so that Maddy began to feel slightly uncomfortable.

"What I am about to say to you must remain strictly confidential."

"Of course, you have my word."

"I want to offer you a job."

Maddy felt her heart skip a beat but she tried to remain calm.

"Doing what exactly?"

"Much the same as you're doing now. I want you to reorganise our sales team. Some members of the staff have been too long in the job. They've lost their competitive edge. They wait for business to come to them instead of going out and actively pursuing it. Others have lost interest a long time ago and are simply coasting along relying on old contacts in the industry. That might have been okay once upon a time but not any more. I've watched how you have shaken up Carroll and Shanley. I like your style and the way you have managed to motivate your staff and bond them into a team. I'd like you to do the same thing for us."

He finished speaking and picked up his glass.

Maddy took a deep breath. This was praise indeed, coming from someone of the eminence of Peter O'Leary.

"I'm flattered," she managed to say.

"Don't be. You've worked hard. But some things can't simply be attributed to hard work. Some things are natural, like leadership, for instance. From what I know of you, you've got that in abundance."

She felt the colour rise in her cheeks. "I don't know what to say."

"I know you won't come easily," Peter O'Leary continued. "You've been with Carroll and Shanley for your entire career and you obviously feel loyalty towards them. I admire that. It's a good quality. So I would be prepared to make it worth your while."

"Tell me."

"I know your present salary."

"*Really?*" Maddy was amazed. Peter O'Leary had obviously gone to a great deal of trouble to research her background.

"I'd be prepared to double it."

She struggled hard not to gasp.

"I'd pay you a handsome commission based on all sales."

"All sales? In all your branches?"

"That's right. You'd be responsible for them. If I pay you commission it gives you an incentive to achieve results."

"This all sounds very generous," Maddy managed to say.

"I'm not finished. There would be the usual perquisites such as pension scheme, company car and expense account. Plus, after a reasonable probation period, say twelve to eighteen months, I would be prepared to make you a director."

It was with enormous difficulty that Maddy managed to maintain her composure. This was an amazing offer. The opportunity to continue doing something she loved and with salary and conditions that a few months ago she could scarcely have dreamt of!

"I expect you will want some time to think about it," Peter O'Leary said, rising from the table and producing a card from the pocket of his waistcoat. "That's my personal number. If there's anything you need to clarify, don't hesitate to ring me."

He held out his hand and warmly shook Maddy's.

"Thanks for the meal," she said. "And your generous offer. I'll certainly give it serious consideration."

"I hope you make the right decision. I would thoroughly enjoy working with you. In a few years' time, O'Leary and Partners are going to be the premier agency in the country. I'd like you to be on board. But whatever you decide to do, I expect you to keep this conversation confidential."

She left the Shelbourne Hotel with her head reeling. The lunch with Peter O'Leary was the most amazing thing that had happened in her entire career. She was so excited that her legs could barely carry her down the steps of the hotel. On her way back to the carpark she passed a little bar. She decided to break one of her rules and have a gin and tonic while she tried to digest what had just occurred. She found a quiet corner table and toyed with her drink while she played the conversation over again in her head. Reorganising O'Leary's sales team, doubling her salary, commission, perks. And the opportunity of a directorship in eighteen months' time! It all sounded too good to be true.

She desperately needed to seek advice from someone whose judgment she trusted. But this was a decision she would have to make entirely on her own. She had given her word to keep the conversation confidential although she knew it was going to be one of the hardest things she had ever done.

Her first instinct was to ring Peter O'Leary this evening and accept. An opportunity like this might never come again. But she had learned not to trust first instincts. There were so many things to consider, so many angles. She knew the staff at Carroll and Shanley. She had recruited many of them herself in recent months and they were loyal to her. They understood each other. They worked well together.

On the other hand, people at O'Leary and Partners were bound to resent her. She was a newcomer. People would be jealous and possibly rebellious when she began the work of reorganising the sales team. Peter O'Leary had hinted that dead wood would need to be pruned and that would be painful and potentially bloody.

She knew she could do it. She knew she had the will and the determination for the task. But did she *want* to? Did she need the hassle and the heartache? Did she want the bitterness and the treachery and the inevitable tears when people were told they were going to be demoted, passed over or even lose their jobs? She wasn't sure that she did.

She finished her drink and stood up. This wasn't a decision that could be made lightly. At the very least, she would have to sleep on it.

She walked to her car feeling a little better and more clear-headed. Despite all the conflicting emotions, one thing stood out and it gave her enormous satisfaction. Her work had been noted and approved by no less a person than Peter O'Leary, doyen of the Dublin property scene.

The following morning she rose at her usual hour and went for her jog. She showered and had breakfast and then called the office to say that she was going to be late. She waited till Sophie and Rosie had set off for work then sat down at her desk with a pen and paper and drew a single line down the page. On one side she jotted down the pros of Peter O'Leary's offer; on the other the drawbacks. On one side, she put the salary and conditions, the prestige, the promised directorship and the experience the job would bring. After undertaking this task, she would be able to walk into any auctioneering position in the city and name her terms.

On the other side, she put the cons: the blood, sweat and tears, the drain on her emotions, the hollowness and the inevitable guilt she knew she would feel when the job was done. She stared at the paper for a long time while she struggled to make up her mind. But what convinced her in the end was none of these things. It was her sense of loyalty to her colleagues – to Tim Lyons and Jane Morton, to Marina and the eager-beaver sales team she had recruited and moulded. But most of all she felt loyalty to Mr Shanley who had protected her and given her her first job as a fresh-faced schoolgirl. How could she leave them and walk away to join the opposition? How could she live with herself after doing a thing like that?

Part of her said she was a fool, that this was a once-in-a-lifetime opportunity. Nevertheless, she lifted her phone and dialled the number Peter O'Leary had given her and after thanking him profusely, she politely turned down his offer.

Chapter Seven

But Maddy's job promotion wasn't all excitement and glamour. There was a dull side too. Now she had to sit through boring meetings where people talked endlessly about projection targets and revenue graphs. She knew that much of it was necessary if the firm was to plan ahead but she was itching to get into the thick of things and do what she liked best – selling property.

By now, Rosie had settled smoothly into the household at Auburn Grove. The house-sharing was working out brilliantly. Everyone was respectful of the other person's space and privacy. They all mucked in with the household chores. They shared the bills and they had each other for company and support. It was ideal. And her friends were capable of pleasantly surprising her as she discovered one weekend a few weeks later.

It was a sunny Saturday morning and normally Maddy would have begun the day with a brisk jog. But Tim Lyons had organised a seminar for the staff at a hotel in County Meath and Maddy was expected to attend. To complicate matters further, the three friends had spent a boisterous night pubbing and clubbing so Maddy was still fast asleep when the alarm-clock sounded at eight o'clock.

The seminar was to be an all-day affair with lunch. Maddy had doubts about the usefulness of these events. She was firmly convinced that the best way to motivate the sales staff was by encouragement and the prospect of handsome commissions but Tim had insisted they all attend. If nothing else, he said, it would give them an opportunity to bond, a buzz word that seemed to be doing the rounds quite a lot recently.

Maddy cursed the fact that she was doomed to spend such a lovely day in a stuffy conference room instead of in her back garden where she was hoping to start work on the patio she had planned. She had gone as far as drawing up some designs and getting quotes from Paddy Behan. But first, the garden had to be licked into shape.

Since she had moved in, the garden had almost reverted to its primitive state and already they were halfway through the summer. So, before she could do anything, she knew she would have to spend a couple of weekends hacking and digging. The one positive feature was that the weather was now drier and the days were longer and the builder had assured her that the work of laying the patio would take a few days at most.

She arrived at the conference venue slightly out of sorts, to find that most of the staff had got there before her and were sporting large delegate's badges with their names printed on, which struck her as silly since they all knew each other already. She had a bad feeling that this was going to be one of these seminars where they were bombarded with reams of information but learnt very little. She grabbed a cup of coffee and an information pack with a shiny new pen stuck in the flap. More waste of money, she thought as she took a seat at the back of the room beside Tim Lyons.

"You're going to enjoy this," he said, grinning all over his face. "I'm told this guy is hot stuff."

I hope you're right, she thought grimly. Otherwise, I've wasted my Saturday.

The man conducting the seminar was a middle-aged Londoner in a loud suit. He was described on the promotional material as a consultant. Maddy had learnt to be wary of that word. Too often in her experience, it meant the man had been let go from his previous job and had decided to set up on his own.

He began by telling a couple of ribald jokes about an Englishman and an Irishman which drew some astonished looks from the staff. Don't tell me he's going to patronise us on top of everything else, Maddy thought with a sinking heart. But despite her misgivings, she gradually began to warm to him. He clearly knew what he was talking about. She glanced once more at the man's biography in the information pack and discovered that he had been the chief negotiator for a leading firm of London auctioneers. She recognised the name. They were a top-drawer agency who dealt in the kind of properties that Arab sheiks on a spending spree in London might be interested in.

"Remember at all times that you're working for your client," he said. "The client is the person who is paying your fee. That means that you always go for the best deal and not the quickest deal. But you also have a responsibility towards the purchaser. A person who believes he got good treatment will spread the word. A person who believes he was cheated or conned will also tell others. And believe me, he will tell more of them. And he'll speak with more conviction. That's why I keep stressing that you go for the *best* deal – the deal where all the parties are happy."

Maddy glanced around the room. The audience was sitting up and paying attention. Some of them had already brought out their pads and were taking notes. When the time came for a coffee-break at eleven o'clock, the speaker was surrounded by people wanting to ask questions.

Maddy found herself standing beside Tim Lyons.

"Well?" he asked, cautiously. "What do you make of him so far?"

"I think he's very good," she confessed. "I had my doubts but I must admit this guy seems to know the business."

Tim was delighted with her praise. His face broadened into a smile.

"Just goes to show," he laughed. "You *can* teach an old dog new tricks."

She got home shortly after six o'clock, feeling jaded after the drive and the long day sitting in the conference room. Now, she was looking forward to a nice cool glass of wine and a chance to put her feet up and empty her mind in front of the television for a couple of hours.

But instead she found Sophie and Rosie in the back garden wearing old tee shirts and jeans, busily pruning back branches and digging out brambles and weeds. Already they had assembled a large pile of dead wood in the centre of the lawn. They stopped to wipe the sweat from their eyes when they saw Maddy get out of her car.

"What on earth are you doing?" she asked.

"Cleaning up the garden," Rosie said with a grin.

"Yes," Sophie added. "It was such a nice day that we thought we'd make a start."

Maddy took a look at the progress they had made. Already the garden was beginning to take shape. A couple of sparrows and an aggressive little robin were hopping about in the debris in search of food.

"You didn't need to do this, you know. I'm sure you had better things to do."

"Like what? Ironing our clothes? We live here too, remember," Rosie said.

Maddy gave each of them a hug.

"I'm very grateful. It looks fantastic. You must have been working very hard."

"We've enjoyed it," Sophie said. "Besides, we thought we needed some exercise."

"Why don't you take a break and we'll have a couple of beers?"

While they pulled off their gardening gloves, Maddy went back into the house and returned with some ice-cold Buds. She brought some of chairs from the kitchen and they sat on the lawn and watched the huge orange sun begin to sink in the sky.

"How did your seminar go?" Sophie asked.

"Better than I thought," Maddy admitted. "The guy who was taking it certainly knew the ropes. And the staff seemed to enjoy it."

"So it wasn't a total waste of time?"

"Not at all, I picked up a lot of tips. But you know, selling property is just like anything else. You can only absorb so much theory. In the end, you've got to go out and do it." She stretched her legs and took a long pull from the beer. "This is beautiful. Think what it will be like when we get the garden cleaned up and the patio laid."

"Do you feel like continuing tomorrow?" Rosie asked. "I checked the weather forecast. It's going to be another good day like today."

"That's a great idea. Why don't we take advantage of the dry spell? Between us, we'll make a huge dent in the work."

"We'll start early," Sophie added. "Say nine o'clock?"

"You're on," Maddy said as she closed her eyes and sighed.

The following morning they were up early and ready for action. After breakfast, they began the task of clearing the remaining debris. They worked steadily till six o'clock and by the time they had finished, the job was almost completed. They had managed to dig out all the rambling creepers and briars, trim back the hedge and build a rockery at the bottom of the lawn. As a result, the garden now looked about twice its original size.

"I think that's all we can do for now," Maddy said as they packed all the waste into large black bin liners. "Once Paddy Behan has laid the patio, we can reset the lawn and we'll have our little oasis of calm. I'll ring him first thing Monday morning."

Sophie had agreed to cook dinner, so she had a quick shower then disappeared into the kitchen while Maddy and Rosie sat in the garden and drank beer. By the time they too had showered and changed their clothes, the meal was ready.

"Hope you like it," Sophie said. "It's nothing special."

"I don't care," Rosie announced. "I'm starving. I'm so hungry I'd take a bite out of a baby's leg."

Sophie had cooked a coq au vin and the succulent smell was all over the house. To accompany it, she had made a plain salad with French dressing and cut a basket of fresh bread.

Rosie took one mouthful and rolled her eyes. "My God, this is absolutely delicious. I'd be happy to live here just for the food alone."

"Have some wine," Sophie said, filling her glass and clearly pleased at her reaction.

"Let's have a toast," Rosie said.

"Okay, what do you suggest?"

"Let's toast ourselves. To us."

"To us," Maddy said. "Forever friends!"

The phrase seemed to strike a chord. Everybody laughed and touched glasses.

"Forever friends!" Sophie said. "May nothing ever come between us!"

The builder came and laid the patio. The three women reset the lawn and before long a nice green carpet of grass swept down to the rockery where the shrubs and plants were already taking root. Maddy had her oasis of calm and tranquillity where she sat in the evening after work and enjoyed the warm summer sun. She had her two best friends around her and they were all getting along famously.

They gave dinner parties and weekend lunches and had great fun matching the guests. And Maddy's career continued on its successful path. She was working very hard but achieving results and her financial situation was healthier than it had ever been. The summer slowly blended into a glorious autumn and the leaves began to fall from the trees.

One evening, she sat on the patio and watched the sun setting like a ball of fire in the western sky. The air fell silent and the only sound was the chirping of the birds on the lawn. She watched as the sun slowly slipped below the horizon.

I have never been happier, she thought. Never have I felt as contented as this.

Chapter Eight

It was a balmy afternoon towards the end of September. It had been a bumper season for sales, good prices achieved, including several record figures for properties in the Dublin 4 area, healthy bonuses and commissions earned and everybody happy. Now they were into the autumn again when the days grew shorter and darker and even the smartest house looked drearier than it had in the bright days of summer.

Maddy was busy taking an inventory of properties that had somehow got left behind and were now languishing on their books, properties that would need an extra bit of effort to shift in the next few months before December drew near and everything went flat.

She looked up quickly as Marina approached her desk.

"I've got a Mr Delaney on the phone."

Maddy gave a start. The only Mr Delaney she could think of was Greg and she hadn't heard from him for over a year.

"Did he ask for me, personally?"

"Yes. He says he's a friend."

"Put him on."

The minute he came on the line she recognised the deep, masculine, self-assured voice. It was Greg all right.

"Hi, Maddy," he began. "How is life treating you these days?"

"Very well, thank you. And how are you?"

"I'm working too hard, as usual. But I'm not complaining. In my business, that's a good way to be."

"You must be well settled into The Beeches by now, Greg. You must be one of the longest residents."

She heard him laugh.

"You got it. The units have all been snapped up. Not a single one left. You were right, Maddy. You told me if I got in early I could have my pick of the crop. And that's exactly how it turned out."

"Well, I'm very pleased. We always try to keep our clients happy."

"You've certainly got one contented bunny right here," he chuckled. "Actually, it's about The Beeches that I'm ringing you."

"Oh?"

"I want you to sell it for me."

She caught her breath. It was barely sixteen months since Greg Delaney had bought the penthouse. He had been over-the-moon about it, regarding the purchase as a triumph for his investment skills. And now he wanted to sell it. She wondered what had happened in the meantime.

"Certainly, I'll put you in touch with one of my colleagues."

"You don't understand," he said. "I want *you* to sell it."

Maddy paused. "That isn't possible, Greg. I don't conduct individual sales any more."

"Why not?" he demanded.

"I've got a different job now. But my colleagues are all skilled negotiaters. I can vouch for every one of them."

"No," he said firmly. "It's you I want, Maddy. I bought it from you and I was very impressed with the way you handled it. Now I want you to sell it for me."

"But I just explained . . ."

"I could take it to another agent – but I don't want to do that. I'd prefer if Carroll and Shanley had the business. But it has to be you, Maddy. No one else will do."

She hesitated. Greg Delaney's penthouse had undoubtedly risen in value since he bought it and shouldn't be too hard to sell despite the lateness of the season. And she didn't want to lose the business to a rival firm. It looked as if he had her in a corner.

"All right," she said at last. "I'll make an exception in your case. But first I'll have to view it again."

"That's no problem," he said, brightening up. "Just tell me when would suit."

They made an appointment for the following afternoon at three. Maddy wanted to see the penthouse in daylight to get a firm idea of its potential, particularly since Greg had got professional help with the décor. He said he would take the afternoon off and work on some business from home.

She put the phone down with an uneasy feeling. Something about Greg's manner had alarmed her, particularly the threat to take the business elsewhere. It sounded a bit too close to bullying for her liking. Nevertheless, she turned up the following afternoon at the appointed time and parked her silver Audi in the bay outside the apartment block. She was dressed in one of her usual work outfits – a smart, black business suit with white blouse and scarf and a pair of stylish designer shoes. As she emerged from the car, she stood for a moment to take in her surroundings.

She hadn't been here for some time, not since the original sale to Greg when the complex was in the final stages of completion. Now it had the confident look of a mature development. The rose garden was still in bloom. Parked around her, she saw the signs of wealth and success – the BMWs and Volvos and Mercedes which were the trophies of the new rich. Her trained eye told her immediately that she would have little difficulty selling Greg's penthouse if they pitched the price right, particularly since it was one of the best in the development.

She pressed the entrance-hall buzzer and immediately heard his voice on the intercom.

"Hi, Maddy, come on up."

There was a click as the doors opened and she entered the hall. It was spotlessly clean. A bank of letterboxes ran along one wall while a couple of plants in large ornamental tubs stood guard on the white marble floor beside the gleaming lifts. She pressed the button and the doors slid open and she stepped in. A minute later, she was emerging on the top floor.

The door to his apartment had been left ajar but she knocked politely before hearing his command to enter. He was emerging from the smaller bedroom, shaved and groomed and wearing casual slacks and a navy golf shirt. He looked as handsome as ever and was still sporting his trademark grin. He immediately took her hand and clasped it warmly.

"You look . . . marvellous," he said, staring deeply into her eyes.

"You look good too, Greg."

"For how long?" he chuckled. "The rate I'm working, I'm going to go down with a coronary any day soon." He smiled. "Coffee?"

"No, thanks. I'll just look over the apartment if that's okay and then we can discuss the details of sale."

"Fine, fine. Where do you want to start?"

"Why don't I begin right here in the hall?"

She took out a notebook and pen and began to make notes. Immediately, she could see around her the evidence of Lorna Hamilton's handiwork – the sleek, modern, minimalist furniture that graced the spacious hallway, the large abstract painting on the wall opposite and the clean lines of the décor. It was the same thing in the lounge and the bedrooms, the smaller of which Greg had converted into an office with a desk, word-processor, fax machine and filing system. Ms Hamilton had certainly done a good job. Maddy would have to give her full marks for that.

They finished up on the terrace where Greg had installed a wrought-iron table and four chairs. Maddy glanced at the breathtaking view over the bay and the city sparkling in the afternoon sun. This was the feature that had most impressed him when he was buying.

So far, he had been silent. Now he spoke.

"So, what do you think?"

"I think it's magnificent. That lady you got to advise you certainly has very good taste.

"Lorna?"

"That's right. Your apartment looks like something out of the pages of *Homes and Gardens*."

He beamed with pleasure. "What do you think it would make?" he asked eagerly.

"You bought it for £83,000, right?"

"Correct."

"Sixteen months ago?"

"Yes."

"I'd say you should double your money."

"How much?"

"£160,000 with a bit of luck."

At once, she saw a look of disappointment come over his face.

"Maybe £165,000," she added quickly.

"I was hoping it would get more," he said.

"It might if you held off till the spring but right now we're heading into the flat season. People don't normally buy property in the winter. They have too many things on their minds, including Christmas. Besides, properties look better in the spring. Any chance you could hold it for six months?"

He was vigorously shaking his head. "Not possible."

"It has to go now?"

"Yes."

"Okay," she said. "There are still a few punters about and I know several people I can contact personally who might be interested. I'll get to work at once drawing up a brochure and placing some ads. I suggest we put it on the market at £170,000 and see what response we get. We can always reduce the price if we don't get a bite."

"I would prefer £200,000."

Maddy stopped. Two hundred thousand was far too much. Even for an apartment as good as this. She just hoped Greg wasn't going to be one of those vendors who thought they knew better than the auctioneer. They had made her life a misery in the past.

"That might be too high," she said carefully.

"It's worth it. I don't want to give my apartment away for less than its true value."

"But we have to be realistic. There's no point pitching the price higher than the market will bear."

"Two hundred thousand," he insisted.

She glanced at him. He was determined. It was obvious that he wasn't going to be persuaded to lower the price.

"All right," she said. "I take my instructions from you. Now are you planning to include the furniture in the sale?"

"What do you think?"

"It's beautiful furniture," she conceded. "It will certainly improve the selling potential. I suggest you leave it open. Some people prefer to install their own furniture while others like to buy a place they can walk straight into. If we get a buyer and they show interest in the furniture we can do a side deal."

"Perfect," Greg said, brightening up.

"Now for our terms. We charge 1.25% of the selling price plus VAT at 21%. Plus we will bill you for any advertising we place on your behalf."

"And how long do you think it will take?"

She shrugged. "Who knows?"

"I'd like it all wrapped up by Christmas," he said.

Maddy felt another dart of apprehension. "Christmas?"

"Yes. That's my deadline."

"Well, I'll certainly do my best."

She drove straight back to the office and spent the next hour working on a sales brochure. She had all the room dimensions from the original sales material but now she added her own creative flourishes, describing in glowing terms the sleek décor, the exclusivity of the development, the modern kitchen and bathrooms with their gleaming appliances and the *coup de grâce* – the terrace with its stunning views over the city. The first objective was to entice people to view the apartment. Once they had seen it, they couldn't fail to be impressed.

When she had finished, she handed her notes to Marina and asked her to arrange with Greg to have publicity photographs taken and then get all the material over to the printer. It was after six thirty when she finally left the office and headed for Auburn Grove. Neither Rosie nor Sophie was at home so she had the house to herself. She had a shower, got out of her work clothes and dressed in some casual things, then went into the kitchen and rustled up a mushroom omelette and salad for supper. She poured a glass of wine and settled down in front of the television to catch up on the news.

She was feeling strangely uncomfortable. The reappearance of Greg Delaney had unsettled her. She wished he hadn't come looking for her to sell his penthouse. She had a bad feeling about it. Something in her bones told her there was trouble ahead.

The following morning she returned to work on the backlog of properties that remained unsold – the job she was doing before Greg had diverted her. She was planning a final advertising push and had convinced several owners to lower their prices a little in the hope of luring in some potential purchasers. And she was also hoping to persuade her favourite property journalist, Paula Matthews, to give her some editorial coverage in return for the advertising spend.

At half ten, when she judged that Paula would be safely at her desk with a mug of coffee, she rang her number.

"Hi, Paula. It's Maddy here. I've got good news. We're planning to take out a three-page spread with you in next week's property supplement."

"Well, that will certainly cheer up the accountants," Paula replied in her usual tone of tired cynicism.

"I was hoping you might be able to give us a bit of a write-up. Give the properties a little push."

"Hang on while I open my Dictionary of Superlative Clichés. *Bijou residence in quiet cul-de-sac* to describe a damp bed-sitter in Harold's Cross? Is that the sort of thing you have in mind?"

"Yes, Paula. That's it exactly. Just brighten up my tired old prose. Sprinkle a little of your creative stardust."

"Get out of here," Paula groaned. "One of these days you'll get me prosecuted by the Trades Descriptions police for assault and battery on the English language."

"All we're doing is bringing the properties to the attention of the general public. We're not forcing anyone to do anything they don't want."

"I'll see what I can do."

"And I have a special favour to ask. This one won't need any jazzing up. I have a fabulous penthouse coming on the market in Sandymount. The Beeches. You know it?"

"Of course, everyone knows The Beeches."

"Well, this is one of the best units in the development. Less than two years old and furnished exquisitely. Fantastic views, fitted kitchen. Believe me, it will write itself."

"When can I view it?"

"I'll give you the vendor's number. Why don't you ring him and make an appointment?"

"Okay."

"And Paula . . . be prepared to have your socks knocked off."

She put down the phone with a satisfied smile. Despite her cynicism, Paula knew how the property market worked. The day her supplement came out, sales of the paper increased dramatically because even if they weren't interested in buying, people still loved to read about houses.

She spent the rest of the morning ringing around several potential buyers. The first call was to a recently retired doctor called Charles Murphy who wanted to sell his large house in Dun Laoghaire and move to something smaller and closer to the city.

"Hi, Charles," she began. "I have a property that might interest you."

"Yes," he responded, eagerly.

"The Beeches in Sandymount."

"I know it. Good location."

"And this one is a beauty, a two-bed penthouse with amazing views. It might be exactly what you're looking for."

"What are they asking?"

"It's going on the market at £200,000."

"That's an awful lot of money for an apartment."

She heard the enthusiasm drain out of his voice.

"But this one is special, Charles. You really have to see it."

"I could have bought one a couple of years ago for £85,000 except I wasn't ready to move."

"There's been a lot of inflation in the market in the meantime."

"But not that much. That's more than double what they sold for."

"It has the DART train practically on the doorstep. No need to drive into town."

"No," he said, finally. "It's too rich for my blood. I think I'll pass. But keep me posted. Try something a little cheaper next time."

The next few calls elicited the same response. People just thought she was asking too much. Even for a penthouse in The Beeches. Even for one that Maddy pitched with such enthusiasm. Damn Greg Delaney, she thought. She was going to have a struggle on her hands to sell his penthouse for anything approaching £200,000. And he wanted it all wrapped up by Christmas. Why didn't he listen to what she had to tell him?

By a quarter past one, she was feeling hungry. She left the office and drove into Ballsbridge where she had a pub lunch in one of the local hostelries. The bad feeling she had the previous evening, was beginning to return. Selling this apartment was going to be a mammoth task which would eat up a lot of her time and energy. She wished she had told him to take a hike when he first called instead of allowing him to bully her into taking on a job she didn't want.

By five past two when she returned to the office, Marina was waiting.

"Mr Delaney rang when you were out."

"Oh!"

"He wants you to ring him back immediately. He says it's urgent."

"Right," Maddy said, slipping off her jacket and hanging it in her closet.

She got Greg at once.

"Hi," she said. "You were looking for me."

"Yes, I was," he snapped. "What the hell is going on?"

"How do you mean?" she gasped.

"I got a call half an hour ago from some hack wanting to come and tramp all over my apartment. And before that I had someone else wanting to come and take pictures."

"That was Paula Matthews. I asked her to give you a call. And the pictures are for our sales brochure."

"Well, you had no authority. I don't want people walking in and out of my home as if it was the Dandelion Market!"

Maddy recoiled in shock.

"You should have consulted me. I have my privacy to think about," he continued in an agitated voice.

"She is doing us a favour," Maddy managed to say. "I'm trying to persuade her to give us a write-up in her property supplement. It will help with the sale. But she can't write about something she hasn't seen."

"I'm paying *you* to sell my apartment," he barked. "Not some scruffy journalist."

"You haven't paid me anything," Maddy retorted angrily.

"You'll get your commission from the sale."

She had heard enough. Greg Delaney hadn't bought her. She didn't have to sit here and take this abuse.

"That's *if* there is a sale. And the way you're behaving there won't be. Now if you want me to continue with this transaction, I strongly suggest that you get off the stage and let me handle it my way. Otherwise you can find someone else to sell it."

There was a stunned pause on the other end.

"I'm sorry," he said at last. "I've never sold a property before. I didn't realise."

"It's more complicated than you think," Maddy said, still furious. "When you're selling your home you've got to be prepared for some disruption. In fact, the more disruption you have, the better, because it means people are interested. Now, can I ask you to relax and let me take care of this? And would you please arrange an appointment for Paula Matthews to come and see the place?"

"Okay," he said in a sheepish voice.

"And one other thing. Why are you selling? People are going to ask me."

"Oh, didn't I tell you?"

"No, I'm afraid you didn't."

"I'm getting married."

Chapter Nine

The news that Greg Delaney was getting married left Maddy stunned. Somehow, it had never occurred to her. She had convinced herself that he was destined to remain a bachelor – a charming, handsome, spoiled and occasionally arrogant man – but definitely not a marriage prospect. Now, she realised how foolish she had been. Greg was much too fine a prize to remain unclaimed for long.

She put down the phone and stared off into space. Now the events of the last few days were beginning to make sense. She assumed that the wedding was scheduled for some time around Christmas which would explain the mad rush to get the apartment sold before then. But she was also annoyed to discover that the news had unsettled her and in her confusion she hadn't even congratulated him.

She wondered who the lucky woman might be – probably some high-flying financial whiz-kid like himself. Instead of pillowtalk, they could discuss investment strategy, she thought bitterly. And where was he planning to live once he had disposed of The Beeches? He had made no mention of buying another place.

She decided to put the matter out of her mind. What Greg Delaney did with his life was his own business. But now she was glad that she'd had that little altercation with him. As a rule, she avoided arguments with clients but there were occasions when you simply had to tell people where to get off. And Greg Delaney certainly needed taking down a peg. He had begun to treat her as if she was some office junior. Hopefully, he had got the message and would let her get on with the damned business of selling his apartment. And with a bit of luck that would be the end of it.

She spent the rest of the afternoon finalising her campaign for the unsold properties that remained on her books. There was always a handful of smart investors waiting for the winter when they might pick up a bargain. She was hoping to interest some of them. Indeed, she remembered with a smile, it was around this time of year that she had bought Auburn Grove and that had certainly proved to be a bargain. My God, she thought, another year has almost flown and I've barely noticed.

At four thirty she got a phone call from Paula Matthews.

"Hi," she said. "I've just got back from viewing that penthouse in The Beeches. You were right. It's a stunner."

"I knew you'd like it," Maddy said, brightening up. "How was Mr Delaney?"

"Greg? He was nice as pie. He couldn't have been sweeter. Picked us up and drove us out to Sandymount. Even gave me and the photographer a glass of wine. Said he appreciated the big favour we were doing him. Although, I have to say he sounded rather grumpy when I rang him earlier."

"You probably got him at a bad moment. He's an investment analyst. Those guys seem to live in a permanent pressure cooker."

"Anyway, you'll be pleased to learn that I'm planning to lead the supplement with it. Plenty of big pictures and a nice jazzy write-up as you requested. That's another drink you owe me."

"You help me sell this apartment and I'll send round a bottle of best Moët," Maddy laughed.

"Just one question, you don't think £200,000 is a bit on the high side?"

Maddy paused. So she wasn't alone in her view that Greg was asking too much. Paula's sharp eye had spotted it too.

"It's certainly at the upper end of the scale," she conceded.

"It's just that you don't want to scare people off. A lot of them are on tight budgets."

"You're right. But he insisted."

"Okay. We'll get it sold or go down fighting. Talk to you. Byeee."

Maddy smiled to herself as she put down the phone. The lead story in Paula's property supplement was bound to generate interest. And she knew her friend would give the apartment a nice breezy write-up.

She had just finished speaking when she saw a motorcycle courier arrive at the door with a large bouquet of roses. What the hell is this about, she wondered as Marina hopped up smartly and intercepted him. She watched the secretary scribble her signature on the courier's pad and accept the flowers. Then she turned and walked straight for Maddy's desk.

"They're for you," she said.

"Me?" Maddy replied in amazement.

"That's what he said. Looks like you've got a secret admirer."

There was a card tucked underneath the cellophane wrapper. Maddy pulled it out.

Please accept my heartfelt apologies for my rude behaviour and receive these roses as a token of my remorse. Greg.

She was gobsmacked. She stared at the roses. They were beautiful. Already their heady scent was beginning to fill the room. There was no question: Greg Delaney could certainly turn on the charm when he wanted. But there was no way she was accepting his flowers.

She slipped the card in her drawer, gathered up the roses and walked back to Marina's desk.

"Take them."

"Me? They were addressed to you!"

"I know but I'm giving them to you. You've been working very hard recently. These are to show my appreciation."

True to her word, Paula wrote a dazzling feature about the penthouse which took up half the front page of her property supplement. It was accompanied by stunning photographs displaying all the best features of the property including a magnificent shot of the view from the terrace. The article coincided with the advertising campaign planned for the properties which had got stuck. If this didn't pull in the punters nothing would. Maddy anticipated a busy couple of weeks.

She wasn't disappointed. Paula's write-up elicited twenty-four inquiries and sixteen firm appointments to view. Maddy knew that some of them would be sightseers just wanting to have a look at the apartment so they could talk about it to their friends at their next dinner party. But most of them would be genuine.

She decided to schedule them in groups of four in the afternoons when it was still daylight. This was partly to cut down on time but also to give the viewers the opportunity to see the apartment at its best. And there was another more subtle reason. Doing it this way, the viewers would know they weren't alone. Others were interested in the apartment too. They had competition.

Meanwhile she was busy with her other properties. As expected, the advertising campaign had produced renewed interest. In a matter of days, her team of negotiators had secured firm offers on five of them. But it took a bit longer for bids to come in for Greg's penthouse. By the end of the second week, she had received just three and none of them was inspiring.

The first was from a thirty-something young man who said he worked in computer technology – whatever that was. He put in a ridiculous bid of £120,000 and he also wanted all the furniture included. Maddy thanked him but said she thought the offer was a bit on the low side. She didn't even bother to put it to Greg since she knew he would explode. Out of courtesy, she rang the young man back and told him his bid had been turned down but if he cared to increase it substantially, they would reconsider. She didn't hear from him again.

A better offer came in from a couple who were moving from London to live in Dublin for employment reasons. But there was a snag. They couldn't complete the deal until the following February when the man was due to take up his new appointment. Maddy stressed that the vendor had given specific instructions that the property must be sold before Christmas. The couple said they would go away and think about it. But when Maddy rang them a week later, they had changed their minds.

The best offer was for £150,000 and came from another couple who were trading down. It was close to Maddy's original estimate of what the apartment might fetch and she knew with a bit of haggling she could probably bring it up. But again there was a hitch. The couple couldn't complete the deal till they sold their own house. In normal circumstances, she would have been happy to go along with this, even offer to sell their house and earn another commission but Greg's damned deadline was getting in the way.

By now, three weeks had passed and she hadn't heard a word from him. He had obviously taken to heart her demand for no interference. It was time to ring him and bring him up to date. He came on the line sounding slightly reserved like a bold child who has recently been chastised for some misdemeanour.

"I thought I'd give you a call, let you know what's happening."

"Yes," he said, eagerly. "I was wondering how things have been progressing."

"I've been very busy on your behalf," she continued. "The good news is that we've had a very brisk response to the ads and Paula's wonderful write-up. To date, almost twenty people have viewed it."

"That sounds fantastic. Any firm offers?"

"I have several people who are definitely interested. But there are problems."

"Yes?"

"Price for one thing. Timing for another."

Now he sounded apprehensive. "How do you mean?"

"I haven't secured an offer that comes anywhere close to the asking price. And trying to close this deal before Christmas is a major headache. I was wondering if there is any room for manoeuvre."

"You mean lower the price?"

"Or extend the deadline. Or both."

She heard a loud sigh on the other end of the line.

"Look, Maddy, this is a bad time for me. I have a meeting in five minutes and I need to think. Is there any chance we could sit down somewhere and go over this?"

She was reluctant to face him again but he was her client and she could hardly refuse to discuss the sale of his property with him. Besides, she sensed the time had come for some serious talking.

"Okay," she said.

"How about a quick lunch in O'Hara's? It's close to your office."

"What time?"

"Say one o'clock. In the meantime, I'll give this matter more thought."

"Right," she said. "I'll be there."

At ten to one, she left the office and drove the short distance to the restaurant in the centre of Ballsbridge. Fortunately O'Hara's had parking so she smartly swung her Audi into the bay. As she locked up, she noticed Greg's black BMW sports car already parked.

He was sitting a table at the back of the restaurant and stood up as she came in.

"This should be discreet," he said, as she joined him. "Give us a chance to talk without being overheard."

She glanced at him. He looked dreadful. There were tired lines in his face and dark rings beneath his eyes. Greg Delaney had certainly lost some of the sparkle she had come to associate with him.

"What do you want to eat?" he asked. "Their roast beef is excellent."

But Maddy decided to have a warm chicken salad. This was supposed to be a short business lunch and she was anxious to get it over as quickly as possible.

As soon as they had ordered, he turned to her.

"Firstly, allow me to apologise for upsetting you. I'm really sorry. Did you get my flowers?"

"Yes, I did. It was a really nice gesture."

He smiled. "So we're friends again?"

We were *never* friends, Maddy thought but kept it to herself.

"Of course."

"So tell me what's happening with the apartment."

"I have to be blunt," she began. "I don't think there's any possibility of selling it for the price you're asking in the time you've given me. We're now into October. Even if I got an acceptable offer tomorrow, it would still be a mad rush to get the finance and the legal work completed before Christmas."

Immediately, he looked downcast. "That long?"

She nodded. "Remember how long it took when you were buying it? The banks are very slow about lending money. And the solicitors take forever."

"But we've still got three months."

"No, we don't. With holidays and so on, we've got about nine weeks. But more important, we don't have an offer."

"So, what do you think we should do?"

"Take it off the market and put it up again in March."

He shook his head. "That's completely out of the question. Why don't you reduce the asking price a little? Say £190,000."

"No, Greg. You'd need to reduce it by a lot more if I'm to have a realistic chance of selling it."

"How much?"

"What I originally suggested. £165,000."

He looked aghast. "I couldn't possibly accept that."

"Then you're not going to sell it."

His face went pale. He glanced down at his plate as if he had just been told he had an incurable disease.

Suddenly Maddy felt sorry for him. It was obvious that the man sitting across from her was under enormous pressure.

"I need a drink," he said.

She reached out and touched his arm. "I'm sorry, Greg. But we have to be realistic. This is not the best time to sell property and I really think you're handicapping yourself with the Christmas deadline. My strong advice is to withdraw the apartment and put it up again in the spring. I'd be much more confident then."

"You don't understand," he said. "Lorna is insisting."

"Lorna?"

"My fiancée."

She stared at him. "You mean Lorna Hamilton? The woman who advised you on the décor?"

"That's right."

Maddy was shocked. So he was marrying Lorna. She certainly hadn't wasted any time getting her clutches into him.

"I don't get it. She did such a beautiful job for you. Why on earth does she want to sell?"

He let out a weary sigh. "She just doesn't like it. She's got her heart set on this large house in Dalkey. It's a beautiful place with gardens and terraces, all that sort of thing. But we can't move on the Dalkey house till I've sold my apartment."

"When is the wedding?"

"December 20th. The plan is that we go off on honeymoon and come back to our new house in Dalkey with everything done and dusted."

It was a crazy plan and whoever devised it needed their heads examined but Maddy couldn't say that to Greg. She stared across the table feeling a mixture of sympathy and incredulity. Greg attracted a waiter and ordered a double whiskey. As soon as it arrived, he swallowed it in one large gulp.

"Let me get this straight," Maddy said. "You need to get around £200,000 for your penthouse in order to buy the Dalkey property? Is that right?"

He nodded and wiped his mouth. "That's it in a nutshell. The vendors are asking £250,000 for the Dalkey house. Lorna has some finance of her own which will make up the balance."

At last, it was all becoming clear. Now she could understand his insistence on asking a ridiculous price for his apartment and then tying a noose round his neck by demanding the sale be finalised before Christmas.

"Couldn't you talk to the auctioneer and explain your situation? Perhaps you could come to some arrangement with him to buy the property in the spring once you've sold The Beeches. Perhaps you could offer to pay him a deposit to show good faith?"

But Greg was shaking his head again. "I don't think that would work. He says he's got other people interested."

And he's probably bluffing, Maddy thought. "It might be worth a try."

Greg looked at her with a hopeful gleam in his eye like a pup that's just been offered the opportunity of a walk. "You think so?"

"Yes, I do. And if it facilitates matters for you, I'd be prepared to relinquish the sale of The Beeches and let the Dalkey auctioneer handle both."

"Oh, no," Greg said. "I couldn't do that. You've put in so much work."

"But I haven't sold it. And to be honest, I don't think I will, given all the constraints."

"Are you absolutely sure?"

"Yes, I've just told you. But I will have to bill you for the advertising we've already placed."

"Of course."

He sniffed and ran his fingers across his chin. For the first time since they sat down, he was beginning to cheer up.

"I think I'll ring him this afternoon. Thank you, Maddy. You're a star."

I'm a bloody fool, Maddy thought ruefully. That's what I am. I had a feeling this business was going to be trouble from Day One and I was right.

Chapter Ten

Greg rang a few days later to say he had spoken to the Dalkey auctioneer and the man had accepted her suggestion. He was going to hold the house for Greg and take over the sale of his apartment in The Beeches. He thanked her profusely for her advice and for the work she had already put in on his behalf. He sounded genuinely contrite about the way everything had turned out.

"I feel like an absolute heel for doing this to you," he said.

"Well, don't," Maddy replied. "It was my idea after all."

"But it all seems so unprofessional. I should have explained everything to you right from the start."

"That might have made matters easier," she conceded. "But don't beat yourself up over it. I just hope everything works out smoothly. And I wish you the very best for your wedding. I hope you will both be very happy."

Privately, she was delighted to have Greg and The Beeches off her hands. The project had been a mess from the word Go. But the following day she was surprised to find a magnum of champagne, a large box of chocolates and a note from him apologising once more. She sent the champagne to Paula Matthews as a thank-you for her assistance and passed the chocolates around the staff. Then she put Greg Delaney out of her mind and got on with her work.

The next few weeks were extremely busy as Carroll and Shanley tried to finalise the remaining sales and prepare for the spring campaign. Already they had a number of properties on their books from vendors who were anxious to get their homes on the market early. It looked like the new year would start where the old one was leaving off – in a maniacal rush.

But as the holiday approached, Maddy had a fresh concern to occupy her mind – where was she going to have Christmas dinner? Rosie had suggested that instead of going home to their families, they should have the meal at Auburn Grove. Sophie thought this was an excellent idea. She was anxious to try out her culinary skills on a full-scale dinner with roast turkey and stuffing and all the trimmings and offered to do the cooking. But Maddy had doubts. It was a tradition to eat Christmas dinner with her family and she was loath to break it. It made the departure from home appear much too final and she was sure her mother, in particular, would be upset.

In the end, they reached a compromise. After much discussion, they agreed to go home to their families on Christmas Day and then on St Stephen's Day, they would all eat together at Auburn Grove.

It was an inspired decision. Instead of having turkey again on St Stephen's Day, they agreed to have duck. After foraging among her cookery books, Sophie came up with a recipe for Duck a l'orange which she served with roast potatoes, string beans and rice. Like all her recent adventures in the kitchen, this one was a resounding success. They drank white wine and ate Bailey's Cream cake for dessert.

Afterwards, Rosie suggested they ring round their friends and invite them over for drinks. The result was a hilarious evening that went on till the wee small hours.

But soon the holiday was over and it was back to work. Maddy spent a frantic few weeks designing brochures and organising her sales team for the expected rush. The industry had been surprised by the keen uptake of the early apartment developments and many builders were now scrambling to get into the market. Across Dublin, the skyline was becoming cluttered with cranes and gantries. Her prediction was coming true. Dubliners were discovering the appeal of apartment life, particularly young, single, professional people who wanted stylish living close to the city centre. And Carroll and Shanley were benefiting as a result.

But the biggest demand was still for houses. One evening, as she was preparing to leave work, Tim Lyons approached her.

"Are you in a hurry to get home?" he asked.

Maddy was wary. Was he about to ask her to take on some difficult task?

"Depends on what you've got in mind."

"I'd like you to look at a property. It's actually quite close to where you live. We can do it on the way home."

"Okay," she agreed.

The house was in Munster Road in Rathmines. It was a tree-lined street of Edwardian red-bricked houses. Maddy immediately recognised it as one of the properties that had been stuck on their sales list since the previous summer. As they parked their cars outside, she was reminded of Auburn Grove and the resemblance increased as Tim Lyons took the keys from his pocket and opened the front door.

Inside, they were met with the same gloom and decay. Dust gathered in corners, the windows were dark with grime and cobwebs festooned the walls. But as he led her from room to room, her sharp eye took in the house's positive features. It was bigger than Auburn Grove, with three large bedrooms and a smaller room that had once been a maid's quarters in the days when people kept domestic servants. In addition there was a kitchen, bathroom, living-room, drawing-room and gardens front and rear.

"What do you think?" Tim asked, turning to her at last.

"It's got definite potential. But it's going to need a lot of work."

She tried to remember the asking price.

"We're looking for £20,000 for it," he said, as if reading her mind. "That's reduced from an original asking price of £25,000. It's almost a repeat of your own situation. An old man lived here all his life. It was his family home. He's only got one surviving relative – a brother who is now seventy-six and just wants the house sold at any reasonable price."

"And we still can't shift it?"

Tim shook his head. "It's a damned shame, really. I agree with you. The house is a bargain and you could do a lot with a little bit of imagination. But we've had it so long it's beginning to become an embarrassment. I was wondering if any of your friends might be persuaded."

She looked around the drawing-room where they were now standing. She could see how it would look with the floors sanded, the window frames replaced and maybe the wall between the dining-room knocked down to make the room even larger. She immediately thought of Sophie and Rosie. They were earning good salaries and both had asked her to keep an eye out for a bargain like Auburn Grove. She wondered if they might be interested.

"Let me have a think about it," she said. "I'll make some inquiries."

When she got home, she found Sophie in the kitchen preparing pasta for supper and Rosie lounging in front of the television in the living-room with a glass of Valpolicella in her hand.

"Just getting in the mood for our baked lasagne," she said. "Why don't you join me? Grub will be served in ten minutes."

"Let me take a quick shower first," Maddy said, disappearing off to the bathroom. When she returned Rosie had set the table and lit the candles. A large bowl of salad sat in the middle of the table beside a basket of fresh bread.

"Smells delicious," she said as Sophie emerged carrying the pasta in a large baking tray.

"Just a few things I threw together," she replied with a grin.

A couple of minutes later, they were all tucking in.

"I've something to tell you," Maddy began, as she probed the pasta with her fork. "Remember how you both asked me to watch out for a bargain house for you, something similar to this place?"

They had both stopped eating and were staring at her.

"Well, I might have found something."

"Where?" Rosie demanded.

"Not far from here. Number 26, Munster Road, in Rathmines. The house is bigger than this one and it has definite potential."

"How much?" Sophie asked.

"Twenty thou. Reduced from twenty-five. You might even get it for a bit less. Are either of you interested?"

"I am," they said in unison and then broke out laughing.

"I'd need to see it, of course," Sophie said. "And it would depend on how much work needs to be done but I would certainly be interested."

"Me too," Rosie confirmed.

"In that case, why don't I arrange a viewing for Saturday? And I'll ask Paddy Behan to come along as well. He can give us an idea of what needs to be done and how much it would cost."

"Brilliant," Rosie said, excitedly polishing off her wine and refilling the glass again.

The idea of buying a house had now fired their imaginations and they spent the rest of the evening discussing mortgage rates and repayments and legal fees and all the attendant details that would be involved.

By the time Saturday morning came around everyone was on edge at the prospect of viewing the house.

Maddy had already got hold of the keys and, after a hurried breakfast, they drove the short distance to Munster Road.

Paddy Behan was waiting.

"Be prepared for a shock," Maddy warned as she opened the front door. "The house is in a terrible state. It's the main reason it hasn't sold."

The smell of decay was waiting for them as soon as they entered. Maddy wandered out to the back garden and left the others to view the house at their leisure. There was an ancient potting shed whose roof had collapsed and a rusting lawnmower slowly disintegrating in the long grass. But she could see the possibilities once the garden had been cleaned up. She was examining some fruit trees at the bottom of the lawn when she saw the trio emerge at last. She hurried through the tangled grass to meet them.

"Well," she asked. "What do you think?"

They started talking together, then Sophie took the lead.

"It's a lovely old house but it's going to need an awful lot of work. The floorboards in the drawing room are rotten. And I think the bathroom hasn't been touched since the house was built. As for the kitchen, it would need to be completely demolished."

"But if it was knocked into shape it would be beautiful," Rosie added excitedly, "and there's plenty of room to extend. I can just see the house with new windows and central heating and nice bright colours on the walls."

They all turned to Paddy Behan.

"Tell us the bad news," Maddy said. "What did you find?"

He slowly scratched his chin. "How old is the house?"

"About a hundred years old."

"Well, it certainly looks it. But the good news is it's basically sound. They knew how to build houses back then. The walls and foundations are as solid as the day it was put up."

They were all listening eagerly now.

"However, whoever buys it will need to install a new roof, new floors, new plumbing, new electrics."

With each job he mentioned, their faces fell.

"I would recommend a new kitchen and a new bathroom. You might also consider knocking down the wall on the ground floor to make one big lounge area like you have in Auburn Grove. You could turn that house into a palace if you had the money to spend."

There was silence for a moment as everyone digested Paddy's bad news.

"How much money?" Maddy asked at last.

"Off the top of my head, you'd be looking at £15,000 minimum."

They stared at each other in disbelief.

"That much?" asked Maddy.

"There's at least three months' work involved. Not to mention materials. If you're seriously interested, I could do a detailed breakdown for you. But you won't have much change left out of £15,000."

Maddy looked briefly at her two friends. Their enthusiasm had completely drained away. Now their faces were gloomy with disappointment.

"Okay, Paddy, thanks for your time. We'll keep in touch."

They watched the builder climb into his van and drive away, leaving a sad scene behind. Maddy glanced at her watch. It was a quarter to one. She turned to her friends.

"Right, girls, it's time to cheer up. We're going to have a good lunch. And this one's on me."

Chapter Eleven

They drove to a new bistro that had recently opened in Ranelagh village. The atmosphere had turned to gloom. Maddy knew that Sophie and Rosie were busy doing calculations in their heads and arriving at the same conclusion – there was no way that either of them could afford to buy the house *and* pay for the improvements required.

Once they were seated in the restaurant, she ordered a round of drinks. While they waited, they glanced distractedly at the menus. Rosie ordered moussaka and Sophie opted for spaghetti carbonara with a side salad while Maddy decided to treat herself to pork chops.

"Now," she said when the food arrived along with a bottle of house red, "let's conduct the inquest. According to my calculations, it's going to require nearly £40,000 to buy and renovate the house. That's including all the legal costs and taxes."

"There's no way I could afford that sort of money," Sophie said with a look of sad disappointment.

"Me neither," Rosie agreed shaking her head vigorously and dipping into her moussaka. "Why don't we just forget all about it?"

"Mind you, I could have fallen in love with it," Sophie added. "I could just see how cute it would look when all the work was done.

93

Unfortunately, it's way out of my league."

"But you would have a property that's worth around £70,000," Maddy pointed out.

"And debts to match. We have to be reasonable here."

"Have either of you got any personal savings?" Maddy probed.

"I've got a few bob in a savings account," Rosie admitted. "A *very* few bob."

"How about you, Sophie?"

"Zero. I might be able to borrow a few bob off my parents."

"Could you manage to scrape together a deposit?"

"Possibly."

"Ummhh," Maddy said. On the drive to the bistro she had been doing some serious thinking. "There just might be a way round this."

"Like what?" Rosie asked. "Rob a bank? Print our own money? Maybe we could kidnap someone and hold them to ransom?"

"You could buy it between you."

The two women put down their cutlery and stared at each other.

"Can you do that?" Sophie asked after a pause.

"Married couples do it all the time."

"But we're not married. We're not even going out together," Rosie giggled, nervously.

"How exactly would it work?" Sophie wanted to know.

"You'd own the house between you."

"And split the costs down the middle?"

"Yes. I don't see why it shouldn't be possible. I'll tell you what. Why don't I make some inquiries? And on Monday morning you guys make an appointment to see your bank managers."

"If we do manage to buy the house," Rosie said, "you're going to lose your lodgers. How will you manage?"

"The way I managed before you came along. Don't worry about me. I'll survive."

Maddy's suggestion seemed to cheer them up. Sophie refilled the wineglasses and five minutes later they were deep in conversation, excitedly planning how they would redecorate the house once they had succeeded in getting their hands on it.

Over the weekend, Maddy rang Conor Black at his apartment in Seapoint.

"I'm sorry to bother you like this," she began apologetically."

"Not at all. It's always a pleasure to hear your cheerful voice, Maddy. Got a problem?"

"No, thank God. I just need some advice."

"Shoot."

"Is there any legal reason to prevent two people who aren't married or otherwise related buying a house together?"

"Not that I'm aware of. It's rather unusual. But it's perfectly feasible."

She explained the situation regarding Rosie and Sophie.

"How are they going to finance it?" he asked.

"With a mortgage."

"I see," Conor Black said ominously.

"Is that a difficulty?" she asked.

"It could be. The banks are extremely cautious. But to answer your original question, there's nothing in law to prevent them doing it."

Maddy thanked him, put down the phone and got out her calculator. Assuming that Sophie and Rosie had to borrow the full £40,000, the repayments would come in around £450 a month. Between two people that would mean £225 each. She dealt every day with customers whose repayments were double that and more. It was a lot of money but perfectly affordable provided they tightened their belts a little.

On Monday morning, in quick succession, Rosie and Sophie rang to say they had fixed appointments with their bank managers for the following day. Maddy had already briefed them that the banks would require statements of income from their employers so on Tuesday, armed with this information, they set off. That evening over dinner at Auburn Grove, they related their experiences. Both interviews appeared to have gone quite smoothly.

Maddy reported back to Tim Lyons that her friends were

interested but wanted to secure finance before proceeding further. He seemed relieved at the prospect of finally getting the property off his books.

"One thing's for certain," he said, cynically. "There's no danger of anyone nipping in and stealing the house from under their noses."

One week slipped slowly into another until everyone was in a state of nervous tension.

"Try to relax," Maddy advised. "Waiting for mortgage approval is the worst part. Once that is out of the way, it will be all plain sailing."

Rosie was the first to hear. Maddy returned from her jog one morning to find her dancing up and down the hall clutching a letter from her bank saying she had been approved for a loan of £20,000 repayable over twenty years subject to all legal requirements being met. She flung her arms around Maddy and kissed her.

"I can't believe this is really happening," she croaked with tears in her eyes. "Oh, I'm so excited!" Then she stepped back and sobered up abruptly. "But, of course, it can't happen unless Sophie gets her mortgage too."

Two days later, however, a similar letter arrived for Sophie.

"We have to celebrate," she said, barely able to restrain herself. "I know what I'll do! I'm going to cook a special dinner tonight. I'll make something really nice. What about lamb? I've never cooked lamb before."

"And we'll buy a bottle of champagne!" Rosie said.

Maddy laughed with joy. "Don't go mad," she said with a grin. "Don't spend your entire mortgage before you even get it!"

They celebrated in style that evening, with many a toast to their success, and didn't once discuss the practicalities of the matter.

Then next day it was back to business.

It was time to make an offer.

On Maddy's advice, Sophie rang Tim Lyons and put in a bid for £18,000. He seemed so pleased to get the offer that he didn't even haggle with her. Later in the afternoon, he rang back to say the offer had been accepted and a contract would be drawn up at once.

Maddy then rang Conor Black to engage him and tell him what was going on.

"Are you telling me the banks have actually agreed?"

"Yes," Maddy said. "They've both secured mortgages of £20,000. You sound surprised."

"I'm more than surprised. I'm amazed. Maybe the banks are moving into the twentieth century at last."

"Now it's over to you. I'm told you can expect a contract in the next few days."

"Congratulations," Conor replied. "I'll keep you informed of developments."

But the celebrations were premature. The first sign of trouble came a few days later in a phone call from Conor.

"I'm afraid we've run into a problem."

Maddy's heart sank. "What's happened?"

"Sophie's bank is beginning to get cold feet."

"Why?"

"They're claiming they weren't aware that this was going to be a joint purchase."

"But Sophie told them."

"I know. But there seems to have been a mix-up. I'm going to speak to them this afternoon and try to sort it out."

"And what happens if they refuse the loan? What do we do then?"

"We'll cross that bridge when we come to it," Conor said warily. "Meanwhile, let's just deal with one problem at a time."

It was ten to five when he finally got back to her. Immediately, she heard the gloom in his voice.

"It's bad news, I'm afraid," he said, glumly. "They're withdrawing their offer."

"*What?*"

"They say they've found something in the small print that prevents them lending in situations like this."

"But they've already sent her a letter of approval," Maddy said, astounded. "Can she sue them or something?"

"I wouldn't advise it. They're claiming she misled them about the circumstances."

"That's outrageous. Surely that's a libel?"

"But how do we prove it? It's their word against hers. Anyway, it's all academic. At the end of the day we can't compel them to lend her the money."

Maddy felt the crushing disappointment return.

"So where do we go from here?"

"She could try another bank. But my fear is that once word gets around they'll all take the same line."

"What if she was to try Rosie's bank? They've granted *her* a loan."

Conor didn't sound optimistic. "It will mean moving her accounts and that's going to take time but it's worth a try, I suppose."

"We'd better give it a shot. After all, we don't have any other options."

"Looks like it," Conor said.

"Who's going to tell Sophie the bad news?" Maddy asked at last.

Conor let out a loud sigh. "I suppose I'd better do it. I *am* her solicitor after all."

That evening, poor Sophie came home with a sad face and as soon as she plumped down on the settee, she began to cry.

"There, there," Maddy said, trying to comfort her. "It's not the end of the world."

"But I had my heart set on that place," she sobbed. "I had even planned the first dinner party."

"We won't give up yet. Conor says you can try Rosie's bank."

"That's just prolonging the agony," Sophie replied, the tears running down her cheeks.

But she took Maddy's advice and transferred her accounts to Rosie's bank. It took ten days and a lot of paperwork to cancel all her direct debits and set them up again. But once she had completed the transaction, she immediately made an application for a loan.

The outcome was a complete body blow. A few days later, her application was refused. And worse was to follow. The following day, Rosie also received a letter saying that, due to unforeseen circumstances, the bank had been forced to review its lending policy. As a result and with deep regret, it was withdrawing its offer too.

Chapter Twelve

In the days that followed, they were plunged into mourning for the death of their dream and the atmosphere in Auburn Grove turned grey and oppressive. Maddy blamed herself. She was the one who had encouraged them in the crazy belief that the banks would change the policy of a lifetime and lend them the money to buy the property. She should have known better. It was only recently that some of them had even allowed women to open accounts without their husbands' consent.

They had set their hearts on buying the house and now their hopes were dashed. For Maddy, the situation was made worse by the knowledge that the property was an absolute bargain. Some lucky client would inevitably come along to claim the prize.

Conor had little solace to offer when she eventually picked up the courage to ring him.

"I'm not really surprised," he admitted. "I was afraid something like this would happen. The word has obviously got around."

"I still don't understand what the problem is. They both have steady jobs. They're earning good salaries. And they will have the house to use as collateral."

"I told you the banks are ultra-cautious. They're worried that if one party defaults on the loan they won't be able to take possession of the house because the other party will own half of it."

"But why would anyone want to default? It will be their home, for God's sake."

"Maddy, you really can be very naïve at times. Nobody sets out to default. They just get into trouble, that's all. It happens every day of the week."

"So, is there anything more we can do?"

"Afraid not," he said, gloomily. "It's their money. If they won't lend it, we can't force them."

But the subject continued to linger like an oppressive presence over the household.

"I knew we would never be able to afford it," Sophie said one evening. "Women like us are not cut out to be homeowners."

"Nonsense," Maddy retorted. "Stop thinking like that. You were just unlucky. Next time, things will be different, you'll see."

"How?" Sophie asked bitterly. "A rich aunt will die and leave us the money or maybe you think we'll win the Lottery?"

"You might find another house, something you can afford without having to ask the damned banks for money."

Sophie gave her a withering glance. "We'll never find anything like Munster Road. And besides we haven't got any money of our own. You know it's impossible."

"Oh, stop moaning! Something will turn up," Maddy snapped before realising that she didn't have the faintest idea what she was talking about.

Tim Lyons was equally disappointed when he heard the news.

"I'm beginning to have nightmares about that house," he groaned. "I wish some kind person would simply come along and take it off our hands."

"We'll give it an extra push in the spring campaign," Maddy promised. "We'll manage to sell it. You know everything sells in the end."

"I wish I had your confidence," he said wearily.

It was the spring sales campaign that eventually shifted Maddy's mind away from the problem. It was now April and the gardens were in bloom. All along Auburn Grove, the cherry trees were shedding their lush piles of pink and white flowers. Bright boxes of scarlet geraniums and yellow pansies were appearing on windowsills and the whirr of lawnmowers filled the evening air.

In her own garden, the shrubs she had planted in the rockery were sprouting and the trees were in leaf. The lawn she had laid down was now pushing up a thick carpet of green baize. One weekend, she dusted down the patio furniture and went out and bought some hanging baskets. In a few weeks' time, it would be warm enough to sit out here once more and enjoy a cool glass of wine in the bright evening sunshine.

At work, events had taken a manic turn. Every day brought an avalanche of enquiries and viewings and the sales team was run ragged. At one stage, the activity reached such a peak that Maddy was forced to abandon her policy of not getting directly involved in sales and took on a number of prestigious properties to relieve the pressure. She also crossed an important watershed in her career. She conducted her very first auction.

This was something she had never attempted before. Auctions were strictly the preserve of the senior executives and demanded great skill and experience. They were usually reserved for properties that were expected to attract exceptional interest.

But they could easily go wrong. Many buyers disliked the auction process because they could never be sure what they might end up paying. They preferred the safety of a private treaty sale where the price was agreed and they could work out their finances in advance. As a result, some auctions failed to attract any bidders at all and the property had to be withdrawn and put on the market again leaving everyone looking foolish.

Most of the houses that Carroll and Shanley decided to auction were large period residences in the plusher parts of Ballsbridge and Sandymount where there was usually fierce competition to buy. It was one of these – a fine Victorian home with five bedrooms, two bathrooms, several drawing-rooms and large gardens front and rear – that Tim Lyons asked her to take on one day.

"Why me?" she asked, nervously.

Tim was blunt. "I don't want to hurt your feelings, Maddy. But if you want me to be honest, it's because we've got no one else to do it."

"What about you? Couldn't you handle it?"

"I'm already auctioning five properties. I just can't give it the attention it deserves."

"But I've never done it before. What if I make a mess of it?"

He smiled. "You and I both know that's not going to happen. I wouldn't have asked you if I didn't have confidence. Just regard it as a learning curve. There's always a first time for everything."

But he did agree to coach her in the process.

"The first thing is to decide on a reserve price. I've already spoken to the vendor and he's looking for £350,000. It sounds a lot but the way the market is going at the moment, he might just get it."

"And then we prepare a brochure and organise some advertising?"

"Precisely. Just like any other sale."

"I suppose I'd better take a look at it," Maddy said, without much enthusiasm.

She rang and made an appointment to inspect the house that afternoon. It was called Elsinore and stood on a leafy road off Merrion Avenue – a street of large, well-maintained houses and carefully tended gardens that exuded an air of wealth and privilege. The vendor was a plump English businessman called George Cooper who had spent several years in Dublin and was being transferred back to head office in London. He didn't attempt to hide his disappointment that the job of selling his house had been entrusted to a woman – and a young one at that.

"Like it?" he asked gruffly, after Maddy had been given a tour of inspection through the magnificent rooms with their exquisite furnishings and gleaming chandeliers. It was easily the grandest house she had ever been asked to sell.

"It's beautiful."

"Think we'll get the price?"

She hesitated before replying. Experience had taught her never to give a commitment in case it wasn't realised.

"It's a lovely property, Mr Cooper. I don't think we should have any problem attracting interest."

"That's not what I asked you. I want to know if you'll be able to sell it for £350,000."

"It's certainly worth that," she ventured, cautiously.

Her reply only seemed to infuriate him.

"Dammit, woman! Can't you give me a straight answer?"

"No, I can't," Maddy said, looking him squarely in the eye. "Not until we've put it on the market and judged the response."

"So why am I employing you?"

"To get you the best price. I will certainly guarantee to do that. And if it's any comfort to you, I believe I can secure the reserve. But I won't promise you something I might not be able to deliver."

The answer took the wind out of his sails. He sniffed and Maddy moved swiftly to the subject of viewings.

Half an hour later, she was relieved to drive away from Elsinore and its gruff owner, her mind filled with foreboding about what problems might lie ahead.

In the next few days, she got busy with the advertising campaign. They had settled on May 2nd as the date for the auction. George Cooper was anxious to have the property sold as soon as possible and Tim said that a short, sharp campaign would concentrate minds and force the punters to get their wallets out. The timing was also fortuitous as Elsinore's magnificent gardens would be displayed to their best advantage.

She immediately despatched the maintenance team to erect a large board outside the house bearing the legend: *Magnificent Period Residence On Circa Half Acre. Auction May 2nd. Viewing Strictly By Appointment,* followed by the firm's logo and phone number. Next, she got to work designing a beautiful brochure with lavish photos of the property and gardens. She booked a series of half-page ads in *The Irish Times* and *The Independent* and rang the property editors to ensure some accompanying editorial.

As usual, Paula Matthews was keen to help.

"That's the best house I've seen in a very long time," she said, after a viewing arranged by Maddy. "They'll be murdering each other at the auction."

"You think so?" Maddy asked, eager to seek any reassurance she could find.

"Maddy, my dear, wake up and smell the coffee! That house is a stunner. It's located in the best neighbourhood in Dublin. Beautiful gardens, needs no work. And I'm going to give it a dinky write-up next Wednesday. Why wouldn't it walk out the door?"

"I'm just nervous," Maddy conceded. "It's my first auction."

"Really? I thought you were a seasoned campaigner."

"The senior excutives always handle the auctions."

"Well, believe me, this is one you don't have to worry about. Why don't you just sit back and enjoy the experience?" she laughed as she rung off.

The ads and the write-ups meant that Maddy's phone was soon hopping as people sought appointments to view. But she knew that some of them would be mere gawkers. It had become a pastime with certain members of the Dublin public to spend their afternoons looking over other people's bedrooms. Ballsbridge Porn, some wit had dubbed it. But she had no way of knowing who was serious and who was not, so she was forced to treat every caller as a potential buyer.

Consequently, she had twelve parties waiting to view on the first public showing of the property the following Saturday afternoon between three and five. To assist her, she had dragooned three of her sales team to help keep an eye on things. It was not unknown for ornaments and small household items to go missing on occasions like this. As a potential deterrent, each person who turned up was asked to sign a register with name, address and phone number before being given a brochure and escorted around the house.

Some people took a quick inspection and were gone in ten minutes as if they had a train to catch. Others lingered, admiring pictures and pieces of furniture or wandering in the gardens as if they were in a public park. It was a gruelling couple of hours as Maddy and her assistants struggled to answer questions on everything from the dimensions of the en-suite bathroom to the curtain fabrics in the drawing-room while still continuing to smile and appear bright and cheerful.

But finally five o'clock arrived, the last visitor was despatched out into the warm afternoon sunshine and Maddy was able to lock up and secure the house.

"Phew!" she said as she walked across the gravel to her car. "That was some experience! I think I need a drink. Anybody care to join me?"

They all set off for a nearby bar where Maddy was glad to sit down, kick off her shoes and sip a cool glass of wine while she recovered from the ordeal.

"How many more of these have we got?" a bright young woman called Sue Donovan asked.

"Three. And then we've got the auction. But I expect today was the worst. There's usually a mad rush in the beginning."

"Well, the vendor should be pleased," said Sue. "The house has certainly stirred a lot of interest."

"But how many of them will turn up on the big day? That's the crucial question."

As anticipated, the next three viewings drew smaller crowds but they were still tiring affairs. In the end, Maddy felt she knew more about Elsinore than George Cooper himself.

But of the thirty or so parties who had come to view, she calculated that only half a dozen were definitely interested and would come to the auction. No doubt they were now talking to their bank managers and arranging their finances.

But when she mentioned this to Tim Lyons, he smiled knowingly and said: "There's absolutely no way of telling, Maddy. Auctions are a lottery."

Nevertheless, she was relieved to get the final viewing out of the way. The following Wednesday was the day of the auction when she would have to stand up in front of the crowd and attempt to coax them to outbid each other. Tim had spent a couple of hours guiding her through the routine and advising about the pitfalls. But his soothing words did little to reassure her. Wednesday's ordeal was not something she was looking forward to.

On Monday morning she came into work prepared to concentrate once more on the spring sales campaign which was now approaching its peak. But she had barely settled down at her desk when the phone gave a loud ring. She glanced up to see Marina silently mouthing the word Elsinore and pointing to her.

She lifted the phone and pressed it to her ear.

"Maddy Pritchard," she said.

"Forgive me," a cultured male accent announced. "My name is Peter Drake. I'm calling about Elsinore. The house you have for auction."

"Yes?" Maddy said.

"I'd like to view it, if that could be arranged."

"We had the last viewing on Saturday, Mr Drake. The auction is going ahead this coming Wednesday."

"Oh dear," she heard him say. "I was away on business and have just learnt about it from my wife. Is there any possibility you could make an exception?"

Maddy was faced with a dilemma. George Cooper had already suffered serious disruption during the past few weeks and was likely to blow a fuse if she suggested putting him out of his house once again so that Peter Drake could browse through it.

"I don't really think …"

"I'm genuinely interested," he cut in. "We've been waiting some time for a house to become available on that road. If we liked it, we would certainly be prepared to bid."

Something told her that the man on the telephone was no idle tourist anxious to see round a neighbour's home. She remembered Tim's remark about an auction being like a lottery. What would happen if none of the viewers she had earmarked turned up and she had sent this man away?

"Would you mind giving me your number?" she said at last. "I'll ring the vendor and see if it's possible to fit you in."

"Thank you very much," Peter Drake said and rattled off his phone number.

It was with trepidation that she dialled George Cooper and listened to the impatient ringing tone. At last, she heard the phone being picked up.

"Yes?" a voice barked.

"Mr Cooper, it's Maddy Pritchard here. From Carroll and Shanley."

"Yes?"

"I'm sorry to bother you like this. But I've got a gentleman who is anxious to see Elsinore. He was out of the country and missed the scheduled viewings."

She braced herself for the expected explosion.

"My God!" she heard George Cooper groan. "Have you any idea of the pain this has caused us? We've had people tramping through our home for the past three weeks as if it was the main hall of the RDS."

"I wouldn't have bothered you but I think this man is genuinely interested."

"They all say that. Most of them are just nosy parkers with nothing better to do on a Saturday afternoon."

"But why take the gamble? This could be the man who will buy it. I'll make sure to keep the disruption to a minimum."

"When do you suggest?" Cooper said with a weary sigh.

"Tomorrow afternoon?" Maddy asked, brightly. "Half an hour?"

"Oh, all right," he groaned. "After all the inconvenience we've suffered already, one more sightseer won't make any difference. I'll arrange for the house to be vacated between three and four. My wife will be picking up the children from school."

"I'll be gone when she gets back. I promise."

She heard the line buzz as George Cooper put down the phone.

Peter Drake turned out to be a thin man in his early forties whose dark hair was turning prematurely grey. He was apologetic when Maddy met him the following day at Elsinore.

"I'm sorry to have caused this inconvenience," he began as he warmly clasped her hand. "I'm very grateful you could fit me in."

"That's okay," she replied. "It's just that poor Mr Cooper seems to have spent more time out of his house than in it during the past few weeks. And he thought he had finished with the viewings."

She opened the heavy front door and led Peter Drake into the large hallway. He stood for a moment looking around before following her into the main drawing-room with its brilliant chandelier and heavy drapes. But his eyes betrayed no emotion as they travelled around the room. Then he was quickly following her again into the dining-room. Fifteen minutes later, he had seen the entire house. Throughout the inspection he hadn't uttered a single word.

"Would you like to see the gardens?" Maddy asked.

"No, thank you," he replied. "I've seen enough."

"You have our brochure. The auction is tomorrow. If there is any information you need in the meantime, please give me a call."

"Yes, I'll do that," Peter Drake said, as he climbed into his grey Mercedes car and drove away up the road.

Maddy stared after him. What a strange man, she thought. I wonder if I've just wasted my time?

The auction had been scheduled for three o'clock in a function room of Jury's Hotel. Maddy arrived at two, with two of her sales team and Tim Lyons who had agreed to accompany her for her first foray into auctioning. For the occasion, she had decided to wear a smart navy business suit, white blouse and scarf, dark stockings and black shoes.

"Feeling nervous?" Tim asked as they looked around the empty room.

"What do you think? I've been dreading this moment for weeks."

"Just relax," he said with a reassuring squeeze of her arm. "It will all be over before you know."

"You sound like my dentist."

He grinned. "Nothing can go wrong. And even if it does, I'll be here to pick up the pieces."

"Thanks a million for that vote of confidence," Maddy said and turned to go.

"Aren't you forgetting something?" he asked. "You're going to need this." And he presented her with a small gavel.

Sue Donovan had ordered a pot of coffee and some sandwiches. But Maddy had no appetite. Her stomach felt like a nest of butterflies. She tried to pass the time by standing at the back of the room and sipping coffee while they waited for the bidders to arrive.

They came in ones and twos, looking furtively around like shoplifters before taking their seats. When Tim Lyons finally closed the doors at two minutes to three, there were fifteen people in the room. Maddy took a deep breath. Now the moment of truth had arrived. With quivering legs, she walked to the lectern and gazed out over the room.

At that moment, the door opened again and she saw Peter Drake enter. He smiled apologetically as he slid into a seat near the back of the room.

Maddy summoned all her courage for the task that lay ahead. Tim Lyons had coached her several times in the drill but nothing prepared her for the dread that came over her as she faced the assembled audience. If she made a mess of this it would mean a black mark against her. She felt her mouth open automatically and the words begin to come out.

"Thank you all for your attendance. We are here today to auction the property known as Elsinore at St Margaret's Road, Ballsbridge. This is a prime property with mature gardens on approximately half an acre of land. Will anyone open the bidding at £350,000?"

In the silence of the room you could hear a pin fall. Maddy felt her stomach turn a somersault as she stared at the mute, impassive faces. Her worst nightmare was coming true. If she couldn't even get the bidding started, the auction would have to be abandoned and all the time and effort of the last few weeks would have been wasted. Not to mention the humiliation she would suffer as a result.

For several awful moments nothing happened. She felt her heart pound like a drum.

"Three hundred and fifty thousand pounds," she repeated. "Do I have any offers?"

A few people coughed and then in the middle of the room a hand slowly began to rise. She craned her neck to see a man in a blazer and open-necked shirt. He was one of the people she had earlier marked down as a serious contender. A wave of relief washed over her.

"Three hundred and fifty, I'm bid," Maddy said, feeling her confidence return. "Will anyone offer me three sixty?"

Again the silence. People fidgeted in their seats and glanced nervously at each other.

"Any improvement on three fifty?" she coaxed.

A man in a pin-striped suit who was sitting near the door raised his folded newspaper.

"Three sixty, I'm bid. Three sixty. Anyone offering three seventy?"

The bidding had finally started and Maddy could feel a wild adrenalin buzz course through her veins. She was beginning to enjoy this experience.

The first man hesitated before raising his hand again.

"Three seventy. Any advance on three seventy?"

The man in the suit signalled again.

"Three eighty. Will anyone offer me three ninety for this excellent property?"

She gazed down at the first man but he was shaking his head. He'd had enough and was getting out. The man in the suit was now smiling. He had seen off his rival and was looking confident.

Maddy waited a second and raised her gavel. Peter Drake stared impassively towards her. He had taken the trouble to come to the auction but he hadn't entered the bidding. Perhaps he found the stakes too high.

"Three eighty. Going once."

She brought the gavel down on the desk before her.

"Going twice."

She saw Peter Drake's hand quickly go up. She took a deep breath and continued.

"I'm bid three ninety. Any advance on three ninety?"

The smile had gone from the man in the suit and now he was looking concerned. He glanced round to see who his new competitor was.

"Will anyone offer three ninety-five?"

The man in the pin-striped suit raised his newspaper.

"Three ninety-five. Anyone offering four hundred?"

The silence in the room was deafening. She had managed to push up the price to £395,000. Even if the bidding stopped now, she had pulled off an amazing achievement.

She looked at Peter Drake and saw him nod.

"Four hundred I'm bid. Do I hear four hundred and five?"

The man in the suit was looking extremely uncomfortable. Beads of sweat were starting to roll down his cheeks.

"Four hundred once," Maddy said and brought down the gavel.

The man in the suit had his newspaper up again. Maddy was feeling giddy with excitement. Now she knew how those high-rolling gamblers must feel when they risked everything on the throw of a dice. Where was the bidding going to stop?

"Four hundred and five. Will anyone offer me four hundred and ten?"

The atmosphere in the room was now electric. People waited expectantly to see what would happen next. Maddy hesitated for a second and raised the gavel again.

Peter Drake's hand went up.

"Four hundred and ten I'm bid. Any advance on four hundred and ten?"

She looked at the man in the pinstriped suit but he was shaking his head in disgust. He had no more stomach left for the contest. He had made his final bid and been defeated.

She looked round to see if any other brave soul felt like entering the fray, then raised the gavel. The room was silent as the grave. Not a finger stirred.

"Four hundred and ten once. Twice."

She brought the gavel down with a resounding crack.

"Sold for four hundred and ten thousand pounds to Mr Drake."

Her legs felt like jelly as she stepped down from the lectern and walked to the back of the room to shake hands with Peter Drake. She felt drained of emotion. The last few minutes had been the most exciting of her entire career and now she felt exhausted.

"Congratulations," she said, warmly clasping his hand.

"Thank you," Peter Drake replied. He had taken out his cheque book already in preparation for paying his deposit.

"I hope you enjoy your new property," Maddy continued. "You seemed quite determined."

"Oh, I was. We've waited a long time for a house like Elsinore."

"Well, you can relax now. Sue will take good care of you. Just let us have the name of your solicitor and we'll pass it on to the vendor."

With a smile and wave, Maddy walked out of the room to join Tim Lyons who was waiting with George Cooper in the lounge.

Cooper hadn't attended the auction but was ecstatic at the news that Maddy had secured such a hefty price.

"I'm absolutely delighted," he said, grabbing her hand and pumping it furiously. "I had my doubts, you know."

Maddy smiled tightly. She resisted the temptation to tell him she had promised to get the best price and she had delivered.

"Yes," Tim chimed in. "You carried it off like a virtuoso. I believe you've achieved a record for a property such as this."

"That's nice to know," Maddy said sweetly.

Tim wanted to buy drinks to celebrate but Maddy excused herself. After the excitement of the auction, she felt exhausted. Now she just wanted to get home to the peace and serenity of Auburn Grove.

Twenty minutes later she was relaxing in a warm bath. She had encountered another challenge in her career and passed with flying colours.

She felt on top of the world.

Chapter Thirteen

It was a few days later and Maddy was busy at her desk when she received a phone call from Mr Shanley's secretary to say that the managing director would like to speak to her. Since the auction, she had been walking on air. The price she had achieved for Elsinore was indeed a record as Tim Lyons had surmised and the fact was duly recorded in the property supplements which trumpeted the news along with prominent mentions of the firm. It was all excellent publicity and everyone was delighted.

Fergus Shanley was a founder of the company along with his lifetime friend Paddy Carroll who had died a few years earlier. It was Mr Shanley who had given Maddy her first job and he had always taken a keen interest in her career. But he was getting older and now only came into the office a few times a week, leaving the day-to-day running of the business to the senior partners. An interview with him was a rare event.

"When would he like to see me?" Maddy asked respectfully.

"Right now," the secretary announced. "He's waiting for you."

She immediately stood up, straightened her skirt and made a beeline for the bathroom where she quickly brushed her hair and repaired her make-up. Then she climbed the stairs that led to the managing director's office. She knocked politely on the door before hearing the command to enter.

Fergus Shanley was sitting behind a large mahogany desk, staring intently at some reports. He was wearing a dark sports shirt and a warm cardigan around his thin frame. Maddy's eyes took in the walking stick that rested against the desk. Mr Shanley had been a fit man all his life and a keen golfer until arthritis had curtailed his activities. Recently he had undergone surgery to replace a hip and a knee. He looked up when he saw her framed in the doorway.

"Ah, Maddy. Good to see you. Come in, my dear. Take a seat." He pointed to an empty chair across the desk from him. "You're looking very well," he continued as she sat down. "And working hard. I heard all about your triumph the other day."

She blushed with pride.

"A record price. Congratulations. And your very first auction, I understand. Were you nervous?"

"A little," she conceded. She wasn't going to tell the managing director that she had been terrified.

He smiled. "I well remember *my* first auction. I was as nervous as a kitten. All those expectant faces staring up at me. It was like going on stage at the Olympia Theatre. But you carried it off with aplomb and, of course, we're all very pleased. The resultant publicity has done the company no harm at all."

Maddy lowered her eyes to conceal her triumph as he continued.

"Some people believe that conducting auctions is a man's job, too rough for a woman. But I don't hold with that nonsense. There's no job in this industry that a woman can't do. And you have proven me right." He beamed across the desk. "I hear that your spring campaign is already achieving heartening results."

"Yes," Maddy replied. "Sales are up again."

"There's more confidence in the market and people have a bit more money to spend. But that doesn't mean we can rest on our laurels. We've got to keep plugging away."

"I agree."

He opened a drawer, took out an envelope and pushed it across the desk.

"I want you to accept this as a small token of my appreciation."

Maddy stared at it.

"Go on, pick it up. It's not going to bite you," he laughed.

She took the envelope and slipped it into her pocket.

"I'm very grateful. Thank you very much."

"No need to thank me. You've earned it."

He leaned forward in his chair and examined her closely.

"Tell me something, Maddy. Are you happy here?"

The question took her completely by surprise.

"Oh, yes, Mr Shanley. I'm very happy."

"I'm pleased to hear that. We like to keep our staff happy. I'm a firm believer that contented staff make productive employees. Don't you agree?"

"Certainly."

"So if you ever feel unhappy, I hope you will feel free to come and talk to me."

"Of course! Did you have any reason to think I might be unhappy?" she ventured.

Fergus Shanley smiled once more. "No. But I know that others are interested in you. I heard about your lunch with Peter O'Leary in the Shelbourne Hotel."

She felt herself blushing again. How on earth had he learned? She hadn't breathed a word about the lunch.

"Peter is a cunning old fox but not as clever as he thinks. He mentioned the lunch to someone and that person told me. I know the terms he offered you to join his team."

Maddy's face was now red with embarrassment. She felt as if she had been found out in an indiscretion. Or worse, an act of disloyalty!

"I also know you turned him down."

"I wanted to stay here," she replied.

"You don't have to explain," Fergus Shanley went on. "It was a very generous offer. Any young person in your position would have found it extremely attractive. But you put your loyalty to this company ahead of your ambition and that is very much to your credit. I will make sure that it doesn't go unrewarded." He shifted in his seat. "I'm getting too old for this business. I'm not so fit anymore. One of these days, I will retire and then the company will be reorganised. Someone else will take my place."

His face had taken on a grave look. "The industry is changing fast. It's no longer a gentlemen's club. Competition is growing fiercer by the day. The time is coming for younger hands at the helm."

He paused and looked directly at her.

"I want you to know that you have a bright future with Carroll and Shanley, Maddy."

"Thank you," she heard herself say.

"Yes, indeed. The company depends on people like you."

She finally left the managing director's office and made her way downstairs again. Once she got to her desk, she quickly tore open the envelope he had given her. She could hardly believe her eyes. It contained a cheque for £6,000. Fergus Shanley had given her the entire commission the company had earned from the auction of Elsinore!

With the auction out of the way, Maddy was free once more to concentrate on the main job of directing her sales team. Every day brought fresh properties to the market. The window of their office was crammed with houses for sale and their board with its bright blue and red logo was seen increasingly in gardens and fences all over the area.

But one property remained solidly stuck, ignored and forgotten by sales people and buyers alike. Despite their best efforts, the house on Munster Road remained unsold. Maddy was beginning to feel guilty. She had promised Tim Lyons to give it a special push but so far nothing had happened. Those people who had been persuaded to view had come away unimpressed. The house was just too gloomy. It needed too much work. It lacked the bright, well-maintained appeal of other properties. Why spend good money on a house that was only going to bring problems and headaches?

But the house remained on Maddy's mind. One sunny afternoon towards the end of May, she decided to drive over to Rathmines to view it again. It was beginning to bug her. She was determined that the season wouldn't end without it being sold. She parked outside and looked along the tree-lined avenue. The neighbouring houses sparkled in the bright sunshine, their lawns neatly trimmed, their gardens blooming with bright flowers, the driveways swept neat and clean. All except No 26.

By comparison, it looked drearier than ever. The windows were grimy and dirty and the paint was peeling from the front door. Unlike its neighbours, the garden had reverted to nature, and weeds nourished by the winter rains had now grown to monstrous proportions. There was even grass sprouting from the crooked gutters. The house looked dismal and depressing. Maddy could understand why any prospective purchaser would immediately want to run a mile from it.

The gloomy impression was reinforced as soon as she opened the front door. It was a dreadful shame to see the old house falling apart like this. It had so much potential. As she walked through the rooms, she kept reminding herself how they would look with a little bit of imagination and some tender loving care. She recalled what people had told her after she purchased Auburn Grove. How they had envied her. How they wished they'd had her vision. She remembered their astonished looks at the house-warming party as she showed them round the rooms and told them what she had paid.

This house could be the very same. It could be transformed. It would be a labour of love. Before the paint was even dry, it would have doubled in value. It was in a very good part of town and it was going for a song. A flash of inspiration came to her. Why didn't she buy the house herself!

She paused as the thought took root in her brain. With the cheque which Fergus Shanley had given her, she now had almost £18,000 saved in a deposit account. She would only have to borrow the £15,000 for the renovation work plus a bit more for legal fees and stamp duty. Since her promotion, her salary had practically doubled. What was stopping her? Suddenly she felt that if she didn't buy the house and someone else did, she would never forgive herself.

She gave the place a final look-over and locked up. Now she was determined. She *would* buy it! She drove back to the office in a lighter mood, her mind teeming with excitement at the plans that were rapidly taking shape in her head. But she kept her counsel. Before she made another move, she still had some work to do.

That evening, while Rosie and Sophie went off to see a movie, Maddy fixed a mug of coffee, sat down at the kitchen table with a pen and paper and did some calculations. Now that she had decided on a course of action, she wanted to be totally sure that nothing could go wrong. The sad experience of her friends still rankled. She began with her salary and disposable income. She counted projected bonuses and commissions. She subtracted her living expenses, current mortgage repayments, legal fees and the extra money she would be required to repay on her new borrowings. With every calculation she made, she felt more convinced. It would be a very tight squeeze but it was possible. She *could* buy 26 Munster Road, if the bank could be persuaded to lend her the money.

It was now half past eight. Conor Black would be at home. She didn't like bothering him after working hours but this was something of an emergency and he had always been very accommodating in the past. She lifted the phone and rang. He answered at once.

"Hi, Conor," she began.

"Maddy!" he replied in a jaunty voice. "To what do I owe this pleasant surprise?"

"I wonder if you could advise me about a query I have. I'm thinking of buying another house."

She heard him laugh.

"So you've decided to become a property tycoon?"

"Nothing so grand, I'm afraid. It's the house in Munster Road that Sophie and Rosie tried to buy."

"You mean you still haven't managed to sell it?"

"No. And it's an absolute bargain. I just know I could do so much with it."

"So what's the problem?"

"I'll have to get a mortgage. Before I start building up my hopes, I want to be sure there is no impediment that would cause the banks to turn me down."

"You're buying it for yourself?"

"Yes."

"With your own money?"

"Most of it. I'll have to borrow around £20,000."

"And you'll be the sole owner?"

"That's right."

"Well, I can't see any difficulty. The reason your friends were turned down was because they were buying it jointly."

"I have to confess I'm apprehensive."

"Maddy, there's an old saying. Nothing ventured, nothing gained. I think you should go for it. All you have to do is convince your bank manager."

"Thanks, Conor. You're a gem."

The following morning as soon as she arrived into work, Maddy rang the bank and made an appointment to see the manager the following day. Next she went to see Tim Lyons.

"The house in Munster Road," she said.

His ears immediately pricked up.

"I'm thinking of buying it myself."

He let out a whoop and seized her by the shoulders.

"Oh, Maddy! That's the best news I've heard in ages. That house has been haunting me like Marley's ghost."

"I'm thinking of bidding the £18,000 that was accepted the last time."

"But how are you going to finance it? You've already got a mortgage on Auburn Grove."

"Leave that to me. What I need from you is another statement of income. And I'd like you to use your creative accounting techniques again."

"You're going to look for a second mortgage?" Tim asked, clearly bowled over by her audacity.

"That's right. But I don't want to do anything till I get the all-clear from the bank. I'm seeing the manager tomorrow."

"I'll get working on it right away. Oh, Maddy, you really are a brave woman."

"No, I'm not. I'm just someone who can't resist a bargain."

The following lunch-time, armed with a glowing salary statement from Tim, Maddy went to see the new bank manager. He was a former rugby international called Alan Semple who was clearly uncomfortable in his tight business suit and stiff collar. She had the distinct impression that he would feel much happier togged out in track-suit and runners. But he was a pleasant man without formality and a refreshing change from the rigid bureaucrats she had dealt with in the past.

For the next five minutes Maddy made her pitch.

At last, Alan Semple sat back in his chair and stroked his chin.

"You want to borrow £20,000?"

"Yes."

He scribbled some figures on a notepad and did some rapid calculations.

"I think we can manage that."

Maddy felt her heart leap.

"I'll forward your application right away," he said, "with my personal recommendation."

"When will I know?"

"Within fourteen days."

"It's in very bad repair," she said then, adding quickly, "but it's basically a solid structure – and I plan to carry out extensive renovation work."

"We'll take all that into account, Miss Pritchard."

Alan Semple stood up and shook hands with her.

"I'll ring you with the decision as soon as I get word."

Maddy hurried back to the office, feeling buoyed up by the interview.

"How did it go?" Tim Lyons whispered as he went past her desk later in the afternoon.

"Okay, I think. I'll know for sure in the next fortnight."

He gave her a thumbs-up sign. "Good luck."

The next two weeks crawled by. Despite having gone through this experience before, Maddy still found the waiting period excruciating. Then one morning, having spent twenty minutes discussing the progress of a sale with a client, she put down the phone and immediately heard it ring again.

"Have I got Miss Pritchard?"

It was Alan Semple.

"Yes," Maddy replied.

"Alan Semple here. Your loan application has come back."

She felt a nervous tingle run along her spine. "Yes?"

"It's good news, Miss Pritchard. Your loan has been approved."

Within five minutes, she had found Tim Lyons and put in a formal bid for the property. She knew by now it was only a formality. But there were still a number of hoops to jump through before she could finally become the legal owner of 26, Munster Road.

That evening at dinner she dropped her surprise. Sophie had cooked a shepherd's pie with string beans and salad. Maddy waited till they were all seated round the dining-table before making her announcement.

"I hope you guys haven't given up on Munster Road?" she said casually as she forked up some of Sophie's pie.

Rosie stared at her. "What do you mean?"

"I mean, how would you like to live there?"

Rosie gave her an odd look. "What is this? Some kind of weird joke?"

"No. I'm perfectly serious. So would you like to live there or not?"

"But the bank turned us down," Sophie said.

"I know that. Now, *I'm* in the process of buying it."

There was a loud clattering sound as Sophie dropped her fork.

"You're *what?*" she said, staring across the table.

"I'm buying the house and I'm asking if you'd like to be my tenants."

She paused and looked around the table.

"That's if you still want it."

Next moment, there was uproar. Sophie jumped out of her chair and hugged her and was quickly joined by Rosie. Next minute, the three women were dancing around the dining-table with their arms entwined, singing at the top of their voices: *"Happy days are here again!"*.

The next few weeks were a crazy rush of form-filling, contract-signing and numerous trips to Munster Road to take measurements and photographs. The three women spent their evenings huddled round the dining-table excitedly making drawings of how they wanted to redesign the house. Maddy had firm ideas about what she planned to do but she also wanted to hear what the others had to say. They were going to live there after all.

When they had finished and Sophie had been promised the blue tiles she wanted for the bathroom, Maddy called in Paddy Behan who said he could start work as soon as the sale went through. With a bit of luck, he would have the reconstruction finished by August.

"Aren't you going to miss us?" Rosie asked one evening after they had spent the day in town looking at furniture.

"Why would I miss you? You'll be less than half a mile away. Anyway, I'm looking forward to having Auburn Grove all to myself again. It's the reason I bought it in the first place!"

It was a madly exhilarating time. The gloom that had hung over the women for the past few months had now completely evaporated and was replaced by a wild expectancy. Everyone was on tenterhooks, eagerly making plans while they waited for the sale to go through and the building work to begin.

Then, just when she thought she couldn't handle any more excitement, Maddy's life took another twist.

Chapter Fourteen

It was a bright Saturday afternoon and Dublin was thronged with tourists and shoppers. She had gone into Grafton Street for a hairdressing appointment in preparation for a dinner party she was attending that evening. It was being hosted by a well-known property developer and promised to be a glittering occasion. But she was only going because Carroll and Shanley were hoping to secure the sales rights to an apartment complex he was building and she wanted to look her best.

After spending several hours having her hair tossed, trimmed, washed and blow-dried, she returned to her car about four o'clock and was just about to open the door when she felt a gentle tap on her shoulder. She turned and found Greg Delaney smiling at her.

She gave a start. The last time she had set eyes on him was the previous October. And in the meantime, a lot had happened to remove him completely from her mind.

But he seemed pleased to see her.

"I thought it was you," he said, "but I wasn't sure. How are you?"

"I'm fine, Greg," she replied, quickly regaining her composure. "And how are you? How did the wedding go?"

A frown passed over his handsome face. Something warned her that she had wandered into dangerous territory.

"It didn't," he said, abruptly.

She stared at him for a moment. "You mean...?

"I mean we didn't get married. It was called off."

Maddy was shocked. "Has it been postponed?" she managed to say.

"No. It's been cancelled."

"I'm sorry. I hope . . ."

He shrugged. "It's a long story, Maddy. And I haven't got time to go into it, right now. But all round, I think it was for the best."

"And what about The Beeches? Did you manage to sell it?"

"No. I've taken it off the market." He glanced quickly at his watch as if he was suddenly anxious to get away. "Look, I have to see someone in twenty minutes. I've got to run."

"Okay," she said. "Nice meeting you."

"You too," he said, rushing away.

She watched him go. What on earth had happened? It must have been horrific to have to cancel the wedding. Apart from whatever heartache was involved, she thought of all the preparations that would have had to be dismantled, all the people who would have to be contacted, not to mention the terrible embarrassment. No wonder he didn't want to talk about it.

Which of them had broken it off? It must have been Lorna Hamilton, she decided. Maddy had never met the woman but she didn't like the little she had learnt about her. She had sounded like the type of bossy, domineering woman who would drive any man insane with her constant demands. Maybe Greg had a lucky escape, she thought as she got into her car and prepared to drive back to Auburn Grove.

The dinner party turned out to be the sort of occasion that Maddy hated. It was terribly snobby with brash men and brittle women attempting to outdo each other with their jewellery and their dresses and their talk about holidays and clothes. She felt very uncomfortable and when it came midnight, was glad to make her excuses and leave, her duty done.

But over the next few days she found her thoughts wandering back to that chance meeting with Greg Delaney. Her curiosity had been aroused. She wondered what had happened with Lorna Hamilton to cause the wedding to be cancelled and the apartment sale abandoned.

She found her attitude to Greg beginning to soften. His problem was that he was too impulsive. The episode with The Beeches was a good example. If he had listened to her advice, he would have realised that selling the property for such an exorbitant price in such a short period of time was impossible. But he had gone about it like a bull in a china shop. Now he was left with the embarrassment plus the costs. She had already billed him for several hundred pounds in advertising fees and doubtless the Dalkey auctioneer would have done the same. And that was nothing compared to the nightmare of the abandoned wedding. Poor Greg, she thought. Despite his faults, it was hard not to feel sorry for him.

Meanwhile, she had her hands full with 26, Munster Road. After weeks of excited discussion, they had finally decided how they wanted the house to be restored. The wall separating the two ground-floor rooms was going to be removed to make one large living-room. The bedrooms would be completely renovated along with the bathroom and at Sophie's request the kitchen was going to be enlarged and extended. After much haggling, Paddy Behan agreed that the work could be done for £16,000. Now they just had to wait for the contract to be signed and the legal work completed.

However, a few weeks later, Maddy was surprised to answer the phone and hear a familiar voice on the line. Greg Delaney came on, sounding bright and chirpy like an eleven-year-old boy on the first day of the school holidays.

"Greg," she said. "It's nice to hear from you again."

"And you."

"So how are you?"

"I'm fine. Up to my neck in work but I enjoy that as you know."

"Well, I'm very glad to hear it."

She wondered why he was ringing. She hoped he wasn't going to ask her to sell The Beeches for him again. She hadn't the stomach for all that hassle once more. But it was something else entirely.

"I've got a colleague who's looking to buy something in your neck of the woods," he said, cheerfully, "and I took the liberty of giving him your name. I hope you don't mind?"

"Not at all," she said with some relief. "We're always glad of new business."

"He's called Ed Clancy. You can expect a call from him any day soon. He'll explain exactly what he's looking for. I told him you were the best estate agent in Dublin and he'd get star treatment."

"You're in the wrong business, Greg. Ever think of a career in PR?"

He laughed heartily. "You know, we should get together for a drink some time," he mused. "I've an awful lot to tell you. We sort of lost touch for a while."

"Sure," Maddy said. "I'd like that. Why don't you call me when you're free?"

"How about next Monday?"

The speed of the invitation caught her on the hop. "I'm not sure if . . ."

"Or Tuesday, if that suits you better. I'm free both evenings."

There was an almost pleading quality in his voice. He sounded lonely and Maddy felt her heart go out to him. Besides, she was dying to find out exactly what had happened with the wedding.

"Okay," she said.

"So which day will it be?"

"Monday is fine."

"Brilliant. How about Charlie's Bar in Baggot St? You know it?"

"Sure."

"I'll meet you in the lounge at six o'clock."

"Okay."

"Excellent. I'm looking forward to it, Maddy."

"Me too."

She put down the phone and stared off into space. Now she wondered if she had done the right thing agreeing to see Greg Delaney again. Her previous experiences with him had not been good. But she told herself it was merely an innocent drink. He probably needed a shoulder to cry on after his ordeal at the hands of Lorna Hamilton. If he attempted to take it any further, she would politely decline.

Ed Clancy rang later that afternoon and made an appointment to see her the following day at twelve. He turned out to be a large, heavily built man in his early forties who had a home in Dundrum but wanted to move closer to the city. He was looking for a four-bedroom house near to schools and shops and within walking distance of the sea.

As luck would have it, Maddy had the perfect place – a smart detached villa in Blackrock with mature gardens. She gave Ed the sales brochure and arranged with one of her staff to show it to him and his wife at the weekend. For good measure, she added a few more properties that might interest him. He left the office extremely satisfied and with a promise to give Carroll and Shanley the sale of his house in Dundrum. Altogether it was good morning's business.

Meanwhile, events were now proceeding rapidly with 26, Munster Road, and Conor Black had called to say he expected to wrap up the purchase in the next couple of days. Maddy's long-term plan was to use the house as an investment. She had agreed with Sophie and Rosie to pay her the same rent as before, £50 a month each, which would help to offset the mortgage.

Before she knew it, it was time for her drink with Greg. She decided not to dress up for the occasion in case she sent out the wrong signals. This was merely a social occasion, an errand of mercy and she was determined to keep him at arm's length. So she wore a simple knee-length skirt with black boots and a little cotton jacket. However, before leaving the office she spent five minutes in the bathroom carefully applying lipstick and repairing her make-up.

She found him standing at the counter, deep in conversation with the barman. She thought he looked elegant in his well-tailored white linen suit and neatly groomed hair. As soon as he saw her, he set about making a big fuss before whisking her off to a corner table.

"Now, what are you having?" he asked, once they were seated.

"I think I'll stick to coffee," Maddy said. "I don't like to drink and drive."

"Oh c'mon, we haven't seen each other in ages."

"All right, I'll have a glass of red wine. A small one, please."

He gave their order to the barman, then turned his attention back to her again.

"You look wonderful," he said, staring deeply into her eyes.

"Thank you."

"Tell me everything that has happened to you. How is the job?"

"The job is going extremely well, I'm pleased to say. I'm probably every bit as busy as you are."

"No, that wouldn't be possible," he replied, flashing the boyish grin that Maddy remembered. "Nobody works harder than me. Except my boss, as he keeps reminding me." He laughed then stopped and looked seriously at her. "It's so good to see you again, Maddy. You don't know how many times I was tempted to ring you in the last few months. I desperately needed someone sensible to talk to."

"What was stopping you?"

"Pride, I suppose. I didn't want to admit that I'd made an awful hash of things."

"You mean the wedding?"

"Not just the wedding – the romance, the sale of the apartment, the whole damned lot. You've no idea what a mess everything was." He sighed. "But it's over now, thank God, and nobody got killed."

"We all make mistakes, Greg. Nobody's perfect."

"This wasn't a mistake. It was a disaster. I don't know what came over me. It was as if I had taken leave of my senses." He shrugged. "Anyway, you don't want to listen to this stuff."

"Please," she said. "You can talk about it if it makes you feel better. I don't mind."

The barman appeared with the drinks and Greg paid him.

"I don't know where to begin. Normally, I'm a very sensible guy but within weeks of meeting Lorna I seemed to have fallen completely off my trolley. I'd agreed to sell my apartment, buy a house in Dalkey that I couldn't afford and marry her. When I look at it now I can see that I must have been crazy."

"It's called love," Maddy said.

"You think so?"

"Well, I certainly hope so. You don't normally go around proposing marriage to someone you're not in love with, do you?"

"But I didn't propose to her," he said quickly. "*She* proposed to me. Or to put it more accurately, she insisted."

Maddy stared.

"You've never met her, have you?" he asked.

"I don't think so . . ."

"If you did, you'd remember and you'd know exactly what I'm talking about. Lorna is a very strong-willed woman as well as being extremely beautiful. I think I'm attracted to women like that," he said, glancing at her.

She felt a blush creep into her cheeks.

"From the moment she came out to advise me about the apartment," he went on, "she took complete control. Everything you saw there – the colour of the walls, the size of the settee in the living room, everything right down to the flower vase was Lorna's decision. I just went along like I'd been hypnotised."

"Well, she certainly did a very good job. I've told you that already."

"And that would have been fine if she had stuck to what she was being paid for. But once she had finished with the penthouse, she started in on me. On our very first date, she told me I would have to get married. She said I was a disorganised workaholic with nothing to live for outside my job and needed a woman to impose some discipline on my life."

Maddy listened with fascination. It was exactly what she had suspected. But Lorna Hamilton had set to work even faster than she'd thought.

"In no time at all, she had decided that no one could organise my life better than she could so she proposed that we get married. And like a fool, I agreed. I suppose I was dazzled by the fact that such a beautiful woman would ask me to marry her. Then she made up her mind that apartment living was unsuitable and we needed to buy a house. But not just any house. It had to be a large house. In Dalkey of all places which you know is one of the most expensive locations in Ireland. And that's where you came on the scene."

"The idea of buying the Dalkey house was fine," Maddy said. "If you'd had the cash to fund it. The problem was you were asking far too much for The Beeches and giving yourself too little time to sell it."

"I know, I know," Greg said, burying his head in his hands. "I just wish I had listened to you at the beginning. It would have saved me an awful lot of heartache, believe me."

She took a sip of her wine. This story was incredible. She still couldn't understand how someone as smart as Greg could have allowed himself to be railroaded like this.

"Do you want to tell me how it all ended?"

"In disaster and woe," he said. "We couldn't sell The Beeches and we couldn't buy the house despite letting the Dalkey auctioneer take it over. He was completely useless, by the way. Not a patch on you. In all the time he had the penthouse I think he brought one person to view it."

Maddy stifled a smile of satisfaction.

"Meanwhile," he went on, "Christmas was fast approaching but it wasn't bringing tidings of joy. Lorna was going ballistic that something she had planned wasn't coming right. She had finally met a situation she couldn't control. And she didn't like it one little bit. Every day she was on the phone to me about when The Beeches was going to be sold. She was obsessed with it. She would ring seven or eight times a day.

At the same time she was trying to organise our wedding with all the attendant stress *that* involved. And the wedding was going to be the grandest affair that Dublin had ever seen, hundreds of guests, gallons of champagne, acres of flowers. I couldn't sleep with worry. I was losing weight. I couldn't concentrate on my job. Something had to give. In the end the whole thing collapsed like a house of cards."

"What happened?"

"I woke up one morning and realised that I just couldn't go through with it. I couldn't live with the thought of Lorna controlling every aspect of my life no matter how beautiful she was. It would be like living in hell. I decided to call the wedding off."

"*You* did?"

"Yes. You look surprised."

"It just sounds so incredible."

"Incredible doesn't even begin to describe it. She went berserk, of course. Here was something else she couldn't handle. There was a dreadful weeping scene. I was accused of being everything from Charles Manson to Adolf Hitler. Then I had to begin the nightmare of cancelling the wedding service, the reception, the honeymoon and taking The Beeches off the market. I lost about £20,000 on the whole ghastly business. But I consider it a small price to pay for having escaped."

"Where is she now?"

"London. She said she was so shamed by what had happened that she couldn't possibly work in Dublin again. I got blamed for that too, of course."

He drained his glass then signalled to the barman for another.

"I'm terribly sorry," Maddy said at last. "I had absolutely no idea."

He shrugged. "I was foolish. I just wish I'd had the good sense to talk to you. I'm sure you would have advised me."

Yes, Maddy thought. I would have told you to drop Ms Control Freak like a hot potato. But would you have listened?

"Put it behind you, Greg, and start afresh. Learn a lesson from it. Be more careful next time."

She glanced at her watch. The time had flown. It was now almost half seven.

She stood up.

"Thanks for the wine," she said. "I'd better be going."

"But you've only just arrived."

"That was over an hour ago."

"My God, you're right. I hope I didn't bore you?"

"No, Greg. I was fascinated."

He clasped her hand. "Thanks for listening to me. After telling you the whole horror story, I feel an awful lot better." He leaned forward and politely kissed her cheek. "Maybe we could meet again?"

Maddy paused. Now was the time to tell him that she didn't want the relationship to develop any further. "I'm not sure that would be a good idea."

"Please? It's been such a relief talking to you."

She looked at him. He looked so lost and vulnerable. Something deep inside her wanted to protect and comfort him.

"Okay," she said. "Give me a ring. You've got my number."

She drove back to Auburn Grove, amazed by the story she had just heard. Greg was an intelligent guy but he was like a lot of men she had known – a sucker for female charm. And in Lorna Hamilton he appeared to have met an expert in the art of manipulation.

But he seemed to have survived and she had enjoyed talking to him again. She felt the beginning of a smile cross her lips. It might be fun getting to know Greg Delaney a little bit better.

Chapter Fifteen

The following morning, Conor Black rang to say the contracts were in order, the mortgage was agreed and he was ready to complete the purchase of Munster Road. When would suit her to come in and sign the necessary papers?

Maddy had been waiting for this day for a long time and was anxious to get started.

She quickly glanced at her appointments diary for the rest of the day and saw that it was blank.

"This afternoon?" she asked, hopefully.

"Why not? No time like the present," she heard him say. "This afternoon at three."

She worked through lunch and at three o'clock she was once more in Conor's office, seated across his vast untidy desk while he pushed over pieces of paper for her signature.

At last, when all the paperwork had been completed, he put his pen away, stood up, presented her with a set of keys and firmly shook her hand.

"Congratulations. You're building up quite a nice little portfolio," he said. "That's two fine properties you own."

"This one was a bargain. They both were. I would have kicked myself if I had missed it."

He smiled warmly. "I suppose you and your boyfriend will go out tonight and celebrate?"

"No," Maddy replied.

"Oh?"

"I don't have a regular boyfriend."

He looked surprised as he regarded her with renewed interest. "Indeed? I would have thought an attractive woman like you would have hordes of admirers. Fighting them off, I would have thought."

Maddy simply laughed. "Thanks for the compliment, Conor. But I have my hands full with other commitments. Boyfriends are low on my agenda right now."

"Well, you've certainly made a very wise investment," he said, becoming serious again. "Just between ourselves, I had a client last week who sold a house on that very same road for £95,000."

She stopped in the act of putting on her coat. "Really?"

"Yes. Just a few doors away from yours in fact."

"That's interesting," she said as she slid into her coat and said goodbye.

How odd, she thought as she got into her car and prepared to drive away. For a brief moment back there I thought Conor Black was flirting with me. But the news that he had just given her had certainly cheered her up. £95,000 for a similar house on the same road! It vindicated her decision and confirmed her judgment. But right now she had to contact Paddy Behan and organise the building work.

After a series of convoluted phone calls she managed to track him down to a noisy pub in Cabra.

"I've got the keys to Munster Road," she said. "It's all finalised."

"That's brilliant. Congratulations."

"When can you start?"

"Let me see!" Paddy shouted above the din. "I've a job to finish out here which will take another few days. I suppose I could start next Monday morning, eight o'clock."

"Right," Maddy said. "I'll be there to meet you. You won't let me down now, will you?"

"Get away out of that!" Paddy chuckled. "You're dealing with professionals here. Anyway, if I did something like that your brother Brian would never speak to me again."

That evening, Maddy and the girls sat around the kitchen table and drank wine and ate a chicken curry that Sophie had prepared. It wasn't quite the wild celebration they had the last time she had purchased a property but it was no less important for that.

"Drink up, girls. Paddy Behan starts work on Monday morning. In a few months' time, you'll have your own pad."

"You've been very good to us, Maddy," Rosie said. "How can we ever repay you?"

"It's called friendship," Maddy replied. "Forever friends, remember? We stick together."

"Forever friends," they said and tipped their glasses in a toast.

They spent the next few evenings in a lather of activity, attempting to prepare the house for the arrival of the builders. First thing was to clear away the old-fashioned furniture which the previous owner had left behind. Maddy contacted a firm that specialised in house clearances and they came with a van and took everything away.

Then at lunch-time on Friday, she got a surprise phone call from Greg Delaney.

"Doing anything tomorrow?" he asked.

"Nothing special."

"How would you like to come to a barbecue with me?"

"What is it exactly?" she asked.

"Just a colleague from work. He has a cottage in Enniskerry and has invited a few friends over. It'll be completely informal. A few beers, a burnt hamburger and some limp salad. You've been to barbecues before, Maddy."

A day in the countryside would be a pleasant diversion, she thought. And Wicklow would be at its best just now.

"Okay. What time are we talking about?"

"I could pick you up around eleven. No point taking both cars. Then we'll have a nice relaxing drive through Wicklow."

"I'd better tell you how to get to my place."

"I know where you live. Raheny."

"I've moved, Greg. I'm now living in Ranelagh."

"Oh! Is the north side not good enough for you any more?"

"Closer to work," she said with a chuckle.

She gave him directions and put down the phone. That evening, instead of meeting Sophie and Rosie for their regular Friday-night drinks, she went straight home, cooked a nice supper, had a long soak in the bath and was in bed with a good book by eleven o'clock.

The next day was bright and sunny. While her housemates slept off the excesses of the night before, she got up and tidied the house. She was just finishing breakfast when she heard the bell ring. When she opened the door, she found Greg standing on the step dressed in chinos, loafers and a casual shirt underneath a smart leather jacket.

"So you found it all right?"

"Yes. I used to live in a bed-sit near here when I was a student."

"Come and have some coffee," she said.

He stepped inside and she saw his eyes quickly darting around the hall as he took in the surroundings. She brought him into the living-room and he gave a whistle of approval.

"This is a nice place you've got here, Maddy. What are you paying for it?"

"£185 a month."

"You're getting a good deal for a whole house. I would have thought rents round here would be a lot more."

"That's not rent, Greg. That's my mortgage."

She saw his jaw drop.

"You mean you own it?"

"Yes. Why do you sound surprised?"

"It's just...well it looks so expensive."

He walked across the room to examine a framed print that was hanging above the fireplace.

"It's beautiful. I'm very impressed."

"Let me show you my pride and joy."

She led him to the end of the room, pulled back the sliding doors and took him out to the patio. It was bathed in light and the geraniums and pansies were opening to the sun. The garden was sparkling with life, the daffodils tossing their yellow heads, the buds on the trees bursting into leaf.

"Why don't you sit here and I'll get the coffee?" she said, pointing to the carved wooden bench she had bought at a garden centre.

When she came back, she found him bent over the roses.

"They need pruning," she said. "I've been so busy lately that I've fallen way behind with the spade work."

"This is magnificent," he said, gazing down the lawn. "It's so relaxing. You know the big thing I miss about The Beeches is a garden."

"It's a lot of hard work."

"But it's worth it. Listen to the birds. Look at the flowers. It's so …"

"Tranquil?"

He turned to her and smiled. "Exactly. You know, I envy you having a place like this."

She was delighted at his praise. She loved it when people admired her handiwork.

"You're a very lucky woman," he continued. "Most people would give their right arm for somewhere like this."

"It wasn't just luck. There was a lot of risk involved too. You should understand that."

"Do you mind me asking? Was the house expensive?"

"It cost me £15,000."

He stared. "*What?*"

"Plus another £7,000 to have it renovated and furnished. When I bought it, it was a wreck. It had been on our books for ages and we couldn't find a buyer."

"But it must be worth four times that by now."

"I don't know. It's not for sale."

He looked at her with increased respect. "You're a genius, Maddy."

"No, I just took a chance. I could see the potential."

"But that's what it's all about. Seeing what no one else can see.

You're one smart cookie. We could do with your talent in our business."

She shook her head. "I'd be completely lost. I'm afraid I haven't got a clue about stocks and shares."

"You'd pick it up in no time."

"Are you offering me a job?"

"Are you available?"

She laughed. "I think I'll stick to what I know. And that's property. I'll leave the stock market to the financial wizards like you."

The drive down to Wicklow was exhilarating. Greg was particularly attentive to her. His compliments about her house and her investment skills had left her feeling warm and satisfied and now she leaned back and allowed the breeze to toss her hair as the car negotiated the narrow country roads around Enniskerry.

At last they stopped outside a gateway with two large stone pillars and he slowly manoeuvred the car along a bumpy path till they found themselves outside a stone bungalow with a sign that read: *Whinbush Cottage*. A young man in Levis and golf shirt came out to meet them.

"This is Maddy," Greg said, hopping out of the car. "Maddy, meet Marc McCarthy who happens to be one of the dynamos of our operation."

Marc gave a grunt. "Dynamo? More like a flat battery, if he was telling the truth."

He was a sturdy young man about Greg's age with a square chin and solid shoulders. He clasped her hand in a firm grip and told her she was very welcome.

"We're out the back," he said. "Come through the house. How were the roads? Traffic okay?"

"Remarkably free," Greg replied. "We did the trip in an hour."

They went through the cottage and out to the back lawn where a group of people were standing round a smoking barbecue drinking bottles of beer.

"Let me introduce you," Marc said. "This is my wife, Sally."

A plump, contented-looking woman with red hair and freckles smiled at Maddy and took her hand.

"You must be Maddy," she said. "Greg has told us about you."

"Oh?" she replied. "I hope it was nothing bad?"

"On the contrary, he was singing your praises. Apparently you fixed Ed Clancy with a house?"

"That's right."

"Well, if you managed to satisfy Ed you must be good."

A couple of tousle-headed children had approached and were now examining her intently.

"These are the offspring," Marc said. "Jemima is eight and Toby is six. Say hello to Maddy and Greg."

The children muttered their hellos and immediately ran off giggling.

Marc drew them towards the circle round the barbecue and introduced them. Greg seemed to know most of the people already.

"Lovely day for a barbecue," he remarked, accepting a can of beer from Sally. Maddy asked for a glass of wine.

"Fingers crossed," Sally replied. "Last time we attempted this we were washed out and ended up eating Chinese carry-outs round the stove in the kitchen."

"I don't think there's any danger of that today," Greg responded, staring at the cloudless sky where the sun hovered like a blood-red orange.

The other guests crowded round and once they discovered that Maddy was an estate agent, the conversation immediately turned to property while the sausages spluttered and spat on the grill.

"What do you think?" a plump man asked. "Are prices going to stabilise?"

"I think they'll continue to rise," Maddy said.

"Oh, why do you say that?"

"Well, the population is growing and people have to find somewhere to live. And interest rates are beginning to fall."

"The reason I ask," the plump man continued. "I have my eye on a place over near Glencullen."

"I can't advise you without seeing it," Maddy replied diplomatically, "but my instinct would be to buy now."

"Hmmmh," the plump man said. "That's what I was thinking myself."

Sally reappeared with a large glass of wine for Maddy.

"I hope they're not picking your brains," she said. "They always do that whenever someone interesting turns up. Dr Jameson absolutely refuses to give any medical diagnoses at our parties. He tells them to come to his surgery and pay like everyone else."

The group broke into laughter and Maddy found herself grinning happily. She sipped her wine and looked along the garden where the children were now chasing each other through the bushes. The sun was slanting across the lawn and in the valley below the house she could see a flock of sheep grazing contentedly.

Greg caught her eye and smiled.

"Enjoying yourself?" he asked, his arm falling protectively across her shoulder.

"Yes."

"That makes me happy. Now come and eat. I think the hamburgers should be sufficiently incinerated by now."

They stayed till eight o'clock when the air began to cool. Some of the diehards had donned woollen jumpers and pullovers and were preparing to remain drinking on the lawn till it got dark. But Maddy and Greg had an hour to drive before they reached Dublin.

Dusk was beginning to fall as they approached the outskirts of the city.

When they finally came to Ranelagh, Greg glanced at her and said, "It seems a bit early to be calling it a day. Why don't we go off somewhere and have a quiet drink?"

But Maddy was suddenly feeling tired. "I think I'll go home, Greg. I've got some work to catch up with."

Immediately, she saw the disappointment on his face but he quickly recovered.

"How about coming out with me again?" he asked.

"Sure. Give me a ring and we'll arrange something."

He brightened up. "I'll certainly do that."

"And Greg, I really enjoyed myself. Thanks for a lovely day."

"My pleasure."

He reached out and drew her close. Next moment he was kissing her and she was yielding to his warm, sensuous touch.

Eventually she pulled herself away and placed a finger across his mouth.

"That's enough for one night," she smiled.

"But there'll be more? Promise me there'll be more."

"That depends on how well you behave," she laughed and pushed open the car door.

Chapter Sixteen

A couple of weeks went past and Maddy didn't hear from Greg. She wasn't too concerned. He was a very attractive man but there were aspects of his personality such as his impetuousness and occasional arrogance that made her pause. She knew if he was seriously interested in her he would come back. Besides, she had other things to occupy her mind. Paddy Behan had begun work on 26, Munster Road, which meant a series of meetings and inspection tours so that the builder was totally familiar with the jobs she wanted done. In addition, Tim Lyons had asked her to undertake another auction.

"Isn't there someone else to do it?" she asked when he approached her about it.

"Of course, there are several."

"So why are you coming to me?"

"Because the client specifically asked for you."

This was a pleasant surprise. "Really?"

He nodded.

"But I've only conducted one auction in my entire career," she protested.

"That may be so. But you achieved a record result. And people aren't stupid. They read the property supplements and they want you to perform a similar miracle for them."

"I'm gobsmacked," Maddy said. "I don't know whether to feel honoured or blackmailed."

"I'd feel honoured," he replied with a smile. "This means the punters are sitting up and taking notice."

The property to be auctioned was a modern bungalow in Booterstown. Maddy rang the vendor and made an appointment to view the following morning. When she arrived, she was met by a small, frothy, bottle-blonde woman in her early forties who said her name was Mamie McCarthy. She was obviously proud of her house. She quickly took Maddy to see the four bedrooms, the large lounge-cum-dining-room, spacious modern kitchen, two bathrooms (one en-suite) and gardens front and rear. It was a very nice house and extremely tastefully furnished but it was hardly exceptional. Maddy couldn't help wondering why it was being offered for auction.

"I'm emigrating," Mrs McCarthy announced once they had finished viewing and were seated in the kitchen drinking coffee and sampling some of her home-baked apple cake. "I'd like you to put that in the paper."

"Put in the paper the fact that you're emigrating?"

"Yes. I can't wait to get far enough from the cheating no-good lowlife I married. I thought I'd settle in the Canaries. The weather is fantastic and you can live on a quarter of what it would cost you here. Have you ever been there?"

"No," Maddy replied.

"You'd love it. Palm trees, golden beaches and the sun shines all day long. We used to go out to Tenerife every January before I caught him at his dirty tricks."

"I see."

For the next ten minutes, Mamie McCarthy regaled Maddy with all the gory details of her marital situation. How she had caught her businessman husband having an affair with his secretary who was young enough to be his daughter. How he said he was in love and wanted a separation and after a lengthy legal wrangle, Mamie's solicitors had secured the bungalow as part of the settlement.

"I'm sorry," was all Maddy could think to say when she had finished.

"I'm not. I'm better off without him. Now I can start living my life again."

"And why have you decided on an auction?" Maddy asked.

"It's a public statement, isn't it? I want everybody to know. And you're the best in the business. I saw your photo in the papers so I asked for you."

"I'm flattered," Maddy replied.

"Why? If you're good at something, you should make the most of it. Now what do you think I'll get?"

This was the tricky question. Before the appointment, Maddy had undertaken some research and discovered that a similar house a few streets away had achieved £190,000 in a private-treaty sale a few months earlier.

"What are you expecting to get?" she countered.

"Well we paid £30,000 for it eight years ago and I know it's gone up a lot since then. I suppose if I got £150,000, I'd be happy."

Maddy breathed a sigh of relief. At least Mrs McCarthy didn't have an inflated opinion about the value of her bungalow. £150,000 was certainly attainable. Indeed with a bit of luck, they should be able to get much more.

"Have you absolutely ruled out a private-treaty sale? There are certain advantages, you know."

"Like what?" Mrs McCarthy asked.

"Well, a lot of purchasers won't touch auctions. They like to know exactly how much they're going to spend. We usually auction houses where we expect a great deal of interest."

Mrs McCarthy immediately looked offended.

"Not that there won't be lots of interest in your house," Maddy hastened to add. "It's a beautiful property and it's in excellent condition. You've certainly kept it very well. I've no doubt there will be stiff competition for it. I just wondered if we might do better in a private sale."

"No," Mrs McCarthy said firmly. "I want it auctioned. I want ads in all the papers. I want that miserable husband of mine to know exactly what he's lost by his hanky-panky."

"All right," Maddy said, sweetly. "If that's your decision, we'll auction it."

The next ten minutes were taken up discussing viewing times, reserve price and the finer details of the transaction. It was decided to auction the property in three weeks' time and hold public viewings twice a week. They fixed the reserve price at £170,000 which sent Mrs McCarthy into a paroxysm of delight.

"Are you sure?" she asked. "It seems a bit on the high side."

"We'll find out soon enough from the level of interest," Maddy replied. "This is a bit like a game of cards. But one thing I have to warn you. You've got to be prepared for some disruption. For the next few weeks, people will be walking in and out of your house as if it was the Phoenix Park."

But far from being unhappy, Mrs McCarthy seemed tickled at the prospect of strangers trooping through her house and the attendant publicity it would bring.

"And you'll make sure there's plenty of ads in the papers?" she insisted.

"Certainly. But you know you'll be paying for them?"

"That's all right. I want everybody to know. You can deduct the cost from the sale price."

Maddy left the house thinking how happy she would be if all her clients were as agreeable as Mrs McCarthy. Once back at the office she arranged for an advertising board to be placed outside the house and a photographer to take pictures for the brochure. She rang her friends on the property supplements and got agreement for editorial write-ups to accompany the adverts. By lunch-time, most of the preliminary work had been completed.

"How did it go?" Tim Lyons asked as he passed her desk later in the afternoon.

Maddy told him about her meeting with Mrs McCarthy.

"It's rather odd," Tim mused. "I can't remember a public auction for a house like this before."

"I did point out the drawbacks," Maddy said, "but she was determined. Nothing would do but an auction."

"Well, she's in the driving seat," he replied. "You'll just have to pull out the stops."

Her afternoon was taken up by a meeting with the developer whose dinner party she had attended some weeks earlier. He was constructing an apartment complex and marina in Malahide and had appointed Carroll and Shanley as sole selling agents. As an incentive, he had come up with the bright idea of giving a berth in the new marina to each purchaser. It was a coup for the company but it added considerably to Maddy's workload.

In addition, Paddy Behan called after four to say he had encountered a plumbing problem at 26 Munster Road and would have to delay work for a few days while he sourced new materials. She was feeling drained when the phone rang at ten past five and she heard Greg on the line.

"Hi," he said, sounding upbeat.

She was surprised at how pleased she suddenly felt to hear his voice.

"How have you been?" he inquired.

"Extremely busy."

"That makes two of us. I've been in Brussels on business for the past ten days."

So this explained why she hadn't heard from him. She was flooded with relief.

"I'm working on a major deal for a client but now I'm back in Dublin and eager for some intelligent female company. I wondered if you might be free to have dinner with me tonight?"

"What did you have in mind?"

"I thought we might go to Hennessy's restaurant and have a nice relaxing evening, a bottle of wine and some pleasant conversation."

"That sounds ideal."

"I'll call for you about eight. How does that sound?"

"Fine."

"Excellent. We'll have a good night, Maddy. I've got so much to tell you."

She put down the phone and smiled. She was glad he had called. She realised she was looking forward to seeing Greg Delaney's handsome face again.

She left the office at five thirty and drove straight home to Auburn Grove. Sophie had called to say she was going to a birthday party for a colleague and Rosie was attending a record launch with her boyfriend, so she had the house to herself. She pulled off her shoes and went upstairs to run a bath. As she relaxed in the hot suds, she thought how chance was intervening once more in her affairs. She was almost twenty-seven and had no regular man in her life. And now Greg Delaney had suddenly reappeared. Was Fate trying to tell her something?

Greg was handsome – there was no question about that. From the very first day she had seen him she had been taken by his good looks; his mop of fine blond hair, his broad shoulders, his boyish grin that could instantly charm the most reluctant heart. But it wasn't his looks alone. Greg had oodles of personality. He could brighten any company by his presence. He was a rare combination of charm and style. Maddy knew that many women would give their right arm for a man like Greg Delaney.

She showered and dried herself then went into her bedroom to get dressed. She chose a wine-coloured party dress. She would wear it with a white jacket and high-heeled shoes. She put on the dress and then attended to her hair and make-up. When she had finished she considered her image in the wardrobe mirror. She looked good – really good. She was just putting on her jacket when she heard the doorbell chime. She glanced at her watch. It was smack on eight o'clock. Greg was punctual as usual.

He was standing on the doorstep with a bouquet of red roses in his hand.

"For the beautiful lady," he said, giving her the flowers and kissing her gently on the cheek.

"For me?" she said, a little taken aback.

"Well, I don't see any other beautiful lady," he said with a smile that immediately had Maddy laughing out loud.

"Let me put these in some water," she said, disappearing into the kitchen.

"Are you hungry?" he shouted after her.

"Let's say I'll give a good account of myself."

"I think you'll like Hennessy's. Ever been there?"

"No!" she called over the noise of the kitchen tap.

"Trust me, you're going to like it," said Greg as she came back from the kitchen with the roses in a vase.

She placed the flowers on a table in the hall.

"All right," she said. "What are we waiting for?"

Hennessy's turned out to be a small intimate restaurant in a narrow cobbled lane off Dame Street. It held about thirty people but the candlelit tables were diplomatically spaced to allow for privacy. A pianist tinkled old Hoagy Carmichael tunes as they came in and the head waiter took their coats. Maddy quickly glanced around to see a handful of couples already seated, their heads bent together in soft conversation. Just the sort of place for that romantic rendezvous, she thought as she took her seat.

They studied the menu and the wine list and ordered.

"It's great to see you again," Greg said when the waiter had hurried away. "You look absolutely ravishing."

"Thank you."

"Being busy clearly agrees with you."

"Sometimes I wonder," she said. "Sometimes I think work is taking over my life."

"But you obviously enjoy it. And you must be good at it."

"I do enjoy it but there's such a thing as balance."

She told him about the recent developments in her career and her first auction.

"That must have been scary," he said with a grin.

"It was terrifying."

"I remember the first big deal I ever did. I put on a brave face and pretended I was totally on top but inside I was shaking like a leaf. There was a lot of money at stake."

"But you pulled it off?"

"Yes. And the client was delighted."

"And if you hadn't?"

"I would have been toast and we wouldn't be sitting here tonight. But you see, Maddy, life always presents us with challenges. And you have a choice. You can play safe or you can confront them. It's by accepting the challenges that you learn what you're capable of."

Greg had ordered a sirloin steak with broccoli and baby potatoes while Maddy, who had been overindulging on Sophie's gastronomic delights of late, contented herself with sole and a tossed green salad. While they ate, Greg told her about the project that had recently taken him to London.

"This is all terribly hush-hush," he said, adopting a conspiratorial tone.

"My lips are sealed."

"I've been asked to act for a consortium of businessmen who are thinking of making a bid for an exploration company." he explained.

"What sort of exploration?"

"Oil."

"Sounds intriguing."

"It is. But they have to get it right. Exploration companies are notoriously risky. Get it right and they stand to make a killing. Get it wrong and they could end up losing their shirts."

"And you have to do the background research?"

"Exactly. And believe me, it's not easy."

"I don't think I'd have the courage for a job like that," Maddy said. "My nerves would never stand it."

He shrugged and poured some wine. "It is high-wire stuff all right. But there's a tremendous excitement. It gets addictive."

A bit like my own job, she thought.

After their main courses, he tempted her into choosing a dessert and it was almost eleven o'clock when they finally made their way out into the balmy night air.

"Feel like shaking a leg at a club?" Greg asked.

Why the hell not, Maddy thought. I haven't been to a club for months.

"Sure."

He took her arm and steered her in the direction of the Electric Palace on Westmoreland Street where she seemed to get a second wind that kept her on the dance floor till the wee small hours. It was almost three when Greg finally deposited her back at Auburn Grove.

"I had a wonderful evening," she said, as he took her in his arms.

"Me too. Why don't we do it more often?"

"My thoughts exactly," she said.

He kissed her and she could feel her blood stir, a warm thrill of pleasure running up and down her spine. At last, they separated.

"Goodnight," she said as she gently pushed him away.

He looked at her longingly.

"Goodnight," he said. "I'll call you."

Later, as she curled up in bed and the waves of sleep engulfed her, Maddy pondered on the evening she had just spent. She had been so happy that she could have danced all night. No other man had ever had this effect on her. What was happening? Was this the kind of challenge that Greg had talked about? Was she about to find out what she was capable of?

Chapter Seventeen

After that night, events seemed to move with whirlwind speed. Greg rang a few days later and invited her for a romantic supper at the Trocadero restaurant in South Andrew Street. The following weekend he took her to a rugby match at Lansdowne Road where Maddy tried and failed to follow the strange gyrations on the pitch, before they joined a crowd of happy supporters in Kitty O'Shea's pub when the game was over. Before she knew, they were seeing each other almost every day.

But these alterations to Maddy's life did not escape the attention of her housemates. It was obvious that a man had entered the picture.

Rosie, with her usual bluntness, got straight to the point one evening as they were enjoying a glass of wine on the patio.

"Come clean," she said. "You can tell us his name."

"Who?" Maddy retorted, pretending to be confused by the question.

"This guy you're seeing. And don't give me any baloney. Recently, you've been behaving like a giddy mare."

Maddy suppressed a smile. "All right, I'll tell you. Not that it's any of your business. He's a guy I used to know. And recently our paths have crossed again. We've been seeing a little of each other."

"More than a little," Sophie joined in. "Every evening. Where did you meet him?"

"He met *me*. He was one of my clients. He just walked in off the street."

"I think I remember. Didn't you sell him a house in Sandymount?"

"You're getting warm. It was an apartment. In The Beeches."

"He's a stockbroker or something. Isn't that right?"

"He's a financial analyst. He investigates companies. He decides if they're a good investment."

"Sounds very technical," Rosie said. "But he must be loaded to afford a place in The Beeches."

"I've never asked him about his income," Maddy replied. "Let's just say, I believe he's comfortable."

"Are you fond of him?"

"Mmmmm."

"You must be," Rosie pressed on, "or you wouldn't be seeing so much of him. I know you, Maddy. You don't waste time on also-rans."

Maddy grinned. "You pair seem to have taken a great interest in my romantic life all of a sudden."

"It gives us something to talk about," Sophie replied. "I'll tell you what. Why don't you invite him to dinner? I'll cook a nice meal and we can run him up the flagpole and tell you what we think."

"Okay," Maddy said, realising that they would have to meet Greg sooner or later. "I'll ask him."

Meanwhile, the work on 26 Munster Road was now back on track. Paddy Behan and his men turned up faithfully each morning with their concrete mixer and tools and luckily the weather held fine. The large skip they had hired rapidly filled up with old rusted pipes and pieces of wood and bricks and ancient bathroom fixtures. Once Maddy was confident that they knew exactly what changes she wanted, she stayed out of their way. But each Sunday she drove over to see how things were coming along.

They began by stripping off the roof and the old rotted window frames so that the house looked like a skeleton, just four bare walls and a large black tarpaulin where the roof used to be. For a while nothing seemed to happen and then, slowly, she began to notice the changes. Gradually a new roof started to take shape, the clean black slates shining in the bright morning sun. Then the window frames were put in place. Then a new front door appeared. By July, the outline of the new house she had planned was clearly emerging and she began to look forward to the day she could gain possession.

At work, the relentless selling pace continued with no sign of a slowdown. The auction of Mamie McCarthy's bungalow in Booterstown was drawing closer and Maddy had been pleasantly surprised at the level of interest it attracted. The large ads she had commissioned had duly appeared in the property supplements with accompanying editorial articles. A company board had been erected in the front garden announcing the auction, a lavish brochure had been produced and the property was prominently displayed in the window of the firm's office. The net result was that forty people had been to view the property.

Mrs McCarthy was thrilled. Hardly a day went by that she didn't ring to find out the state of play till Maddy began to get heartily sick of her voice. But at least she didn't interfere or try to influence events. She seemed happy just to have the bungalow at the centre of attention.

Sophie suggested the following Saturday night for Greg's dinner invitation.

"What sort of food does he like?" she inquired.

"He's not particular. He'll eat anything."

"Is there anything he doesn't like?"

"I don't think so."

"I want this dinner to be a success. Maybe I should just stick to something tried and trusted."

"Oh, no!" Maddy insisted. "I want this to be a special occasion. Give vent to your creative instincts."

Sophie cast an uncertain look. "Are you sure?"

"Absolutely. Break out. Cook something memorable."

"I'll try," Sophie said without too much enthusiasm.

The following evening as Maddy and Greg were driving back from a movie, she said casually: "You're invited to dinner on Saturday night."

"Oh! Where?"

"My house. My pal Sophie is cooking."

"Is it a special occasion?"

"Yes. *You're* coming. But there will only be the four of us. Sophie likes to cook."

He smiled. "I get it. They want to inspect me. See if I measure up."

"Yes," Maddy said. "That's exactly what it is. They're dying to meet you."

"I suppose I should regard it as an honour. So, I'll just have to be on my best behaviour."

Saturday afternoon found Auburn Grove in a state of excitement. Rosie had undertaken to tidy the house while Maddy drove Sophie to the supermarket to buy provisions.

"Have you decided on the menu yet?" she asked as she parked her Audi.

"Yes. We're having tomato and mozzarella cheese for a starter. And for the main course I'm cooking a pork and vegetable casserole."

"Sounds delicious," Maddy said and she headed for the wine department, leaving Sophie to her own devices.

Half an hour later when she returned to the car, she found her friend loaded down with bags of vegetables and parcels of meat. She stacked the wine and the bags into the boot and they headed back home.

"I hope you're not nervous," Maddy said. "Greg really is a very laid-back guy. He's not the least bit fussy. So just relax. This isn't a cookery competition."

But her soothing words didn't have any effect. As soon as they returned, Sophie donned her apron, poured a glass of wine and locked herself into the kitchen with her bags of groceries and soon

Maddy could hear the sound of chopping and scraping. Before long, an appetising aroma began to seep out into the living-room where Maddy and Rosie were watching television.

At six o'clock, Sophie finally emerged.

"Everything's ready," she announced, wiping her hands on her apron.

"*Everything?*"

"Yes. All I have to do is serve the food. Now I'm taking a shower. Will somebody set the table?"

By half seven, all was in place. The table was set and the glasses and cutlery sparkled. The patio doors were open and a warm breeze carried the scent of the garden into the dining-room. They were all dressed up to the nines and Sophie had put a Van Morrison tape on the stereo set. Now all they had to do was wait for Greg to arrive.

At eight o'clock, they heard the sound of his car pulling up outside. Sophie jumped up to peep out the curtains but Maddy immediately pulled her back.

"Behave yourself!" she scolded. "We don't want him thinking he's some kind of exhibit in a zoo."

Reluctantly, Sophie sat down again and a minute later the doorbell chimed. Maddy, who had put on her short red cocktail dress for the occasion, strolled casually out to the hall. A moment later, she was back in the room with Greg. He was wearing a smart suit with open-necked shirt and clutched a bottle of wine and a large box of chocolates.

"Let me make the introductions," Maddy said, turning to her friends who were eagerly ogling the new arrival.

"So you're the chef?" he said to Sophie, warmly grasping her hands and gazing into her face while she fluttered her eyes as if she was meeting a pop star. "I've heard all about you from Maddy. I believe you're a wizard in the kitchen."

"More like a witch," Sophie joked.

Greg laughed. "Well, these are for you," he said, pressing the chocolates into her hands before turning to Rosie and kissing her cheek with a beaming smile

"Drinks anyone?" Maddy said, grabbing a bottle of wine that was chilling in an ice bucket and ushering them like a flock of sheep out to the patio.

Before long, they were sitting in the warm evening sunshine chatting gaily as if they had known each other all their lives. Greg was in sparkling form, making little jokes, doling out praise and compliments, firing off witty remarks while he stretched his long legs and sipped his wine. Maddy couldn't help feeling proud of him. He looked so strong and handsome and she could see from the smitten looks of her friends that they thought so too. Sophie in particular seemed to have fallen under his spell and gazed at him like a helpless kitten in awe of its mother.

"I'd better see to the food," she said at last, dragging herself away from the company and going off to the kitchen. "I hope everybody has an appetite."

Ten minutes later they were seated at the dining-table and tucking into the starter.

"This is wonderful," Greg announced, spearing a forkful of cheese. "What is the dressing?"

"Just olive oil and soy sauce," Sophie said modestly like a television chef being complimented on a culinary coup.

"I think simple dishes are best," he continued with a warm smile. "That's where the creativity gets to shine. And this is excellent, Sophie. You have my compliments."

Sophie lowered her head to hide her blushes.

The main course followed – a rich infusion of carrots, onions and tomatoes and succulent chunks of tender pork on a bed of rice. It was delicious and once more Greg was lavish in his praise. The meal finished with a chocolate layer cake that Maddy had bought earlier at the supermarket. By any standards, the meal was a triumph and she was delighted, not least for her friend who had laboured all afternoon in the kitchen to produce it.

Afterwards they sat around the table while Greg entertained them with funny stories about life in the fast world of high finance. Before anyone realised, it was half one and he announced that it was time to go. He said he was expecting an urgent phone call from London the following morning.

When he had left and the sound of his car had died away, Maddy closed the door and went back in to her friends.

"Now, you've seen him. What do you think?"

"What a hunk!" Rosie exclaimed. "Are there any more like him?"

Sophie looked as if she was floating on a cloud.

"He's absolutely gorgeous. And such excellent manners. Did you hear what he said about my starter?"

"You're so lucky," Rosie added. "Men like Greg don't grow on trees."

"For God's sake, hold on to him," Sophie added. "Any woman would die for a man like that."

"I'll certainly try," Maddy grinned.

"And if you ever think of giving him up, please let me know."

Maddy couldn't help the smile of satisfaction that slowly crept across her face. The evening had been a brilliant success and she was deliriously happy. And the praise of her friends for Greg only served to reinforce a feeling that was already growing steadily in her heart.

It was now Wednesday and the auction of Mamie McCarthy's bungalow was scheduled for Friday. But strangely, for a woman who had called Maddy practically every day since the sale had been announced, Mamie had suddenly fallen silent. Maddy thought it was odd but she was grateful for the respite. She checked the hotel where the auction was due to take place to ensure that everything was in order and got on with other pressing business.

Then on Thursday morning, Mamie lobbed a hand grenade into their midst. Maddy had barely settled at her desk when the phone rang and she heard her unmistakable tones on the line.

"I'm taking it off the market," she announced.

"*What?*"

"I've decided not to sell," Mamie said.

For once, Maddy lost her professional cool. She couldn't believe what she was hearing. She had put hours of work into the preparation for this auction. Over the past three weeks, she had organised adverts and publicity, designed a brochure and escorted dozens of prospective clients around the house and now Mrs McCarthy was blithely announcing that she was taking it off the market. What on earth had happened?

"Johnny's coming back," she explained, barely able to contain her delight.

"Johnny? Who's Johnny?"

"My husband."

"But I thought you were thrilled to be free of him? I thought that was the reason you were selling? You said you were going to live in Tenerife or somewhere."

"I know. But he rang me on Monday and said he wanted to talk. It was all the publicity, you see. People were telling him he was mad to sell his lovely house. And that got him thinking about everything he was giving up for that little floozy. So we had a meeting and now we've patched it all up. He's sorry for what happened and he's moving back in with me this evening. So I can't sell the house now, can I?"

"I see," Maddy replied, murderous thoughts gathering in her mind.

She set off immediately to explain the situation to Tim Lyons. Nothing like this had ever happened before. She couldn't remember an occasion when a house had been taken off the market before an offer had even been made, still less one that was lined up for auction.

Tim listened patiently, then shrugged his shoulders. "There's nothing we can do. We'll bill her for the advertising of course."

"But what about all the work I've put in? Can't we bill her for that?"

"I'm afraid not, Maddy. You'll just have to take it on the chin."

She was furious. "It was a fix. I know it. I always wondered why she wanted an auction and now I know. It was all the publicity. She was using us to lure her philandering husband back."

"You could be right but you can't prove a thing."

"I know I'm right. What a devious old cow! No wonder he ran off with his secretary. Grrrr," she growled through clenched teeth as she stormed back to her desk and began the tiresome business of cancelling the hotel room and placing adverts to announce that the auction had been called off..

It took Maddy a few days to calm down but on Sunday morning Greg called to take her for a spin in his car. It was a beautiful sunny day and they planned to drive across to Howth and walk the cliffs before having lunch and taking in a jazz session in one of the local hotels.

As she settled beside him in the passenger seat, she had a sudden impulse and said: "Would you mind taking a short detour? I want to show you something."

She directed him out of Ranelagh and a few minutes later they were entering the leafy stretch of Munster Road.

"Stop here," she said when they arrived at No 26.

He pulled the car in to the kerb.

"What do you think?" she said, pointing to the house which now boasted a shiny new roof and gleaming window frames and all the modern appearance of a newly built home.

"It's very smart," Greg replied. "Why are you showing it to me?"

"It's my house. I own it."

His mouth opened in surprise. "*Your* house?"

"Yes. I bought it several months ago and now I'm having it restored. It was another of those houses that we couldn't sell because it was in such a terrible condition. So I got it cheap. C'mon, let me show you inside."

He quickly locked the car and followed her.

Inside, there was a smell of fresh paint and varnish. The whole bottom half was now one huge room. New floors had been laid. The old kitchen had been ripped out and extended and a modern one was taking shape. The walls were being plastered. Upstairs, the small maid's room had been converted into an en-suite bathroom to adjoin the main bedroom. There was still work to be finished but it was now possible to see the lovely new house that was beginning to emerge.

Greg stared around him in wonder.

"So what do you think?" she asked.

"I'm lost for words. It's fantastic."

"Wait till it's finished. You're going to love it."

"Do you mind if I ask what you paid for this one?"

"Eighteen thousand pounds."

"You can't be serious!" he exclaimed.

"I am. I paid £18,000 and another £15,000 to get all this work done. When you count in legal fees and taxes and the cost of furnishing the house, I'll have spent the guts of £40,000."

"But it must be worth double that."

"One close by sold recently for £95,000."

He turned to her. "I'm amazed. What are you going to do when it's finished?"

"Rosie and Sophie are moving in. They're going to be my new tenants."

"You could always sell it. Take your profit."

"No, Greg, I would never do that. You don't know the whole story. They tried to buy it and couldn't get a mortgage."

"So you bought it for them?"

"Sort of."

He took hold of her shoulders and stared into her eyes.

"You're very good to your friends, Maddy, aren't you?"

She shrugged. "They're good to me."

"And you're loyal."

"Yes," she said. "I place great store by loyalty."

"I admire that. Loyalty is a quality that is rapidly going out of fashion."

The following day, Paddy Behan rang to say he hoped to get the house finished in three weeks' time and she should start thinking about furniture. It was something the women had spent a lot of time considering and most of the furnishings had been selected already. But over the next few weeks they spent a couple of enjoyable weekends driving around stores and retail warehouses, choosing wall hangings and rugs and lamps. When Paddy Behan finally vacated Munster Road, Sophie and Rosie would be ready to move in.

Meanwhile, Greg and Maddy were becoming inseparable. He had taken to ringing her every morning at work and dropping into Auburn Grove in the evenings. They spent most of their free time going out to restaurants and drinks parties and for walks along the river and drives out to Killiney and Sandycove. Gradually, their lives became entwined.

Then one sunny Sunday morning, she woke in his bed at The Beeches and realised she was in love.

Chapter Eighteen

Falling in love was a new experience for Maddy. The nearest she had ever come before was with a tall, gangly boy called Seán whom she met one summer at the Connemara Gaeltacht when she was thirteen and he was fifteen. He was tall with a head of dark hair and long curling lashes and he came from a little town in Sligo. Seán was the first boy who ever asked her to dance and he clutched her hand tightly as they negotiated the *Walls of Limerick* at the ceildhe and afterwards he told her she had done very well for a city girl. Maddy was smitten.

She thought she had met the love of her life. One night after the ceildhe, he brought her outside to the back of the hall on the pretext of getting fresh air and awkwardly kissed her. Maddy went around for the rest of the month in a swoon. She had a boyfriend and that made her special. The other girls looked up to her. Then she returned to Dublin and the letters that Seán had promised to write never arrived and after a fortnight she had forgotten all about him.

There had been lots of boys in her teenage years because she was growing into a striking young woman with her fine figure and flashing eyes. Spanish eyes, somebody said one time, and she had taken it as an enormous compliment remembering the dark, sensual señoritas with combs in their hair whom she had seen dancing the flamenco on a television programme. She was never short of admirers but by now she had become aware of the power she had over men and it made her haughty and proud. If a boy hadn't sustained her interest after a couple of dates he was quickly dismissed. Maddy didn't have time for lengthy courtships with so many suitors tripping over themselves to gain her attention.

By now she was getting interested in sex. Suddenly it seemed to be everywhere – in the magazines and books she read and the films and television programmes she saw. All her friends were talking about it and Maddy began to think that maybe she was missing out on something. So at the age of seventeen, she set out deliberately to lose her virginity. The young man who was chosen was twenty-one and she met him on a package holiday to Majorca with her school friends after they had finished their Leaving Cert exams. He was from London and his name was Keith.

One evening when they had all been out drinking sangria at a party organised by the holiday reps, Keith brought her back to his hotel room. After they had spent some time kissing, he got undressed and slipped on a condom. Maddy had never seen a real live naked man before. Or a condom either. But she braced herself as he laid her on the bed and removed her underwear and began pumping at her while she lay back and offered no resistance. She felt nothing except a slight pain when he entered her. After a few minutes, Keith rolled off again and said it was brilliant and told her he loved her. Maddy was left wondering what all the big fuss was about.

She didn't tell anyone about her experience with Keith but now whenever one of her friends raised the subject of sex, she felt at least she knew what they were talking about. And as she got older, she met more experienced lovers – men who took their time to arouse her and give her pleasure. Gradually the experience started to improve. She began to realise that perhaps there was something in it after all. But she never really tasted the joy of sex till she met Greg Delaney.

Greg was a practised lover and had a healthy sexual appetite. He was skilled and patient, slowly caressing her till she felt every nerve in her body tingle with expectation before pressing on to a climax that left her sated. But it wasn't just the sex. There was so much more to admire about him. He was handsome. At over six feet tall with broad shoulders and hair like corn, he was easily the best-looking man she had ever gone out with.

He was charming. He was considerate. He had a droll sense of humour that made her laugh. He was confident and self-assured. He was relaxed in the company of women and didn't monopolise a conversation with talk about himself like so many of the men she had known. He listened to what she had to say and sought her opinion. As a result, he made her feel that she was the most important person in his life. And she in turn thought him extremely sophisticated.

She knew he had faults. He was impulsive. He could be arrogant. He liked to get his own way. Maddy had seen all these defects in action. But gradually, as they got to know each other better, these flaws of character didn't seem to matter so much. Maddy was prepared to overlook them. She had plenty of faults herself, if she was honest. No one was perfect. And Greg's failings were small things when weighed against all his good qualities. Before she realised, she had put aside her caution and thought Greg the most marvellous person she had ever met. So it was little wonder that she woke up in his bed that morning and discovered she was in love.

She lay staring at the sun as it came streaming in through the bedroom curtains to bathe the room in a brilliant light. She turned to look at the man who was sleeping beside her. He was lying on his side with a hand curled up towards his face. She stared at the fine blond hairs at the base of his neck, the down-like stubble on his chin, the slope of his shoulders, the strength of his arms. He is so beautiful, she thought, so perfect. And now I have fallen in love with him.

As she watched, Greg slowly began to stir. First a hand went to his forehead and gently began to rub. His eyes slowly opened and he looked at her. He yawned and shifted his legs in the bed and finally he pulled himself up.

"You were watching me," he said with a smile.

"Yes. I was admiring you. You're so handsome when you're asleep."

"Only when I'm sleeping?"

"No. All the time."

He laughed and curled his arm around her shoulders and drew her close.

"Beauty is within, Maddy. Surely you know that?"

"Yes, I do know it. But with you it's everywhere."

"You'll turn my head if you go on like this."

"I know I shouldn't tell you. I hate vain men. But I can't help it."

He laughed again as he pulled her down and kissed her.

"You're a strange woman, Maddy."

"Am I?"

"Yes. You never cease to intrigue me."

"Is that good or bad?"

"Oh, definitely good. I don't think I would ever get bored with a woman like you."

His fingers gently caressed her spine and moved down to her thighs. She felt her body stir and pressed closer so that she could feel his hot breath on her neck as he kissed her again, passionately this time. He stroked her hair and gazed into her dark eyes and then his mouth moved to her breasts and along the curve of her belly and she felt herself tremble with pleasure.

"What time did you arrange to meet the girls at Munster Road?" Greg shouted from above the noise of the shower.

"Twelve o'clock!" Maddy replied.

Today was moving day. On Friday evening, Paddy Behan had finished work on the house and after they had jointly inspected it to make sure everything was in order, she had paid him the outstanding money. He had done an excellent job and completed it with only a short delay.

"I think you'll find it's exactly what you ordered. I followed your instructions to the letter," he said as they trooped through the empty rooms and Maddy checked light switches and taps and inspected corners and cupboards. "If you discover anything when I'm gone, just give me a call and I'll come back and fix it right away."

"It seems fine, Paddy," she said. "I have to say you're a very tidy worker."

She looked with relief at the clean-swept floors, the ledges and windowsills free of dust. Someone had obviously gone over the place with a powerful industrial vacuum cleaner.

"I learnt that from my old father, God rest him. He always insisted that we leave a job looking spick and span."

"Well, it's certainly going to save us a lot of housework, that's for sure!"

Sophie and Rosie had been eager to move in right away but Maddy had urged patience. The furniture they'd ordered had to be delivered, curtains had to be put up and electrical appliances installed. There was still a lot of work to be done before the house would be habitable.

"I suggest you wait till Sunday unless you fancy dossing on the floor in a sleeping bag," she said and Rosie and Sophie, who both loved the comfort of their warm beds, reluctantly agreed.

On Saturday morning, the first of the deliveries arrived in a large van – the living-room suite and dining-table which had been purchased from a leading store in town. These pieces had been the subject of much discussion because Sophie rightly pointed out that they were the most important items in the room. They had finally settled for a huge cream-coloured settee and two armchairs which took up much of the space before the fireplace. The dining-table was circular and seated eight and had been placed beside the patio doors so that people could look out at the garden while they dined.

This arrival had been the prelude to a steady stream of deliveries throughout the day. In rapid succession, the fridge, cooker, washing machine, tumble-dryer and dishwasher arrived. And after the deliverymen had finished installing them, the bedroom furniture came in another van. While all this was going on, the women had dressed in track-suit bottoms and old tee shirts and commenced washing windows, hanging curtains, putting up paintings, arranging plants and brushing the paths at the front and back of the house.

By eight that evening they were exhausted but all the major work had been done. There were some minor items that still remained to be purchased but at last the house looked cosy and habitable.

Now all that remained was for Sophie and Rosie to move their personal belongings from Auburn Grove. Sophie's brother had undertaken to transport them in his van this morning and Maddy had agreed to meet them at the house at midday.

At last, Greg came out of the bathroom vigorously drying his hair with a towel.

"What's my role in all this?" he asked with a grin. "I thought you said all the heavy-lifting work had been done?"

"So it has. Your role is to look elegant and handsome and to cast a cool eye over everything and give it your seal of approval."

"I think you're more qualified for that than I am."

"I just want you to see it," she said, giving him a quick peck on the cheek. "The place has been completely restored. You're not going to recognise it. Paddy Behan has done a marvellous job."

"You should hold onto that guy," he said with a knowing grin. "You never can tell when you might need him again."

Outside, the sun was blazing. It was going to be another glorious day.

While Maddy showered and dressed, Greg went into the kitchen and began to prepare breakfast.

"Grub's up!" he shouted as Maddy emerged from the bedroom wearing faded Levis and an old check shirt. In the kitchen, she found him pouring coffee. Two plates of bacon and eggs sat on the breakfast bar beside a freshly made stack of toast.

She pulled out a stool and sat down.

"So you're finally getting Auburn Grove to yourself," said Greg.

"Yes," she replied. "But it's kind of sad in a way. Sophie and Rosie are my best friends."

"They're not going very far."

"I know," she said with a sigh, "but it won't stop me missing them."

When they arrived at Munster Road, they found the two women anxiously waiting. Sophie's brother had already unloaded the van and taken off again saying he had to meet his mates in the pub to watch Liverpool playing Arsenal. Now their suitcases and boxes were strewn all over the driveway as if there was a car-boot sale in progress. God knows what the neighbours are going to say, Maddy thought as she stepped out of the car and strode quickly towards them.

"I can't wait to get in," Rosie announced, giving a little shiver of delight as Maddy approached.

Both women had wanted the master-bedroom with its en-suite bathroom and in the end it was settled by tossing a coin. Rosie had won and now she wanted to gain possession and stamp her personality on the room as quickly as possible.

Maddy marched to the front door and took three sets of keys from her handbag. She gave the girls one each.

"I suggest you get a spare set made just in case you lose them," she said as she pressed them into their eager hands.

"Shouldn't we have a ribbon for you to cut?" Sophie gigged nervously. "Like an official opening ceremony?"

"What a brilliant idea," Maddy replied sarcastically. "And we could have got the local photographer round to take pictures. And the Lord Mayor to make a little speech. C'mon, let's get inside before somebody decides that we're breaking in and calls the police."

She opened the door and they all piled into the hall. Rosie and Sophie immediately headed upstairs to the bedrooms, pulling their bags behind them. Maddy glanced at Greg to gauge his reaction. The last time he had seen the house, it was only half-finished. This time, his approval was written plain on his face. He strode into the living-room and stared at the plush new furniture, the exposed brickwork above the fireplace, the freshly-painted walls and the tasteful prints that the women had chosen.

He came out again and walked into the kitchen, gazing in admiration at the gleaming new fridge, the sparkling taps and sink unit, the marble-topped work surface, the bright cupboards, the washing machine nestling beside the dishwasher. At last, he turned to face her.

"Do you like it?" she asked.

"Like it? It's amazing. I'm lost for words."

He took her in his arms and kissed her. "Oh Maddy, my beautiful, creative genius, you've performed a miracle."

"I had a lot of help," she said, smiling with pleasure. "Me and the girls planned it together. And we mustn't forget Paddy Behan. He did all the real work."

"But you were the inspiration. You saw the potential. And you took the risk. And now you've created a dream home. I'm proud of you," he said, kissing her again.

Meanwhile, the sound of Abba singing 'Money, Money, Money' could be heard booming out of the master bedroom where Rosie had taken possession.

Sophie came back downstairs and made straight for the kitchen.

"I suppose the first thing is to make everybody a nice cup of tea?"

"Hold on a minute," Greg said, producing a carrier bag. "I've got a better idea."

He opened the bag and took out a bottle of champagne.

"We've got to christen the new house properly. I take it you've got glasses, Maddy? You seem to have thought of everything else."

"Of course."

She opened a cupboard and took out a set of sparkling wine glasses.

At the sound of the cork popping, Rosie suddenly reappeared and held out her glass to be filled.

"To the new house!" Greg said as he poured.

"I'm beginning to grow fond of this bubbly," Rosie remarked, taking a large sip. "We'll have to move house more often."

By the time Greg had tuned in the television and the women had finished unpacking their belongings into the ample cupboard space and had neatly stacked their records and books on the shelves, it was three o'clock. Sophie suggested cooking a celebratory lunch but Greg had another suggestion.

"You've had a busy weekend. Why don't we all head down to Rathmines and I'll buy you a nice meal? It'll be my treat."

"What a good idea," Rosie agreed. "Why don't we do that? You'll have plenty of opportunities to cook in the future, Sophie. Besides, I've got a confession to make."

They turned to stare at her.

"I forget to get any groceries. We've got nothing to eat."

She made a face and Sophie let out a groan. "Oh, Rose! That was your job. How could you do that?"

That settled it. They all piled into Greg's car and drove to a little Italian place on Rathmines Road. He ordered a bottle of Valpolicella and soon they were sipping wine while their heads bent over the menus as they tried to decide what to order.

Maddy glanced around the table at her two best friends and her lover all chatting happily together. She felt as if she had reached some kind of milestone in her life. Everything was falling into place. Her job was going well. She had the house in Auburn Grove to herself at last. And she had Greg now firmly established in her life. She felt a warm contented glow spread over her and suffuse her with joy.

Chapter Nineteen

"What I need is a professional man," Sophie announced one Friday evening a few weeks later as they were gathered in the packed lounge of the Pink Parrot pub.

Maddy had just joined them, having first taken her sales team for their end-of-week drinks to a pub near the office. It was now the middle of July and the frantic selling season had finally tailed off as customers departed on holidays. At last they could relax although the hectic pace would soon pick up again in the autumn. But for now, she could afford to take her foot off the pedal.

She was in a light-hearted mood. She was seeing Greg later at a farewell party for one of his colleagues and then they were going for a quiet supper somewhere. As a result, she was restricting herself to mineral water. Knowing Greg, he would want to unwind with a couple of beers and she would probably end up driving him home.

At Sophie's announcement, Rosie's mouth had fallen open and now she stared across the table at her friend.

"A *professional* man? Are you talking about a gigolo? Surely you're not —"

"No, not a gigolo, you fool! I mean a man with a profession. I've given this matter some serious thought. I'm almost twenty-seven years old. Don't you think it's time I settled down?"

"You're thinking of getting married?" Rosie's voice had now taken on a shocked tone. "We've just moved into our new house. Surely you're not contemplating leaving me for some man?"

"Well, maybe not getting married," Sophie admitted. "Not quite yet. But at least get *serious.*"

Rosie caught the eye of a passing waiter and indicated another round of drinks.

"I don't think I follow you," she said, glancing nervously at Maddy.

"What I mean is," Sophie said, swallowing the remains of her gin and tonic, "it's time I formed a steady relationship instead of bouncing around with all these deadbeats I've been seeing. The last guy I had worked in a record store but he really wanted to be a drummer in a rock band as if that was ever going to happen, for God's sake. And he certainly wasn't steady. He was flirting with every young one that came into the store."

"I don't know what you saw in him, to tell you the truth," Rosie said. "He wasn't exactly Robert Redford."

"You should talk," Sophie retorted. "You went out with that Paul guy for six months and he was never around when you needed him."

"That was just a phase," Rosie said as the waiter arrived with fresh drinks. "Now I've got Adam. He's very reliable."

With this remark, Rosie had got to the nub of the situation. Maddy, who had been listening intently, could immediately spot Sophie's dilemma. Both Maddy and Rosie now had steady boyfriends. Rosie had recently fallen in with a young accountant called Adam Gray whom she had met at a PR party and he was pursuing her relentlessly. Maddy thought he was a bit dull but no-one could say that he wasn't steady. And now Sophie was feeling left out.

"I think you should relax," Maddy said, trying to be helpful. "You shouldn't rush into anything. You're a very attractive woman, Sophie. You have a lively personality. You're good fun. You're excellent company."

"You think so?"

"Of course. You wouldn't have any trouble attracting a suitable man."

"But it's the type of men I seem to attract," Sophie said sadly. "They're not exactly into serious relationships. That's why I think it's time I changed direction. A professional man with good career prospects would be more interested in settling down, don't you think?"

"Ummmmm," Maddy said, nursing her glass of Ballygowan. "I'm not so sure about that."

"No? You've got Greg and he's just about the most adorable man I've ever met. And he's absolutely devoted to you."

"I think it all depends on the man. Some of the so-called professional guys I've met are just as footloose as those deadbeats you talk about. Just give it time, Sophie. Mr Right will eventually come along."

But Sophie wasn't to be put off.

"Where's the best place to meet these professional types?" she asked Rosie. "Where do they congregate?"

"How would I know? I just met Adam by accident at a party. I didn't go out searching for him."

Sophie turned again to Maddy. "What about Greg? Has he any single friends? I think someone in financial services might be exactly what I need."

"I wouldn't bet on it," Maddy replied. "They're always working. You might see even less of him than Rosie saw of Paul."

"I could cope with that," Sophie said, beginning to sound desperate. "The way it is now, I'm just drifting along expecting things to happen to me. It's time I took control of my life. I've got to shape my own destiny. I can't just hang about waiting for Fate to come knocking on my door."

Maddy and Rosie exchanged a glance across the table and Rosie rolled her eyes.

"Let me have a chat with Greg and see what he comes up with," Maddy said, glancing at her watch and realising it was time she was gone.

Sophie took hold of her hand. "Oh Maddy, would you, please? Greg knows me. He knows what a solid, reliable person I am. All he has to do is introduce me to someone and I'll do the rest. Just tell him I'm looking for someone nice. Someone like himself, in fact."

"Leave it with me," Maddy said, standing up and putting on her coat.

But Maddy didn't get an opportunity to pass on Sophie's request before Greg surprised her with an announcement of his own. It occurred the following morning as they were eating breakfast on the patio at Auburn Grove. It was half ten and the sun was shining. The roses and geraniums were in bloom and from the trees at the bottom of the lawn the sound of birdsong filled the air. Maddy sipped her coffee and felt the sun warm on her face.

By now Greg had taken to spending weekends with her and had moved in several changes of clothes and some shaving stuff. The arrangement suited her well. It was one of the advantages of having the house to herself, now that Rosie and Sophie had gone.

"I've been thinking," he said, stretching his long legs and cradling his coffee cup in his hands. "We've both been working extremely hard recently. What would you say to a break?"

"You mean a holiday?"

"Sure. I've got a friend called Joe Spence who owns an apartment in Marbella. He says I can have it whenever I like. The weather should be marvellous down there at this time of year."

Maddy hesitated. This suggestion had come right out of the blue. She had never been away on a holiday with a man before. She felt it would definitely move their relationship up a gear.

"When did you have in mind?"

"No time like the present," Greg said, finishing his coffee and setting the cup down on the table. "I'm sure the company could spare me for a week. What about you?"

"Business has slackened off," she agreed, "and I was actually thinking of taking some leave."

He suddenly sat forward, excited now by the possibility. "So why don't we do it? You'd love it down there. You could spend the days working on your tan and the nights . . ." A grin spread over his handsome face. "I'll leave the nights to your imagination. But I guarantee one thing. You won't be bored."

Maddy felt his enthusiasm infect her too. She flung her arms around him and hugged him tight. "Oh Greg, it sounds brilliant. Let's do it!"

On Monday morning, as soon as she got into work, she went to see Tim Lyons.

"I'm sure the office could run without you for a while," he said with a grin once she had outlined her request. "I won't say it will be the same but we'll probably survive. When did you want to go?"

"Next week?" she asked hopefully.

"That shouldn't be a problem," he said, getting serious again. "I'll ask Jane Morton to cover for you. You just go off and recharge the batteries. You deserve a rest."

Maddy went back to her desk and rang Greg. Now that the prospect of the holiday was starting to become real, she was seized with anticipation. She thought of the balmy days, lazy lunches at some little beach bar, cocktails on the terrace overlooking the sea, dinner in some pavement restaurant with the scent of mimosa hanging in the air. It would be the perfect way to unwind.

"Good news," she said. "I've got next week off. How does that sound?"

"It sounds brilliant. Give me a couple of hours to work on it. I'll ring you this afternoon."

She went off to lunch with a light heart, already thinking of the things she would need to pack – a new bikini, some light summer dresses, a good tanning lotion, her running shoes and vests. And she would need to make an early appointment at the beauty salon for a leg wax and facial. By the time she returned to the office she had a list made out in her head. Just thinking about the holiday might turn out to be almost as exciting as the holiday itself.

At four o'clock, Greg rang to tell her it was all arranged.

"Already?" she said, amazed at his speed.

"We've got the apartment for six nights. And the flights are booked and paid for. We fly out of Dublin airport on Saturday morning at eight o'clock. It's early but the good news is we'll be able to eat lunch on the dock in Puerto Banus."

"Yipppeee!" she said, so excitedly that several heads turned to stare.

The next few days seemed to race past. Maddy rang Sophie to tell her they were going and to ask her to drop into Auburn Grove occasionally and water the house plants.

"You lucky cow!" Sophie exclaimed. "A week in Spain with that gorgeous hunk. Can I come along to carry your suitcase?"

"Only as far as the check-in desk," Maddy laughed.

She spent a morning clearing away the small backlog of work that remained. Finally, she rang her mother to tell her not to expect her for Sunday lunch.

"Where are you going?" Mrs Pritchard wanted to know.

"Spain."

Her mother, who had never been further than Bray sounded almost as excited as Maddy.

"Be careful you don't get sunburnt. I'm told it's very hot over there. They have oranges growing from the hedges."

"I think it's the trees, Mum. But you don't have to worry. I'll be well prepared. I'm bringing loads of sun cream."

"And watch what you eat. They go in for all sorts of strange food in those foreign places. You don't want to catch a tummy bug."

"I'll be thinking of your delicious roast beef," Maddy said.

"Who are you going with?"

Maddy knew her mother would be shocked at the thought of her going on holiday with a man. It would be easier to tell a little white lie.

"A girl from work. We got a last-minute cancellation."

"Well, you go off and enjoy yourself. I don't suppose there's any point sending us a postcard if you're only going for a week. You'll probably be home before the card."

"I'll ring and let you know how I'm getting on."

"Yes, do that. We'll all be thinking of you. And watch that sun."

"Bye, Mum. Give my love to Dad."

Before she realised, Friday had arrived. She took her staff for a farewell drink and they surprised her by presenting her with a goody bag containing a paperback novel, a pair of RayBan sunglasses, a mini-bottle of champagne and a star-spangled G-string which she drew out of the bag to gales of laughter. Then it was a mad dash to say goodbye to Rosie and Sophie at the Pink Parrot before meeting Greg at a pub near his office.

The following morning at five the alarm clock jolted them both awake. Outside the window it was still dark but an early glimmer of dawn was beginning to brighten the sky. Greg, who was usually a heavy sleeper, immediately jumped out of bed and went straight into the kitchen to make coffee while Maddy took a shower. By a quarter past six they were on the road and by seven, Greg had deposited the car in the long-term carpark and they were checking in their luggage.

They had half an hour to wait before boarding so he suggested they go to the coffee dock. Outside the big windows, the sun was high in the sky. Maddy was now wide awake and twitching with excitement. She was really going to enjoy this holiday. They had just finished coffee when the announcement came booming over the public address system to say their plane was boarding.

The flight was short – just two and a half hours – and for most of the journey Maddy buried her head in the paperback novel her colleagues had given her. She looked up when she heard the captain say they were commencing the descent into Malaga airport. From the window, she watched the coastline come slowly into view, the ring of mountains and the white surf lapping at the yellow sand. Next moment, Greg was holding her hand as the plane landed with a shudder and began to taxi along the runway.

Stepping onto the tarmac was like opening the door of a furnace. The heat came at them like a wave as they hurried into the welcoming shade of the terminal building. Here, they quickly passed through passport control before collecting their bags and making their way to the car-hire desk. Half an hour later, they were cruising along the motorway towards Marbella.

Maddy lay back and let the breeze toss her hair. Down below, she could see the roofs of the little whitewashed houses and the blue of the sea. She could smell the salt air and the scent of flowers. She couldn't wait to get to their apartment. She couldn't wait to get out of her clothes and into her bikini and stretched out in that glorious sunshine.

The apartment was in a modern block near the yacht club. The moment Greg turned the key Maddy gave a squeal of delight. It had a massive bedroom with en-suite bath and a spacious lounge and kitchen. Everything in the apartment was white: the walls, the comfortable settees, even the little coffee table that sat before the huge open fireplace.

But it was the terrace that really caught her breath. It had a long, wrap-around balcony with wicker furniture and a couple of sun beds stacked neatly against the wall. She ran to the rail and gazed out at the ocean, shining like glass in the bright sun. She could see palm trees and golden sand and in the distance, a couple of yachts bobbing like corks on the vast expanse of sea.

She turned to Greg who took her in his arms and kissed her.

"Welcome to Marbella!" he said. "Do you think you're going to like it?"

"I love it. Oh, Greg, this place is marvellous!"

He smiled. "I said you'd be happy, didn't I? Now, why don't you make out a list of provisions while I unpack and then we'll go out to the supermarket? Are you hungry?"

"Sort of."

"We can grab a bite of lunch at the same time."

"And then I want to get into the sun," Maddy said. "I don't want to waste a single moment."

The afternoon drifted by. Maddy covered herself in sunblock and stretched out on one of the recliners while Greg settled in the shade with a book he had found in the lounge. It felt so relaxing that eventually Maddy closed her eyes and before long, she was dozing.

She woke to find Greg standing over her and shaking her arm.

"You were sleeping," he said. "That's a dangerous thing to do in this hot sun. No point getting burnt on your very first day."

She quickly sat up. "What time is it?"

"Quarter to six. We should discuss dinner," he said. "What would you like to eat?"

"I don't mind."

"There's plenty to choose from and lots of lovely restaurants."

"Why don't you pick somewhere? You know Marbella."

"I could take you to Caprani's. It's an Italian place down at the seafront. You can get practically anything there. I think you'd like it."

"Okay," Maddy said. "Let's go there."

She poured a cool glass of wine and watched the sun begin its slow descent. It was so peaceful here far from the hectic pace of the office. Time was her own and she could do what she liked. To cap it all, she was sharing this idyllic holiday with the man she loved. She sighed as she felt a breeze cool her face. Sophie was right. She was one lucky girl.

They ate a lovely dinner at Caprani's where the head waiter seemed to know Greg and gave them a pavement table where they could watch the promenaders stroll by. It was after ten o'clock when they left. They walked back to their apartment in the moonlight, listening to the waves pressing against the shore. Once they arrived, Greg led her out onto the terrace and silently took her in his arms.

She felt his warm lips caress her throat and breasts. She closed her eyes and sighed with pleasure. This was the perfect ending to a perfect day, to stand here on this moonlit terrace in the arms of her lover.

At last, he took her hand.

"Come," he said. "It's time for bed."

Chapter Twenty

And so the week passed in a blur of sunshine and pleasure. Each morning at seven thirty, Maddy rose with the dawn, pulled on her running gear and went for a jog along the beach. On the way back, she called at a little bakery she had discovered to buy croissants and bread rolls. Then they ate breakfast on the terrace as the sun slowly lit up the sky. By eleven o'clock the temperature was touching 35 degrees.

The days were spent sunbathing, swimming, reading, and eating lazy lunches in little bars and cafes. Some afternoons, they drove along the coast to Fuengirola or Benalmadena and once they ventured up into the mountains to visit the old Moorish town of Ronda. In the evenings they ate wonderful dinners in delightful restaurants while flamenco guitars played and the stars twinkled in the bright heavens. It was a perfect existence and the most magical time that Maddy had ever experienced.

One evening as they sat on the terrace in the moonlight, a thought came into her head. She hadn't forgotten the way the waiter at Caprani's restauarant appeared to know Greg. It was a crazy thought but it had been bothering her for the last few days.

"When was the last time you were here?" she asked.

"Last year. I came for ten days."

"With a woman?"

He paused. "Yes."

"Was it Lorna?"

He lowered his head and looked away. "Yes," he said. "As a matter of fact, it was."

She felt a stab of jealousy. She knew it was irrational but the hurt was real and now she regretted asking him. The thought of another woman sharing him filled her with an insane suspicion.

Now it was her turn to lower her head and look away.

"What does it matter?" Greg asked, gently taking her hand. "It's all over now. You're the only one I care for."

She clung to him as she struggled to hold back the tears.

"Promise me you'll never come here again without me," she said.

"Of course. Now that I've found you, Maddy, no one else matters."

"Oh Greg, do you mean that?"

He laughed and gently stroked her hair. Above them, the moon hung like a silver lamp in the sky.

"Put this nonsense out of your head," he said. "No one will ever take your place, Maddy. No one could ever measure up to you."

At last the glorious holiday drew to a close. The lazy carefree days and languid nights came to an end and it was time to go back to Dublin. The evening before they left, Greg took her on a shopping expedition.

"I want to buy you a little present," he said. "Something to remind you of this trip."

"You don't have to do that," she protested.

"But I want to. What about a piece of jewellery?"

Despite her protests, he insisted on taking her to a shop in Marbella. It was filled with expensive jewellery: beautiful diamond earrings and sapphire brooches and silver bracelets. In the end, she chose a simple gold chain for her neck.

"Are you sure this is all you want?" he asked.

"Yes. It's perfect."

He stood behind her and she felt the gentle touch of his hand as it brushed her skin. He clasped the necklace round her throat. She looked in the mirror and saw how well it complemented the golden tan of her skin.

He bent and kissed her neck.

"You're so beautiful," he whispered and Maddy felt her heart throb with joy. "You're the loveliest creature I have ever seen."

She turned to him and he took her in his arms and kissed her while the young saleswoman politely looked away.

They arrived back in Dublin to grey skies and a downpour of rain but it couldn't dampen her spirits or the fond memories of the wonderful week she had spent with Greg. They quickly located his car and splashed off into town.

The following morning they were back at their posts and the dreary reality of work.

There was a mountain of post waiting for Maddy and then at eleven a meeting with Tim Lyons to begin preliminary work on the autumn sales campaign. It was midday before she returned to her desk to find a message from Sophie welcoming her back and asking her to call.

Sophie came on the line in a chatty, exuberant voice.

"How did the holiday go? What was the weather like?"

"Wonderful," Maddy replied. "It was the best holiday I've ever had."

"Lucky you. It hasn't stopped raining since you left."

Maddy glanced out the window and saw the spots of rain dappling the pane and thought briefly of the sunshine she had left behind.

"Did you ask Greg?" Sophie said abruptly. "Remember what we talked about? Did you ask if he has any suitable friends?"

Maddy was immediately brought back to earth. In all the excitement of the holiday, she had completely forgotten Sophie's request for Greg to help find her a partner. She fumbled desperately for a response.

"Oh, yes."

"And what did he say?"

"He . . . er . . . said he would think about it. He has several single friends but he wants to make sure he gets the right guy."

"At this stage, I'll take practically any man provided he's not already married or gay. I'm not choosy."

"But you want to do this right," Maddy said, playing for time. "You've got your self-esteem to think about. You don't want to sell yourself short."

"Oh, to hell with self-esteem. Where's it got me so far?"

"I'll tell you what – let me get back to you. I'll talk to him again."

"Don't forget," Sophie said. "I'm relying on you."

"Relax," Maddy said, in her most soothing voice. "We'll find somebody."

She put down the phone and heaved a sigh. Sophie had sounded desperate which wasn't necessarily the best frame of mind in which to go looking for a partner. But she *was* one of her best friends. She would have to do something to help her.

The following evening when they were having a drink in the Harbourmaster bar after work, Maddy raised the topic with Greg.

"I was talking to Sophie yesterday," she began.

"Oh yes. How is she?"

"She's envious as hell about our holiday."

"Does that surprise you?"

"She was wondering if you've got any friends who might be interested in meeting her."

He stared. "Does she mean romantically?"

"I think so."

"That's an odd request, isn't it?"

"I think she feels left out," Maddy explained. "You see Rosie has a steady boyfriend and I've got you. And well . . . she's got no one at present."

Greg slowly scratched his chin. "I have a lot of single friends but I'm not sure I would recommend them. They're not exactly reliable types when it comes to women. I'm very fond of Sophie. I wouldn't like to see her get hurt."

"She's tougher than you think," Maddy said quickly. "Don't let that innocent exterior fool you. Sophie is well able to hold her own."

"So why does she need my intervention? Can't she just find a partner for herself? Isn't that what most women do?"

"A lot of women rely on their friends. It may appear accidental but you'd be surprised how many romantic relationships are actually engineered."

"Really?" Greg said with a grin. "And all along I've been under the illusion that it was the work of Cupid and his little bow. Who engineered *our* relationship, might I ask?"

"No one," she smiled. "Our relationship was made in Heaven – a true meeting of hearts and minds. But not everyone is so lucky. Now, are you going to dig up someone for Sophie or not?"

"I'll find her a guy," he said. "But after that they're on their own. I will take absolutely no responsibility for how it turns out. Now, how about another drink?"

The man Greg selected was called Arthur Brady and he was a thirty-five-year-old stockmarket trader who worked for Greg's firm. He agreed to make up a foursome for a visit to a restaurant a few nights later.

Sophie was ecstatic at the news when Maddy rang to tell her.

"What's he look like?" she asked, eagerly.

"I haven't met him," Maddy admitted, "but Greg tells me he's thirty-five, about five feet eight inches tall and dark-haired. And he's a stockbroker. That's what you asked for, isn't it?"

"He sounds ideal," Sophie trilled. "When do I get to meet him?"

"Tomorrow evening. We're going to Hennessy's restaurant off Dame Street. Do you want us to pick you up or can you make your own way?"

"I'll come alone," she said. "It looks less obvious. What time?"

"Eight o'clock."

"I'll be there. Thanks a mill. You're a real pal, Maddy."

"Thank Greg. I had nothing to do with it."

"He's a darling. You don't know how fortunate you are to land a hunk like that."

"Oh yes, I do."

The following evening, Maddy arrived home from work at six thirty, had a quick shower and got dressed. At half seven, she heard Greg's car arrive.

"How was Arthur?" she asked as she settled into the passenger seat of his BMW. "Did he need much persuasion?"

"Not at all," Greg announced. "He was very keen."

"Well, that's a good sign, I suppose."

Hennessy's was the restaurant where Greg at taken her for their first proper date and it was ideal for the business in hand. Candles flickered on the tables and the pianist tinkled out soft romantic music. There was only a handful of diners when they arrived. They were shown to a table near the back.

They had barely sat down when the door opened and Sophie appeared. She waved at them, then slipped out of her coat and gave it to a waiter. She was wearing a figure-hugging turquoise dress that showed plenty of bosom, and sheer stockings. Her blonde hair was piled high on her head. She had obviously spent some time getting ready and Maddy thought she looked quite stunning. She saw Greg glance at her approvingly as she came in.

"You look marvellous," he said, politely kissing her cheek and pulling out a seat for her.

"Thank you," she replied. "Where's Arthur?"

"He's on his way. What would you like to drink?"

They decided on a bottle of wine while they studied the menu. Maddy was starving. She had skipped lunch in order to have an appetite for this meal and now she thought she could hear her stomach begin to growl. But by half past eight there was still no sign of Arthur and Sophie was beginning to get restless.

"He *is* coming, isn't he?" she asked, glancing for the umpteenth time towards the door.

"Relax," Greg said. "He's probably been delayed."

"Should we order?" Maddy asked, feeling the hunger pangs bite.

But before anyone could reply, the door flew open and a plump, untidy figure in a pin-striped suit came bustling in. Greg stood up and waved. The figure immediately began making his way across the restaurant towards them.

Maddy's heart sank. Arthur Brady was definitely no oil painting. She just hoped Sophie wasn't going to be disappointed. But when she glanced at her friend, she saw that she was beaming with delight.

"Sorry I'm late," Arthur said, after they had all been introduced. "I got held up at the office."

He squeezed in beside Sophie, straightened his tie and ran his fingers distractedly through a mop of unruly hair. Across the table, Maddy caught the distinct whiff of alcohol.

"Last-minute rally on Wall Street," he said to Greg by way of explanation, then grabbed a menu and began to read it.

"I'll have the steak," he announced, putting down the menu and helping himself to a glass of wine from the bottle they had ordered.

"So, you two are friends, right?" he said, pointing from Sophie to Maddy.

"Yes," Sophie replied with a sweet smile. "We've known each other since school."

"And what do you do to earn a crust?" he asked.

"I'm in the travel business."

He raised his bushy eyebrows. "That sounds interesting. What exactly do you do?"

"Marketing."

"Ohhh, marketing! The cutting edge of business!"

"More like the blunt edge in my case," Sophie said and Arthur laughed heartily.

Meanwhile, Maddy had taken the opportunity to observe him more closely under the pretext of studying the menu once more. He was at least a stone overweight and she could see his stomach bulging against his shirt. His face was plump and florid and his hair was beginning to thin along the temples. And if that wasn't enough, he had clearly neglected to shave and now a ring of black stubble darkened his pudgy cheeks.

But if Maddy found Arthur less than electrifying, he seemed to be making a more positive impression on Sophie. Across the table, their heads were now bent in animated conversation. Whatever turns you on, Maddy thought as the waiter appeared at last to take their order and Arthur seized the opportunity to ask for another bottle of wine. By the time her food arrived, Maddy was ravenous and she fell on her medallions of pork like someone who had just been let out of prison.

For the rest of the evening, Arthur and Sophie remained steadfastly cocooned in each other's company. Arthur made little jokes and Sophie laughed uproariously as if he was the wittiest man in Dublin. She patted his plump cheeks and he smiled. They gazed soulfully into each other's eyes as if they were the only two human beings left on the planet. Maddy found the scene amazing and when the meal finally came to an end and the bill had been paid, she wasn't surprised to see Arthur gallantly collect Sophie's coat and hold it out for her and, with one arm clutching at her waist, escort her into the dark night in search of a taxi.

"Well, that seems to have gone off quite smoothly," she said, as she settled into the front seat of Greg's car for the drive home.

"It was bizarre. You would think neither of them had seen a member of the opposite sex before."

"What does it matter so long as they're happy? Let's hope it all works out for the best."

"Yes," Greg said enigmatically. "Let's hope it does."

But she didn't have long to wait before she heard a first-hand account of the evening from Sophie. She rang the following morning just as Maddy was leaving for work.

"What did you think of him?" she demanded. "Tell me honestly."

"You're asking *me*?"

"Well, you were there."

"But I hardly spoke two words to the guy. You monopolised him all evening."

"That's because I didn't want to waste time on chit-chat. I wanted to give him my full attention."

"You certainly did that."

"What did you think of his looks?"

Does she want to hear the truth, Maddy thought? That he could have done with a haircut and shave as well as losing about a stone of weight? I don't really think so.

"Not bad. He was quite handsome in a dark, mysterious sort of way."

Sophie squealed with delight. "My thoughts exactly. And he's extremely passionate."

"You didn't sleep with him?" Maddy said in horror.

"Are you kidding? On our very first date? I intend to keep that prospect dangling enticingly before him till I'm convinced that he's well and truly landed."

"So, is Arthur the type of man you were looking for?"

"Oh, definitely. He's right up my alley."

Well, thank God for that, Maddy thought as she put down the phone.

A few days later, as they were sharing a drink after work, Greg casually dropped a hint that he would like to meet her family. This same thought had periodically crossed her mind. By now they had been seeing each other for four months and they still hadn't been introduced to their respective families. Greg had a better excuse than she did for his parents lived in Galway which would have entailed a three-hour car journey and an overnight stay, whereas the Pritchard family were living only twenty-five minutes away in Raheny.

Her immediate reaction was to delay. Introducing him to her family was a big step and it was fraught with dangers. Greg would be the first man she had ever brought home. While she was now certain that she loved him, she still wasn't sure if the feeling was reciprocated. He had recently had a bad experience with Lorna Hamilton and that was bound to colour his views about long-term relationships. What would happen if they broke up? It would leave her with a lot of explaining to do when her family started asking embarrassing questions.

But the decision was unexpectedly taken out of her hands a few weeks later when she arrived for Sunday lunch in Raheny. She had noticed an air of anticipation as soon as she sat down at the big dining-table in the kitchen beside her brother, Brian. Her sister Helen seemed in particularly triumphant mood as she preened herself like a cat that had just caught a rather large mouse. Maddy wondered what could have happened. Maybe she had got a promotion at work.

But it was nothing like that.

"Helen has an announcement to make," Mrs Pritchard said when everyone was comfortably seated with plates of steaming roast beef before them.

Mr Pritchard, who was clearly looking forward to his lunch, groaned softly until his wife shot him a withering glance that silenced him at once.

"Go on, Helen," Mrs Pritchard urged. "Tell them your good news."

Everyone put down their knives and forks and stared at Helen who fluttered her eyelids and tried to look demure.

"It's just ..." she began, then stopped and fluttered her eyes some more.

"What?" Mr Pritchard said. "Spit it out for God's sake! Me dinner's getting cold."

Mrs Pritchard nudged her husband in the ribs and Helen gave him a murderous look.

"It's just . . ."

"What?" Maddy prompted.

"Joe Fuller's asked me to marry him and I want you to be my bridesmaid."

Chapter Twenty-one

Everyone around the table stared. This was indeed a surprise! While Helen and Joe Fuller had been going out together for over two years, the on-off nature of the relationship had always placed a large question mark over its long-term durability and Maddy had often wondered if they would *ever* manage to get married. The last time she had been home for Sunday lunch, the pair had been having one of their regular rows and Helen was sulking. Now she was announcing her engagement.

"Oh Helen, that's marvellous news!" she said, leaping up and enveloping her sister in a warm hug. "I'd be delighted to be your bridesmaid!"

"I'm having three altogether," Helen said, rather smugly. "Majella Malone and Bernie O'Rourke are the other two."

"That's fantastic," Maddy replied. "When's it to be?"

"November."

"You must be thrilled to bits. And Joe's such a wonderful guy. You really are a lucky woman getting a man like that."

"He's lucky to get me," Helen responded tartly.

"We need something to celebrate," Maddy said. "Will I drive over to the off-licence?"

"You'll do no such thing," Mrs Pritchard said, taking charge of the situation. "I've already bought a nice bottle of wine in the supermarket. It's cooling in the fridge."

She got up and returned with the bottle and five glasses. To Maddy's relief it was a decent enough Chardonnay and not a bottle of cooking wine since her mother knew absolutely nothing about the subject. Mr Pritchard struggled with the cork and filled the glasses and Mrs Pritchard proposed a toast.

"To Helen and Joe!" she said. "Long life and happiness!"

"Long life and happiness!" everyone said, drinking their wine and smiling benignly at Helen who was clearly enjoying her moment of triumph.

Mr Pritchard coughed to clear his throat.

"I'm sorry to put a damper on the proceedings but there's something I have to ask," he said, wiping his mouth with his napkin. "How much is this hooley going to cost me?"

"Nothing."

"Well, that's good news. How are you managing that?"

It turned out that Joe and Helen were paying for the wedding themselves which greatly relieved Mr Pritchard who was now able to eat his lunch with a lighter mind.

"Where are you going to live?" Maddy wanted to know. Now that the reality of the situation was beginning to sink in, there were so many questions to ask.

"We're buying a house in Baldoyle," her sister replied, basking now in all the fuss and attention. "It's a new development."

"Smart move," Maddy said. "You won't regret it."

"It's nearly built," Helen continued. "It's a semi-detached with three bedrooms, garage and gardens front and back. Joe's signed up and put down a deposit."

"Will it be ready in time for the wedding?"

"Oh, yes," her sister replied. "We got a guarantee from the builder."

"And where are you going for your honeymoon?"

"Fuengirola."

"I know it," Maddy declared. "It's just along the coast from Marbella. Oh, Helen, you'll love it! The sun, the sand! And the weather will still be nice in November."

"It better be," Helen replied. "We're paying enough for it."

The following Sunday when Maddy turned up for lunch, she found the household abuzz with Helen's wedding plans. Her mother was hopping around like a contented hen while her father sat quietly in his chair by the window his head buried in a newspaper and her brother Brian attemped to watch the television.

"Joe's such a lovely man," Mrs Pritchard purred, giving Maddy an extra helping of vegetables because she still wasn't convinced that she was feeding herself properly in Auburn Grove. "He's so considerate and so good with his hands. They'll never need to hire a handyman for that house, that's for sure. Joe will do everything himself."

"That's lucky," Maddy said. "You'd be surprised at the number of little jobs that need to be done."

"We're all so excited," her mother went on. "Our very *first* wedding. Although I knew from the minute I set eyes on Joe that he was the one. You can tell he's such a solid, dependable sort of man."

She glanced pointedly at Maddy and laid heavy emphasis on the word *first* as if to indicate that she expected her to follow her sister's example and find herself a partner pretty soon.

"Do you need any help to choose your wedding dress?" Maddy asked Helen.

But Helen, who had been going around with a smirk on her face ever since the engagement was announced, merely tossed her head.

"No. That's all taken care of. I'll let you know when the time comes for your fitting."

After that, each time Maddy returned to Raheny, the atmosphere was more frantic. The wedding was only two months away and there was so much to do. By now, the church had been booked along with the reception which was being held in a nearby hotel. But there were such a lot of details still to be organised.

The wedding dress had to be made and the bridesmaids' outfits.

The cake had to be ordered, flowers had to be arranged, the choir had to be engaged and a lady to sing as Helen came down the aisle on her father's arm. Then there was the organist, the photographer, the man to shoot the video, the band to play at the reception, wedding transport, the rehearsal, and the bride's going-away outfit. And finally, there was the guest list to be decided.

Helen wanted a big wedding with as many as two hundred guests. She was determined to make a splash and have people talking about her long after the event was over. And she kept adding to the list till before long it had grown to two hundred and sixty. It was at this stage that Joe Fuller finally put down his foot and said there was no way they could afford anything on this scale unless they wanted to begin married life in the bankruptcy court.

That's when the tears began.

Maddy arrived at St Margaret's Lane one weekend to find the house in turmoil, Helen sulking in her bedroom, her father buried deep in his newspaper, Brian looking as if he wished he was down in the pub and Mrs Pritchard wringing her hands in desperation in the kitchen and no sign of any Sunday lunch.

"What's going on?" Maddy asked, putting her arm gently around her mother's shoulders and pulling out a seat for her to sit down.

"The wedding's off," Mrs Pritchard said, bursting into tears and burying her head in Maddy's breast.

"What?"

"She told him this morning on the phone. She said if she couldn't invite who she wanted to her own wedding then she wasn't going ahead with it."

"This is crazy. I'll go and talk to her."

"No," Mrs Pritchard said, quickly restraining her. "This is something she has to sort out with Joe. Interfering won't do any good."

"But she can't call off the wedding for such a stupid reason after all the preparations. She'd be the talk of the neighbourhood. Surely that's not the sort of publicity Helen wants?"

Half an hour later, an ashen-faced Joe Fuller arrived.

"Where is she?" he demanded, when Mrs Pritchard let him in.

"Up in her room."

He gave a scowl and bounded up the stairs.

Mrs Pritchard put on the kettle. "I think I need a strong cup of tea," she said.

Joe Fuller remained upstairs talking to Helen for almost an hour. Down below they could hear raised voices. Mrs Pritchard and Maddy exchanged glances and Mr Pritchard kept his head buried in the sports pages. He had long ago said he was having no hand, act or part in Helen's wedding except to give her away and he would do that with a glad heart. Mrs Pritchard thought you could take that comment two ways.

Eventually, the noise upstairs subsided and Joe and Helen came down again. Helen looked rather sheepish and downcast.

"We've agreed to cut the list to a hundred and fifty," Joe announced. "It was either that or no house."

"Does that mean the wedding's back on?"

"Yes," Helen muttered.

"Thanks be to God," Mrs Pritchard said.

But reducing the number of guests didn't herald the outbreak of peace. At her first attempt to trim the list, Helen removed most of Joe's guests so that all that remained were his parents, his five brothers and sisters, his boss from work and an elderly aunt.

"Are you trying to start a civil war?" he asked when he saw her handiwork. "If we go ahead with this, my mother will never speak to either of us again. Give me that list."

He ran his eye down the platoons of guests.

"Who's Maria Higgins?"

"She's a girl I went to school with," Helen mumbled.

"Well she can go for a start," Joe said, drawing a line through her name.

"But she was my best friend," Helen protested.

"That was ten years ago. Now who exactly is Assumpta O'Toole?"

"She works at the checkout in the Spar."

"Out!"

"You can't," Helen screeched. "I promised her."

"You're proposing to invite her and not my Uncle Christy?"

"But what am I going to tell her?"

"You can tell her the dog ate the wedding cake. She's not coming," Joe said. "And that's final."

It took nearly a week to restore the guest list to some semblance of balance but it meant that the numbers had crept back up again to a hundred and eighty. By this stage, Joe Fuller and everyone else was worn out with all the arguments.

"With a bit of luck some of them won't be able to come," he said with a weary sigh. "I swear to God this is the last time I'll ever get married."

Maddy, who had realised that the wedding would provide the perfect opportunity to introduce Greg to her family, had managed to get him included on the list of guests. But she gave up any hope of adding Sophie and Rosie. Thankfully, both of them were very understanding when the time came to tell them.

"It's your *sister's* wedding after all," Rosie said with a grin. "If it was yours and we weren't invited that would be a completely different story."

Maddy sniffed but made no reply.

The invitations were eventually sent off and, with this hurdle overcome, the work of organising the myriad other details proceeded more or less calmly. Maddy tried to distance herself as much as possible from the stress of it all but she couldn't avoid one last involvement when the summons came for the fitting of her bridesmaid's dress.

As part of the negotiations, Helen had increased the number of bridesmaids to six which everyone thought was way over the top and also meant that Joe had to engage six groomsmen. But on this point, she was adamant and couldn't be moved. She was already thinking of the photograph in the *Northside People*.

The dresses, which were of pink taffeta, were being made at a boutique off Grafton Street and involved several visits for measurements and adjustments. Maddy shuddered each time she thought how much this was going to cost. But she turned up faithfully for her appointments until finally, about two weeks before the big day, the dressmaker announced that she was satisfied. It was with a huge sigh of relief that Maddy left the wedding and all its complications behind and fled to the peace and quiet of Auburn Grove. Now all that remained was the comparatively straightforward rehearsal and then the ceremony itself.

Meanwhile, Sophie's relationship with Arthur Brady had taken off like a barn roof in a storm. In their frequent phone conversations Sophie could talk about nothing else but Arthur's scintillating conversation, his witticisms, his encyclopaedic knowledge of the stock market, his taste in music, his sense of humour, his familiarity with good food and wine and his insight into the grubby machinations of the political world.

She made him sound like the most sophisticated man in Dublin so that Maddy often wondered if they were talking about the same person. Arthur had certainly kept these qualities well hidden on the one and only occasion she had met him.

A measure of how far he had managed to captivate Sophie came a few weeks later when she announced that she would be unable to join the others for their regular Friday night outing to the Pink Parrot lounge. Arthur was taking her to visit his ailing grandmother in St Benedicta's nursing home in Stillorgan.

"Something's definitely happening to her," Rosie said in hushed tones to Maddy. "She never stops talking about him. I've never known her get so excited about a man before."

"She's in love!"

"Must be."

"But you've seen Arthur. He's hardly the sort of man to sweep a girl off her feet, now is he?"

"Not this girl, anyway," Rosie replied, tartly.

"Maybe she's going through some sort of crisis?"

"What do you think we should do?"

"I don't know. But it's all very odd."

On Monday, Rosie rang to report that Sophie had spent the entire weekend at Arthur Brady's apartment in Donnybrook and only came home early that morning to change her clothes before going into work. "I hope she's not thinking of moving in with him permanently. Who will I get to share the house with?"

"Do you think we should have a talk with her?" Maddy asked, recalling Greg's remark that some of his friends were not entirely reliable when it came to women.

"Well, it's not really any of our business."

"But I wouldn't like her to get hurt. People can do silly things when they're in love."

"We don't know if she is truly in love, do we?" Rosie said. "It might just be a passing infatuation."

"I feel sort of responsible. I introduced them after all."

"Why don't we give it more time and see what happens?" Rosie suggested. "If she's still behaving like this in a few weeks' time, we'll reconsider."

At last the morning of Helen's wedding arrived. It had been a struggle but all the formalities had finally been taken care of. There had been occasions during the last few weeks when Maddy thought ruefully that a presidential inauguration would have demanded less effort. But they had made it.

The cake was baked and was now stored in the fridge of the local hotel. The church was decorated with flowers. The choir and the organist and the singer had all been booked and paid. The transport was organised, the priest was engaged and now Helen sat in the bedroom of the house in Raheny on the verge of tears because someone had stepped on the edge of her train and torn it.

"Oh, for God's sake," her Aunt Connie said, "it's only a little tear. No one will notice it."

"*I'll* notice it," Helen burbled. "And think of all the money I paid for it!"

"Get me a needle and thread and I'll have it fixed in a second,"

Aunt Connie said, appealing to Maddy for help. "And for heaven's sake put a smile on your face. Brides are supposed to be happy on their wedding day. The way you look, people would think you were being led off to the firing squad."

The three upstairs bedrooms and the bathroom were filled with excited females – the six bridesmaids, Mrs Pritchard, Aunt Connie and the lady from the local beauty parlour who had been hired to fix their hair – all flitting about and getting in each other's way. Downstairs in the parlour, Mr Pritchard, squeezed into a tight-fitting morning suit and waistcoat with a white carnation in his button-hole, fidgeted in his seat by the window while the minutes ticked away and he did his best not to explode with nervous tension.

Earlier, Maddy had got up at seven o'clock and immediately gone into the bathroom to get showered. She had got her hair styled the previous afternoon and now she admired the hairdresser's work as she quickly got dressed. She made coffee and smeared marmalade on a couple of croissants and brought some in to Greg.

"You can lie on, if you like. You don't have to be at the church till half eleven."

"No, I'll get up. I've got some calls to make. How do you feel? Excited?"

"Yes but, believe me, this has been no picnic. I'll be relieved when it's all over." She glanced in the mirror. "How do I look? Do you like my hair?"

"It's lovely and you look radiant, as always. I hope you don't steal all the attention away from the bride."

"I don't think there's any danger of that," Maddy said, caustically. "You don't know Helen."

Greg chuckled and took a bite out of his croissant.

"I'm looking forward to meeting your folks," he said.

"And they're looking forward to meeting you."

She glanced at her watch. "I'd better be going. You know where the church is?"

"Sure."

"Okay. See you later."

She gave him a quick peck on the cheek and departed for the mayhem of St Margaret's Lane.

Now it was ten to twelve and the only people remaining in the family home were the bride, Maddy, Aunt Connie and Mr Pritchard whose patience had been stretched to breaking point. All the others had departed for the church.

"Are you ready yet?" Mr Pritchard bellowed up the stairs. "The car is waiting. If you don't come now, the priest will go home."

"Just a minute!" Helen shouted as Aunt Connie made some last-minute adjustments to her hair.

"My God," Mr Pritchard groaned, "I think I'm going to have a heart attack."

At that moment, Helen appeared at the top of the stairs with Maddy and Aunt Connie holding up her train. She made a regal descent, oblivious to all the panic her delay had caused while Mr Pritchard fidgeted nervously with the keys to the front door.

"You didn't say how I looked," she remarked to her father.

"You look brilliant. Now get into the back seat of the car while I lock up the house and just pray that there's no traffic on the road."

After a mad dash, they were at the church for five past twelve. Maddy quickly went to join the other bridesmaids while Aunt Connie slipped into a seat at the back. At last the organ began to play and Helen, clutching her father's arm, began her stately progress down the aisle.

She looked spectacular. Maddy had to concede that the dressmaker and the hairdresser and all those who had attended Helen had done a magnificent job. She even managed a tight little smile as she nodded and waved to the assembled guests like a queen on the way to her coronation. When they reached the altar, Mr Pritchard handed her over to Joe Fuller with the grateful look of a man delighted to be finally relieved of a heavy burden.

Afterwards, they all retired to the hotel where the reception was being held. The guests headed for the bar while the bride and her party went out to the garden for photographs. Maddy caught sight of Greg, clutching a pint of Guinness and deep in conversation with her brother, Brian.

"Everything okay?" she asked.

He grinned. "Splendid."

"I have to pose for some photographs but I'll join you later."

"Take your time. I'll be fine."

Eventually it was time for the lunch and then the speeches. Maddy was dying to get out of her bridesmaid's dress and into something more comfortable but Helen at the head of the table appeared to be enjoying herself enormously. This was her big day and she was the centre of attention. She was relishing every moment.

At last, the tables were cleared away and the band began to play. Joe Fuller led his new bride onto the floor for the first dance and the room burst into applause. Maddy slipped away and joined Greg at his table.

"How are you holding up?" he asked.

"With great difficulty. I feel utterly whacked."

"Nothing that a gin and tonic won't cure," he said, signalling to a passing waiter.

"Thank God it's finally over," she sighed. "You've no idea what a nightmare this has been."

But Greg had an enigmatic twinkle in his eye. "Oh, I don't know," he said. "I've thoroughly enjoyed it. I think everyone should get married at least once in their life. Don't you?"

Chapter Twenty-two

Maddy's hectic workload was showing no signs of letting up. Indeed, it was about to get even heavier. A developer, who was planning a block of luxury apartments on the site of an old warehouse in the docklands, had decided to award the selling rights to Carroll and Shanley. It was a prestigious contract and could open up even more business for the firm. Maddy was flattered when Tim Lyons asked her to take personal charge of it.

The man who was developing the site was a former football player from Mayo called Mick McCann. The first time she met him, Maddy was taken by how young and fit he looked. Most of the developers she had dealt with were middle-aged and decidedly overweight. But McCann was thrusting and energetic and seemed determined that his development was going to be the finest yet built in the city. The apartments he was planning were going to be bright and airy and he was committed to using the best materials – finest Italian marble, Howth stone fireplaces, polished hardwood floors, designer bathrooms and kitchens.

For Maddy, the project entailed exploratory meetings with Mick and his development team to agree on a sales strategy. The apartments were being aimed at young professionals and she already had some ideas about how they should be marketed. The site was ideal. It was near the city centre and close to rail and transport links. And it fronted onto the river which she decided should be the main selling point. But there was still something missing. She worried about it for days until suddenly the answer came to her like a blinding flash. What the project needed was a commercial centre.

At her next meeting with the development team she made this point.

"Don't you think you should include some shops and restaurants? Maybe even a bar or two?"

Around the table, McCann and his colleagues glanced at one another.

"What do you have in mind?" the chief architect asked. He was a fussy little man called Denis Sharkey who clearly believed Maddy was butting into an area that didn't concern her. She could immediately sense his resentment.

"We should see this development as a community," she said. "It's not just a place for people to sleep. They have to live here too, spend their recreational time here."

Mick McCann was now looking at her with renewed interest.

"There's no demand for that sort of thing," Sharkey replied, sharply.

But Maddy wasn't going to allow herself to be sidelined so easily.

"I think there *is* a demand," she went on. "I've thought about this and I keep asking myself the same question. 'Would I buy one of these apartments?' And the answer I keep getting back is 'no.' The location is perfect but if I was buying, I would want a deli on my doorstep where I could pick up small grocery items like bread and milk and maybe newspapers. I'd want a bar where I could meet my friends in the evening and at weekends. I'd want a restaurant where I could eat from time to time. And the type of client we are aiming for will have the very same requirements as me."

"This is ridiculous," the architect retorted. "We're supposed to be building apartments."

But McCann waved him to be quiet.

"Go on," he said, giving his full attention to Maddy.

"The site would be ideal for a restaurant," she continued. "It's right on the river. It would draw people from all over town. It could be a major selling point."

"It would mean redrawing the plans," Sharkey objected, his cheeks growing red with indignation.

"So, what's the problem?" McCann asked. "We want to get this project right. If we have to redraw the plans, then that's what we'll do."

"But we'll be able to build fewer apartments."

"We'll gain on the shops and it will make the remaining apartments easier to sell," Maddy pointed out. "And think of the publicity it will bring. Everyone will be talking about it."

The architect was about to raise fresh objections but McCann quickly silenced him.

"I think Maddy has a valid point," he said. "I need more time to think about this."

Sharkey shot Maddy a thunderous glance and gathered up his papers and plans.

"Same time next week," Mick McCann said. "We'll make our final decision then."

The following morning, he rang her at work.

"I've been thinking about your suggestion," he said. "I'd like to discuss it further with you. Are you free for lunch?"

"When?" Maddy asked.

"Today, if possible."

She had planned to grab a quick sandwich but this project was important and here was an opportunity to impress her views on McCann in a one-to-one situation.

"Okay," she said. "Tell me where."

They agreed to meet at Peppers restaurant in town at one o'clock. McCann gave her directions and at five to one she was pushing open the front door of a large, noisy brasserie which was quickly filling up with sharp-suited executive types. She saw Mick's athletic figure already seated at a table near the back with a bottle of wine open before him and a glass already poured. He stood up as Maddy approached and pulled out a seat for her.

"Want a drink?" he asked when they were both settled.

She shook her head. She hadn't come here for a boozy lunch. She wanted to get some serious work done.

"What are you eating?" he continued. "They do a good steak. I can recommend it."

She quickly perused the menu. When she looked up again, she saw that McCann was studying her.

"Well?" he smiled.

"I'll have the grilled chicken."

He quickly got hold of a waiter and gave their order.

"You sure you won't have a glass of wine?" he asked, reaching for the bottle.

"I try not to drink during the day," she explained.

"Well, I find it helps me relax," he continued, topping up his glass. "After a morning spent on building sites, I like to pamper myself. Now, I've been thinking about this idea of yours."

"Yes?"

"I'm inclined to go with it. But Sharkey has a point. If we go for a restaurant and shops, it will mean fewer apartments. There's a limit to what they'll allow us to build on that site."

"But the big gain will be on the prestige the project will attract. I think people would be prepared to pay a premium to live in a development like this."

"And what if I can't lease the shops?"

"You will lease them."

Mick McCann's handsome face broke into a smile. "That's easy to say. But I'm already mortgaged to the hilt. I'd frighten you if I told you how much I owe the banks and we haven't even got planning permission yet."

"But you want this to be your signature project, the one that will make your name. You're committed to making it the best development in the city. Why not go for the whole hog?"

At that moment, their food arrived and McCann fell on his steak with obvious relish.

"If you're worried about leasing the shops," Maddy continued, "I could make some discreet enquiries for you."

"Would you?"

"Sure. And if we don't get a positive response, we can rethink it. But I'm convinced this idea will take off. It's what people want, Mick. It's the future."

"You're a very shrewd woman," McCann said, studying her once more. "This is a male-dominated business. We don't have many women in the construction industry."

"Yet at least half your customers are women. And in my experience, women are more interested in property than men."

At that moment, their conversation was interrupted by a brash voice. Maddy looked up to see an untidy figure towering above her.

"Enjoying your lunch?" Arthur Brady asked.

She was caught off guard. She hadn't seen Arthur since the meal in Hennessy's restaurant several months earlier when he had been introduced to Sophie.

"Arthur!" she exclaimed. "How are you keeping?"

"Oh, I'm fine," he said, swaying slightly and looking intently at Mick McCann. "I just popped in to replenish the old nosebag." He seemed to hesitate.

Maddy quickly introduced the two men and they shook hands. She noticed McCann looking at Arthur's slightly dishevelled figure, his crumpled suit and untidy appearance.

"Mick and I are business colleagues," she explained. "He's a developer."

"Ah," Arthur replied, "now I get it. You're plotting some property coup. Well, I'll let you get on with your conversation. Got to get back to the office. Toodleoo."

He waved a hand and made his way unsteadily towards the door. Mick watched him go.

"Who was that?" he asked.

"He's a stockbroker. He's going out with my girlfriend."

He nodded.

"So," he said, getting back to their discussion. "You're going to check out the potential of these shops for me?"

A few nights later, Maddy was enjoying a quiet drink with Greg when he unexpectedly brought up the meeting.

"Arthur tells me he ran into you recently."

"That's right," she replied. "Pepper's restaurant. I was having lunch with a client."

Greg sniffed. "Handsome devil by all accounts. Arthur says you seemed to be enjoying yourselves."

Maddy stopped and put down her glass.

"He said *what*?"

"He said you appeared to be very cosy. In fact, he mistook you for lovers until he realised it was you."

She felt her face redden with indignation. "I hope you told him to get lost?"

"I didn't know what to say, quite honestly. I was taken aback."

"It was a business lunch, Greg. With a very important client called Mick McCann. He's a property developer."

"I didn't know that."

"Well, now I'm telling you. And Arthur Brady should mind his own damned business instead of running around spreading malicious gossip. Besides, I introduced them so he knew who Mick was."

"Calm down," Greg said.

"But you raised the subject. I deal with lots of men in the course of my business. Do you expect me to account for every one?"

"No, of course not."

"Do you find me questioning you about your lunch appointments?"

"Look, I'm sorry," he said, taking her hand. "It's just that I care very deeply for you, Maddy. I suppose when he told me, I was a little jealous. You're a beautiful woman. I'm sure lots of men find you every bit as attractive as I do."

She looked into his face.

"Listen, Greg. There's something you must understand. If our relationship is to develop, we have to trust each other. I could never accept a man who was jealous."

"I understand. I won't raise the matter again."

"Please don't," she said.

But the incident upset her. Greg had betrayed another side of his nature that she hadn't seen before. If he could be suspicious over a simple thing like this, what else would make him jealous? It didn't bode well for the future.

And there was something else that bothered her. He still had not told her that he loved her. Yet the incident had provided him with the perfect opportunity to express his feelings. He hadn't taken it. She wondered why. Was it because he still wasn't sure?

The next afternoon, Greg rang to say he had organised a special treat. He was taking her somewhere immediately after work. He sounded like the old Greg, confident and brimming with enthusiasm.

"I don't want any excuses," he said. "I've gone to great trouble over this and I won't take 'no' for an answer."

"What is it?" she asked, her curiosity aroused.

"You'll find out when you get there."

"Can't I even go home to get changed?"

"No. And you'll be leaving the car at work – we're travelling by taxi. I'll call for you at six o'clock sharp. Byeee!"

She heard a click and he was gone.

What on earth could this be, she thought? But something inside her was pleased. Whatever Greg had planned for her, it showed he cared. And it meant that their relationship was back again on an even keel.

She worked steadily throughout the afternoon, ringing contacts in the restaurant and shopping trade and sounding them out about the possibility of leasing a commercial unit in Mick McCann's development. The overwhelming response was positive. Everyone she spoke to thought it was a great idea. But her big achievement was securing the interest of Paul Le Brun.

Le Brun was a native of Normandy who had married an Irishwoman and settled in Dublin where he had opened a restaurant providing up-market French cuisine. The restaurant was called Pigalle and was located in a lane off Baggot Street. It was an immediate success. It had even secured a prestigious Michelin star which only served to enhance its already swollen reputation.

After outlining her plans to Le Brun, the restaurateur indicated he would be very interested in purchasing a lease if the terms were right. Maddy was euphoric. The response had vindicated her. Now she was convinced that Mick McCann would have no difficulty off-loading the units if he decided to go with her suggestion.

She was in excellent mood when she finally put down the phone and glanced at the clock to see that it was now a quarter to six. She quickly tidied her desk and applied some make-up in time to see a taxi pull up at the door.

Greg was seated in the back, wearing a smart business suit with blue button-down shirt and tie. His hair had been freshly groomed.

"Can't you tell me where we're going?" she asked as she settled in beside him.

"No."

"Can't you at least give me a clue?"

"Afraid not. You'll just have to be patient."

"This is like a magical mystery tour," she said, as the taxi headed south along the coast in the direction of Booterstown. "It better be good."

But Greg remained tight-lipped as they focussed on the road ahead. "Let's just say that I think you're going to enjoy it."

At last, they found themselves in Blackrock. The taxi turned off the main road and drove a short distance before stopping outside a restaurant that Maddy instantly recognised.

"The Chalet d'Or?"

He turned to her with a wide smile.

"That's right, the scene of our very first dinner. Remember?"

"Of course, I do. I talked about it for weeks afterwards."

"So, let's hope we can repeat the experience. I've been lucky enough to secure a table for seven which explains the tight schedule."

She threw her arms around his neck. "Oh, Greg, I'm thrilled! Did you have much trouble getting a reservation?"

He shrugged and grinned. "I had to grovel, of course. You know Marco O'Malley's reputation for eccentricity. He made me feel that he was doing me an enormous favour. But the main point is I got a table. Are you hungry?"

"I am now."

He checked his watch. "It's a quarter to seven. Let's go in. We can have a drink while we wait."

He paid for the taxi and it sped away.

The restaurant was filling up. Marco O'Malley, a huge man in a white apron, glared at his customers from his eyrie in the kitchen but his grim attitude immediately changed when his eyes fell on Maddy. He left the kitchen and advanced towards her, gently lifted her hand to his mouth and let his lips brush her fingers.

"Madame, it is my exquisite pleasure to meet you."

Maddy was amused to hear his pseudo-French accent – she knew he was in fact Irish. Marco turned to Greg.

"And you, sir, may I ask? Who are you?"

Greg gave his name.

"Ah, the young man who requested a table because it was a special occasion!"

The chef beamed at Maddy and leaned his head sideways. "Now I understand. Any meal with a woman as beautiful as this would be a very special occasion. You are a lucky man, sir. Now if you would come with me, please."

Greg raised his eyebrows at Maddy as they followed the chef to a table at the top of the room where they could see out across the whole restaurant. It was easily the best table in the house and, with a smart bow, Marco O'Malley seated them and presented two menus.

"What would you like to drink?" he asked.

"Could we have two kir royales?" Greg asked.

"Certainly, sir."

Smiling once more at Maddy, he left and made his way back to the kitchen, pausing for a moment at the bar to give instructions to the wine waiter.

"What was that all about?" Maddy asked, once he was out of hearing.

"I think he's smitten by you. And who would blame him? You look exquisite tonight."

"In my working gear! With only a lick of make-up! I don't think so! You should have warned me, you know."

"You always look exquisite." He took her hand. "This is my way of saying sorry for what happened the other evening."

But she attempted to brush the apology aside. "Let's not talk about it, Greg. Let's just enjoy ourselves."

"No, we have to talk about it. I don't know what came over me. I suppose I *was* jealous at the thought of another man having lunch with you. But that's no excuse. You must understand, Maddy, that I still haven't fully recovered from my experience with Lorna."

"I do understand."

"Arthur has admitted that he was half-cut the day he met you. He'd been drinking heavily the night before and he was still hungover. But I want to apologise. I don't want to lose you, Maddy. I promise it will never happen again."

She looked at him. He seemed so abject and contrite that she felt her heart go out to him. "Why don't we both forget all about it? Let's put it behind us and never mention it again."

"Are you sure?"

"I'm certain."

She looked up as a waiter arrived at the table bearing a small tray.

"Your kir royale, madam – sir," he announced setting the sparkling glasses of champagne on the starched linen tablecloth.

It was a wonderful meal and a memorable evening. Greg insisted that they order the house speciality – suckling pig – thick juicy slices of tender pork, accompanied by side dishes of haricot beans, roast baby potatoes and creamy whipped spinach. To accompany the meal, he ordered a bottle of Beaune, a delicious light red Burgundy wine.

Throughout the occasion, Marco O'Malley hovered like a benevolent presence, enquiring if the food was to their satisfaction, topping up their wineglasses, straightening the cutlery till the other diners in the restaurant began to gape as if they were minor celebrities. They ended the meal with a mouth-watering confection of berries and fruits and flowing glasses of a rare French liqueur that Marco poured with an extravagant flourish.

"Did you enjoy your meal" he asked at last, presenting Greg with the bill.

"It was perfect."

"And you, madame?" the chef enquired, turning to Maddy.

"Oh, I sure did," she replied, realising that her head felt light after drinking the liqueur.

"I am so pleased," he replied, taking her hand again and kissing her fingers. "And you will return?" he asked as he helped them on with their coats.

"We certainly will."

"*Enchanté*," Marco said as he escorted them to the door and the waiting taxi.

Maddy was giggling as she settled into the back seat and they headed off for Ranelagh.

"Why does he go on like that?" she asked. "He's Irish, for God's sake. You'd think he was some exotic Latin."

"He's a chef," Greg replied. "And chefs are supposed to be eccentric. It's all part of the mystique."

"Well, he certainly treated us like royalty." She cuddled closer to Greg and rested her head on his shoulder. It felt so warm and comforting. "Thank you for a wonderful evening."

"My pleasure."

His breath was hot against her cheek.

"There's something else I want to say, Maddy."

"Yes?"

"I think I'm falling in love with you."

The words were like music to her ears.

He drew her tight and their lips met in a passionate kiss.

Chapter Twenty-three

At last, Greg had declared his love. All the lingering doubts that had troubled her were suddenly dissolved in the wave of joy that swept over her. Her relationship was on solid ground. Her love for Greg was being returned and it was a wonderful feeling that infused her and gave her life new purpose.

She was in fine form next day when she reported back to Mick McCann on the positive reaction she had received about the shops.

"That's fantastic," he said. "So the people you spoke to think it's a good idea?"

"They think it's an excellent idea.."

She told him about Paul Le Brun's interest in a lease on the restaurant if the terms were right.

"He's a big name," she added. "Once he's on board, I'll bet the others will come flocking in."

McCann was delighted. "I've been running over the figures again. If we include a commercial development we'll lose a dozen apartments so the shops will have to take up the slack."

"Do you think you might go with it?"

"Yes. I'll speak to the bank right away."

"What about Denis Sharkey's objections?"

"Leave Sharkey to me," Mick said in his gruff, businesslike manner. "I'll be paying his fee. In the end of the day, he'll do what he's told."

Tim Lyons was also excited when she broke the news to him.

"Good work, Maddy. That sounds marvellous. It also opens up possibilities for us."

She could see the way his mind was working. So far, Carroll and Shanley's business had been confined to residential property. But this venture provided an opportunity to get a foothold in the commercial market.

"Stick with it. If McCann goes with this, I want us to be the firm that negotiates those leases. Keep me informed."

But it wasn't all work. Now she was spending practically all her free time with Greg. She began to take him for Sunday lunch to her parents' house in Raheny where Mr Pritchard was pleased to have someone who shared his interest in football. The house was a lot quieter now that Helen was gone but Maddy would sometimes catch her mother weighing up Greg as a future son-in-law.

As Christmas drew near, they began to make plans. One evening, Greg suggested that she might like to come with him to Galway to meet his parents.

"We could go down on Stephen's Day and stay over. What do you think?"

"I'd love to meet them," she said.

"I think you'll like them."

"Will they approve of me?"

"Of course they will. They'll be delighted to find that I'm dating such a wonderful woman." He gave her his boyish grin.

"And we can have Christmas dinner with my mum and dad," Maddy said, getting excited now. "Mum's planning a family reunion with Helen and Joe."

He put his arm around her waist and drew her close. "And maybe in the New Year we might escape again to Marbella."

Maddy felt her heart leap. Marbella sounded wonderful. A break in the sun would be the ideal way to start off the year.

"Oh, Greg! That would be fantastic."

He winked. "Let me have a chat with Joe Spence and we'll see what we can do."

But while Maddy's relationship was going from strength to strength, Sophie's was beginning to show signs of wear and tear. Maddy began to notice small hints of tension but it all came pouring out one Friday evening as the three friends were relaxing in the Pink Parrot after work.

"I'm worried about Arthur's drinking," Sophie confessed with a doleful face. "I think he might have a problem."

Rosie and Maddy exchanged a glance but neither spoke.

"How bad is it?" Rosie eventually asked.

"Pretty bad. He seems to be half-drunk most of the time. I even found a bottle of whiskey in his briefcase the other day. I don't think it's normal to carry a bottle of whiskey around. Do you?"

"Have you tried talking to him?" Rosie asked.

"Talking is a waste of time. He just denies it. He says he has a couple of drinks at lunch-time and another couple after work. But I've seen him in action. He can put away enough to sink a battleship." She let out a loud sigh. "I'm worried sick about him. I don't know what to do. I'd get rid of him except I care for him too much. But having a drunk for a boyfriend is no fun, I can tell you."

She turned to Maddy.

"Do you think he might listen if Greg talked to him?"

"I could ask him," Maddy said doubtfully.

"Oh, would you? I'd be really grateful. I don't want him to get into trouble."

That evening when she was alone with Greg, Maddy raised the subject.

"Sophie's very concerned about Arthur's drinking."

Greg raised his eyebrows. "She's not the only one. His boss is worried too."

"So other people have noticed?"

"Of course. With Arthur it's hard to escape."

"She wondered if you could have a chat with him."

He rubbed his chin. "Would it do any good? I've seen this sort of thing before. Problem drinkers have a great capacity for denial."

"But he's your colleague. He might pay more attention if you spoke to him. Can't you tell him that people are beginning to talk about it?"

"Look, Maddy, I'm very fond of Sophie. I think she's a wonderful woman and a brilliant cook and I know she's one of your best friends. But I did say at the beginning that I wouldn't take any responsibility for how this thing turned out."

"I know you did. But all she wants is for you to have a quiet word with him."

"All right," he said finally. "I would only do this for Sophie. And don't be surprised if Arthur tells me to take a hike."

A few days later, Greg came back with the good news that he had spoken to Joe Spence and the apartment in Marbella was available in March.

"It's a good time to go," he said. "The temperature should be around 20 degrees. Not too hot and the weather will be nice and sunny."

"That's fantastic. I'll speak to Tim Lyons about getting time off."

"And I had a serious talk with Arthur. I told him that people were getting worried about his drinking. After a lot of huffing and puffing, he promised to slow down."

"Oh, Greg, that's marvellous. Sophie will be delighted." She gave him a quick peck on the cheek. "Thanks for everything. You really are a wonderful man."

Greg grinned. "Let's face it," he said. "We're a wonderful couple."

As Christmas approached, the weather turned cold and wet. Maddy would often gaze from her patio window at the sodden, grey picture the garden presented in contrast to the splendour it had shown in the summer. But now she had March to look forward to and the trip to Marbella.

The days passed quickly. At work, the sales pressure eased off as the holiday drew near. Mick McCann called to say that he was postponing any decision on the apartment development till the architects had redrawn the plans and he had gauged the reaction of the planning authorities. But if the verdict was favourable, he was going ahead with her suggestion. He also gave her an undertaking that Carroll and Shanley would get the rights to negotiate the leases for the shops as well as being sales agents for the apartments. All in all, it was a good piece of work.

Before she knew, the holiday was upon them.

On Christmas Eve she went over to Munster Road to deliver her presents to Sophie and Rosie.

"Another year gone by. Doesn't time fly?" Rosie said.

Maddy thought of the year that had passed. A lot of things had happened. She had bought another house and taken up with Greg. And her career had continued its upward trajectory. She had so much to be grateful for.

"How is Arthur?" she asked Sophie.

"Good," she replied. "I don't know what Greg said to him but it seems to have worked. He's really cut down on his drinking."

"I'm pleased," Maddy said and squeezed her hand.

"What about Adam?" she asked Rosie.

"He's fine. We're going out to Killiney the day after Stephen's Day to visit his parents. They're a nice couple and they absolutely dote on Adam. He's an only child so he gets spoiled."

"That's a coincidence," Maddy said. "Greg's taking me down to Galway on Stephen's Day to meet his parents. I have to admit, I'm a little nervous."

"Why?"

"I want to make a good impression. I want them to approve of me."

"Oh for God's sake!" Sophie put in. "What does it matter? Greg approves of you. That's the main thing."

"No, she's right," Rosie said. "I know exactly how she feels. It's important to have the in-laws on side."

"In-laws?" Maddy said with a laugh. "You're talking as if we were planning to get married."

Sophie and Rosie looked at each other.

"Well, that's the next logical step, isn't it?" Sophie said. "Anyone can see that. It's plain as day."

Christmas Day at St Margaret's Lane turned out to be a happy family occasion. Mrs Pritchard had cooked a large turkey and a ham and dishes of roast and mashed potatoes, Brussels sprouts, carrots and peas and chestnut stuffing. And she was determined that no one would leave the table until they had done justice to the large plates of food that she placed before them.

There were eight people sitting down to eat: Maddy and Greg, her brother Brian, Aunt Connie, Mr and Mrs Pritchard and Joe and Helen, who Maddy was pleased to note was on her very best behaviour. She was pleasant and polite and seemed to have subdued her tendency to complain and demand attention. She even offered to help her mother in the kitchen which was highly out of character.

After the main course, Mrs Pritchard served plum pudding and custard followed by tea and Christmas cake by which stage even the hardiest eaters like Mr Pritchard were holding their stomachs. Everyone adjourned to the parlour and the whiskey and sherry bottles came out.

Mrs Pritchard called on Joe to sing 'The Fields of Athenry' and he duly obliged while Helen held his hand and gazed soulfully into his eyes. Something has definitely happened to her since she got married, Maddy decided. She's behaving like a different woman. When she finally left with Greg at ten o'clock the party was still in full swing and Aunt Connie was crooning 'The Charladies' Ball' while Mr Pritchard attempted to accompany her on a mouth organ.

"What a day," Greg said as he settled into the driving seat of his car and fastened his belt.

"Did you enjoy it?"

"I had a blast," he said. "I thought television had wiped out all that home entertainment."

"Not in St Margaret's Lane, it hasn't," Maddy said with a quiet feeling of satisfaction that the day had gone so well.

The following morning, they were up at eight o'clock for the journey to Galway.

"Don't expect anything as raucous as yesterday," Greg said as he shaved at the bathroom mirror and Maddy brewed coffee while attempting to pack an overnight bag. "Sorry to say, lunch with the Delaney family will be a much more subdued affair. And one other thing, it's separate bedrooms, I'm afraid."

"Of course," Maddy retorted. "I didn't expect anything else. I don't want your parents to get the idea that you've fallen into the clutches of some Jezebel."

"I could think of a worse fate," he replied, ducking to avoid the rolled-up tights she flung at him.

By nine o'clock they were on their way. Because it was a holiday, the roads were mercifully free of traffic and they made good progress. By eleven o'clock they had passed Athlone and were heading westwards with hopes of reaching Galway by one.

As the city drew closer, Maddy's apprehension grew. She was still nervous about meeting Greg's family for the first time. From what he had told her, his parents were a respectable middle-class couple in their mid-sixties. His father had been a bank manager for his whole career while his mother had stayed at home to raise Greg and his three siblings – one of whom, his brother, Toby – was expected to join them with his young family. She desperately wanted them to like her. She knew if they took against her, it could make life difficult.

At last, Greg swung the car into the driveway of a neat bungalow on the western outskirts of the city. It was a quarter past one. His parents were waiting at the front door to greet them. Greg made the introductions and Maddy presented them with the presents she had brought – a cashmere cardigan for Mrs Delaney, who turned out to be a petite woman with blue-rinsed hair, and a bottle of Redbreast whiskey for Mr Delaney. He looked like an older version of Greg with his broad shoulders and stiff military bearing.

Mrs Delaney took the gifts without comment.

"You're late," she said, turning to Greg. "You said one o'clock and it's now a quarter past."

"I said I was aiming for one o'clock. I got here as soon as I could."

"Well, you've kept everyone waiting. I hope the lunch isn't ruined."

She brought Maddy into the house where she opened a door to reveal a small fussy little bedroom with a wash-hand basin and towel in a corner.

"Do please hurry up and join us. Everyone is hungry."

Maddy felt her apprehension increase. How odd, she thought as she quickly rinsed her face and combed her hair. She hasn't seen her son for months and the first thing she does is scold him. But worse was to come.

She quickly applied fresh make-up and, with beating heart, hurried back to the large dining-room where Greg and his parents had now been joined by a young woman, two children and a man who she took to be Greg's older brother, Toby. Fresh introductions were made and she took her seat while she waited for the meal to begin.

"We're having poached salmon for lunch." Mrs Delaney announced, as she passed the plates around the polished mahogany table. "I hope you like it?"

"Oh yes, salmon is fine."

"Seámus has a problem with his heart," she explained. "His doctor has recommended fish. It's good for his cholesterol."

Mr Delaney nodded self-consciously.

"I'm sorry to hear that," Maddy said. "But I like salmon. It will make a change from turkey."

Greg's mother passed her a plate. On it rested a piece of salmon, two potatoes and some string beans. It made a pale comparison with the heaped platter she had faced the previous day at St Margaret's Lane.

There was a silence while everyone stared at her and Maddy was forced to lower her eyes. She could tell this was going to be an awkward lunch. Maybe they were expecting her to continue the conversation.

"How was the journey down from Dublin?" Toby put in, after a pause.

Maddy immediately turned to him. He was a tense man in his 30s with a pale face and a white expanse of forehead. Greg had told her he was a civil engineer. Across the table, his wife, Gráinne, a plump dark-haired woman with narrow, inquisitive eyes sat beside their two little boys.

"It was fine," Maddy replied. "There was very little traffic."

"Greg tells us you're in the property business?" he continued.

"That's right."

"Are you busy?"

"Very busy. There's a lot of building taking place right now."

"Here too," Toby added.

"Maddy is the best in Dublin," Greg interjected. "She sold me my apartment."

They heard Mrs Delaney cough loudly and her husband began to eat which was the signal for everyone to fall on their plates.

After a while, Mr Delaney turned to her.

"What exactly do you do in the property line?" he asked.

"I'm in sales."

"And how did you get into this business?"

He managed to make it sound like something not quite respectable.

"By accident. When I left school, I was looking for a job and this one was available. So I applied and they took me on."

Mrs Delaney looked up, sharply. "Did you not take a degree?"

"No," Maddy said, picking at her salmon as she felt a chill run through her. "I didn't particularly want to go to university. I was keen to start earning money. To be honest, I don't think I've missed anything."

An ominous silence followed the remark.

"All our children went to college," Mrs Delaney said firmly. "Besides fitting a young person for a career, a university education broadens the mind."

Maddy could feel her face grow red with embarrassment. The conversation was not going at all well.

Mr Delaney sniffed. "This job you do, Miss Pritchard? Does it pay well?"

"It pays reasonably well. I earn a basic salary plus I also get commission."

"And do you like it?"

"I love it. But it *can* get quite hectic at times."

"Maddy is being modest," Greg interjected. "She was recently promoted. She's now in charge of the sales team."

"It seems to me that houses practically sell themselves these days," Mrs Delaney interjected.

Maddy flinched at the implied put-down. But before she had a chance to defend herself, Mr Delaney spoke once more.

"What do your parents do, Miss Pritchard?"

"They're retired."

"And your father?"

"He was a labourer. He worked for Dublin Corporation."

If she had said her father was the local ratcatcher she couldn't have received a more frigid response. This time there was an even longer silence and the faces turned away and studied their plates.

Maddy couldn't help the feeling of indignation that was beginning to well up inside her. Had Greg brought her all this way to be interrogated by his family? Why should she apologise for not going to university or for her father's occupation? He might not have earned much money but he had given them love and security and they had never known a hungry day. And why was Greg sitting there like a dummy and making no attempt to defend her?

The questioning had started up again.

"Which part of Dublin do you come from?" Toby asked.

"Raheny."

"That's on the north side?"

"Yes."

"Is it safe?" Mr Delaney asked. "Dublin has become so violent."

"It's perfectly safe," Maddy replied.

"We have friends who live in Dublin," Mrs Delaney added, "but they're out in Foxrock. It's beautiful there, very refined, very quiet. Their neighbour has a senior job in RTÉ."

The meal was turning into a nightmare. She felt her frustration approach boiling point. If she didn't act soon, she was going to say something she might regret. She glanced at Greg, appealing to him for help but he lowered his face.

"Seamus met our friend through the bank," Mrs Delaney continued. "He has a very senior position. He has a degree in Economics, of course. In the bank, a third-level education is essential if you want to get promoted. Without it, you're no-one."

Maddy stared across the table at her tormentor. She carefully laid her napkin beside her half-eaten plate and stood up, her hand shaking with indignation.

"I'm not feeling well," she said. "Will you please excuse me? I think I need to lie down."

Greg followed her immediately to her room.

"What's the matter?" he asked.

"Matter? Haven't you been listening to that inquisition?"

"Don't take it personally," he said. "They don't mean any harm. They're old-fashioned, that's all."

"Take it personally?" she exclaimed. "What else has it been? I've never been asked such personal questions in my life."

"I'm sorry, Maddy, honest I am."

She stared at him, struggling with all her might to keep her anger under control.

"Did my family grill you when you came out to my house? Of course, they didn't. They may not have been to university but they certainly know what good manners are."

"Please try to calm down."

"I'm trying hard, Greg. Believe me. But I've known since I sat down at that table that your parents didn't like me. What's more, they feel I am not good enough for you. And I haven't come the whole way to Galway to be told that."

They left early the following morning before anyone was up. Maddy had spent a restless night just waiting for the dawn so she could escape from this awful house. Greg sat beside her at the wheel, pale-faced and tense. She knew that for him too the trip had been a disaster. He had hoped his parents would take to her. Instead they seemed to resent the hold she had on their son.

By the time they reached Ranelagh it was almost midday. She was feeling exhausted but her anger had finally cooled. She was looking forward to a hot bath and something to eat.

As she opened the front door, she heard the phone ringing. It was Sophie.

"Thank God I got you," she said, her voice sounding desperate. "This is the third time I've called."

"What's the matter?" Maddy asked.

The next words sent a chill running down her spine.

"It's Arthur. He's unconscious and I can't wake him up."

Maddy was stunned.

"Stay right where you are. We're coming over," she said and immediately turned to Greg who was coming through the door with the bags.

"Arthur's taken some kind of turn. We have to get over there."

Chapter Twenty-four

Arthur was lying fully dressed on the bed, covered with a blanket, when they arrived at Munster Road five minutes later. His eyes were closed and his face had the colour of cement. His breathing was slow and laboured. A strong smell of alcohol permeated the room.

Sophie stood beside the bed, wringing her hands in distress.

Greg bent over him and prised open one eye. It was lifeless. He tried slapping his face but Arthur only muttered and a trail of white spittle dribbled from his mouth.

"How long has he been like this?" he asked.

"I found him half an hour ago. I had to go into town and when I came back, there he was." Her body trembled with shock. "Oh Greg, I'm terrified. Is he going to die?"

"I don't know. But we'll have to get him to hospital immediately. Where's Rosie?"

"She went off this morning with Adam."

"Okay. Let's see if we can shift him. You two grab his legs and I'll take his shoulders."

It was a struggle but they managed to lift Arthur off the bed. Unconscious, he was a dead weight. With great effort, they eventually manhandled him out to the street and into the back seat of the car. Maddy and Sophie sat on either side of him while Greg settled in behind the steering wheel.

"Tell me what happened," he said as he started the car and headed across town to St James's hospital.

Sophie bit her lip and fought back the tears. "He started drinking on Christmas Eve. It was only supposed to be a celebratory glass of wine. But he continued right through Christmas. I couldn't get him to stop. I pleaded with him but he kept insisting it was only a few drinks and he could handle it. When I left him this morning, he seemed okay but he must have had booze hidden somewhere in the house. I found this."

She took an empty whiskey bottle from her bag.

Maddy stared in horror. "You mean he drank a whole bottle of whiskey in a couple of hours?"

"No wonder he passed out," Greg said as the sprawling hospital complex came into view.

The Accident and Emergency department was crowded but once Greg reported the situation to the duty nurse, a couple of medics immediately sprang into action. Arthur was taken from the car and placed on a trolley and wheeled off to the casualty ward while they settled down to wait.

Maddy went off to find some cups of strong tea.

By now, Sophie was silently weeping into her handkerchief.

"Thank God you came when you did. I didn't know what to do. I just started to panic."

"Drink the tea. You'll feel better."

"I should have done more to stop him."

"Don't blame yourself," Greg said. "He would have found a way. He's an alcoholic. Once he starts to drink, he can't stop." He put his arm around her and gently caressed her cheek. "I'm sorry, Sophie. But that's how it looks to me. I don't think Arthur has any option now but to stop drinking completely."

After what seemed an eternity, a doctor came to see them. He questioned Sophie about how long Arthur had been drinking and what exactly had happened.

"How is he?" she asked when the doctor had finished taking notes.

"He's sleeping now. We had to pump out his stomach."

Sophie shuddered. "Is he going to be all right?"

"Yes. He'll survive. But it was a close call. He's lucky you found him when you did. We'll keep him here for a few days till he's back on his feet and then he can go home."

"When will I be able to see him?"

"Ring tomorrow. We should know by then. Are you his partner?"

"Yes."

"I'm going to repeat this to Mr Brady when he sobers up. He can't continue to drink like this. If he does, I'm afraid it will only be a matter of time before…"

He left the remainder of the sentence hanging in the air.

The journey back in the car was conducted in silence. Everyone was thinking of what the doctor had said. If Sophie hadn't found him in time, Arthur could now be dead.

As they approached Munster Road, Maddy put her arm round her shoulders and cuddled her. "Why don't you stay with me tonight?"

But Sophie shook her head. "Rosie will be home soon. I'll be okay."

They stopped at No 26 and Sophie hugged them both.

"I don't know what to say. Thanks for everything."

"Are you sure you don't want to stay with us?"

"Yes. I'm calm now."

"Get a good night's rest. I'll call you in the morning."

Arthur was discharged from hospital two days later. Greg drove Sophie to pick him up and then brought them back to Munster Road where Sophie was going to take care of him.

"How did he look?" Maddy asked when she spoke to Greg later in the afternoon.

"Pretty ghastly. I think he's had a shock. The doctor had a long talk with him and told him if he didn't stop drinking he was going to kill himself. He recommended that he start attending Alcoholics Anonymous meetings."

"Do you think he'll listen?"

"He says he will but who knows? At least he's got a medical opinion so he has no excuse for fooling himself any more."

"Poor Sophie," Maddy said. "She finally finds a man she's interested in and this has to happen."

"I've talked to her," Greg said. "If Arthur doesn't shape up, I'm sure she's going to leave him."

Arthur rested up at Munster Road till he was well enough to return to work. Each evening on his way to see Maddy, Greg called to visit him and reported on his progress. After a week, he started back at the office. He told anyone who enquired that he'd suffered an attack of food poisoning. Only Greg and his boss knew the truth.

But he did make a serious effort to stop drinking and he took up the doctor's recommendation to attend AA meetings. He seemed to get better. He began to take exercise and lost weight. Gradually, a fresh colour returned to his cheeks. His eyes seemed brighter and clearer. His colleagues and friends began to relax and Sophie declared herself delighted with the way everything had turned out.

"Maybe it was the best thing could have happened to him," she told Rosie and Maddy a few weeks later in the lounge of the Pink Parrot. "He's got all this literature and I've been reading up on it. Did you know that alcoholism is a recognised illness? I used to think it was only down-and-outs but it affects all sorts of people. And often they have to get a severe shock before they accept their situation."

"Is he finding it difficult?" Rosie asked.

"He still misses his booze. But he says that will pass with time. The main thing is he knows he's got a problem and he's determined to do something about it."

Meanwhile, Maddy was plunged back into the hectic whirlwind of work. Mick McCann had spoken to his bankers and they had agreed to provide the extra finance for the commercial development. The revised plans that Denis Sharkey and his team had reluctantly drawn up received initial planning approval with some minor alterations and now Mick was bullish about getting his project off the ground.

"I've set a target date of twelve months to opening and I don't want any slippage," he told Maddy one day.

"There won't be any slippage from our side," Maddy replied. "You've seen the preliminary marketing plans for the launch. I've booked space in all the property supplements and arranged write-ups. And I've lined up a bright young media advisor called Annie McNamara. She's talking about getting us radio and television exposure. And she's already working on the launch party."

"How about the leases for the units?"

"That's going ahead. I told you the initial response was extremely positive."

"Then get to work on it. Every day we fall behind schedule costs me money."

"And the terms?"

McCann waved his hands. "I'll leave that entirely up to you. I'm trusting you to get me the best deal you can."

Negotiating leases for commercial property was virgin territory for Maddy but instead of feeling apprehensive, she relished the challenge. This was a learning curve and she was looking forward to it.

She began by conducting some quiet research. For the next few days, she buried herself in the property files to get a feel for current prices in the sector. When she had boned up sufficiently, she rang Paula Matthews.

"I want to pick your brains," Maddy began.

"You can pick them if you can find them," Paula laughed.

"Don't put yourself down. You're the smartest property journalist in Dublin. What you don't know isn't worth enquiring about."

"Well, thanks for the compliment. I feel flattered. What did you want to ask me?"

"I'm speaking to you totally in confidence," Maddy continued. "Which means I don't want a word of this conversation to go any further."

"Scout's honour," Paula said. "Now you've got me curious."

"I've talked to you about Mick McCann's development down at the docklands. We've already booked advertising space with your paper."

"Go on."

"Well, he's changed his plans slightly. Now he's going to include a commercial development to provide shops and a restaurant. He wants this to be a landmark project."

"That's a brilliant stroke," Paula enthused. "I'm surprised no one thought of it before. It's bound to be a major selling point."

"That's the whole idea. He's given us the leasing rights for the commercial units."

"I see. That's a new departure for you, isn't it?"

"Exactly and that's what I want to ask you about. I want to get top-drawer clients at the best prices. How do you think I should pitch it?"

"Ummmm . . . Mick McCann is probably up to his neck in debt so he'll want to recoup some outlay pretty fast. On the other hand, it's a new venture and people will be cautious. They mightn't want to commit themselves to something that could backfire."

"It won't backfire," Maddy said. "McCann will make sure of that. What do you think we should ask?"

"It depends on the size of the unit. But for a prestigious development like this one, I'd pitch them around £60,000. You can always revise the figure depending on the response."

"Thanks, Paula. I owe you. And remember, this conversation never took place."

"I don't even know who you are!" Paula laughed and put down the phone.

Armed with this information, Maddy got to work. She had agreed with Mick McCann that the restaurant was going to be the flagship unit. With Paul Le Brun already expressing keen interest, she decided he was the person she should start with. But getting hold of him wasn't easy. She made numerous calls and left messages but he didn't get back to her.

This was a problem. She needed to have him on board before she could proceed. Once she had his agreement, she would use it as a lever to work on other prospective clients. She made up her mind. The restaurant opened for business at seven o'clock which meant he would be there now getting the kitchens ready. Instead of speaking on the phone, she would pay him a visit.

The restaurant was dark and locked when she arrived at five thirty but, undeterred, she pressed her thumb on the bell. Eventually, she saw a figure in chef's apron emerge from the back of the building to open the door.

"The restaurant is closed, madam," the figure said, peering out into the dark lane.

"I know that," she replied. "My name is Maddy Pritchard. I've come to see Mr Le Brun."

"Do you have an appointment?"

"No. But I spoke to him on the phone a few weeks ago. He should remember me."

"Wait a moment, please."

The figure closed the door and disappeared once more into the dark recesses of the restaurant. A few minutes later, she saw Le Brun himself coming towards her.

"Yes?" he said, opening the door and giving her a curious look.

"I know you're busy right now," she began. "I'm sorry to bother you but I couldn't contact you by phone and since I was passing by I decided to call in person."

"What did you want to see me about?" Le Brun interrupted.

"The restaurant at the docklands that we talked about? You expressed an interest in taking a lease."

"Ah yes," the restaurateur said.

"I wondered if you could spare a moment to discuss it?"

But Le Brun clearly wasn't in the mood.

"It isn't possible. I have a dinner party arriving at half past seven. I must prepare."

"This won't take long," Maddy pressed. "We're going ahead with the development and I wanted to be sure that you're still interested."

"I will discuss it with you another time. Not now."

There was a firmness in his tone that brooked no argument.

"Okay," Maddy said. "But I'd like to talk as soon as possible."

"I will telephone you," Le Brun said and began to close the door.

"When?" Maddy asked.

"Tomorrow. The next day."

The door closed with a loud snap and Maddy stood in the cold lane watching Paul Le Brun's small figure retreating once more to his kitchen.

But he didn't ring the next day. Or the day after. Maddy was now faced with a dilemma. Until Paul Le Brun made up his mind, she was effectively stymied. She was counting on his name to encourage the others. To make matters worse, Mick McCann rang a few days later to ask how she was getting on.

"I'm making progress," she said. "I'm conducting some preliminary research on the market. We need to get the terms exactly right.

"What about Le Brun? Have you got him on board yet?"

"I've spoken to him. He said he'd get back to me."

"Maybe it's time to start leaning on him. We need Le Brun and his restaurant as our anchor tenants, Maddy. You said so, yourself."

"I know. I'm working on it. Just give me some more time."

"Don't take forever," McCann said with a hint of impatience as he put down the phone.

Damn Paul Le Brun, she said to herself. Why doesn't he have the common decency to return my phone calls? She tried to distract herself with other work in the hope that the chef would keep his promise and call her but as the day wore on, hope began to fade. By late afternoon, she knew she was left with no option. She would have to call him again.

This time, she got him at the second attempt.

"Hello, Paul," she began in her brightest, cheeriest voice, although her heart was hammering in her breast. "It's Maddy Pritchard. I wondered if you've had an opportunity to consider our proposal."

"I've been very busy," he began with a hint of annoyance.

"Would it be possible to sit down and discuss terms? Then we will know where we stand. It shouldn't take more than half an hour."

"I just told you I am busy," he repeated, his voice beginning to sound angry.

"I'm sorry. But I need to get a decision."

There was a pause and she heard him taking a deep breath.

"All right, I will give you a decision. I am not going into your development. Now are you happy?"

Chapter Twenty-five

She put down the phone with a trembling hand. She could still hear Le Brun's sarcastic voice echoing in her ear. He had pulled out and now she was left with no anchor tenant. She felt devastated. How was she going to break the news to Mick McCann?

She got up quickly and made her way to the washroom. She couldn't let anyone see her like this, least of all her boss, Tim Lyons. She would have to pull herself together. Once in the washroom, she locked the door and splashed some cold water on her face. She glanced at her reflection in the mirror. A pale, shocked version of herself stared back.

Now she regretted her decision to ring Le Brun. It had been a mistake. She should have given him more time. But she had been under pressure and now it had all blown up on her. What was she going to do?

She glanced at her watch. It was a quarter past five. She would have to get away from the office to somewhere quiet where she could think. She went back to her desk and began to tidy up as Marina watched her.

"Are you all right?" her assistant asked. "You look pale."

"I'm fine but I've got to go out. If anyone is looking for me tell them I've got an appointment. Take a message and I'll get back to them tomorrow."

She drove straight home to Auburn Grove, got undressed and filled the bath. Then she got into the hot tub and tried to think her way through the problem. There was no point approaching Paul Le Brun again. If she did that he would assume she was desperate. Worse still, he might tell others and word would get around that she was panicking. Instead, she would have to remain calm and focussed. She would have to find another way out.

Eventually, she got out of the bath, dried herself and went into the kitchen to make a cup of tea. She took the tea into the living-room and sat there watching the evening grow dark outside the window as she wrestled with her dilemma.

She was facing a crisis. Mick McCann would be back to her tomorrow wanting to know what was going on. She had to have something plausible to tell him. But what? No matter which way she looked at the situation it remained bleak. She had lost the only anchor tenant for the development and she had no one to replace him. Despite her best efforts, Maddy felt a black depression settle over her.

It was in this mood that Greg found her when he turned up at the house around six thirty.

"Hey" he said as he came into the lounge. "What's the matter with you? You look like you've seen a ghost."

"That's exactly how I feel. Oh Greg, I've just had terrible news."

She told him what had happened as he sat beside her and gently stroked her wrist.

"The arrogant bastard," he muttered under his breath when she had finished. "Who does he think he is, treating you like that?"

"It was partly my own fault. I didn't read the signals correctly. I should have handled him more delicately."

"Rubbish. You had to get a decision. You couldn't just sit around forever waiting for him to make up his mind."

"Well, now he's made up his mind all right. And it wasn't what I was expecting."

"Look," he said. "You need cheering up. Why don't I take you for a nice meal?"

"I've no appetite."

"Oh c'mon," he said, standing up and taking her arm. "Go and get dressed. We'll go somewhere we can talk. You know what they say about a problem shared?"

Reluctantly, Maddy allowed herself to be persuaded. She went into the bedroom and pulled on a heavy skirt and warm sweater. Fifteen minutes later, they were seated in a cosy little bistro off the Rathmines Road.

"Now," Greg said when the waiter had taken their order and poured the wine, "in my experience, there is no problem that cannot be solved if you approach it properly. Your big dilemma is to find someone to replace Le Brun, right?"

"But not just anyone. We're relying on this person to be the anchor tenant. It has to be someone with prestige, someone who will attract other tenants. And most important, it has to be someone who will enhance the development and make it easier to sell the apartments."

"That's a tall order, isn't it?" Greg mused. "It narrows the field considerably."

"Yes," Maddy said, looking glum as the waiter arrived with their food.

Throughout the meal, they tossed names across the table but none of them was suitable. They were people she had already approached who had shown no interest or else they were people who weren't sufficiently well known to fill the role required.

At last, as the waiter appeared with the dessert list, Greg suddenly clapped a hand to his forehead.

"My God," he exclaimed. "Why didn't we think of him sooner?"

"Who?"

"Marco!"

"Marco O'Malley?"

"Of course! He'd be ideal. He ticks all the right boxes."

"But he's already well established in Blackrock."

"You'll be offering him a place in the centre of the city. And it will be bigger. He'd be able to feed more people, make more money."

"I don't know," Maddy said doubtfully. Marco O'Malley seemed to inhabit a rarefied world that made him totally unapproachable. It would be like trying to sell encyclopaedias to the Queen.

"He'd be the perfect tenant. And you can't say he doesn't have prestige. Marco must be the best-known chef in Dublin. He's the man. I'm telling you."

"You think so?"

"I'm positive. And besides, he took a big shine to you the last time we ate there. I'll bet you could persuade him. Why don't you ring him? What have you got to lose?"

"It would be fantastic if we got him," Maddy conceded. "He'd certainly create a buzz."

"So what are you waiting for? Give him a call in the morning."

It was with a lighter heart that she went to bed that night. Marco O'Malley offered the ideal solution. It would be a tremendous coup if she managed to recruit him. But she was determined not to repeat the mistakes she had made with Paul Le Brun. She was quickly learning that the prickly reputation of chefs was not the stuff of fiction. It was real. And Marco O'Malley was already well-known for his eccentricity. She would have to approach him on tiptoe and wearing kid gloves.

The following morning, she rang the office and told Marina she would be late then waited till eleven o'clock before sitting down at the phone and calling O'Malley's number. By now, he should be up and about after the labours of the night before. She could hear her heart beating like a drum. The eccentric chef was liable to tell her to jump off a cliff. That was if she managed to talk to him at all.

But after being passed to a number of people, she finally heard O'Malley's gruff voice come on the line.

"Mr O'Malley?" she began with as much saccharin as she could inject into her tone.

"Yes."

"My name is Maddy Pritchard. I had dinner in your lovely restaurant recently with my boyfriend."

"What is his name?"

"Greg Delaney."

"Delaney? Delaney? I don't think I know him."

"It was a special occasion. We had the roast suckling pig. We sat at a table at the top of the room."

"Ah, of course, now I remember! You were the handsome lady with the long dark hair and the beautiful sparkling eyes."

"You're too kind, Mr O'Malley. But that sounds vaguely like me."

"I never forget a good-looking woman. Do you want to book a table?"

"Not this time," Maddy said, quickly. "This is a business call."

"What sort of business?"

Maddy swallowed hard before plunging straight on.

"I'm speaking on behalf of a developer who is building a top-of-the-range apartment complex in the docklands. Part of the development will include a restaurant. We are looking for the top chef in Dublin to be our anchor tenant and naturally we thought of you. I wonder if you would be free to discuss it?"

She stopped for breath. She was amazed at her own audacity but more amazed that she had managed to say so much without being cut off.

"A restaurant in the docklands?" O'Malley repeated.

"Not just any restaurant. This will be one of the very best. It will have marvellous views over the river. And it will be very convenient to town."

"How many people will it seat?"

"As many as you like. That is the beauty of this proposition. If you come in with us now you can design the restaurant to your own specifications. This is a wonderful opportunity to get in at the beginning. And this is going to be a spectacular development, Mr O'Malley."

There was a pause. Maddy wondered if she should press on. But she had already said enough. If she said any more she ran the danger of overkill.

The silence continued.

"Mr O'Malley, are you still there?"

"Oh yes."

"Do you think you might be interested?"

"I think I might be very interested," Marco O'Malley said. "When can we sit down and talk?"

Before she came off the phone, Maddy had made an appointment to see the restaurateur at three that afternoon. She couldn't believe her good fortune. She had completed the first hurdle by getting him interested. Now she had to face the difficult task of persuading him to take a lease on the restaurant. And she was only going to get one shot at it. This called for great skill and nerve and tact. She was going to need all the expertise she had gathered in a career spent selling property. She needed to psych herself up for the challenge. She decided to go for a jog.

She stripped off and donned her running gear, then drove across town to Sandymount Strand. As luck would have it, the tide was out. Across the bay, she could see the white battlements of the Baily lighthouse perched atop of Howth Head. The beach was deserted. The golden sand stretched for miles towards Dun Laoghaire. It was perfect. She flexed her leg muscles against the promenade wall and then set off at a steady pace along the strand.

As she ran, she rehearsed the arguments she would make. She would stress the location, the up-market clientele, the publicity, the freedom to design the restaurant, the favourable terms they could offer if he signed up now. Then she tried to place herself in Marco O'Malley's shoes. What would he be looking for? What objections might he raise? How would she answer them? Backwards and forwards she considered the various angles as her feet pounded the sand. By the time she finally returned to her car three-quarters of an hour later, she had a coherent strategy worked out in her head.

Now it was one thirty. She rang the office again and spoke to

Marina. She told her she had another important appointment for the afternoon but would call into the office later to check on any outstanding business. Then she drove back to Auburn Grove and had a hot shower.

For this meeting, Maddy decided she was going to look her most seductive. Marco O'Malley had already commented favourably on her looks and appearance. Well, she would capitalise on it. It might appear unethical to some people but this was no occasion for scruples. When she walked into the Chalet d'Or restaurant for her appointment, she wanted the famous chef to sit up and take notice.

She spent a long time on her hair and make-up. Then she rummaged in her closet till she found the perfect dress, a slinky black number with a plunging neckline. It would hardly pass as a business outfit but so what? Maddy was determined to play every card she possessed. She applied the reddest lipstick she could find. It perfectly complemented her dress and hair. She finished with a gentle spray of *L'Amour* perfume then stood in front of the full-size mirror to examine the effect.

She looked like she had just stepped out of a fashion shoot. The dress emphasised her elegant figure, her hair glittered and shone, her skin glowed with vitality. If Marco O'Malley had been impressed the last time she had visited his restaurant, dressed as she had been in her business suit and worn out after a day's work, he was going to be completely knocked out today.

By five to three she was pulling her car into the parking bay outside the Chalet d'Or, having first called to confirm that she was on her way. A waiter in a black suit was waiting for her. He bowed politely and led her to a small room at the back of the restaurant that served as an office, then took her coat and hung it on a stand for her. She was barely seated when the door opened again and the massive bulk of Marco O'Malley in his white chef's uniform was framed in the doorway.

He stopped and stared as Maddy rose and stretched out her hand. Slowly, without once taking his eyes off her, O'Malley raised her hand to his lips and gently kissed her fingers.

"*Enchanté*," he murmured.

"Thank you for agreeing to see me at such short notice."

But he waved his hand in a dismissive gesture. "The pleasure is all mine, Miss Pritchard." He beamed at her. "Before we begin, would you care for a glass of wine?"

"I'd prefer coffee," she replied. She was determined to remain focussed, to concentrate all her attention on the task that lay before her.

O'Malley lifted the phone and made a call.

"You look even more beautiful than before," he said.

"Thank you. You're too kind."

"I merely tell the truth. I see many good-looking women in my restaurant. But none as handsome as you."

At that moment, the door opened once more and the waiter appeared with a pot of coffee and two cups. O'Malley poured while continuing to smile at her.

"Now," he said. "Tell me about this restaurant you're planning."

Maddy had prepared an information pack and now slipped it from her briefcase.

"Everything you need to know is contained in here. This development will be the most luxurious in the city. It will be constructed with the very finest materials and will cater for high-worth clients. Many of them will be young professionals – lawyers, accountants, business people. And the centrepiece will be the restaurant. It will face out onto the river with views across the city. It will have a large patio for outside dining when the weather is fine. And it will be fifteen minutes from the city centre. With someone as skilled as you at the helm, I guarantee it will immediately become Dublin's premier restaurant."

The chef purred with delight at her brazen flattery. He peered closely at the drawings she had provided. Maddy could sense that he was excited.

"When will it be ready?"

"In twelve months. That should give you sufficient time to dispose of your present premises, if that's what you want to do."

O'Malley continued to study the plans. "How many apartments are you building?"

"Two hundred."

"You're confident you can sell them all?"

"Certainly. We have already received inquiries from many interested clients and we haven't even launched our publicity campaign yet. I wouldn't be surprised if these apartments are sold completely off-plan."

The information seemed to reassure him.

"And I can design this restaurant myself?"

"Yes."

He leaned back and stared at her. She could read the conflicting thoughts that were careering through his mind. He already had a highly successful restaurant here in Blackrock that was booked out for weeks in advance. Why take a gamble?

She moved immediately to convince him.

"This is a once-off opportunity for you to be associated with this prestigious development, Mr O'Malley. You can double your capacity and move the Chalet d'Or onto a completely higher plane."

She paused for a moment.

"You're the chef we would prefer but if you decline we will naturally find someone else."

Marco O'Malley's face immediately grew dark. "Someone else?"

"Of course. We are determined to have a restaurant."

"You mean there has been interest from another party?"

"Yes," she said. It wasn't the entire truth but it wasn't a lie.

"That charlatan Le Brun, was it him? Was he the one?"

She felt her heart jolt. Had Marco got psychic powers as well as everything else?

"You must appreciate that I can't discuss confidential information with you."

Marco was now working himself into a lather of indignation.

"That bastard is a complete fraud. He knows nothing about cooking. He is conning people with that greasy spoon café he operates in Baggot Street."

"Mr O'Malley, you're universally acknowledged as the finest chef in the country. Nobody doubts it. There is no other chef who can hold a candle to you."

"Naturally," Marco responded without a shred of modesty.

"That is why we have come to you. We want the very best chef for our restaurant."

"Indeed. You're quite right. And you have found him."

"So are you interested?"

"Of course, I'm interested," Marco O'Malley said. "Why do you think I am sitting here?"

The next half hour was taken up with discussion about practical issues such as capacity, design and time-scale. These were all items that would ultimately be decided in negotiations with the architects and Mick McCann. But Maddy felt a warm feeling of satisfaction. She had achieved what she set out to accomplish. Marco O'Malley, the best-known restaurateur in the country, was now on board. When they finally stood up, she felt like throwing her arms around the burly chef and hugging him. But instead, she politely proffered her hand again to be kissed.

"I'll make sure Mr McCann rings you tomorrow," she said, as Marco gently released her fingers.

"It has been my great pleasure," he announced. With the business out of the way, Marco had now reverted to flirtation. "I am so pleased that we have reached agreement."

"So am I," Maddy replied. "I know that together we can forge a successful partnership. If I may say so, I think you're making a very wise decision."

Marco smiled and his eyes drooped languorously. "Let us hope so," he said.

It was coming up to five o'clock when she finally arrived back at the office to find a pile of phone messages spilling over her desk.

"Mr McCann has been on," Marina said with a warning look. "Twice. He wants you to ring him immediately."

"Anything else?"

"Mr Delaney rang. And Mr Lyons wants to talk to you when you're free. That's the urgent stuff. The rest of the messages can wait."

"Thank you, Marina," Maddy said. "Do you think you could organise a strong cup of tea?"

She rang Greg at once.

"Good news," she said. "We've got Marco in the bag."

"*Whaaat?*" He sounded amazed. "You didn't waste any time."

"No point beating around the bush. You know me, Speedy Gonzalez. Listen, I've got other calls to make. I'll give you all the low-down when I see you later. Byeee!"

The next call was to Mick McCann. He came on the line sounding irritable and impatient.

"I've been trying to reach you all day," he grumbled. "Why didn't you call me back?"

"I've been busy."

"Have you got Paul Le Brun yet?"

"No," Maddy said. "He's pulled out."

She heard McCann gasp.

"Tell me this is a joke."

"Afraid not. It's deadly serious."

"But he was going to be our anchor. What the hell are we supposed to do now?"

"We've got someone better."

"Better? Who is better than Paul Le Brun? He's got a bloody Michelin star, for God's sake! I was counting on him to bring in the other tenants."

"I've got Marco O'Malley."

There was silence on the line.

"Did you hear me, Mick? I said I've got Marco O'Malley."

"If you're pulling my leg, I will not be pleased."

"I'm not pulling your leg. I've been dealing with him all day. I've just got back from the Chalet d'Or. He's coming in."

"Is this serious?"

"Damned right it is."

She heard McCann let out a whoop.

"Maddy, I don't know how you did it but I am absolutely gobsmacked."

"It's called business know-how, Mick."

"With O'Malley in we'll be beating clients away with a stick."

"I said you'd call him tomorrow to discuss the technical details. As part of the bait, I told him he could design the restaurant. Are you happy with that?"

"Of course, I'm happy. At least he'll know what he's talking about unlike some of the people I've been dealing with."

"I have also negotiated a price of £120,000 for the lease plus an annual rent of £20,000 to be reviewed after five years. I told him that was subject to your final agreement. What do you think?"

"Think? I think I've died and gone to heaven."

"Don't do that just yet, Mick. At least wait till we've got the development launched."

She heard him laughing as she put down the phone.

Her boss grinned when she told him of the coup.

"What was he like? Marco O'Malley?"

"He was fine. We got along like a house on fire."

"I've heard stories about him. He's supposed to have chased some poor devil through the streets of Blackrock with a carving knife."

"Ah yes, but that guy was asking for it," Maddy said with an enigmatic smile.

"Why? What did he do?"

"He said his steak was underdone. What do you expect, Tim? Chefs are sensitive people."

Once Marco O'Malley had signed the contract and paid his deposit, Maddy gave Paula Matthews the news. It was Maddy's way of repaying her for all the favours she had done in the past.

The story appeared the following day under a banner headline which read: TOP IRISH RESTAURATEUR FOR PRESTIGE DOCKSIDE DEVELOPMENT.

Ireland's most famous chef, Mr Marco O'Malley, has just completed a deal to open a brand-new restaurant at an up-market site on Dublin's trendy docklands. Mr O'Malley, who owns the chic Chalet d'Or in Blackrock, is planning a spacious up-market venue which will provide a five-star dining experience for his guests.. The development which will also house shops, cafés and a bar as well as 200 luxury apartments is being built by Mr Mick McCann. The selling agents are the successful Ballsbridge firm of Carroll and Shanley.

The story appeared with a grinning photograph of Marco in chef's uniform outside his Blackrock premises. It had the effect she anticipated. Within half an hour of sitting down at her desk, the phones began to ring with potential tenants and purchasers anxious to sign up for units in the development.

But one particular call took her completely by surprise. That afternoon, she lifted the phone to hear Paul Le Brun's voice. But this was a different man to the one who had closed his door in her face. Now, he sounded contrite and subdued.

"I'm ringing about the restaurant," he began. "I've been thinking about it and now I want to come in."

"The option is gone," she said. "Mr O'Malley has taken it."

"I read that story. I thought if I offered more you might change your mind. Whatever he has agreed, I will pay £50,000 more."

"But I gave you an opportunity and you turned it down."

"You got me at a bad time. I wasn't thinking properly."

"Mr Le Brun, I don't believe you understand how we conduct our business. We have a contract."

"Contracts can be broken. I am offering more." He was beginning to sound aggressive. "I want into that development. It is imperative."

"I'm afraid you're too late," Maddy said. "You had your opportunity and you rejected it."

"But —"

"I'm sorry," Maddy said and put down the phone.

Chapter Twenty-six

In the weeks that followed, she was extremely busy. As anticipated, Marco's restaurant had proved a massive draw for the development. By early in March, most of the commercial units were gone and a quarter of the apartments had been sold off the plans. And so far, not a brick had been laid on the site. But sadly, her relationship with Greg was about to enter choppy waters.

It wasn't just the pressure of her workload. Ever since the disastrous visit to his parents at Christmas, there had been an unspoken tension between them. Maddy resented the implied criticism that had been levelled by his parents and the fact that he had done nothing to defend her. This tension surfaced a few weeks later when Greg announced that he was going to Galway again and asked her to come with him.

"I can't Greg. I have to complete the details of two leases for the shops. It's more complicated than you might think and Mick McCann is anxious to have them first thing on Monday morning."

"Please come with me," he begged. "I want you to get along with my parents."

"But they'll only make me feel uncomfortable."

"They're old-fashioned. They'll come around."

"I'll go some other time, but not this weekend. I really do have a lot of work to get through."

"All right," he said, in a hurt tone. "If that's how you feel, I'll go alone."

He went off in a huff on Friday evening. Maddy felt a pang of regret for the dilemma he faced, torn between his family and her. Maybe, in time, she could summon the courage for another visit but not just yet. The memory of that awful lunch was still too fresh in her mind.

So she put it behind her and got on with her work.

So far, Mick McCann hadn't got round to the important business of finding a name for the development despite numerous promptings.

"What do you think of The Wharf," he said to her one day. "Do you think it conjures up the right image of the docks and the sea?"

"I think The Wharf is an excellent choice," she agreed. "But you had better decide soon. In fact, we're already way behind on this. We have to get promotional brochures printed and the advertising finalised. I've already booked the space."

"I'm also thinking of applying for another fifty apartments on the site."

Maddy stopped in her tracks. This was a new suggestion and she didn't like the sound of it.

"Do you think that's a good idea?" she said.

"Why not? We'll easily shift them now that the development has taken off."

"But this is meant to be your signature project. If you squeeze in another fifty apartments something is bound to suffer. You won't have the space for the gardens you had planned. It will be just another cramped apartment complex like all the others."

"Not if it's designed properly."

"No matter how you design it you'll lose that spacious feel you were aiming for. And clients will believe they've been cheated. You're able to charge top prices, Mick, because you're offering them something different. Believe me, there will be a backlash."

"You're too cautious," he said. "This is a chance to make some serious money."

"It's also an opportunity to enhance your name and reputation. Which is more important?"

McCann gave her a sour look. "There's no reason why I can't do both."

"Yes, there is. Something will have to give."

Greg got back from Galway on Monday and they met for a drink after work.

"How did the trip go?" Maddy asked.

"Fine. My mother asked about you. She wanted to know if you were feeling better."

"How is she?"

"Oh, she's the usual. She spent the whole weekend arguing with my father about where to go for their summer holiday. Which reminds me, are you all set for Marbella? You haven't forgotten? It's only a few weeks away."

Maddy hadn't forgotten. She had been eagerly looking forward to their break in the sun. But what seemed perfectly feasible a few months before now looked a lot more uncertain with the pressure of work that had suddenly descended on her shoulders.

"I'm hoping to make it," she said, doubtfully.

Greg looked appalled

"*Hoping*? But I thought this was all agreed. I've arranged with Joe Spence to have the apartment for a week. I was going to book the flights tomorrow. You have to do it early."

Maddy heaved a gentle sigh. The last thing she wanted right now was an argument with Greg.

"Can you leave the flights till later? Till I'm absolutely sure I can go?"

"But you've known about this since December. What's holding you back?"

"A little four-letter word called work. I'm up to my chin at the moment with Mick McCann's development."

Greg was working himself into a lather.

"You can't let them walk all over you, Maddy. You work hard enough as it is."

"There is no one walking over me," she retorted, angrily.

"Then just tell them that you're going and let them get on with it. They're taking advantage of you. And the more you let them get away with it, the more they'll do it."

His last remarks stung her because in her heart, she believed they might be true. Since the turn of the year, she had been working flat out, taking work home in the evenings and giving up some of her weekends. And Tim Lyons had got her a new mobile phone which meant that she could never escape his attention. She began to wonder if she was being asked to work harder because she was a single woman who was supposed to have no other demands on her time.

Nevertheless, she approached Tim Lyons and asked if she could have some time off to take a short holiday.

"I don't see why not. How is Mick McCann fixed?"

"He seems happy. He's finally decided on a name. He's going to call it The Wharf. It means we can now press ahead with the publicity campaign. But there is one thing that bothers me."

She told him about McCann's idea to build another fifty apartments on the site.

"So what's the problem?" Tim Lyons said. "It will mean more commission for us."

"It will also mean that he won't have an exclusive development any more. He'll be short-changing the clients who've already committed to buy. I know I wouldn't be happy if I'd bought into something and then learnt it was going to increase in density by 25 per cent."

But her boss only laughed. "You're too ethical, Maddy. The way that place is buzzing, people will be delighted to buy into it. In fact, I wouldn't be surprised if McCann is tempted to put up the prices."

She shrugged in defeat. "So I can take a break?"

"Sure. Be my guest."

She told Greg and he booked the flights. Now she had something to look forward to. A week in Marbella with nothing to do but relax in the sun would be the ideal antidote to the stress she was under.

And it would give them an opportunity to work on their relationship.

Meanwhile, Arthur Brady was sticking to his resolve. Sophie was becoming more relaxed with each passing day that he continued to be sober. One evening, Greg and Maddy dropped into Munster Rd to find Arthur doing some work in the garden. He had lost weight and looked fit and healthy. There was a tone to his skin and clarity in his eyes. Maddy could never remember him looking so well.

"Are you finding it difficult?" she asked as they chatted on the patio. "You were quite fond of your booze."

"Fond?" he laughed. "I was addicted to the stuff. I'm an alcoholic for God's sake. But alcohol can be a bitter enemy. It can turn on you and take away everything you possess." He pulled Sophie closer and kissed the top of her head. "Including the person you care most about."

"He's doing fine," Sophie said with a big smile. "I'm very proud of him."

"If I keep to my routine, I should be okay. I'm going to AA meetings and I'm learning a lot about this disease. The secret is not to take that first drink. You might not believe it but that's the one that gets you drunk."

"I'm glad for them," Maddy later confided to Greg. "Arthur seems like a completely different person since he stopped drinking."

"And his work has improved. You know, I was really worried about him. I think they were on the verge of firing him if he didn't get his act together."

She cuddled closer. "I'm sorry we've been snapping at each other. It's my fault. I should listen to you more often."

"I was wrong too," Greg said. "I shouldn't interfere in matters that don't concern me. But you're so willing that people turn to you with jobs that they could do perfectly well themselves. I see it happening all around me, every day of the week."

"You're right, she said. "Maybe it's time I did something about it."

Mick McCann had decided to press ahead with his plan for another fifty apartments on The Wharf site and had now lodged his planning application. It reinforced something that Maddy had long suspected. Developers would seek to extract the last penny of profit from every scheme they were involved in. She had thought Mick was different. She had thought he was a man with a brave vision to do something courageous. Now she could see that his talk about making The Wharf a prestige, signature development was so much hot air and it made her sad.

But it didn't take long for the reaction to set in. One morning, a few days later, she took a phone call at the office and heard an angry voice on the line. It was an investor who had paid deposits on three apartments at The Wharf.

"What's this I hear about McCann building more units on that site?" he demanded.

"Who told you?" Maddy countered.

"Never mind who told me. Is it true?"

"It's er . . . not quite true."

"Don't talk gobbledygook." The man sounded furious. "Is he building more apartments or isn't he?"

"He might be."

"What the hell does that mean?"

Maddy felt cornered. The man had the right to know what was likely to happen to his investment and she wasn't going to lie to him.

"He's considering it," she said.

"How many?"

"Another fifty."

"That many? Has he applied for permission?"

"Yes," Maddy said.

"That's it," the man retorted. "I'm cancelling. I want my deposits back."

"But…" Maddy began.

"But nothing. If McCann wants to turn his development into a chicken coop for battery hens, that's his business. But it's not what I bought into and I want no part of it."

"We've got a contract," Maddy reminded him.

"A preliminary contract which gives me the option to withdraw. McCann is changing the terms of our agreement and I'm exercising my right to pull out."

There was a loud thump as the phone went down.

The following days brought more cancellations – all of them serious investors who had snapped up luxury units on foot of the article that Paula Matthews had written. These were the men with the big money that Mick McCann had been counting on to get the project off the ground. Now, the worry was that word would get around and other players would panic as well and cancel their contracts. She decided to ring McCann and warn him.

But he seemed unfazed by the news.

"How many have cancelled so far?" he asked.

"Eight."

"That's nothing. We'll replace them."

"But these are serious players, Mick. Between them, they account for nearly twenty of your best apartments."

"Look, Maddy, you were right to warn me and I appreciate it. But let's get this thing into perspective. Every development I've ever built, I've got cancellations. It happens all the time. People change their minds or they can't raise the cash. You know that."

"Not these kind of people. I'm worried if word gets out, there'll be more. People can behave like sheep sometimes."

"Calm down. We haven't even launched our publicity campaign yet. When those write-ups you've promised start to appear, they'll all be back in again."

"I wouldn't count on it."

"Leave it to me," he said. "I think I know what I'm doing."

But Monday morning brought more bad news. Paula Matthews rang shortly after ten o'clock.

"I hear the heavy-hitters are pulling out of The Wharf," she began.

Maddy immediately felt herself tense.

"Some people have cancelled, that's true," she said.

"How many?"

"Are we on the record?"

"Yes, we're on the record."

"Where are you hearing this, Paula?"

"Industry sources."

"Rival developers, you mean?"

"That's irrelevant. Is it true or not?"

"You're not going to write this, surely?"

"Of course, I'm going to write it! It's news."

"Look, I'd appreciate it if you didn't," Maddy pleaded. "Something like this could cause us a lot of damage. You would be doing me a big favour."

There was a pause.

"Maddy, I'm surprised at you. How long have you known me?"

"Six years."

"Then you must know by now that I can't do that. My credibility is on the line, here. You can't expect me just to write puff pieces for you and then suppress something you don't like. Besides, it wouldn't matter. The word is out. Somebody else will write it and then I'll look stupid."

"Okay, I'm sorry. Forget I said that. You know the Orinoco Coffee Bar? I'll see you there in ten minutes and give you the whole story."

For the next hour, Maddy sat with Paula and answered her questions while their caffè lattes grew cold. She calculated that this way she would at least have some control over the story and be able to put the best possible spin on it. When she had finished, Paula sadly shook her head.

"I can't believe he'd be so stupid. I always had Mick McCann marked down as a smart operator."

"So did I. But he just got greedy."

"Don't they all?" Paula said, snapping her notebook shut and finishing her coffee. "Look, Maddy, I'm sorry it has come to this. I know it's going to cause you grief. But I've no option. You understand that, don't you?"

Maddy reached out and hugged her friend.

"Sure, I understand. You've got to do what you've got to do. Go right ahead. I'm a big girl now. I can take it."

Paula's report appeared the following day and was quickly followed by similar stories in the other papers. Mick McCann was outraged. He rang Maddy wanting to know what the hell was going on and why she hadn't used her influence to stop it.

"It doesn't work like that," she said.

"Of course, it does. Why didn't you send her a bottle of champagne or something to keep her mouth shut?"

She stifled a bitter laugh. "You've got a lot to learn about how the media works, Mick."

At first nothing happened. Then she began to notice that inquiries about The Wharf had dried almost to a trickle. Then the cancellations started in earnest. By the end of the second week, the number who had pulled out had passed twenty which was almost half the people who had signed up.

On top of that, Maddy was now dealing with media questions on a daily basis. The story had taken on a life of its own. If something didn't change soon, it was obvious they were heading for a crisis. The following Monday she came into work to hear the worst news of all.

"I need to talk to you urgently," Mick McCann said, after she had taken his call.

"Go ahead."

"Not on the phone. It's not safe. Can you come over here right away?"

She got into her car and drove straight to the headquarters of McCann Construction in Donnybrook. She found him pacing the carpet of his office. His face was like thunder.

"What is it?" she said, sounding breathless.

"Sit down. You're not going to like this."

"What?"

"Marco O'Malley is pulling out."

Chapter Twenty-seven

Maddy sat dumbstruck and stared at Mick McCann. This was what she had feared the most. This was what frightened her so much that she hadn't even allowed herself to think about it. With Marco O'Malley pulling out they were facing disaster. It would undo months of hard work and deliver a blow from which they might not even recover.

"When did this happen?" she managed to say.

McCann glared at her. "He rang this morning at nine o'clock. He said he'd been thinking things over and in the light of media reports he wasn't coming in. He said he couldn't risk his reputation on a development that might not succeed."

Well, at least one man is keen to safeguard his reputation, Maddy thought bitterly.

"I blame you for this," McCann continued, his face growing red. "You're supposed to look after the media. If those stories hadn't got out, none of this would ever have happened."

Maddy gasped in astonishment. She couldn't believe what she was hearing. She was the person who had recruited Marco O'Malley. She was the person who had come up with the idea of a restaurant in the first place. And she was also the very person who had advised him not to apply for the extra apartments. Now she was being blamed because Mick McCann had allowed his greed to get the better of him.

"I think that remark is totally uncalled for," she said. "If you were half a man you would withdraw it."

"It's true. If that bitch hadn't written that story, none of this would have happened." McCann was now apoplectic with rage.

"I take it you're referring to Paula Matthews, the same bitch who got the development off the ground with her original story about Marco?"

"That's right. And it's your job to keep her sweet and stop this kind of stuff getting into the papers." He banged his fist on the desk. "But you couldn't even do that right, could you? And now we've got this fiasco on our hands. I want to know what you're going to do about it."

Maddy had heard enough. She pulled herself out of the chair and stood up.

"I'll tell you exactly what I'm going to do. I'm going back to my office."

McCann's face fell. He quickly moved to bar her way.

"You're not going anywhere. I need you to sort this out."

"Tough," Maddy said. "You don't pay me enough money to take this kind of abuse."

She made for the door but McCann followed her and stood with his back against it, blocking her way. There were beads of sweat standing out on his forehead. His eyes were now bulging with a mixture of anger and panic.

"Get out of my way," Maddy said. "Or I'll call the security staff."

McCann stared at her for a moment and then his expression slowly changed.

"I'm sorry," he said. "I apologise. I take it all back. It's just that I'm upset. I didn't know what I was saying. Please don't go."

Maddy folded her arms and glared back at him.

"You've got to talk to Marco," he pleaded. "You're the only one he'll listen to. You've got to make him change his mind."

She looked into his eyes and saw the fear lurking within. Mick

McCann was a man staring into a precipice. He was beginning to grasp the possibility that his whole development could come tumbling down around him.

"I warned you this would happen," she said. "But you ignored me."

"I didn't believe you."

"Do you believe me now?"

"Yes."

"All right," she said. "I'll go back to Marco O'Malley. But there are three conditions. First I want you to withdraw your application for the extra fifty apartments and restore the development to its original plan."

His face went pale and he began to protest. "But –"

"But nothing! I'm not even going to argue with you. If you don't do it, I'm not going to waste any more time."

"Okay I'll do it. I'll ring the planning authorities right away."

"Second. I want you to let me handle the marketing my way. That's what you hired me for and I think I've delivered. You've got more than the extra mile from me, Mick."

"I know, I know. It's true."

"Finally, I want you to keep a civil tongue in your head. If you ever speak to me like that again, I'm walking and I won't be coming back."

"Agreed. I'm sorry, Maddy. Honest, I am. I promise it will never happen again. Now will you please speak to that crazy bastard and convince him to come back?"

"I'll try," she said. "But I can't guarantee anything. Marco O'Malley may be crazy but he's nobody's fool."

But getting hold of Marco was easier said than done. Maddy began by ringing his office and immediately came up against a barrier.

"Who is this?" a polite female voice inquired.

When Maddy gave her name, there was an immediate change of tone. A chill entered the woman's voice.

"Mr O'Malley is not available."

"When could I speak to him?"

"I don't know. He's very busy right now. Why don't you give me your number and I'll ask him to contact you?"

"Would you tell him it's an urgent business matter? He knows who I am."

"I'll make sure he gets your message," the woman said, taking Maddy's number and quickly putting down the phone.

But Marco did not ring back. She tried calling several more times and got the same chilly response. It was obvious he was avoiding her.

She cursed Mick McCann for a greedy fool. But what was done, was done. She had to pick up the pieces and try to rebuild the project. And in the meantime, keep praying that the media didn't get hold of the story. But she knew that time was against her. Sooner or later, the news would leak out and all hell would break loose.

By now, her trip to Marbella with Greg was looming. Every day, he reminded her about it. He was clearly looking forward to the break and the chance to be alone together away from the pressures of work.

"I checked the weather forecast today," he would say. "It's sunny and the temperature is up in the mid 20s. It will be perfect. Think of those beautiful blue skies."

But Maddy could only force herself to smile. She couldn't even contemplate Marbella while she had this crisis on her hands. At work, Tim Lyons had got extremely nervous and had also started to pressurise her. And every day, she had Mick McCann on the phone pleading with her to do anything she could to get the situation back on the rails. In desperation, she rang Paula Matthews and told her that McCann had withdrawn his application and the development was now restored to its original state.

"He's changed his mind, huh?"

"That's right."

"And I suppose you're going to tell me this has got nothing to do with the reaction to his plans?"

"No, Paula. I wouldn't be so foolish."

She begged her friend to give the story a splash.

"I'll do what I can." Paula said, at last. "But you know what us hacks are like. We prefer bad news stories. They sell more papers."

"I just want to reassure the investors," Maddy said. "I think we owe it to them."

"Okay," Paula said without much enthusiasm. "Leave it with me."

The story appeared and had some positive effect. The drain of people out of the scheme slowed down and a couple of investors reconsidered their decision and returned. For the time being, the situation appeared to have stabilised. But Maddy knew that nothing more could be done till they got Marco O'Malley back on board and began to use him for publicity.

It was three days since her original phone call and she'd heard nothing. She considered taking her courage in her hands and going out to Blackrock and confronting him in person. But the memory of her failed visit to Paul Le Brun was still fresh in her mind. Marco was quite liable to have her thrown out on the street and summoning the TV cameras to witness the event. It could turn into the mother of all disasters.

By now she felt totally downcast. For once, she was at a loss what to do. With her phone calls blocked, she was forced to send messages by courier begging him to talk to her. But with each day that passed, the possibility grew more remote. It appeared that Marco O'Malley had made up his mind and wasn't going to be persuaded.

And then, out of the blue, she had a stroke of luck. She was driving along Baggot Street one afternoon on her way to meet a client when she saw a familiar figure emerge from a shop doorway. She glanced in her mirror and felt her heart skip a beat. It was Marco.

Immediately she pulled the car in alongside the pavement and got out. O'Malley was now walking away from her in the direction of Stephen's Green and making good speed for a man of his girth. She ran after him, calling out his name, her high heels clattering on the pavement as she went.

"Marco! Please wait!"

He stopped and turned round and then his face changed expression.

"Marco," she said, finally catching up with him and gulping for breath. "I thought it was you."

"It's me all right," he said, scowling at her from behind his bushy eyebrows. "What do you want?"

"Didn't you get my phone calls?" she said. "I've been trying to reach you for the past week."

"I've been very busy. I've got a restaurant to run."

"I want to talk to you about The Wharf."

"I'm no longer interested," he said, curtly. "I have informed Mr McCann."

"I know. But everything has changed. He's not building any more apartments. The development has been restored to its original state."

This news seemed to take him by surprise.

"When did this happen?"

"Earlier this week."

"Why didn't anyone tell me?"

"I've been trying to reach you but I couldn't get through. Do you think you could spare me a little of your time? Please? It's very important. I'll explain everything to you. It will only take fifteen minutes."

O'Malley glanced at his watch. "It's not possible," he said. "I have to meet someone and I'm already late."

He turned to go.

"Please," Maddy pleaded. "Just give me fifteen minutes of your time. That's all I ask. You don't want to do something you might regret."

He looked at her again and his expression seemed to soften.

He breathed a heavy sigh.

"All right," he said. "I'll see you on Friday at two o'clock. Come out to the Chalet d'Or. Now I really must go. Goodbye, Miss Pritchard."

She watched him walk away. She felt a surge of relief. She had finally convinced Marco O'Malley to meet her. It was a start. Now she had to persuade him to come back on board. And then her joy drained away as another thought struck her.

Friday was the day they were leaving for Marbella.

Chapter Twenty-eight

She was faced with an awful dilemma. She had a choice to make and no matter which way she turned, she was sure to be wrong. But at least the holiday could be rescheduled whereas she would not get another opportunity to talk to Marco O'Malley. It seemed obvious which course she would have to choose.

Greg was furious when she broke the news to him that evening at Auburn Grove. She had never seen him so angry.

"Cancel?" he thundered. "Are you out of your mind? The flights are booked. The apartment is ready. Everything is arranged. You can't do this, Maddy. It's completely out of the question."

"I'm really sorry, Greg. But I've got no option."

"Of course, you have an option. You can come with me as planned. You've known about this trip for months."

"But this is the only opportunity I'm going to get to convince O'Malley. And if he doesn't come back in, the whole project will be in serious trouble."

"So Marco O'Malley is more important than me?"

"You know he isn't."

She tried to stroke his arm but he angrily brushed her hand away.

"Maddy, I've been very patient. I've put up with your erratic behaviour for a very long time. And I've rarely complained. But this time you're just going too far."

"Please, Greg, you're just making it harder for me. I thought you of all people would show some understanding."

"Oh, I understand only too well," he said with a bitter laugh. "Marco O'Malley and Mick McCann have taken over your life. They're the people you *really* care about. Not me!"

"That's just not true," she protested.

"Then prove it. Come away with me and let them simmer in their own juices. McCann brought this problem on himself. Let him sort it out."

She bit her lip and fought back the tears that were welling in her eyes. This was their first serious fight and she hated it.

"I can't," she said.

"Then so be it," Greg said, getting up and striding to the door.

"What are you doing?" she asked.

"I'm going without you. I'll be damned if I'm going to let that fat poseur, O'Malley, ruin my holiday."

There was a thud as the front door closed and Greg was gone.

She was shocked. Not just that he should go away without her but at his lack of sympathy for the situation she faced. She had never once complained about *his* working life and the disruption it caused them – the late nights, the weekends that had to be sacrificed when some urgent business intervened to wreck their plans. Why, all of a sudden was she supposed to be different?

She had a life and a career just the same as Greg. And she also had a future. She had never forgotten the promise of old Mr Shanley after her very first auction: *You have a bright future with Carroll and Shanley.* She knew what those words meant. When Mr Shanley retired and the firm was reorganised, she was looking at a promotion to the top echelons of the firm. Why shouldn't she pursue her dreams? Why was her career less important than Greg's?

If The Wharf failed, Carroll and Shanley would suffer. It was one of the most prestigious projects the company had ever taken on. Apart from the lucrative commissions they would earn, it opened up the potential for a breakthrough into the commercial property market. She couldn't abandon it now at this crucial juncture. Why couldn't Greg see that simple reality?

She went to bed feeling tired and worn but with the hope that overnight, Greg would calm down and see her point of view. But the following morning brought worse news. He rang at ten o'clock to ask if she had changed her mind.

"I can't, Greg. I've already explained. I have to go to this meeting."

"You know what this means, don't you?"

"What?"

"This is the last straw, Maddy."

For the next few days, she was locked in meetings with Mick McCann and her boss, Tim Lyons, but her mind never strayed far from Greg and his final words to her. The vehemence of his reaction had stunned her. Nevertheless, she forced herself to concentrate on the immediate task. On Friday she would have to sit down with Marco O'Malley and convince him to come back in to the development. It was going to be tough. But Maddy found a small grain of comfort in one fact. He would not have agreed to meet her unless he was still interested.

Friday arrived and two o'clock found her outside the front door of the Chalet d'Or, dreading the ordeal that lay ahead. A small, tight-faced woman in a business suit met her and escorted her in sullen silence to the office at the back of the restaurant where she had met Marco on the previous occasion. Maddy wondered if she was the same woman who had so efficiently shielded him from her phone calls.

He was sitting behind his desk, his face dark and stern. There was no offer of wine or coffee and none of the light-hearted flirtation that had marked their last encounter in this room.

"You've got fifteen minutes to convince me," he said as Maddy nervously took her seat across from him.

"I told you that the planning application has been withdrawn," she began, "and the scheme is now back to its original form."

"Well, that's something, I suppose," O'Malley replied, his voice cold. "But why did he make this application in the first place? You told me this was going to be an exclusive development of luxury apartments. Not a Manhattan skyscraper plonked in the middle of Dublin. That's the reason I came in. The Chalet d'Or is associated with prestige. Our clients come from the very top drawer. I don't run a transport café, Miss Pritchard."

"Of course, and that's the very reason we are so keen to involve you. We know you're the natural partner for us."

"So why did he do it?"

"It was an error of judgment."

O'Malley's plump lip turned up in a sneer.

"And what guarantee do I have that Mr McCann won't continue to make more errors of judgment?"

"You can be assured that nothing like this will happen again. Mr McCann realises that he made a mistake and has asked me to apologise to you."

"You must understand," O'Malley continued. "This was a big decision for me. I have an established restaurant here. It's going extremely well. I don't need to move. In fact several people have advised me against it."

"I do understand. But sometimes in business an opportunity comes along that is too good to miss. I believe this is one of them. Think of what we are offering you. If you come in with us you will be the centrepiece of a brand-new project, the most modern development in Dublin. You have already seen the publicity it has generated before it is even built. Think of the location, so close to town. You'll be able to double your capacity. And you have the chance to design the restaurant yourself, exactly as you want it. Where else would you get an offer like that?"

O'Malley slowly stroked his chin.

"I knew all that already," he said. "I'm still not convinced."

Maddy could feel the tension rise as the minutes ticked away. If she didn't persuade him soon, Marco O'Malley was going to get up from the desk and end the meeting. There was nothing for it but to play her last remaining card – the rivalry that she knew existed between O'Malley and Paul Le Brun.

"Mr O'Malley, you're a very shrewd businessman. You have built up your restaurant from scratch. It is the best establishment in Dublin. Everyone admires you."

He sat impervious to her flattery, eying her intently.

"You know quite well that sometimes you have to make a move because if you don't, someone else will do it. That's what I meant when I asked you the other day not to do something you might regret."

O'Malley's eyes narrowed. He leaned forward and stared at her.

"Miss Pritchard, are you attempting to blackmail me?"

Maddy didn't falter. "I'm simply laying out all the information so that you can make an informed decision."

"Le Brun is still interested?"

"I can't tell you that."

O'Malley's face grew crimson with rage. "That bastard, who does he think he is? It is him, isn't it?"

"You know I can't divulge confidential information. But I *can* confirm that we have received another offer, a higher offer than yours. And if you insist on staying out, then naturally we will accept it."

"How much?"

"Fifty thousand more."

"Hell open and swallow him!" O'Malley bellowed.

"We want to go with you," Maddy continued. "You're acknowledged as the best restaurateur in the country. But, of course, we will accept the higher offer if you leave us no choice. I told you before we are determined to have a restaurant at The Wharf."

"If you go with Le Brun he will make a mess of it. You'll rue the day you ever took him on board."

"Mr O'Malley, you're the only one who has mentioned Paul Le Brun. But he is successful and he does have a Michelin star."

The chef stared at her, his face red with fury.

"Oh, to hell with his bloody star! The man's a fraud."

He slumped back in his chair and wiped his face.

"I need time to think."

"That's okay. When will you let me know?"

"This evening."

"All right," Maddy said, standing up and straightening her skirt. "I'll expect your call."

The whole way back to the office, her head was spinning. She had used all her guile and negotiating skills but she still wasn't sure if she had done enough to convince him. As soon as she walked into her office, the phone started to ring. It was Mick McCann wanting to know how the meeting had gone.

"It's hard to say. He's going to call me back."

"Please tell me that he's reconsidering."

"Yes. He'll let me know this evening."

"What way do you think he'll go?"

She could hear the tension in McCann's voice.

"I honestly don't know. But you're the first person I'll call when I hear."

She tried to concentrate on clearing a backlog of files to keep her mind off the one big decision that was hanging over her. But it was almost impossible. She had barely replaced the phone when it rang again. This time, she recognised the voice of Paula Matthews.

"Maddy I've just heard the most incredible piece of news. Is it true that Marco O'Malley is pulling out of The Wharf?"

Maddy's heart skipped a beat. This was turning into a nightmare. Was it possible that O'Malley had pulled a stroke and gone to the media with his story so as to pre-empt any deal with Paul Le Brun? She wouldn't put it past him.

She tried to remain calm. "Where did you hear this, Paula?"

"A good source."

"Can you be more specific? Was it from Marco himself?"

"Oh c'mon, Maddy. You know I can't tell you that."

"It's very important, Paula."

"How do you mean?"

"It could save you from getting egg all over your face."

"Can you simply confirm or deny?" the journalist said, getting tetchy. "I haven't got time for games. I'm up against a deadline."

"Then take my advice and hold off for twenty-four hours. It could save you a lot of embarrassment."

"And then what?"

"Then I'll tell you one way or another."

"You know I hate sitting on stories. You're not going to someone else behind my back?"

"Paula, you've got to trust me on this. Have I ever let you down in the past?"

"No," the reporter conceded.

"Well, then. Twenty-four hours."

She put down the phone and stared off into space. She had bought herself a little grace. But if Marco O'Malley turned her down, the story would soon be all over the papers and they would be staring catastrophe in the face.

The time crawled along. Its passage wasn't made any easier by nervous phone calls from McCann wanting to know if she had heard yet from the chef. By half past five, the staff began to clear their desks to go home until only Maddy and Tim Lyons remained.

At six o'clock, Tim emerged from his office with his overcoat on.

"Feel like a drink?" he asked.

Maddy shook her head. "I'm expecting an important call."

"Marco O'Malley?"

She nodded.

"Let me know at once how you get on," he said, grimly.

At the doorway, he turned and stuck up his thumb.

"And Maddy – good luck."

"Thanks for nothing," she muttered under her breath and watched her boss stride out into the cold evening air.

By seven o'clock, she still hadn't heard. She felt nervous as a kitten but she knew she had to wait. She had made her final pitch. Now it was in the lap of the gods. She took out another file and began to make notes.

The sound of the phone call when it finally came seemed to resonate throughout the empty office. She quickly grabbed the receiver and held it to her ear.

"Maddy Pritchard."

"This is Marco O'Malley."

"Yes?"

"I've given this matter a lot of thought."

"And?"

She felt the tension grip her like a vice. What was he going to say?

"I'm coming back in."

Suddenly, Marco O'Malley's voice seemed far away.

"On one condition. I deal only with you. And if Mr McCann deviates in any way from his original plan, I'm out again and this time I definitely won't be coming back."

Maddy thanked him and put down the phone. She leaned back in her chair and heaved an enormous sigh. She had rescued the development. But she felt no elation. She had done it at a cost and that cost might yet prove too high.

She had jeopardised her relationship with Greg.

Chapter Twenty-nine

Over the next few days, she thought about Greg day and night. She hadn't realised till now how much she loved him and how sorely she missed his presence. She thought about Marbella and the sun and the beach and the flowers in bloom all along the Paseo Maritimo. Why wasn't she there with him? Why was she stuck here in Dublin in the rain, dealing with obstinate chefs and greedy developers?

She decided to join him.

On Monday morning, she rang a tour operator in the desperate hope that there might be a seat available on a flight to Malaga. But she was disappointed.

"All the flights were booked out weeks ago," she was told. "This is a very busy time for winter breaks."

"What about flights out of Manchester or London?"

"I'll try," the weary operator said.

But later in the day, she rang back to say that those flights too were full.

"Is there any point putting me on standby in case someone cries off?" Maddy pleaded.

"Not a chance," the operator said. "I could fill another plane with standby passengers. I could get you a seat for the following week, if that's any use?"

"It's too late," Maddy replied.

"Sorry," the operator said.

Her one remaining solace was that Greg would miss her too and the holiday would provide him with an opportunity to think things over. The words he had spoken had been said in anger. She knew he didn't mean them. In a few days' time, he would be back. They would get together again and hopefully everything would be fine.

Meanwhile, she moved swiftly to capitalise on Marco O'Malley's decision to rejoin the project. She persuaded him to pose for photographs in his chef's apron and white hat at the The Wharf site with the river pictured in the background.

The photos made all the papers. FAMOUS CHEF O'MALLEY INSPECTS SITE OF PRESTIGIOUS NEW RESTAURANT DEVELOPMENT the headlines ran. The radio and television stations quickly got in on the act and Marco appeared on several chat shows talking about his plans to open the classiest establishment in the country providing the most exquisite dining experience outside of London or Paris.

She suspected that he was secretly enjoying himself for there was a large streak of showmanship in the eccentric chef and he was plainly revelling in his victory over his arch rival, Paul Le Brun. But the publicity had the desired effect. Within days, enquiries about The Wharf began to pick up and sales started to climb again. It appeared that they had salvaged the operation. But it had been a close call.

She had expected Mick McCann to be outraged at the chef's refusal to deal with him directly and his insistence on only doing business through Maddy. But McCann seemed quite relieved.

"You're welcome to him," he said, when she told him the news. "The man's a lunatic. I'm just delighted that you've got him back on board."

"But he's only going to stay if you stick to the original plans. And he's right, Mick. Confidence is a very tender plant. I hope you've learnt your lesson from all of this."

"Maddy, I haven't slept for the past fortnight worrying about it.

You think I enjoy this kind of thing? You can relax. Nothing's going to change. Now, can I buy you dinner to celebrate?"

"I think I'll pass," she said. "I'm drained. And I've still got a lot of calls to make."

"Well, thanks for everything you've done. You're a princess."

"Just listen to me in future and maybe we can stay out of trouble."

But it wasn't just her relationship with Greg that had suffered because of the crisis over Marco O'Malley's restaurant. She had been neglecting Rosie and Sophie too. So one evening, she decided to drop over to Munster Road to visit them. When she arrived, she found a roaring fire flaming in the grate and little plates of hors d'oeuvres on a table beside the settee. The house felt warm and inviting. It was obvious they were settling down for a gossipy evening.

"You're not driving, are you?" Rosie asked after she had taken Maddy's coat.

"No. I decided to walk. I needed the exercise."

"Good. We've got a bottle of plonk chilling in the fridge. Now you've got no excuse."

She disappeared into the kitchen and returned with a bottle and three glasses.

"How is Adam?" Maddy inquired, casually.

"Adam is fine," Rosie said with a mischievous gleam in her eye.

"Any developments on the romantic front?"

"Just one."

"What?"

"He wants to get engaged."

"What!" Sophie cried. "You never told me!"

"I was saving it up for later."

"He wants you to marry him!" gasped Maddy.

"Yes. He wants me to marry him. You know, the whole kit and caboodle – rings, bridesmaids, honeymoon, all that stuff."

"How do you feel about it?" Maddy asked, taken aback by the news. She hadn't realised that Rosie's relationship had progressed so far.

Her friend shrugged. "I don't know. I could do worse, I suppose."

"Oh, Rosie," Sophie said making a tutting sound with her tongue, "that's hardly the right attitude. Either you're in love with the guy or you're not."

"I like him well enough," Rosie confessed. "He's got no bad habits that I'm aware of. He's got a good, steady job. And he's nuts about me. So I'd have to give him ten marks out of ten."

"But do you love him?" Sophie pressed.

"I've been thinking about that," Rosie said, "and I'm not sure. How do you know?"

She looked at Maddy. "You're the expert. You've been seeing Greg for yonks. Tell us how you know if you love someone."

"Yes," Sophie pressed.

Maddy blushed. They were asking her about love and at this very moment she wasn't even sure if she had a relationship any more.

"Well," she began, "I suppose it's a feeling of happiness when the object of your affections is around and a feeling of loneliness when he's not. It's waking up in the morning and thinking about him first thing and falling asleep at night with his face printed on your mind."

"And?"

"It's not being content till you're together. And wanting to please him and hating yourself if you have an argument. It's a whole lot of feelings rolled into one. But if you're in love, Rosie, I think you'd know about it."

"Are *you* in love?" Rosie asked.

A crimson tide crept along Maddy's cheek. She tried to laugh the question away.

"Why am I suddenly in the dock?" she said. "I'm not the one who's talking about getting engaged." She saw Sophie looking at her.

"I hear you had to cancel your holiday," Sophie said. "I'll bet that was a downer."

Maddy frowned. Word had certainly travelled fast. Probably Greg had told Arthur and Arthur had told Sophie.

"I wasn't too happy about it, that's for sure. But we had a crisis at work and I had to stay behind to sort it out."

"That's what comes from being top cat," Rosie said. "The buck stops with you."

"And what did Greg say?"

"He went without me."

Rosie and Sophie stared, open-mouthed.

"He did *what?*" said Rosie.

"Went without me," Maddy said, suddenly realising how terrible it sounded.

"You mean to say you let him go?"

"I could hardly stop him," Maddy replied. "He's a grown adult. What was I supposed to do? Tie him to the bedstead?"

"Oh, I love that kinky stuff!" Rosie said and everyone laughed as the tension evaporated.

But the conversation continued to play on Maddy's mind after she got home. The reaction of her friends had plainly told her they thought she was mad to have allowed Greg to go off on holiday by himself. What would a good-looking man like him do in Marbella on his own? He would be like a magnet for every voracious female on the Costa del Sol. Just think of all the temptation that would come his way.

The thought horrified her. And now she began to believe that she had made a terrible mistake. She should have gone with him despite the cost. She thought of the clubs, the bars, the beaches. Everywhere Greg turned he would find willing women with holiday romance on their minds. And he was handsome and charming and, above all, he was single. She must have been crazy.

He was due back in two days' time. She made up her mind. As soon as he returned she would ring him and arrange to meet. She would swallow her pride and apologise. They would put the whole sorry business behind them and move on. And never again would she make the mistake of allowing him out of her sight.

This decision cheered her up and she threw herself back into her work. With The Wharf now back on course, Mick McCann was going around with a happy grin on his face. The glossy sales brochure, complete with artists' impressions of the development, was finally printed and Maddy arranged for copies to be sent out to interested clients.

In addition, she had an important meeting with Marco O'Malley and his architect where they spent an entire afternoon going over the finer details of his new restaurant. And work had commenced on the show apartment which would be central to Maddy's marketing plans. It would be used to give prospective buyers an idea of what the development would be like when it was finished.

At last, Friday arrived and Greg would be flying home. The flight was due into Dublin around lunch-time and Maddy knew he would go straight to his office. She waited till two thirty before ringing but instead of getting Greg she found herself talking to his secretary.

"Can I speak to Mr Delaney?" she asked.

"Who is this?"

"It's Maddy Pritchard."

"Mr McCann isn't here, Ms Pritchard," the secretary replied.

"Oh? Is he still in Spain?"

"No, he didn't go to Spain. He had to cancel the trip."

Maddy reeled from the shock.

"Really?" she managed to say.

"Yes. He went to London instead."

"And when is he due back?"

"He didn't say."

She put down the phone with a worried frown. So Greg had been in London for the past week and he hadn't bothered to tell her. By now, she was feeling totally confused. He had been looking forward to the trip to Marbella. To cancel it and suddenly take off for London was not like him. She wished she could talk to him. She rang his secretary again and asked if she had a number where she could reach him, explaining that the matter was urgent. But the secretary was unable to help.

"He didn't leave any number. He just rings in every couple of days to pick up messages."

"The next time he calls would you ask him to contact me, please?"

"Certainly, Ms Pritchard. I'll make sure to do that."

Maddy worked through the rest of the afternoon with a growing sense of foreboding. What was going on? It was now ten days since the argument with Greg and it was the longest time they had gone without speaking since their relationship had become serious. To add to her feeling of gloom, the sky outside her window grew heavy with cloud and before long it started to rain and a grey, dull mist settled over the scene.

When she finished work, she drove straight home, turned on the central heating and made a bite of supper. Then she settled down to watch some television. But she couldn't concentrate. Her mind kept wandering back to Greg. He must have been very upset to fly to London and break off contact with her. Damn Mick McCann, she thought. Damn Marco O'Malley. Greg had been right. She had allowed them to come between her and the man she loved. And now she was paying the price.

She decided to have an early night, She went to bed and snuggled under the duvet. Outside, the rain rattled against the window and the wind howled. But she couldn't relax. Her mind was now in turmoil. She knew she wouldn't have any peace till she saw Greg again. And then a terrible thought came hurtling into her brain. London was where Lorna Hamilton lived. What if he had gone there to see her?

She felt her stomach heave at the thought. She rushed to the bathroom and was sick into the toilet bowl. She wiped her mouth and flushed the bowl while the terrible thought continued to gnaw at her brain. Surely it wasn't possible? After everything that had happened, surely he wouldn't be stupid enough to go back to Lorna Hamilton again? But he had told her himself how seductive she was. Maybe he had sought consolation in her arms after their argument. It was just the sort of impulsive action Greg might take.

By now, her forehead was burning and she could feel her heart pounding in her breast. She took a cloth and washed her face in cold water. This was crazy thinking. She was allowing her imagination to run riot. She would have to stop it at once before she drove herself insane.

But it *was* all possible. There was nothing about the scenario that could *not* have happened. How she wished she had gone with Greg to Marbella as they had planned and to hell with the consequences. If she had done that, she wouldn't be standing here now, staring at her wretched reflection in the mirror, tormenting herself with these terrible thoughts.

She got back into bed, pulling the duvet tight around her. But sleep didn't come easily. She tossed and turned as the sick video ran in her head and her mind continued to play games with her. She shut her eyes and willed her fevered brain to stop. Eventually, around four o'clock, she at last fell into a fitful sleep.

The clanging of the phone jolted her awake. Outside, a watery sun was breaking through a dull bank of cloud. She glanced at the bedside clock and saw that it was a quarter past nine. Sleepily, she lifted the phone and pressed it to her ear.

"Yes," she said.

"Hi, Maddy," a cheerful voice announced. "It's Greg. I hear you've been looking for me."

Chapter Thirty

She felt a wave of relief wash over her.

"Greg," she gasped. "Where are you?"

"I'm at Heathrow airport. I'm catching the 10 o'clock flight for Dublin. How are you?"

"I'm … okay," she managed to say. "What took you to London?"

"Business. I had a sudden problem to sort out so I thought I'd forget about Marbella and come straight here. How did you get on with the mad chef?"

"I got him back on board."

"Well, that's good news. It should make Mick McCann happy. Look, I have to go straight into the office when I get back."

"Do you have to? I've really missed you, Greg. I'm dying to see you again."

"And so am I. But I have to brief some people. Why don't we meet after work? I've an awful lot to tell you."

"Okay," Maddy agreed.

They arranged to meet in a pub off Grafton Street and then Maddy put down the phone. She threw back her head and let out a shout of joy. Greg was back and he sounded cheerful and keen to see her again. She bounded out of bed and into the shower.

She arrived at the pub for six thirty to find Greg sitting at a table near the bar, looking smart in a crisp blue shirt and double-breasted suit. Immediately, he took her in his arms and kissed her.

"Maddy, I have an apology to make. I've been a selfish brat. Please forgive me."

"Of course, I forgive you."

"It's just that I was so wound up about that holiday in Marbella. I'd been looking forward to it for months."

She gently placed a finger against his lips. "Sssh," she said. "You're home. Let's not talk about it. I'm just so glad to see you again."

"You know I love you," he said. "I want us to be all nice and cosy."

Within minutes they were laughing and drinking happily together as if nothing had happened. Maddy had received a fright but now her lover was back and she felt so relieved. But there was something she needed to get off her mind.

"Greg, please forgive me but there is something I must ask you. Do you ever think of Lorna Hamilton?"

"Lorna Hamilton?" he said, looking incredulous. "Are you mad? That woman caused me enough heartache to last for my entire lifetime. Why on earth would I think about *her?*"

They quickly settled back into their old routine and the dispute over Marbella was forgotten. A group of investors was interested in a new internet technology company called SmartWorld and Greg had been asked to check it out for them. It was a fascinating area where big fortunes could be made overnight but, equally, people could get their fingers badly burned. So the investors wanted to be certain.

The work took him on trips to New York and California but Maddy didn't mind the disruption and Greg kept in regular contact by phone. Besides, she was extremely busy herself. After months of preparation, the show apartment at The Wharf had finally been completed.

It was a beautiful three-bed unit fronting directly onto the river with views across the city. The finest materials had been used in its construction with marble floors and exposed Howth stone above the large open fireplace. The magnificent bathrooms and the spacious kitchen had been equipped with the most modern appliances.

Maddy spent hours agonising over furniture and drapes and organising the décor. No money was spared. This apartment had to look spectacular. It was to be the centrepiece of the development, the first tangible evidence of the scheme's potential. It would be used to convince interested customers that the development really did live up to all the grand claims that had been made for it.

When it was finished, she organised another photo opportunity. This time, she managed to persuade Marco O'Malley to pose with Mick McCann while he presented him with a silver platter on which rested a large red lobster garnished with all the trimmings. She chose a beautiful sunny day. In the background, a yacht drifted languidly on the river. It was perfect. There was only one sour note. Throughout the entire proceedings, the chef pointedly refused to speak to the developer although he did manage a big smile for the camera. But Maddy was happy enough. It made for fascinating photographs and next day they graced all the newspapers.

Meanwhile, life was moving on for Rosie and Sophie. Sophie's relationship with Arthur was firmly back on track and he was managing to stay sober and attend his AA meetings. Maddy soon discovered that Arthur sober was a completely different person to Arthur drinking. He was caring and attentive and he took trouble with his appearance. Now he appeared neatly shaved and groomed and always wearing freshly ironed shirts and ties that didn't look as if they had been used to wipe the dinner plates. And he grew slimmer and fitter.

She also learnt that behind his bluff exterior, Arthur was a sensitive man who had sought refuge in alcohol to escape the relentless pressure of his job. But now that he was sober, he was handling his work much better. And it was paying dividends. The bosses who had recently been on the verge of firing him had regained their confidence and Greg even hinted that Arthur might be in line for a promotion.

Rosie's romance with Adam continued to blossom. Any lingering doubts about being in love had apparently been overcome for at Easter Rosie announced their engagement and decided to throw a party to celebrate. Everyone was excited for the couple but it had a strange effect on Maddy.

By now, she had been going out with Greg for almost eighteen months and he had never once mentioned the possibility of marriage. Whenever she thought about this, she put his reluctance down to his bad experience with Lorna Hamilton. After what he had been through, it was natural that he would be cautious.

But she began to notice something else. Their relationship was changing. She was still in love with Greg. But it was no longer the starry-eyed infatuation she had once felt. Now her love was tempered by the knowledge that Greg was a very complex man and had a dark side to his character. She already knew that he was impulsive but the argument over Marbella had shown him to be demanding and selfish and controlling. Greg liked to get his own way. And he was given to rapid mood swings, sometimes happy and sometimes down in the dumps.

But on balance, his good qualities far outweighed his defects. He was warm and affectionate. And he was capable of great acts of generosity as Maddy was about to find out.

But he still had not asked her to marry him and sometimes she wondered if he ever would.

Rosie's engagement party was scheduled for Saturday night. She had invited about fifty guests, mostly friends and work colleagues and both sets of families. Sophie had agreed to do the catering and serve a buffet supper. Maddy had offered to come over early to give her a hand in the kitchen. Greg was to join the party later.

She arrived at Munster Road shortly after three o'clock, clutching a bottle of wine and the present that she and Greg had purchased between them – a set of Waterford Crystal champagne glasses. She found Sophie in the kitchen frantically chopping vegetables and Rosie in jeans and sweatshirt busily tidying the house.

"I hope you don't mind me throwing a party like this," Rosie apologised.

"Why should I mind?"

"Because it's your house and I wouldn't like anything to get damaged, although I've warned everyone to be on their very best behaviour."

"But Rosie, houses are for living in. I don't mind, so long as they don't set fire to it. Now forget that cleaning," she said, removing a duster from Rosie's hand. "Let me see your ring."

Rosie extended a chubby finger to reveal a brilliant diamond solitaire.

"It's beautiful," Maddy said softly, taking her friend's hand in her own and examining the ring. "Oh, Rose, I'm so happy for you."

"I know you are. You and Sophie are the best pals anyone could possibly wish for."

"Forever friends," Maddy said with a grin. "We've got to stick together, remember. Now tell me how Adam is dealing with all the fuss."

"He's taking it in his stride. You know Adam is really a home bird. He can't wait to get married and settle down. He's already talking about buying a house. That's something you and I will have to discuss one of these fine days."

"Sure. You know I'll be happy to help you. Just let me know when you're ready and we'll sit down and have a chat."

She gave Rosie her present and card and went off to the kitchen where Sophie was busy at the sink, and the cassette player was belting out an old Rolling Stones track.

"Have a glass of wine," she said, pointing to the opened bottle on the counter. "I think you'll need it. This is going to be like the miracle of the loaves and fishes. There are a lot of hungry mouths to feed and I don't mind telling you that I'm as jittery as a new-born lamb."

"Just relax," Maddy said, pulling on an apron and rolling up her sleeves. "If past experience is anything to go on, everything will turn out perfectly well."

The next few hours passed in a frenzy of chopping and peeling. With the casseroles cooking in the oven and a delicious aroma filling the kitchen, they concentrated on the salads and dressings and before long had them prepared, a big platter of bread sliced and the condiments organised. Maddy ferried these out to the living-room where Rosie had spread a large white tablecloth over the dining- table.

By six o'clock everything was under control. The food was keeping warm in the oven and the table had been laid out with little parcels of knives and forks wrapped up in paper napkins. The wine glasses were polished and stood in serried ranks on a side table beside a similar row of bottles. The desserts – chocolate layer cake, pavlova and tiramisu – had been collected from the delicatessen and were now safely stored in the fridge.

Meanwhile, Rosie had been busy organising the furniture so that there were chairs and sofas for those who wanted to sit while the doors had been pulled back to extend the space in the living-room. It seemed like an opportune moment for Maddy to escape to the bathroom and take a hot shower before changing for the evening.

She had brought with her the slinky black dress she had worn on the famous occasion when she had persuaded Marco O'Malley to take the lease on the restaurant. It had worked then and ever since Maddy had regarded it as her lucky dress. It would be ideal for tonight's party. As she towelled herself and began to apply her make-up, she thought of the festivities that lay ahead. She really couldn't stand too much fuss. If the day ever arrived when *she* got engaged, she would simply stick a notice in *The Irish Times* and disappear off to Paris for the weekend. But, she thought disconsolately, the way things were going, that was a very big if.

Her thoughts were disturbed by the chiming of the doorbell as the first guests arrived. She quickly completed her make-up, brushed out her luxuriant hair and straightened her dress. It fitted her like a glove. Yes, she liked this dress. It was a simple off-the-peg garment yet it seemed to have been designed specifically for her, emphasising her figure to fine advantage. Applying a final layer of lipstick, Maddy left the bedroom and headed downstairs.

About a dozen people were gathered in the living-room. Maddy knew most of them already. But among them was a middle-aged couple who she took to be Adam's parents. She went up to them and introduced herself.

"Are you excited?" she asked.

"Not as excited as the bride's parents must be," Mr Gray replied. "They're the people who really feel the stress in these situations."

Maddy thought of the mayhem engendered by Helen's wedding and nodded sympathetically.

"Do you have any daughters?" she asked.

"One," Mrs Gray replied, "but she swears she'll never get married. She says she can't stand silly men."

"Oh? What age is she?"

"Twelve," Mrs Gray said and they all laughed.

By now more people had arrived and the sound of chatter began to fill the room. Maddy left the Grays in the company of one of Rosie's friends while she went off to circulate. She had just poured herself a glass of wine when she heard a familiar voice at her shoulder. She turned to see Arthur Brady beaming down at her. He bent closer and for a brief moment, she thought she smelt something sweet on his breath.

"You haven't seen my lovely Sophie, have you?" he asked.

"She's taking care of the catering," Maddy replied. "You'll probably find her in the kitchen."

She watched him weave uncertainly through the crowd. Was it just her vivid imagination? If she didn't know better, she would have sworn that Arthur had been drinking.

Someone put on the cassette player and soon the floor was a mass of heaving bodies swaying to the music. Suddenly, she saw Greg's face in the crowd.

"Talk about perfect timing," he said, kissing her on the cheek as he caught sight of Rosie and Sophie ferrying large dishes of food from the kitchen. "I'm starving. How is the party going?"

"So far, so good. Everybody seems to be enjoying themselves."

"Sorry I'm late," he apologised, surveying the room. "I got a call just as I was leaving. Someone I've been trying to contact about SmartWorld."

"Well, if you want to get fed, I suggest you get over there fast," she said, pointing to the dining-table. "This lot are about to descend like a plague of locusts. And I can recommend Sophie's casseroles. I helped to make them."

By now the party was in full swing. People were chatting and eating and enjoying themselves. At one stage, Sophie turned off the music and stood on a chair while she made a little speech about one of her very best friends in the whole world, Rosie Blake, and how she was about to forsake the freedom of singledom for the dubious pleasures of married life and how she wished Rosie and Adam all the best that life could offer and many years of connubial bliss. She finished off by proposing a toast and everybody topped up their glasses and drank a health to the lucky couple among much cheering and whooping from the men.

Then somebody formed a conga line and people held onto each other's waists and began to snake around the living-room and finally through the patio and out to the garden. Maddy decided it was time to go home. It was now one thirty and she was beginning to feel tired.

She went to see Rosie and Sophie before she left.

"Thanks for a lovely evening," she said.

"Leaving so soon?" Rosie said. "There are hours of merriment yet."

"Not for this girl," Maddy replied. "I'm feeling bushed. I need to get under the duvet for about eight hours."

Sophie nudged Rosie. "That'll be you in about six months' time. I've seen it happen before. Couples settle down and the next thing you know they can't wait to get into bed."

"You have a filthy mind, Sophie Kennedy," Maddy responded as she waved goodbye.

It was a short drive home to Auburn Grove. Greg was staying over but instead of coming to bed, he decided to type up some notes on his Smartworld project. So Maddy had a shower, got undressed and climbed into bed. Within minutes she was fast asleep.

She was wakened by the loud clanging of the phone. She sat up and drowsily turned on the table lamp. She was alone in bed. She looked at the clock. It was 3.45 a.m. Who can be ringing me at this hour, she thought as she rubbed her eyes and reached for the phone.

But she heard Greg pick it up downstairs and the low murmur of his voice as he answered. A few minutes later, he came into her room with his face looking grim.

"That was Sophie," he said. "She's in a terrible state. Arthur is drunk again."

Maddy felt her heart sink.

"And that's not the worst part. He's having some sort of fit. I need to get over there, right away."

Maddy sank back on the bed, her mind reeling from the shock. Poor Sophie, she thought, as she heard the front door close and the sound of Greg's car starting up. Why did this have to happen now?

Chapter Thirty-one

It was seven o'clock before Greg returned looking pale and exhausted.

"He's in hospital," he announced as Maddy rushed to put on the kettle to make tea.

"What happened?"

"He flipped apparently, tried to smash the place up. We had to call for an ambulance."

"My God! Should I go over there?"

"No. It's under control. The paramedics were able to sedate him. Thankfully, there's not too much damage. A couple of broken glasses, that's all. The girls have cleaned it all up."

"He was drunk?"

Greg shrugged. "Sophie thinks he'd been sneaking drinks at the party."

"You know, I thought I smelt alcohol on his breath earlier. And he seemed a bit unsteady on his feet."

"What time was that?"

"About eight o'clock. But I didn't think any more about it."

"Well, after the guests had left, Sophie found him in the kitchen with a glass of whiskey. When she tried to take it from him, he went berserk. He was completely out of his mind. Arthur's a strong man. It took the three of us to subdue him."

"This is awful," Maddy said, wringing her hands. "How is she coping?"

"Not good," Greg said. "You can imagine. He was doing so well. She thought he had the booze under control and then, bang, this happens."

"I'll go over this afternoon and see her," Maddy said. "I'm sure she could do with some support."

Greg let out a long sigh. "Well, I've had enough excitement for one night. I'm going to bed. What about you?"

"I wouldn't sleep," Maddy said. "Anyway, I've got things to do."

"Okay. Make sure to wake me at midday."

Sophie was in a state when Maddy returned to Munster Road at three o'clock. The house had been tidied up and there was no evidence that there had ever been a party or that a drunken man had been throwing glasses around.

As soon as Maddy appeared, Sophie put her arms around her and began to weep. "I'm so sorry about this. I don't know what to say to you."

"What are you sorry for? It's not your fault."

"I just feel so embarrassed. Ohhhh!" she sobbed. "I could murder him for this. Why did he have to do it?"

"Who knows?"

Sophie wiped away some tears. "He's gone too far this time. I'm not taking any more."

"Don't be hasty." Maddy said, cradling her head. "Just take it easy. He's being looked after now and there's no damage done."

"Yes, there is. There's damage to our relationship. He broke his word. How can I believe him again? How can I trust someone who breaks his promise?" She sniffed between the sobs.

Maddy didn't know how to respond. Like Sophie, she couldn't understand how Arthur couldn't just summon up the willpower to stop drinking completely.

"You don't know how lucky you are to have a good, kind, dependable man like Greg," Sophie went on. "Why can't Arthur be like him? Or like Adam, for that matter? Why can't he just behave like a normal person? I don't want to spend my life tied to a drunk."

"Sssh," Maddy said.

"It's all right for you to say sssh. But what am I going to *do?*"

Two days later, the hospital announced that Arthur would be able to see visitors. Sophie didn't want to go but Maddy persuaded her and Greg offered to drive her there in his car.

"At least go and see him," Maddy counselled. "You can make a decision about your long-term future when he's well enough to be discharged."

Reluctantly, Sophie allowed herself to be taken for a visit. Greg later reported that Arthur was still groggy and had no memory of the violent fit or the broken glasses. And he couldn't explain why he had gone back to drinking after being sober for so long.

A few days later, word came back that he was being transferred to a rehabilitation clinic to receive counselling and treatment for his alcohol dependency. By now, he was overcome with remorse and guilt and filled with resolve to get sober and never to drink again. The course was to last six weeks.

"He's in the last chance saloon," Greg announced to Maddy one evening as they were having dinner together. "His job is hanging by a thread. If he doesn't get his act together this time, they're definitely going to fire him."

"My God! What would he do?"

"It won't be easy for him, that's for sure. This is a small town and word gets around. Besides, they probably wouldn't give him any references."

Maddy was afraid of what the future would hold for Arthur if he didn't seize this opportunity. Apart from his job, his relationship with Sophie was on the brink. She still hadn't forgiven him or decided whether to take him back. But she did agree to visit him. The counsellor in the rehab clinic said it was important for his recovery to have someone stand by him.

Several times a week, Greg picked her up after work and drove her to the clinic to see Arthur. He was punctilious about it. Regardless of other demands on his time, he faithfully made the journey with Sophie. It was then that Maddy remembered Sophie's words. Despite his faults, Greg was a good, kind, generous man. And he was reliable. She was sure of that. He was not the kind of man who would ever let you down.

One evening, after he had come back from the clinic, he said: "I have to go to London this week. It's some work I have to do on SmartWorld. Do you have a problem with that?"

She was surprised by the question.

"No," she replied. Why should I?"

"Well, I just thought. You know who lives there?"

"Lorna Hamilton?"

"Yes. You asked me about her, remember? I don't want you to have any concerns about the true purpose of my visit."

Maddy reached out and pulled him close. "Oh, Greg, if I didn't trust you, do you think I'd still be seeing you? Of course, you can go. You have business to take care of."

"Are you sure?"

"I'm certain. I believe you absolutely when you say that Lorna Hamilton is over."

"Good, he said. "I'm leaving on Wednesday morning. I'll be back on Friday night. I'll keep in touch."

With Greg gone, Maddy agreed to take Sophie to the clinic. She found Arthur looking fit and healthy. The three of them sat in the refectory drinking coffee and Arthur told them about the routine.

"We're not allowed shoes," he said and Maddy looked down to see that he was wearing a pair of carpet slippers. "It's in case we try to escape."

She was shocked. "But it's not a prison."

"No, it's not. But did you notice the high walls and the security gates? And the guards? Not that it stops some people. A guy last week managed to climb over the wall. And then he fell off and broke his leg. But he still managed to crawl to the nearest pub before they picked him up."

Maddy shuddered. It seemed incredible that the craving for alcohol could lead people to such extremes.

"What do you do all day?"

"Plenty," Arthur replied. "They try to make sure we're fully occupied. We've got lectures, counselling and AA meetings. It's very intensive."

"Do you still think about a drink?" she asked.

He shook his head. "Not any more. This time my mind is made up." He looked at Sophie who lowered her eyes. "When I get out of here, I'm never going to touch another drop."

On the way home in the car, Maddy said to Sophie: "Do you believe him?"

"I don't know. Right now, I think he means it. But this is a devious addiction. He's got to be totally determined and when he gets out he's got to go straight back into AA. That's what happened the last time. He stopped going to meetings."

Maddy was bewildered. Because of Arthur, she was learning an awful lot about this terrible illness that seemed capable of taking apparently rational people and turning them into monsters.

"Do you think you'll take him back?"

Sophie closed her eyes and leaned her head back.

"Tell you the truth, Maddy. Right now, I don't know what I think."

By now, the construction work at The Wharf was powering ahead and the buildings were rising storey by storey, bringing a dramatic rise in inquiries. The show apartment proved so popular with prospective clients that Maddy had to assign Sue Donovan full-time to run it. And the traffic through the apartment became so intense that the carpet had to be shampooed twice a week to keep it looking fresh and new.

But her immediate task was to sort out Marco's restaurant and it wasn't proving easy. The chef had turned out to be extremely fussy and *very* indecisive. He couldn't even agree on a name or whether he wanted to maintain his existing premises in Blackrock.

"Everybody knows the Chalet d'Or," he insisted. "It's like a brand. I get letters from people all over the world complimenting me on the meals they've had. There is no question but the name must be retained."

"You could call the new restaurant Chalet d'Or Two," Maddy suggested.

"Ummmm," Marco mused, stroking his fat chin. "I'm not sure about that. It doesn't sound right."

"Or Marco's Place. You're as well known as the restaurant."

"Yes," he said, clapping his hands. "I am, aren't I? I like that. It's got the personal touch."

"Or Chez Marco."

"Yessss! That's good. The French association has appeal."

"And, of course, if you decide to sell the Blackrock premises, you can simply transfer the Chalet d'Or name to The Wharf."

"You're right," he said. "It all hinges on Blackrock. I really must make up my mind what I'm going to do with it."

But if finding a name for the restaurant was a challenge, agreeing the design was quickly turning into a horror story. And it was made twice as difficult because Marco was still refusing to deal directly with Mick McCann so that Maddy ended up acting as an intermediary between the two men.

Allowing Marco to design the restaurant had certain advantages since he was the expert and was going to be working in it. Besides, he had demonstrated a flair for restaurant design in his present premises which exuded a warm, cosy atmosphere which diners and food critics constantly admired. But there was clearly a limit to the amount of space that could be made available if the project was to be viable.

Marco's first attempt at a design produced a vast barn of a place which ran the full length of the ground floor of the commercial block with a kitchen to match. Maddy knew immediately it was a non-starter. If it went ahead, there would be no room left for the proposed shops. But she dutifully brought the design to Mick McCann and when he saw it, he exploded.

"Is he out of his tree?" he bellowed. The dining-room of the *Titanic* was smaller than this. You could fit an orchestra into that space and still have room for a dance-floor. There's absolutely no way we can go with that."

Maddy went back to Marco and broke the bad news. He was not amused.

"But I'm aiming to seat upwards of two hundred diners," he spluttered.

"How many does your present restaurant hold?"

"Seventy at a pinch."

"Maybe you should aim for something just a little bigger? The beauty of the Chalet d'Or – apart from the excellent cuisine," she quickly added, "is the intimacy you have managed to create."

"You think so?"

"Of course! It's what everyone remarks on. If you go for a great big place you'll lose that cosy touch. And there's one other thing to bear in mind. The smaller the restaurant, the lower your running costs."

"Let me think about it," Marco said.

He came back with a new design for a smaller restaurant seating one hundred and twenty guests and taking up about half the space of his first proposal. But when she returned to Mick McCann, he still wasn't satisfied.

"I'll still lose space for two shops. That's two leases and two rents down the drain. Tell him to reduce it."

But this time, Marco refused to budge. Maddy was beginning to get fed up. Why couldn't the two men sit down and negotiate directly instead of behaving like children?

When she told McCann, he was furious.

"He's behaving like a total prima donna. If I allowed every unit holder to design their own premises we'd never get this development built. Who does he think he is?"

"Marco O'Malley," Maddy said. "And he *is* a prima donna. We've known that from Day One. That's what makes him a success. That's why we're so lucky to get him on board. I think you're going to have to concede some ground on this."

McCann grumbled some more but in the end he sent Maddy back to seek some minor adjustments and after another bout of huffing and puffing the design was agreed and the architects got to work. Maddy heaved a sigh of relief. She couldn't wait for the project to be completed so that she could finally part company with Mick McCann and crazy Marco O'Malley.

Meanwhile, Arthur had been discharged from the rehabilitation clinic and was back at work. Greg reported that he appeared to have reformed himself. He was sober and punctual and behaving like an ideal employee. But his relationship with Sophie was not going so well. Whenever she visited Munster Road, she found her friend had lost much of her old *joie-de-vivre*. She was nervy and unsettled and clearly unhappy. She concluded that Arthur's drunken outbreak had inflicted greater damage than she realised.

She confided her thoughts to Greg.

"Something like that takes time to get over," he said. "She's had a shock. And there's also the business of Rosie's wedding. There's a lot of disruption in her life right now."

Greg was now working flat out to complete the research on SmartWorld. The investors were anxious to reach a decision while market conditions were still favourable and were pressurising him to finish his report. As a result, she saw less of him and when she did, he looked tired and harassed and almost as nervy as Sophie.

"You need a break," she said one day. "When this is over why don't we take that holiday in Marbella? I'm sure I can manage a few days' leave."

"Yes, yes," he said but without much enthusiasm. "You're right, Maddy. I *do* need a break. But not right now. I have to get this damned report finished. And what's more important, I've got to get it right. My reputation is on the line."

"Okay," she said, backing off. "Just tell me when you're ready and I'll talk to Tim Lyons."

But the pace of his work didn't let up and whenever she saw him she noticed the old mood swings had returned. Greg was either morose or subdued or he was bubbling with enthusiasm. He became snappy and irritable. She wished he would get his damned report completed so that things could settle down. Then they could have that holiday and discuss their own situation.

But something was about to happen that would alter the whole course of their relationship.

Saturday morning was the time when Maddy usually caught up with houshold chores. And this particular morning, she decided to take some clothes to the dry cleaner's. She opened the closet and rifled through the rows of dresses when it occurred to her that she should take some of Greg's clothes too. He got into the habit of keeping some suits and jackets at Auburn Grove for the times he stayed over. She might as well bring them to the cleaner's too. She laid them on the bed and began to check in case he had left anything in the pockets.

As she did, she felt something rustle in one of the pockets. She fished it out and discovered it was a folded sheet of paper. She opened it and immediately felt her heart stop. What she was holding was a love letter.

Chapter Thirty-two

Darling,

When can I see you? I long for your strong arms around me, your tender touch, your warm embrace. I never thought I could feel like this way about any man.

I count the days till we can meet again.

Love, L

Maddy felt her stomach heave. She stared at the letter till the words began to swim before her eyes. This was a total shock. Her knees felt so weak that she had to sit down on the bed. By now the blood was roaring in her head. No wonder Greg had been acting strangely recently. He had been carrying on an affair behind her back and here in her hand was the proof.

She closed her eyes while she willed herself to be calm then forced herself to read the letter once more. It had been typed on an office computer. There was no address and no date. But there was no doubting the sentiments expressed. This was from some woman who was clearly infatuated with him, some woman who signed herself L.

There was only one person it could be – Lorna Hamilton! Despite his denials he must have continued to see her. He had seen her on his recent trip to London. Maddy felt her shock give way to outrage. Despite all his lies and protestations he had continued to see Lorna Hamilton. How long had it being going on?

She dragged herself off the bed and attacked the suits again, searching the pockets for further information, an envelope or another letter but there was nothing more. She made her way unsteadily into the kitchen and drank a glass of water while she waited for her strength to return and her head to clear. The rage threatened to overwhelm her and it was compounded by the sinking realisation that the man she had loved and trusted had betrayed her behind her back.

She waited for the rage to pass. She knew she must focus. This had been a terrible blow but she must think rationally. She sat down at the breakfast counter and tried to order her thoughts.

Why had he kept the letter? Why hadn't he destroyed it? Because he never expected her to find it! He must have stuck it into his pocket and forgotten about it. Maybe he had more letters like it at his apartment. Now she realised why Greg had been nervy and irritable recently. She had put it down to pressure of work. But it was guilt!

He was still in love with Lorna Hamilton. Despite the break-up of their marriage plans, he had never stopped loving her. The strange behaviour she had witnessed was the result of a man with a bad conscience who was trying to live a lie.

She tried to think what she should do. Her first instinct was to confront him. She had the evidence. Now let him admit his guilt. She would do it right now. She would ring him at once and tell him what she had found and hear him trying to explain it away. But something made her hesitate. Something warned her to think carefully.

A row on the phone was not the best way to handle this. It gave him too much advantage. He could simply terminate the call while he bought time to come up with some excuse. No, the correct way to deal with this was face to face where Greg Delaney would have nowhere to hide. Face to face where he would be forced to look her in the eye and tell her the truth.

Right now, she felt a desperate urge to talk to someone, to pour out all the hurt and bitterness that was raging through her head. She thought of Rosie or Sophie. She should ring them. They were the friends she had always turned to when in trouble. But she couldn't bring herself to do it. The shock was too intense and the grief too private. And there was the shame of admitting that the man she had put her faith in had turned out to be a fraud.

She folded the letter and slipped it into her purse. She put his suit back into the closet and gathered the clothes together for the dry cleaner's. She washed her face in the sink and put on a touch of make-up. She would force herself to be strong even though her heart was breaking. Whatever happened, she must maintain her dignity. She was the person who had been wronged. She was the one who must now hold the high ground.

She drove to Ranelagh and left the clothes in the laundry and then went to the supermarket and picked up some provisions. But it was as if she was living in a dream. She was still in a state of shock. Was it possible that the whole thing was some ghastly mistake? Was it possible that she was imagining the liaison with Lorna Hamilton? But the letter was real. And it had her initial. Logic told her that her suspicions were correct. This was no dream. This was real life and it was happening to *her!*

When she got home, she forced herself to finish the housework. By now it was almost one o'clock. Usually at this time she had a light lunch. But today she had no appetite, so instead she made a cup of tea and went and sat on the patio among the geraniums with thoughts of disaster swirling in her head. Greg was working today, finally writing up his report. He had promised to ring her this afternoon about their plans for the evening. She steeled herself to wait, even though every fibre of her being wanted to confront him immediately without wasting any more time.

She sat in the sun trying to read a novel while her mind kept wandering back and forth. Time and again, she tried to focus on the book but her mind refused to concentrate. And then, just before four o'clock she heard her phone ring.

She grabbed it and clamped it to her ear.

It was him.

"Hi," Maddy," she heard him say.

"Hi, Greg." Her voice wavered.

She wanted to scream. It almost choked her to remain calm.

"Are you okay?" he asked.

"I'm fine."

"You don't sound fine. You sound as if you're ill."

You don't know how ill I am, she thought. You don't know how sick I am to the heart. And it's all because of you.

"I'm tired, that's all," she said.

"Why don't you have a lie-down? It'll do you good. I'm nearly finished this report and I thought we might go out for a meal to celebrate."

"Okay."

"I'll call over at six. Does that suit?"

"Sure. Six is fine."

"Good. I'll see you then. And Maddy…"

"Yes?"

"I love you."

She heard the line go dead and switched off her phone. She glanced at her hand and saw that it was shaking. How can he do it, she thought? How can he talk so calmly as if nothing is wrong? How can he say he loves me when everything is falling to pieces?

At five to six she heard his key in the front door. Finally, the moment had arrived. She put down her book and walked through the living-room to meet him in the hall. He came into the house with a smile, looking like a man who hadn't a care in the world.

"Feeling any better?" he asked as he bent to kiss her cheek.

She felt herself stiffen. "A little," she said.

"Well, I've finished that damned report at last. Do you mind if I pour myself a gin and tonic? I've been working flat out."

"Be my guest," Maddy said. "You know where everything is."

He marched into the kitchen and took down the bottle from a cupboard above the sink.

"Want to join me?" he asked as the gin splashed into the glass.

"Not now. I don't feel like drinking."

He stopped what he was doing and turned to stare at her.

"Maddy, what the hell is wrong with you? You're behaving like a zombie. Are you sure you're okay?"

"Yes," she said.

"Can I do anything?"

"Perhaps."

"What is that supposed to mean?" he said, forcing a nervous smile onto his face.

"It means that you and I have got to talk."

He took a slow sip from his glass as his face darkened. "Why? Is there a problem?"

"That depends on what you tell me."

She walked back towards the living-room.

"Come and sit down, Greg. I've got something to show you."

He was frowning now as he followed her and sat down at the coffee table. She could sense that he was getting defensive. But now that the time had come, she felt her old strength return.

"Okay," he said. "Whatever is bothering you, why don't you just get it off your chest?"

She lifted her purse and took out the letter. She straightened it and pushed it across the table.

"Can you tell me what this is?"

He lifted the letter and the colour slowly drained from his cheeks. He looked up sharply. "Where did you get this?" he demanded.

"In the pocket of your suit. I was getting it ready for the dry-cleaner's."

He gave a nervous laugh.

"Before you run away with some crazy idea. I can explain."

Maddy never took her eyes off his face.

"Go right ahead."

He sighed and ran his fingers quickly through his hair. "It's rather delicate. One of the young guys in work has made a complaint about a female colleague. He's accusing her of harassment. Apparently, they had a brief affair and ever since, the woman has been pestering him with letters and phone calls. My boss has asked me to gather evidence."

She stared at him. It sounded plausible.

"You can understand that we have to be very careful how we handle it," Greg went on. "You can't just discipline someone without proof. That letter forms part of his complaint."

"What's his name?" she asked.

His face turned red. "I can't tell you," he blustered. "This is very sensitive stuff, Maddy."

"I just want him to confirm what you say. If he does, I'll destroy the letter and forget all about it."

"You can't talk to him. This is all highly confidential. If you start asking questions there'll be hell to pay."

"I just need his name."

"No," he said, firmly. "I won't tell you. You can't interfere."

She studied his face. She desperately wanted to believe him but something told her that he was lying through his teeth.

"I'm not a fool, Greg. I'll be very discreet."

"You're not listening, Maddy. I said no. I absolutely forbid it."

"I could speak to your boss myself."

He was angry now. He banged his fist down on the table so that the glass shook. "What is this? An inquisition?" he shouted. "I've just explained the bloody letter. Why are you cross-examining me?"

"I'm simply asking for this man's name. If your story is true then there's nothing to worry about."

"Of course, it's true. Have I ever lied to you before?"

"You tell me."

"Oh for God's sake! This is ridiculous. Either you trust me or you don't." He lowered his eyes and stared at the floor. "I'm not giving you his name."

"Greg!"

He kept his head down and refused to meet her gaze.

"Look at me, Greg."

Slowly, he brought his head up and glanced into her face then quickly looked away.

She knew at once.

"I'm sorry, Greg, but I don't believe you."

"You can believe what you damned well like!" He was shouting again. "You've obviously got your mind made up."

"I think that letter is from Lorna Hamilton. It's got her initial. You're still in love with her, aren't you?"

At the mention of her name, he threw his head back and laughed.

"You are one crazy bitch," he said. "You're completely paranoid. You know, I'm beginning to think you're jealous of her."

"Just prove to me that I'm wrong. It's a simple thing, Greg."

"Maddy, I've no intention of proving anything. I resent the fact that you're even asking me this stuff. It comes down to one simple thing. Either you trust me or you don't. "

He stood up and strode angrily from the room. A few seconds later she heard the front door bang shut.

She went back to the patio. The sun was fading but it was still warm. She gazed down the lawn at the flowers in bloom. The shock had left her now and in its place she felt an intense sadness.

The romance was over. She knew that. She could have saved it by accepting a lie. Lots of women would have been prepared to do that to keep the man they loved. Lots of women would have been willing to turn a blind eye. Perhaps in time, Greg would have given up Lorna Hamilton and returned to her.

But something prevented her. Greg had put the whole matter in a nutshell. She either trusted him or she didn't. And the fact was that trust had been shattered. Nothing could put it together again.

Chapter Thirty-three

She didn't hear from Greg for the rest of the day. But the following morning, just as she was finishing a conference with Tim Lyons, he came on the line sounding brash and chirpy as if nothing had happened. Beneath his bluster, she could detect the uncertainty in his voice.

"I want to apologise," he began. "I shouldn't have called you a bitch. And I shouldn't have said you were paranoid. I was totally out of order. It's just that I've been under a lot of pressure recently."

"I accept your apology," Maddy said.

"You do?"

He sounded surprised.

"Yes."

"Well, thank God for that. So what do you say if I take you to lunch and we forget the whole thing? We've both been under a lot of strain in recent weeks."

Immediately, she could see what he was doing – attempting to spread the blame. *We were both at fault. We were both tired. Sorry I called you a bitch.* And there was no mention of the central issue – the letter and what it signified.

"No," she said.

"No what?"

"I am not going to lunch with you. I don't think you realise, Greg – our relationship is over."

There was a brief pause and then he began to laugh.

"Oh, c'mon, Maddy, I've just said I'm sorry. You don't have to be such a drama queen."

"Greg. You and I are finished. What part of that sentence do you not understand?"

Now he sounded alarmed. "You can't be serious. You're breaking off a perfectly good relationship over a silly argument?"

"I don't want to see you again," she said, firmly.

"Maddy, don't be rash. It's always a mistake to make a big decision when you're angry."

"I'm not angry. I'm perfectly calm. I'm sad, that's all. There are some of your belongings at Auburn Grove, some clothes and books and stuff."

"Please, Maddy."

He was starting to plead with her but she ignored him.

"I'm arranging to have them couriered over to your place. I'd be obliged if you would do the same with my things."

"Maddy, for God's sake, there's no need for this. It's ridiculous."

"And one final thing, please don't ring this number again. If you do, I'll put down the phone. And if you persist, I'll report the matter to the police. Goodbye, Greg."

She replaced the phone, got up from her desk and walked quickly to the bathroom. She entered a cubicle, locked the door, sat down and for the first time in twenty-four hours, she allowed herself to weep.

The weeping did her good. It seemed to unlock all the tension and anger that had built up inside her. For the next few days she survived on a wave of self-righteousness. She was the injured party and she took comfort from the fact that she had been strong. She had stuck to her resolve and hadn't allowed Greg Delaney to persuade her. She told Marina to block any calls from him but there was no need. He didn't ring. And he didn't phone her mobile or write to her at home which she would have been powerless to prevent.

A few days later a parcel arrived at Auburn Grove containing the clothes she had kept at his apartment. There was no note. As time went by, he made no effort to contact her. It appeared that he had finally got the message. He had effectively removed himself from her life. She told herself this was exactly what she wanted and it suited her perfectly.

But Maddy was fooling herself. Letting go of Greg Delaney wasn't so simple. After a while, the feeling of justification began to wear off and was replaced by an aching emptiness which grew in intensity with each passing day. She hadn't been fully aware just how much space he had occupied in her life and, now that he was gone, there was this massive void to fill.

For three or four nights a week, he had shared her bed. Every single day they had talked on the phone or gone out for a meal or a drink. They had spent practically their entire leisure time together. She had consulted him and taken advice whenever she had a major decision to make. Greg had been her partner in every sense. And now, suddenly, he was no longer there.

But in the lonely weeks that followed, she was never tempted to reconsider her decision. She often cursed him for what he had done – selfishly destroying a good relationship. But not once did she think of relenting and inviting him back. She knew that he would come running. She could even tell herself that he had learnt a lesson and would never stray from her again. But she knew it would be the wrong thing. Greg's behaviour had so poisoned the trust between them that nothing could repair it. She would have to put up with the loneliness. Eventually it would pass. In the meantime, she had her work to provide her with distraction and now she threw herself into it with a vengeance.

After weeks of wrangling, the design of Marco O'Malley's new restaurant was finally agreed. It would be a magnificent open-plan dining area with startling views over the river seating one hundred and twenty guests and taking up 600 square metres of floor space. It was less than Marco wanted and more than Mick McCann had been prepared to concede but by now he was anxious to press ahead and the restaurant was holding things up.

At the same time Marco came to a decision about the other outstanding issue. He decided to sell the premises at Blackrock and move the Chalet d'Or in its entirety to The Wharf. So now the new restaurant also had a name. Everyone heaved a sigh of relief that these major hurdles had been successfully overcome.

And then a few days later, Maddy had another remarkable piece of good fortune. The phone rang one morning and she heard a suave, assured voice announce that he was interested in looking at the plans for the penthouses. They were planning to build four and they would be the jewels in the development. Maddy had agreed with Mick McCann an asking price of £400,000 which would make them far and away the most expensive apartments in Dublin. Selling one of them before it was even built would be a major coup.

The man who came to see her that afternoon was in his late thirties, slim, well groomed and confident. He introduced himself as Jack Whittaker. Maddy had already arranged with Tim Lyons to borrow his office and this was where she brought Mr Whittaker and served him coffee and biscuits while she spread the architects' plans out on the large desk for him to study.

As he bent to examine them, she launched into her prepared pitch.

"These penthouses are unique, Mr Whittaker. There is nothing else in Dublin to compare with them, 2500 square feet of floor space, three bedrooms, each with en-suite bathroom, large modern kitchen, separate dining area, superb living-room, plus terraces front and rear giving outstanding views across the entire city."

Whittaker continued to study the plans as she went on.

"The development is situated in one of the best locations, close to all amenities. We are using only the finest materials – Italian marble, polished hardwood floors – and in addition we are including a commercial area with shops, bars and a splendid restaurant which will be operated by Marco O'Malley. You might have read about that in the media? He's the owner of the renowned Chalet d'Or restaurant in Blackrock?"

But the well-rehearsed sales talk seemed to make little impact on Jack Whittaker. He continued to study the plans closely without once looking up. At last, he straightened up and turned to her.

"When will they be ready?" he asked.

"In eight months' time. Construction has already started and we're bang on schedule. But we do have a show apartment which you could see. It will give you an impression."

"How many have you sold?"

"Over seventy apartments so far."

"But none of the penthouses?"

"No."

"So that means I can have my pick?"

"That's right. It's one of the advantages of buying early."

"So tell me, Miss Pritchard, which is the best one?"

Maddy felt her pulse begin to race. Was it possible that he was contemplating buying one of the penthouses straight off the plans without even seeing the show house?

"That's difficult to say. They're all excellent apartments."

"If you were buying one, which would you choose?"

She pointed to the plans.

"That one."

"Why?"

"Because it faces south-south-west. That means it will get the sun afternoon and evening. You can eat on your terrace in the summer. You can have drinks parties while you admire the fantastic view. It should be possible to see as far as the Mourne Mountains on a clear day."

Jack Whittaker looked at her and smiled.

"You've convinced me, Ms Pritchard. I'll take it. Now what do I have to do?"

Maddy swallowed hard. This was amazing. She had never before sold a property as expensive as this one without hard negotiation. But

Jack Whittaker hadn't even attempted to bargain with her. He seemed to regard the transaction as no more exciting than buying a morning newspaper.

"You're aware of the price?" she confirmed, in case there had been any misunderstanding.

"Yes. Four hundred thou."

"Well, in that case, I will require a booking deposit of £20,000. I will arrange for a contract to be forwarded to your solicitor. On signature, we will require the balance of 10% which will be a further £20,000 and the remainder of the purchase price on completion."

"Excellent," Jack Whittaker said. He whipped out a cheque book and quickly scribbled a cheque for the booking deposit. He handed it to Maddy along with a two business cards which he withdrew from his wallet.

"That's my solicitor," he said, giving her one card. "And that's me."

She glanced at the second card and immediately something clicked in her brain. Jack Whittaker was one of the wealthy businessmen who were investing in SmartWorld.

They shook hands and he prepared to go.

"I've enjoyed meeting you, Miss Pritchard."

"Ditto."

At the door, he turned once more as if he had just remembered something.

"You're a friend of Greg Delaney?" he remarked.

"That's right."

"It was Greg who sent me."

"Really?" Maddy said.

"Yes. He said you were the best. He just helped me make a pile of money."

"I'm very pleased."

"Greg is one of my favourite people. Sharp as a knife, hardworking and totally dependable. In fact he's one of the most dependable guys I know. Goodbye, Miss Pritchard. I'll look forward to getting that contract."

By now, several weeks had passed and Maddy had told no one about the break-up. But she knew this state of affairs could not continue much longer. Sooner or later, she would have to tell her family and friends. And it would be better if she did it sooner before word leaked out and people began to ask questions. Indeed, her mother was already getting suspicious at Greg's absence from the Sunday lunches at St Margaret's Lane. So after giving the matter some thought, she decided to start with her.

The following weekend, she drove out to Raheny but the minute she entered the house, she felt her heart sink. The first person she saw was her sister Helen who was already seated at the dining-table with Joe Fuller. Mr Pritchard sat by the window with his head in the sports pages while her mother was busy in the kitchen. This was an unexpected development. Since her wedding, Helen had been an infrequent visitor and Maddy was hoping to find her parents alone.

"On your tod?" Joe Fuller asked with a cheery grin.

"Afraid so," she replied, slipping out of her coat and going into the kitchen to kiss her mother.

"Hello, Maddy," Mr Pritchard remarked, looking up briefly. "It's chilly out today."

"At least it's not raining."

Immediately Helen piped up. "Where's Greg?"

"He's not coming today."

"Why not?"

"Because we've broken up."

There was an embarrassed silence. Helen gave a sharp intake of breath. Joe looked at the tablecloth and moved the salt cellar about. Mr Pritchard quickly turned the pages of his newspaper. Mrs Pritchard came hurrying out of the kitchen, wiping her hands on her apron.

"Did I hear right?" she asked. "Did you say you've broken up with Greg?"

"Yes. That's what I said."

"But you'll be getting back with him?" Helen inquired. "It's only temporary?"

"No. I don't think so," Maddy replied, pulling out a chair and sitting down at the table while she tried her best to look composed. Now she was regretting her decision to come to lunch. It would have been better if she had come some evening when she could have talked to her mother alone without her sister's presence.

"So, what did he do to you?" Helen wanted to know.

Maddy looked at her. "Why do you assume that anybody did anything?"

"That's what usually happens."

"Couples break up for lots of different reasons," Maddy said, with just a hint of irritation. "It doesn't have to be a row."

"Oh, for heaven's sake," Mrs Pritchard said, gently caressing Maddy's back, "leave her alone, can't you? This isn't *Coronation Street*."

But Helen wasn't to be put off. This news was too good to be passed over lightly.

"So what was *your* reason?" she demanded.

"We just decided we weren't suited to each other."

"Well, I hope you didn't let him away with anything. I never warmed to Greg Delaney if you must know. I think he was too full of himself. I don't think he appreciated you."

Maybe you're right, Maddy thought, bitterly. Maybe that's exactly what it came down to. But she resented having to sit here and have her relationship analysed by Helen of all people.

"Give it time," Mrs Pritchard said, soothingly. "You'll be back together again. Everybody has these little tiffs. It's all part of courtship."

"No, Mum," Maddy said, firmly. "I don't think Greg and me will be getting together again. This is final."

"Then I don't want to hear another word," said her mother. "This isn't a wake. We're here to enjoy our Sunday dinner. Now sit up to the table."

"Hear, hear!" Mr Pritchard said. "I'm starving."

She was glad to escape from St Margaret's Lane around three o'clock. Her news had cast a pall over the lunch. She could sense that

Helen didn't believe a word she had said about the separation being mutual. In Helen's view there was always a victim and an aggressor. And the aggressor was always the man. Greg had done something to Maddy and nothing would convince her otherwise. The fact that she was actually right did little to ease Maddy's discomfort.

But at least she had told them. Now she had to break the news to Sophie and Rosie. She decided to invite them over to Auburn Grove one evening for supper. They arrived carrying a bottle of wine apiece with the obvious intention of making a night of it.

"Have you fixed a date for your wedding?" Maddy asked Rosie once they had settled down and she had presented them with plates of smoked salmon and scrambled eggs.

"We're thinking of the autumn," Rosie said.

"Autumn would be a good time," Maddy agreed. "But shouldn't you be making up your minds? There's an awful lot of preparation involved. I know from Helen's wedding."

"Yes, we should," Rosie replied. "But, you see, we can't decide what we want. Adam is all in favour of a small wedding. You know, just family and close friends. He says weddings are a terrible waste of money."

"He's right," Maddy replied, thinking of the extravagance of her sister's wedding.

"But my mother wants a big splash since I'm the only daughter. And my mother is a teeny bit of a snob. She wants to have all the neighbours talking."

"And who is going to pay for it?"

"My parents. But that's not the point. Adam says they could give us the money instead and we could use it to buy a house."

"That's the accountant in him speaking," Maddy said. "And on balance, I think I would agree with him. But what do *you* think?"

Rosie shrugged and took a sip of her chilled Chardonnay. "Well, most girls dream of a big flashy wedding with loads of bridesmaids and everything. And I'm no different. But I suppose we have to be practical."

So far, Sophie had remained silent.

"What's your opinion?" Maddy asked, turning to her.

"My opinion doesn't matter," Sophie replied. "I'm not the one getting married. In fact, the way things are going, I'm not sure I'll ever get married."

"Oh," Maddy said, looking more closely at her friend and noticing how downcast she appeared. "Is it Arthur?"

"Who else?"

"But I thought he was making a good recovery?"

"Yes, he is. And to be fair to him, he's putting a lot of effort into it. He goes to his AA meetings every evening and he takes the whole thing very seriously. But this latest episode has really thrown me. And right now I'm not handling it very well."

"I'm sorry," Maddy said, squeezing Sophie's hand.

"Never mind us," Rosie said, shifting the conversation. "What about *you*?"

"Well," Maddy said, putting on a brave face, "that's partly the reason I asked you over here tonight. I've got an announcement to make."

"You're getting married too!" cried Rosie, jumping up from the settee.

"I'm afraid not, Rose. In fact, it's quite the reverse. We've broken up."

Rosie immediately grabbed her hand. "*Broken up?* I don't believe it."

"It's true."

"But why? What happened?"

Maddy shrugged. She had decided not to tell them about the letter and Greg's treachery. She just wasn't in the mood for a lengthy inquest.

"Incompatibility, I think it's called. We came to the conclusion that our relationship wasn't really going anywhere."

Rosie looked dumbfounded.

"But I thought you were the perfect couple. Everybody did. I thought it was only a matter of time till you were marching up the aisle. I even thought you might get married before me."

Rosie's words brought a lump to Maddy's throat. This was turning out to be much harder than she thought.

"No," she said. "We've been going through a lot of tension recently. Things haven't been working out between us."

"But he's such a nice man. Oh, Maddy, are you sure you're doing the right thing?"

But before she could reply, Sophie started to sob. She sank her head in her hands and began to weep uncontrollably.

Maddy put her arm around her friend and gently patted her shoulder. "Don't cry, Sophie. It's all right."

"But I feel so miserable. Everything is collapsing around us."

"It will get better. It might be hard now but in the long run it will turn out okay."

"No," Sophie sniffed. "It won't get better. It will only get worse."

"Oh, Sophie, cheer up!" Rosie said. "The three of us are still together. We'll support each other. Forever friends, remember?"

Sophie blinked and wiped the tears from her eyes. "That was long ago. We were young and innocent. But now we've grown up and too much has happened."

Chapter Thirty-four

One morning, a few months after the break-up, Maddy came into work to discover that old Mr Shanley had retired and the long-awaited reorganisation of the firm was under way.

Everyone was in a state of excitement because the changes were bound to affect every member of staff. The firm had changed out of all recognition over the years. From a small, closely-knit business, it had grown to be one of Dublin's leading estate agencies with a staff of more than forty and sales of several hundred properties each year.

There was talk about expanding further by opening more offices. There was speculation about a new lettings division to handle the enormous growth in the rental market. Everyone was agreed that change was inevitable and Mr Shanley's departure provided the ideal opportunity. It contributed to the air of expectancy that now hung over the staff. People went around being particularly nice to one another because who knew if the person sitting next to you might end up being your boss?

Maddy tried to steer clear of the office intrigue that suddenly gripped the place. People would gather in small groups at the water-cooler to whisper information. There were frequent reports of certain individuals being spotted having lunch together. The end-of-week drinks session for the sales staff became a hotbed of gossip and rumour.

It was an uncertain time and it induced a palpable sense of uneasiness as people waited anxiously for the outcome. Maddy, however, had plenty to keep her mind occupied. She had used the sale of the first penthouse at The Wharf to garner more publicity for the development. Jack Whittaker had paid the biggest price yet recorded for an apartment in Dublin. It made for a good news story and Maddy skilfully got to work on Paula Matthews and the other property writers.

As a result, two more penthouses were sold in quick succession and another thirty apartments. They were finalising the leases on the shops and the plans for Marco O'Malley's restaurant were now well advanced. Mick McCann was ecstatic. This was a developer's dream. He had sold nearly half of the apartments and he still had four months to go before the completion date.

One day in the midst of all this activity, Maddy was approached by Jane Morton who inquired diplomatically if she expected to be promoted in the shake-up. Jane had been elevated to become Maddy's deputy and was effectively running the sales team since Maddy's energies had been taken up full time with The Wharf. She was a bright young woman in her late-twenties who displayed sharp organisational skills and was clearly ambitious. Maddy had come to rely on her and trust her judgment.

"I try not to think about it," she replied.

It was true. Since she had learnt of Fergus Shanley's retirement, she had made a decision to steer clear of the politicking that was going on all around her. She was all too aware of the dangers of becoming allied with one camp or another and possibly losing out in the process.

But privately, she did harbour ambitions. She had never forgotten Mr Shanley's words of encouragement after her first auction. She had worked hard and productively for the firm and now she hoped her effort would be recognised and she would get her reward.

"Well, you *should* think about it," Jane said, bluntly. "Everyone is talking about you. And people are saying it's time we had a woman in the senior ranks. Two thirds of the staff are female, for God's sake and yet all the bosses are men. It's crazy."

"I'm sure the partners will take all this into consideration when they make their decisions," Maddy said.

"I wouldn't bet on it. I think you should canvass. You have tremendous loyalty among the staff. People want you to succeed. And I'd be prepared to act as your campaign manager, if you like."

"Oh, no," Maddy said, quickly. "Don't do anything like that."

"The others are doing it. They're canvassing like mad. We should let the partners know how strongly the staff feels about this. I promise I'll be discreet."

"Let me think about it," Maddy said.

Meanwhile the date of Rosie's wedding was fast approaching. It was now late August and the wedding was scheduled for the first week in September. Adam had got his way and instead of a big splash with relays of bridesmaids and yards of silk, the wedding was going to be the quiet affair he wanted. About thirty guests had been invited, all family and close friends, and two bridesmaids – Maddy and Sophie. With the money they were saving, they had put a deposit on a small two-bed house in Clontarf which Maddy had helped them find.

"You're doing the right thing," she told her friend when Rosie expressed doubts about the wisdom of their plans.

"But this is my big day. And it's not going to be very big, is it?"

"All the people who matter will be there. And small weddings can be much more enjoyable. They're more intimate for one thing."

"My mother isn't very pleased."

"But your mother had her own wedding. This is *your* wedding, Rosie. You'll have a wonderful day – a real day to remember. We'll all make sure of that."

"Well, this is what Adam wants."

"And you and Adam are the most important people. I think what you're doing is very sensible. You'll be starting married life with your own home. How many brides can say that?"

"You're right," Rosie admitted.

"I know I am. And Clontarf is a very good area. You're making a wise decision buying there. It's got the sea and good transport and you're almost in the heart of the city. Mark my words, Clontarf is a coming place. That house will shoot up in value. You'll never regret it."

"You think so?"

"Rosie! Have you been listening to a word I've said? You're going to have a brilliant wedding and a lovely home to come back to with the man you love. Now, what more could any girl want?"

But Rosie's wedding inevitably caused Maddy to think of her own situation. *She* could have been that radiant bride. Everyone had believed she would be the first of the three girls to marry. In her heart she had thought so too. And now she was going to be Rosie's bridesmaid and would have to stand by and watch the joy on her friend's face while her own dreams were dashed to pieces. It was hard.

Since the break-up, she had never once set eyes on Greg Delaney. But that didn't mean he was far from her thoughts. Occasionally, she would wonder if she had done the right thing. But whenever she began to think like this, she would pull herself up sharply. She had done the *only* thing. Pretending it didn't happen would have only papered over the cracks. It would have been storing up disaster. Without a satisfactory explanation for that letter, the incident would have surfaced again sooner or later with the inevitable consequences. Greg had betrayed her with another woman. She knew that beyond any doubt. To pretend otherwise would have meant she was living a lie.

The approaching wedding also raised another problem. Who was going to take Rosie's place at Munster Road? There was no possibility of Sophie paying the full rent on her own. But finding someone else was not proving easy. Rosie and Sophie had been friends since school and knew each other's little foibles and moods. It was unrealistic to expect a complete stranger to walk off the street and settle into the house. And the search among existing friends and work colleagues had so far drawn a blank.

But, in the excitement of the wedding, this problem was set aside. Even though it was a small wedding there was still a mountain of preparation involved. The dresses had to be ordered and fitted, the church booked, the cake baked, photographs and transport arranged, flowers chosen and a myriad of small details organised. In an effort to keep down costs, they had decided to hold the reception in a restaurant instead of a hotel. The restaurant was owned by a friend of Adam's and he had agreed to prepare a special meal at a good price and close the premises for the evening so they could have it all to themselves. And then Sophie surprised everyone by offering to bake the wedding cake.

"Are you sure?" Rosie asked with a degree of scepticism.

"Yes. I wouldn't have offered otherwise."

"But you've never done anything this ambitious before," Maddy added.

"There's always a first time for everything. Anyway, it's not that complicated. I've got a family recipe I can work from."

"Sophie, I'm very grateful," Rosie said, taking her hand, "but you really don't have to do this."

"Oh ye of little faith!" Sophie replied, scornfully. "Why don't you just trust me? If you get food poisoning, you can sue."

Rosie's mother was horrified when she heard the news. It was bad enough that the wedding was going to be a small affair held in a restaurant instead of a proper hotel! But to be told that a young slip of a woman who had never done it before was going to bake the wedding cake was the last straw.

"I have to say I'm extremely disappointed," she told Rosie. "You're going to make a show of us all. What will the neighbours think?"

"They can think what they like. Do you have any idea what wedding cakes cost?"

"Your father is prepared to pay."

"Oh, Mum, we've been over this before. We're trying to save money for our new house."

"I'm very annoyed. Adam has hijacked the entire affair. The

bride's mother is supposed to play a central role in her daughter's wedding and I've been sidelined. I'll have no more say than one of the waitresses."

"Don't be like that," Rosie said, soothingly. "You'll get to wear your new outfit and your big hat. You'll be in all the photographs."

"Oh, for God's sake!" Mrs Blake said with disgust. "Why don't you just run away to Gretna Green and have done with it?"

But Sophie was determined to show them she could bake that cake. She at once set about gathering the ingredients – the cherries and sultanas, the currants and raisins, the nuts and butter and sugar. Maddy paid a visit to Munster Road one evening and found her in the kitchen wearing an apron and her face covered in flour as she carefully measured sultanas on a weighing scale while keeping one eye on a handwritten recipe torn from a notebook.

"How's it coming along?" she asked.

"We're getting there," Sophie replied, wiping flour from her face with her elbow. "The tricky bit is going to be the icing. It has to be perfect."

Meanwhile, they had been fitted for their dresses. This was one area where Rosie had insisted on splashing out. The two bridesmaids were in blue satin while Rosie looked stunning in a beautiful dress of white silk with a trim of lace. Next came the rehearsal with the priest so that everybody would know exactly what they had to do and there would be no hitches.

"You've no idea what can go wrong," the young priest, who looked not much older than Adam, told them. "Make sure to bring the ring and for God's sake don't kiss one of the bridesmaids by mistake."

The run-up to the Big Day was spent in a hectic rush of last-minute arrangements. A colleague of Adam's had offered to lend him an old Bentley to ferry the bride to the church. Adam had it decorated with white ribbons and posies of flowers and this went some way to pacifying Mrs Blake. Another friend who played in a rock group agreed to provide the entertainment. But Rosie drew the line when a third friend, who was an amateur photographer, said he would take the wedding photographs.

"No way, José," she said when Adam told her. "This is something we *have* to get right. I don't want the photographs turning out with my mother's head missing. I'd never live it down."

And then, suddenly, the wedding day arrived.

The ceremony was scheduled for two o'clock. Maddy slept till nine, had a light breakfast and shower and then drove to Rosie's home in Glasnevin to find the place in uproar as Mr Blake struggled into his tuxedo and his wife ran around like a demented hen trying to organise half a dozen things at the same time.

"Oh, Maddy, thank God you're here!" she said. "Go at once and get into your dress."

Maddy looked at her watch. It was only midday. But she did as requested and went up to the bedroom to find Sophie, who had arrived by taxi, already wearing her bridesmaid's dress and sipping a glass of champagne.

"Welcome to the madhouse," she said.

"Where's Rosie?"

"In the front parlour with the hair stylist. They decided to separate her from her mother before it ended in a screaming match. C'mon, I'll help you into your dress."

Maddy got into her dress and glanced at herself in the mirror. It fitted perfectly. She was just smoothing out some creases when they heard Mrs Blake shouting up the stairs.

"Are you girls ready yet? The photographer will be here any minute."

Sophie rolled her eyes and finished her champagne.

"Let's go," she said. "Battle is about to commence."

But it all went off smoothly in the end. At a quarter past one, after Mrs Blake's hat and costume had finally been arranged to her satisfaction, the bridal party assembled for photographs. There were pictures of Rosie coming down the stairs, standing in the hall, going back up the stairs again. There were more pictures with Mr Blake and without Mr Blake. There were pictures on the back lawn beside the rose bushes and pictures standing outside the front door. When

Rosie and her mother had at last been photographed from every conceivable angle, everyone piled into taxis and drove to the church to await the arrival of the bride and her father.

Adam was already there with his party, looking smart in their hired suits. The church had been brightly decorated with ribbons and flowers and the small knot of guests huddled together in the front rows while some inquisitive onlookers hovered at the back of the church.

And then the organ swelled out the introductory march and there was Rosie coming down the aisle on the arm of Mr Blake to join her husband-to-be. She looked radiant in her beautiful dress with her bouquet of white roses. Maddy could feel her heart fill up with joy for her friend. But it was tempered by a touch of sadness. This is the second time I've been a bridesmaid, she thought. Will I ever be a bride? And then Mr Blake gave Rosie's hand to Adam and slipped quietly into the front row beside his wife.

The wedding service was over much too quickly and then it was off once again to the restaurant and a champagne reception while the photographer got busy with more pictures. By the time they sat down for the meal, it was five o'clock and Maddy was famished. But she was pleasantly surprised to lift the menu and see the excellent dinner the chef had prepared. There were five courses with plenty of choice for even the most fussy appetite. And the food lived up to expectations. It was far better than many of the meals she had experienced with some of her developer clients who had more money than sense.

When they had finished eating and the dishes had been cleared away, tea and coffee were served and the wedding cake was cut. It had sat throughout the dinner in the place of honour at the top table, a lovely tiered confection topped off with two little figures of a bride and groom. Maddy waited while the cake was passed around the guests. Now the moment of truth had arrived. Would Sophie's cake pass the test?

She watched as Mrs Blake cut a piece with her fork and carefully examined it as if it was a dead mouse. Then she sniffed it and lifted it gingerly to her mouth. Maddy watched and waited as she began to chew. And then a smile spread slowly over Mrs Blake's face. Next moment, she was chomping happily and greedily cutting another piece. All around the table, guests were doing the same thing. Maddy felt her own features break into a smile. She felt like cheering. She looked around for Sophie to share the triumph. But she was nowhere to be found.

She located her at last in the Ladies' room washing her face in the sink.

"Oh, Sophie, where did you go? They've just cut your cake and everybody's delighted with it. It's a big success."

"Well, that's good to know," Sophie said, drying her face with a towel.

Maddy looked closely and saw that her friend's eyes were red where she had been weeping. She put her arm around her.

"Oh, Sophie," she said, "what's the matter with you?"

"I'll be all right. I was just feeling a little down. Weddings do that to me."

"Are you sure you're okay?"

"Yes, I'm sure. I was feeling sorry for myself, that's all."

"Come back to the party," Maddy said. "The band's starting to play. C'mon, let your hair down. Enjoy yourself."

Sophie sniffed, took a deep breath and blinked her eyes. "All right," she said. "Let's boogie."

Maddy arrived home shortly after two, tired after the long day and looking forward to collapsing into her warm bed. As she entered the lounge, she saw that the light on her phone was flashing to tell her she had a message.

She lifted it and heard Jane Morton's voice.

"Maddy, sorry to bother you. Can you contact me as soon as possible? Something important has come up."

Chapter Thirty-five

She decided it was now too late to contact Jane. Besides, she was exhausted. Whatever she had to tell her, could wait until morning. So she got undressed, had a quick shower and snuggled gratefully under the duvet. Five minutes later, she was fast asleep.

The phone dragged her awake at eight o'clock. Still dazed, she groped for the receiver and pressed it to her ear.

"I hope I didn't wake you?" Jane Morton said apologetically.

"It's okay."

"It's just that I wanted to get you before you come into work. You received my message?"

"Yes. I was going to call you."

"Well, there's something going on I think you should know. Is there any chance we could meet somewhere for breakfast?"

"The Orinoco in Baggot Street. I'll see you there in half an hour."

"Excellent," Jane said and put down the phone.

Maddy quickly got showered and dressed. Fifteen minutes later she was on the road and thankfully the traffic was light. She reached the Orinoco Coffee Bar at eight thirty to find Jane already waiting, a steaming latte and a half-eaten Danish pastry on the table before her.

Jane began to apologise. "I'm sorry to drag you here so early, but

I think this is important. The rumour mill is in full throttle and the word is out that the board is about to create a new position of Chief Executive. It will be the highest position in the company."

"And who's the front runner?"

"Tim Lyons."

Maddy felt a dart of disappointment.

"He's been canvassing like crazy. Oh, Maddy, if you want to get this job, you'll have to shake yourself into action. You've got to *do* something."

She sat back in her chair. She felt deflated. Tim Lyons had been her boss for a long time. They had always got on well together. But he was not yet forty and if he got this big job, he would have it forever. She would never climb to the top of Carroll and Shanley.

"I would have no problem with Tim," she said at last. "I like him. He would be good."

"That's not the point," Jane said, getting irritated. "He may be nice but he's not the choice of the staff. And he's another bloody man. What sort of signal does that send out? I think it's demoralising."

"But this isn't a promotional vacancy where you apply and get interviewed. You know they don't work like that."

"Can't you at least let them know that you're interested? We'll support you. Oh, Maddy, if they give the job to Tim Lyons without a fight, people are going to feel terribly disappointed."

Maddy sipped her coffee while she struggled to digest the news. This was what she had tried to avoid – getting dragged into a contest which was bound to cause friction and ill feeling. Carroll and Shanley had always been run like a gentlemen's club. Promotions were made on merit and she had received her fair share over the years. Her career had never suffered. Till now!

"What do you think I should do?"

"Write to the senior partners. Tell them you would like to be considered for the job of Chief Executive. If nothing else, you'll be reminding them that you exist. In the meantime, I'll get to work rallying the troops behind you."

Maddy thought for a few moments. Jane was right. Her inaction could well be interpreted as lack of interest. Maybe she should have canvassed like the others. But had she left it too late?

"Okay," she said. "I'll do it."

Jane Morton's face lit up. "Oh, Maddy, you're a champion. It's time somebody put their foot down. I'm proud of you." She quickly drank her coffee and stood up. "I'm off. I'll get to work straight away. See you later."

Maddy sat on at the table, watching the coffee bar fill up with hungry office workers. She wished old Mr Shanley was still around. She knew he would have supported her. But he was gone now and had no more influence. She knew she was engaged on a high-wire strategy. She was challenging the status quo and, if she lost, things could go terribly wrong. But then, she thought ruefully, if I do nothing and Tim Lyons wins, my career is stalled anyway. What choice do I have?

She paid her bill and drove to the office.

She was greeted by a sea of smiling faces. Jane had obviously wasted no time spreading the word that Maddy was finally pitching for the Chief Executive's job. And from the smiles that she encountered, it was obvious her decision had met with approval. But before she proceeded any further, she had a task to perform.

She opened a drawer and selected a sheet of company notepaper then took out a fountain pen and began.

Dear Sirs,

I wish to be considered for the new position of Chief Executive. I have been with the company for eleven years and in that time, have held a number of senior positions in the Sales division. In addition, I have undertaken various special projects including the marketing of The Wharf development which is now successfully approaching completion.

I have a number of ideas for bringing the company forward and streamlining services and would welcome the opportunity to expand on these at your convenience.

Yours sincerely,
Madeleine Pritchard.

She read the letter over. It seemed fine. Not too presumptive or arrogant. She folded it and slipped it into an envelope.

As luck would have it, she had a meeting scheduled for ten with Mick McCann and Annie McNamara, the young media advisor she had hired to give The Wharf a final publicity push. Annie was bubbling over with bright plans for radio and television exposure built around Marco O'Malley. Maddy welcomed the opportunity to escape from the office. The temperature was going to turn up a few degrees when word got around that she had now thrown her hat in the ring.

The meeting had been arranged for McCann's offices in Donnybrook. She arrived to find Annie already there, her face aglow with excitement.

"I've got Marco on the *Late Late Show*," she announced as soon as Maddy sat down. "How's that for a coup?"

"My God, Annie, that's fantastic. They get enormous viewing figures. Well done."

"They want to talk to him about his career and his new restaurant at The Wharf. They've asked permission to do some filming with him on the site. I hope that's okay?"

"Of course, it's okay," Mick McCann said, barely able to contain his delight. "I just hope he doesn't attack Gay Byrne with a carving knife like he did with that other poor bugger."

"I thought all that stuff was made up?" Annie said, looking horrified. "He's not violent, is he?"

McCann was grinning. "Ask Maddy. She's the one he's taken a shine to."

"Marco O'Malley is a perfect gentleman," Maddy replied. "Unless someone criticises his cooking. Incidentally, has anybody told him yet?"

Annie shook her head. "I was leaving that to you."

"All right, I'll talk to him. Now what else have you got?"

Annie passed round a sheet of paper with a list of radio and newspaper interviews she had lined up for the coming weeks with Marco and McCann.

"I'm aiming for saturation coverage. At the end of this campaign,

I don't want there to be a single person in Ireland who hasn't heard of The Wharf."

McCann was beaming. "That's perfect," he said. "Now, what about advertising?"

"All organised," Maddy said. "We've taken full-page ads in all the property supplements to be accompanied by editorial write-ups and interviews. They're set to run in two weeks' time."

"Excellent," McCann said, bringing the meeting to a close. "With this level of publicity, we might manage to sell all the apartments straight off the plans. That would be a record, I think."

On her way out of the building, Maddy contacted Marco on her mobile phone to tell him about the *Late Late Show* appearance.

"Are you comfortable with it?" she asked. "This is major exposure. Annie is prepared to coach you if you like."

"My dear young woman," Marco replied, "do you mean to insult me?"

"I don't understand," Maddy said, growing apprehensive.

"I don't require any coaching. I'm a natural television personality. I will take this in my stride like all my endeavours. I shall simply be myself."

Maddy switched off her mobile and burst out laughing. Marco O'Malley was irrepressible. Thank God they had him back on board.

On her way back to work, she stopped off for a quick bite of lunch. By now, word about her decision to apply for the job would have circulated. But she was unprepared for the reception that awaited her. She had barely sat down at her desk when Tim Lyons came out of his office. She looked up and smiled. But Tim simply stared at her as if he was looking through a pane of glass. Then he lowered his head and without any sign of acknowledgment, strode purposefully past. It was as if she didn't exist.

Worse was to come. For the next few days, the tension in the office was so thick you could cut it with a knife. People kept their heads down and avoided eye contact. The gossiping around the water-cooler came to an abrupt halt. People were afraid to be marked down as conspirators. Any talk about the succession race was confined to out-of-doors and as far away from the office as possible.

By now, Tim Lyons was totally ignoring her which made her working life extremely difficult. Their few contacts were conducted in a frosty atmosphere and consisted of monosyllabic questions and responses. He was treating her as if she was a deadly enemy instead of a loyal colleague. Maddy was amazed. It was as if he had changed overnight into a completely different person. She couldn't believe that a man she had liked and admired for so long could behave like this. But his reaction convinced her that her decision was right. If this was how he treated her simply for applying for the job, then God knew how he would behave if he was appointed Chief Executive.

She tried to stay away from the office as much as possible while she waited for the summons to put her case to the board. Meanwhile, she prepared an outline of her plans to expand and improve the company. She intended to have it printed and bound and to present a copy to each member when she was called to interview. But the summons never came.

Instead, Jane Morton rang her one day and requested an urgent meeting.

"We've got to talk. There have been developments."

"Okay. Where do you want to meet?"

"Somewhere far from the office. There's a pub in College Street called Doyle's. I'll see you in the back snug in half an hour."

"Right," Maddy said. "I'll be there."

Doyle's pub was across the road from Trinity College and she found it easily. She had barely entered when the door opened and Jane arrived, out of breath.

"This is getting ridiculous," Maddy said, as her friend plumped down beside her. "I'm beginning to feel like Mata Hari."

"Well, it's better to be safe than sorry. The secret police are everywhere," said Jane with a tight smile. "Now which do you want to hear first, the good news or the bad news?"

"The good news, of course."

"Well, by my reckoning you've got the support of 75% of the sales staff. And not just the women – a lot of the men are supporting you too. It wasn't easy but I managed to canvass all of them."

This cheered Maddy up.

"I can't be so certain about the managers because I didn't dare approach them directly. But I believe about half of them are behind you too."

"That's fantastic news, Jane. I'm really grateful."

"You haven't heard the bad news yet."

"Go ahead."

Jane pursed her lips and slowly let the air escape. "You've made a deadly enemy in Tim Lyons."

"I knew that already. He hasn't spoken to me for days."

"But do you know *how* deadly? He's blaming you for queering his pitch. He seems to think that if you hadn't declared, he would have strolled into the job. And your intervention has revealed how little support he actually has among the staff which makes his task more difficult."

"Well, there's arrogance for you," Maddy said.

"He's also going round the office bad-mouthing you."

"*What?*"

Jane was slowly nodding her head. "It's true. He's telling people you're lazy and incompetent, that you've been promoted above your ability and that you rub clients up the wrong way. He says you had a flaming row with Mick McCann that almost cost the company The Wharf contract."

Maddy's jaw dropped. This was incredible. She couldn't believe that Tim Lyons would stoop to say things which were so patently untrue.

"Are you sure, Jane?"

"Positive. I heard him myself. He says if by any miracle you managed to get the promotion, you'd close the business in a matter of months and they'd all be out of a job. He says several major clients are already threatening to withdraw their business if you're made Chief Executive."

Maddy gasped. "These are lies. I did have a row with McCann, that's true. But only because he got abusive. Now we're working well together. I had a productive meeting with him only a few days ago."

"I know they're lies. But Tim Lyons thinks he's being clever. He's trying to frighten people and they're nervous enough as it is. People don't like change. It makes them unsettled. And naturally they're concerned about their jobs."

"I'll talk to the staff myself. I'll reassure them. Maybe I should have taken your advice and done it weeks ago."

"No," Jane counselled. "Don't do that. You run the risk of a confrontation and that won't do any good. Then he'll be able to say you're a hysterical woman who can't stand pressure."

"But I can't just sit idly by while he spreads lies about me. I have to do something."

"Stay aloof," Jane counselled, "and let me handle it. People know you, Maddy. They know you're solid and reliable. And most of all, they know you care about them. My hunch is that Tim Lyons will do his case more harm than good if he goes on like this."

But Maddy couldn't stay aloof. The more she thought about the lies Tim Lyons was spreading, the angrier she became. On her way back to the office she decided to ring Mick McCann. He came on the line sounding stressed.

"We've run into a problem," he said. "A delivery of bathroom fittings hasn't arrived."

"Is it serious?" she asked.

"No. They'll turn up. It's just more hassle, that's all. Now what can I do for you?"

"I've got a favour to ask."

"Shoot."

"I've applied for a promotion and I'm looking for references. I wonder if you could find the time to scribble something on my behalf."

She could hear McCann laughing on the line.

"It's going to cost you a glass of champers the next time we meet."

"Write me the right reference and I'll buy you the whole bottle," Maddy replied.

"Okay, I'll fax it over. I'll do it right away."

The reference was waiting with Marina when she got back to the office. Maddy took it eagerly and scanned it.

TO WHOM IT MAY CONCERN

I have had the good fortune to work with Ms Madeleine Pritchard on the sale and marketing of The Wharf development in Dublin's docklands.

Ms Pritchard has worked closely with me from the inception of the project. I have found her assistance invaluable. She has been innovative, imaginative and extremely hardworking. In addition, there have been crucial situations where I have relied heavily on her advice and professional guidance. At all times I have found her totally reliable.

My working relations with Ms Pritchard have always been extremely cordial. She has an easy-going nature which commands trust and respect. Indeed it is no exaggeration to say that without her assistance I doubt if The Wharf would have turned into the successful development it has now become.

Sincerely,

Michael McCann,
Managing Director,
McCann Construction Ltd

Maddy's face glowed as she read the reference. Mick McCann had turned up trumps. She couldn't have come up with a better reference if she had written it herself. This would surely silence Tim Lyons.

She took a copy and attached it to a note for Jane Morton telling her to use the reference at her discretion as evidence of Maddy's good relations with McCann. Then she gathered herself together and marched to the top of the room and knocked on the door of Tim Lyons' office. Heads looked up to stare as she went by.

The moment he saw her, his face broke into a scowl.

"Yes?" he said, in a voice as cold as ice.

"You and I have got to talk," Maddy said.

Lyons showed only disdain. "I've got nothing to say to you."

"Well, I've got plenty to say to you. I understand you have been going around this office spreading lies about me."

"Oh? Have you got witnesses?"

"Yes, I have, as a matter of fact. I would remind you that what you're saying is a slander on my character. I want you to understand that if you continue I will have no option but to take legal proceedings against you."

At these words, something approaching fear entered his face.

"This is ridiculous," he said.

"Is it? I wonder if the board would share your view. I'm certain they wouldn't welcome the bad publicity."

She took the reference she had received and put it down on his desk.

"That's from Mick McCann and it speaks for itself. I can get others if I want. You know what you said about me are blatant lies. You know I have always worked faithfully and diligently for this company. You know I have given one hundred per cent to any job you've asked me to do."

"You betrayed me," he said, bitterly.

"Betrayed you?" Maddy said, scarcely believing her ears.

"I've always been fair to you. You know how much I've wanted this job. And I would have walked away with it if you hadn't decided to interfere."

"So, I'm supposed to restrain my career because you're a man?"

"A *married* man," Tim Lyons corrected her. "With a young family to support. You're a single woman. You don't need this job. I do."

"My marital status has got absolutely nothing to do with this. I have my life to live the same as you. And I'm fully entitled to apply for any job I feel qualified for without having my character assassinated behind my back."

By now, Maddy was trembling with rage.

"I had hoped we could have conducted this competition with a degree of civility," she said. "But I am warning you. If I hear one more word of slander from you, you'll be hearing from my solicitor."

She turned on her heel and walked back to her desk as calmly as she could manage. A deathly silence followed her down the room. Her relationship with Tim Lyons had now erupted into open warfare. But Maddy had little time to think about it.

Sophie was about to drop a bombshell in her lap.

Chapter Thirty-six

Since Arthur Brady's last drinking bout, Sophie had been behaving strangely. She could still reveal flashes of her old happy-go-lucky style but increasingly her mood had turned morbid and depressed. Arthur appeared to be making serious efforts to keep sober but it didn't seem to matter any more. Something had altered between them and Maddy began to fear that the relationship was doomed. But she kept her thoughts to herself.

She hated to see her friend like this. There were many occasions when she longed to take her aside and have a good heart-to-heart talk. It was what they would have done in the old days. But Sophie had also become withdrawn and the few attempts that Maddy made, met with resistance. So she decided to leave her alone. If Sophie wanted to talk, she knew where to come.

But she was totally surprised to return from work one evening to find her friend waiting for her on the doorstep.

"Sophie," she said, "It's good to see you. Have you eaten yet?"

"I won't be staying," Sophie replied, a little defensively.

"Well, at least come and have a glass of wine on the patio. It's nice and sunny out there."

"Okay," she replied, without much enthusiasm.

"Now," Maddy said, once they were seated and she had uncorked a bottle of chilled Chardonnay "to what do I owe this unexpected pleasure?"

"I'm leaving," Sophie said.

Maddy stopped in the act of pouring the wine and put down the glass.

"Leaving? You don't have to do that," she said, quickly. "We'll find someone suitable to replace Rosie. It's only a matter of time."

"You don't understand," Sophie said, staring at the ground. "I'm leaving the country. I'm going to London."

Maddy was shocked. She looked closely at her friend. She hadn't realised she was thinking like this.

"Why? You've a perfectly good job. I thought you enjoyed it."

"I do enjoy it."

"So why are you leaving? What does Arthur think?"

"Arthur and me are finished," she said, looking up into Maddy's face. "That's one of the reasons I'm going."

Maddy immediately put her arm around her friend and drew her close.

"Oh Sophie, why didn't you tell me all this was going on? We could have talked."

"I didn't feel like talking. And anyway, there's nothing you could have done. These things happen. *You* know that." She gave Maddy a sorrowful glance.

"How is Arthur taking it?"

"Not well."

"He's not drinking again?"

"No, thank God."

"I still don't understand. Breaking up isn't a cause to turn your whole life upside down. You could stay in Dublin. You've got the house. We'll find a replacement for Rosie. And I've no doubt you'll find another boyfriend if that's what you want."

But Sophie was shaking her head. "I need a clean break. I want to get away and start afresh. I haven't been happy for some time, Maddy."

"I noticed. And I wanted to say something. But you didn't seem to welcome it."

"You had your own troubles."

"I wouldn't have minded. You know I'm always here for you."

"Yes."

"Is there any chance you could hold off for a while? Maybe things will improve."

"No," Sophie said. "Things won't improve. It's not just Arthur. It's me. I need to get away."

"So you can't be persuaded?"

"No," Sophie said, gazing down the garden at the flowers. "My mind is made up."

Sophie's announcement left Maddy with a feeling that the ground was shifting beneath her feet. In the last few months so many things had happened to shatter the cosy consistency of her life. It seemed like only yesterday that they had all been together, happy in their various ways and the future had looked bright and promising. Now she was surrounded by uncertainty and doubt. And it had all happened with the speed of lightning.

Two days later, Sophie phoned to say she would be leaving Munster Road the following weekend. She had been busy on the phone and had secured several job interviews. One in particular interested her. It was for a marketing position with a travel company that specialised in skiing holidays and she thought she had a good chance of getting it.

Rosie rang later in the afternoon.

"You've heard all the gory details, I suppose?"

"Yes. And I don't know what to say."

"It's what she wants. Maybe she just needs to get this out of her system. But I've been thinking – we'll have to give her a proper send-off. She's having a farewell party at work but it's not the same. I was thinking we should organise something special, just the three of us."

"That's a great idea. Have you got anything in mind?"

"How about a surprise dinner party?"

"That's brilliant, Rosie. We can have it here at Auburn Grove. I'll cook."

"She's leaving on Saturday afternoon. Why don't we have it on Friday night? I can distract her while you get everything ready and then we'll call on some pretext and surprise her."

"That's perfect. I'll get working on it right away."

Over the next few days, Sophie began the task of clearing her belongings out of Munster Road. In the short time she had lived there, she had gathered an awful lot of possessions and it took several journeys in her brother's car to transport all the boxes of clothes and books and records back to her parents' home. When she had finally packed the last box, the two women got busy cleaning the place.

"It seems like only a few weeks ago you were moving in," Maddy remarked. "Doesn't time fly?"

"Tell me about it," Sophie said. "Sometimes it frightens me."

She stopped and looked around the empty bedroom.

"You know, I was very happy here. I wonder if I'll ever be so happy again."

"Of course, you will. You're going through a bad patch. But you'll come out of it."

Sophie looked glum. "I wish I felt so confident."

"Oh, Sophie, you will. It's only in the movies that people are happy all the time."

"*You* seem to be making a pretty good job of it."

"Don't be fooled. I have my black periods too."

"Really?" Sophie said and bent once more to the cleaning.

At last, Maddy received the call for interview. She had begun to wonder if she would ever get the opportunity to put her case to the board. Her letter had obviously thrown them into confusion. But she came into work one morning to find an envelope bearing the company's logo among her internal post. She quickly opened it and read the letter. It was a simple two-line statement signed by the company secretary.

Miss Madeleine Pritchard,
The directors of Carroll and Shanley would be obliged if you would attend
for interview in the boardroom on Thursday next at 2.30 p.m.

She felt relieved. At last the process was moving to some kind of conclusion. It had already gone on too long. Since her confrontation with Tim Lyons, the atmosphere between them had become poisonous. But at least she had put a stop to his campaign of lies against her, and Jane Morton had been busy countering his slanders by showing people the glowing reference from Mick McCann.

Maddy had prepared well for the interview and had her presentation neatly typed up and bound in a handsome folder. She decided not to go into work that morning because the tension would be unbearable. So she put on her running gear and went for a brisk jog to clear her head. Then she had a relaxing shower and got dressed in a sober business suit and white blouse before driving to the office.

Word of the interview had obviously got around because everywhere she looked she saw smiling, encouraging faces. That cheered her up. Maddy knew this was a momentous day for her. Her entire career hinged on the half-hour she would spend with the elderly male panel who would be her interrogators. In those thirty minutes she would have to convince them to change the tradition of a lifetime and appoint a woman to the most senior position in Carroll and Shanley. It would be no easy task.

But it was with a confident step that she made her way to the boardroom at 2.28 p.m. and knocked politely on the door. A voice instructed her to enter.

Four men sat around a large mahogany table and stared at her for a moment. Then one of them smiled.

"Miss Pritchard, you're right on time. Would you care to take a seat?"

He was a small wizened man called Mr Peters. He indicated the vacant chair which awaited her and Maddy sat down while Mr Peters quickly introduced the other board members.

"Now," he continued, "you've requested an opportunity to talk to us about the future of the company after Mr Shanley's retirement and how you see us going forward. We're all ears, Miss Pritchard. You may begin when you're ready."

Maddy began to speak in a strong, steady voice.

"First of all, I'd like to thank you for agreeing to see me. I'm very grateful that you have given me your time. I have outlined my views in this presentation which I will presently expand on."

She gave each member of the interview panel her bound folder and for the next fifteen minutes, took them through it point by point. She talked of the need for the company to open new branches, to establish a lettings division for the growing rental market and to develop the foothold they had gained in the commercial and office sector through their involvement with Mick McCann and The Wharf development.

Throughout her presentation, they listened to her politely. Some of them nodded in agreement from time to time while others maintained an inscrutable silence. Undeterred, Maddy finished off on a rousing note.

"I think Carroll and Shanley are faced with massive challenges. The market is changing dramatically. The economy is booming and the population is growing. There will be a huge demand for property in the coming years. If we are ready for these challenges and prepare ourselves well, we can benefit enormously and consolidate our position. I am confident that I have the resources and the skill to lead the company into the future if you can see your way to appointing me as Chief Executive."

She finished and sat back in her chair. She thought she had done well. Mr Peters spoke again.

"Thank you, Miss Pritchard. That was a masterful presentation. I found myself in complete agreement with everything you had to say." He turned to his colleagues. "Now, has anyone any questions to ask?"

There was silence for a moment and then a thin, balding man with a pale, narrow face cleared his throat. His name was Mr O'Reilly.

"Miss Pritchard, do you mind if I enquire about your marital status?"

Maddy blinked. For the life of her, she couldn't understand the relevance of the question.

"I'm single," she replied.

"And do you have the intention of getting married in the foreseeable future?"

She felt like laughing at the absurdity of the query. "No."

"But that might change? You might decide to get married?"

"I don't know what might happen."

"You see, Miss Pritchard, I'm wondering what would occur if you were married and had a husband and children to attend to. How would you be able to carry on your work as Chief Executive? It would be almost impossible, don't you think?"

Now she could see the drift of his question. As far as Mr O'Reilly was concerned, her rightful position was at home nursing her babies and cooking her husband's dinner and not running a busy auctioneering business.

"I suppose I would have to cross that bridge when I came to it," she said with a tight smile.

"And what if you were to get pregnant?" A red blush enveloped Mr O'Reilly's face at the mention of the word. "You would require considerable time off work, would you not?"

This is getting ludicrous, Maddy thought, as she struggled to maintain a smile.

"Should the circumstance arise, I'm sure we could come to a suitable arrangement," she replied.

But Mr O'Reilly had opened up a rich seam. Another member, Mr Hynes, interjected with a further question.

"Ms Pritchard, do you think you're temperamentally suited for this position?"

"How do you mean?"

"This will be an extremely stressful job. There are a lot of instant decisions to be made, a large staff to run and long hours to work. It's a lot of pressure for a woman to bear. Would your nerves be up to it?"

"But I do all that already. I've been in charge of the sales team for several years. I think I have demonstrated that I'm quite capable of handling stress. I've been personally overseeing The Wharf development at Mr Lyons's request and you'll find a recommendation from the developer included in my presentation."

At the mention of Tim Lyons's name, the remaining panel member, a middle-aged man, called Mr Murphy, piped up.

"Miss Pritchard, Mr Lyons is presently your immediate supervisor. If you were appointed to this position, that situation would be reversed. You would be his superior. Do you think he might find it a bit awkward to take direction from a woman?"

Maddy was running out of patience with this stupid insistence on her gender. Not one member of the board had so far asked a single question about her presentation.

"I think Mr Lyons would have to answer that question for himself," she replied with all the tact she could muster.

"Quite," Mr Murphy said but before he could continue Mr Peters quickly intervened.

"I have no doubt that Miss Pritchard would bring to the position of Chief Executive all the energy and skill which she has so far demonstrated in her career. Now unless there are further questions, I'm sure she'll be anxious to get back to her desk."

The three faces stared mute across the table.

"No further questions? In that case, we will bring matters to a close. Thank you very much for giving us your very interesting views, Miss Pritchard. You'll be hearing from us presently."

Friday arrived and Maddy hurried off from work to prepare the surprise dinner party for Sophie. She had no illusions that she could cook as well as her friend so she wasn't going to waste any time trying. Instead, on her way home, she called into a deli in Ranelagh and bought some smoked salmon and cooked prawns and three generous portions of chicken goulash and little tubs of basmati rice and ratatouille. For dessert, she decided to purchase a chocolate layer cake which she knew Sophie would appreciate. To round off, she bought four bottles of a white Italian wine which was on special offer. The salad she would make herself.

The plan they had agreed was that Rosie would pick Sophie up after her office farewell party and bring her back to Auburn Grove on the pretext of collecting a reference from Maddy in case she needed one for accommodation in London. The party was due to finish around eight which meant she could have Sophie at Maddy's place for eight thirty.

So as soon as Maddy got home, she set about arranging everything. She set the dining-table, placed the candles, put an *Abba* tape on the music player and left several bottles of wine in the fridge to cool. Then she went off to get ready. She had just finished dressing when she heard Rosie's car give two honks which was the signal to tell her they had arrived. She rushed down the stairs and flung open the door to find Rosie and a slightly inebriated Sophie standing on the doorstep.

"Come in," she said. "The wine is chilling, the goulash is heating and your starter of smoked salmon, brown bread and prawn salad is on the table."

Sophie stared uncomprehending. "What are you talking about? I've come to pick up my reference."

"I have it ready," Maddy responded. "But first we're having a little dinner party. Just the three of us."

"But . . . but . . ."

"Oh Sophie, you didn't think we were really going to allow our poor emigrant to brave the wild ocean without saying a proper goodbye, now did you? Come in, you eejit, and don't be standing there."

In a gale of laughter, she pulled Sophie inside, took her coat and bundled her into the dining-room where the lights had been dimmed and the candles glowed invitingly and the sound of *Waterloo* was thumping out of the sound system.

"Now just sit down and I'll pour you a glass of wine. How did your party go?"

"It was brilliant. The boss made a speech and said such nice things about me that I felt like tearing up my resignation letter. Then we all headed for the pub where they tried very hard to get me locked. But listen, you didn't have to go to all this trouble, you know."

"Not another word," Rosie commanded. "Sit down and eat."

For the next couple of hours they sat around the table and talked about old times and reminisced about their first weeks in Auburn Grove.

"Remember the time you burnt the kettle?" Maddy said. "I don't think you paid me for that."

"That was Rosie. And it wasn't a kettle. It was a pot."

"Was it?" Maddy said, bursting out laughing. "I can't even recall."

"Remember your first dinner party?" Rosie added. "How nervous you were?"

"I can remember it," Maddy said. "Jane Morton said it was the best meal she had ever eaten."

"She was just being polite," Sophie said.

"No, she wasn't," Rosie added. "She was right. That's when I decided I just had to move in here."

"I'm going to miss you guys," Sophie said, her eyes misting over. "You've been the best pals any girl could ever have."

"We're only a phone call away," Maddy said. "And you can nip back to Dublin any time you feel like it. There'll always be a bed for you here."

"I feel so sad."

Maddy could see the big tears waiting to fall. Sophie had lately been given to bouts of weeping, so she put her arms around her and hugged her close.

"You'll survive and you'll be stronger. I'll never forget you, Sophie. We shared a lot together. Good times and bad times."

Rosie was busy filling up their glasses.

"A toast," she declared. "Forever friends! May we survive and prosper wherever we go."

Maddy looked at the faces of her two best friends. She wished she had a camera handy so she could freeze this moment in time.

"Forever friends! May nothing ever come between us."

They raised the glasses and drank.

On Saturday morning, Maddy was feeling jaded so she had a late lie-in, then cleaned the house, went for a jog and ate the remains of the chicken goulash for supper while she watched an old black and white movie on television. On Sunday, she drove across to Raheny for lunch where Mrs Pritchard gently probed her for indications that she had found a replacement beau for Greg and a possible husband. And so the weekend passed.

Then on Monday morning she went into work to find a statement pinned on the bulletin board. It was a brief one-sentence announcement. It said that Mr Tim Lyons had been appointed to the newly created position of Chief Executive of Carroll and Shanley to take effect forthwith.

Chapter Thirty-seven

"The whole thing was a bloody fix from start to finish," a furious Jane Morton exploded when they managed to escape for a coffee shortly after eleven o'clock. "They never had the slightest intention of giving you that job. That interview was just a con-job to humour you."

Maddy simply nodded. She was feeling bitterly disappointed even though she had known since the interview that things were not looking hopeful. But she didn't want Jane to know just how badly she felt.

"Well, they've just made a big mistake," Jane continued. "I always thought Tim Lyons was a decent man till all this happened. Then he revealed himself in his true colours, going around the office spreading lies about you. That shows just how ruthless he is."

"Maybe they wanted somebody ruthless. The business is getting tougher every day, Jane."

"But there are civilised rules of behaviour. You can conduct business without being a sneak and a liar. Is the property industry going to become a jungle? I'll tell you one thing. I'll never feel the same way about Tim Lyons again." Jane angrily stirred her coffee.

"Don't be upset," Maddy said.

"I'm sorry, Maddy! We did our best but sometimes the good guys don't win."

Maddy reached out and stroked her colleague's arm. "You've got nothing to be sorry for. You stuck by me and you worked your tail off on my behalf. I will always appreciate what you did."

"So what are you going to do, now?"

"What can I do? I'll just have to accept it and move on."

"Well, let me give you one piece of advice. I'd watch Lyons if I was you. He may have won the top job but he still sees you as a threat and I wouldn't be surprised if he makes life difficult for you."

By now, the news of Tim Lyons' promotion was all over the office. There was relief that the long contest was finally over, mixed with disappointment for Maddy. Throughout the day, several colleagues came to her desk to offer their condolences but she was also surprised at the number of people who avoided her. A new regime was in place and some people had obviously decided there was nothing to be gained by continuing to associate with a loser.

Now she had to face the reality of working for a man who saw her as a rival, a man who had once been a friend but had told her he regarded her as a traitor. After everything that had happened between them, it was not going to be easy. She had to endure the humiliating spectacle of colleagues trooping into Tim Lyons' office to be told of their new responsibilities and emerging with beaming faces while she sat alone at her desk like a contagious patient in an isolation ward.

She knew that her career would advance no further. Tim Lyons was not yet forty and would probably stay as Chief Executive till he retired. The time had not yet arrived for a woman to be appointed to the senior position in Carroll and Shanley. In the days that followed, these hard realities began to sink in and she found herself growing increasingly unsettled.

But at least she had her work at The Wharf to keep her occupied. Construction was almost completed and only the four penthouses and the highest apartments remained to be finished. Marco O'Malley had appeared on the *Late Late Show* and as Maddy anticipated, he had the audience rolling with laughter as he recounted tales of his restaurant experiences and the famous personalities he had entertained. It was a huge success and taken together with Annie McNamara's publicity push, it resulted in the sale of the remaining penthouse and a further thirty apartments.

Suddenly, there was a clamour for units as tardy purchasers woke up to the fact that The Wharf was going to be *the* place to live in Dublin. Each day, Maddy fielded a dozen or more enquiries but by now all the best apartments – those fronting onto the river – had been snapped up. Some of them were even changing hands for increased sums as canny speculators sold on for a profit. And this was happening before the development was even finished. It prompted Mick McCann to suggest one day that they should increase the price of the remaining fifty apartments.

"No," Maddy said emphatically. "That is *not* a good idea."

"But why shouldn't I get the profit instead of some bloody investor?" McCann argued. "I'm the one who took the risk. I'm the person put in the work. I'm the one who had the imagination to develop the scheme in the first place."

"Because it will be bad PR," Maddy said. "We've built up a good head of steam with Annie's publicity campaign and Marco's TV appearances. We've leased all the shops and sold the bulk of the apartments. If you start jacking up the prices you'll undo all that good work."

"I don't see why," McCann argued. "People are burning up the phone lines trying to get their hands on them. Why shouldn't I charge more?"

"It will cause resentment. People will believe they've been conned. They'll be living beside someone who paid maybe £20,000 or £30,000 less for the same apartment. How would you feel?"

"But that's the market. Supply and demand."

"Listen to me," Maddy said. "You have to think long-term. You set out to build your signature development. And you've succeeded beyond your wildest dreams. You've carved out a reputation. Don't throw it away for short-term gain."

McCann scratched his chin and Maddy could see how greed was warring with his better instincts.

"Remember what happened the last time?" she continued. "When you wanted to build more apartments on the site? You nearly scuttled the whole development. I warned you then and you wouldn't listen. Don't make the same mistake again."

The developer shook his head and let out a loud sigh. "Dammit, Maddy, there's times I wonder about you. I hired you to help me sell these apartments, not to cost me money."

"And that's what I'm doing," she smiled. "Now take my advice like a good man and put this silly notion out of your head."

Their immediate attention was now focussed on the opening of Marco's restaurant. He was very excited and wanted it to be a gala affair with loads of famous faces. Maddy and Annie had enthusiastically endorsed his view. This could be a publicity godsend that would help them sell the last remaining apartments.

"I'll design a special menu," Marco trilled. "We'll spare no expense. We'll have lobster and pâté de fois gras, of course. Venison if I can manage to get my hands on some. We'll have partridge, pheasant, hare, salmon and the finest French wines!"

Maddy found herself smiling at Marco's wild enthusiasm.

"How much is this going to cost?" she asked, innocently.

"Who cares?" Marco said, flinging his plump arms wide in a dismissive gesture. "This is to be a banquet fit for royalty. If Marie Antoinette was coming you wouldn't quibble at the cost, would you?"

"If Marie Antoinette was coming, we would have a real publicity coup since she's been dead for two hundred years," Maddy replied. "But Mick McCann might have some things to say."

But when she put the idea to him, McCann surprised her by heartily agreeing to Marco's plan. Recently she had noticed a definite thaw in the relations between the two men. They had even started speaking to each other again.

"I think that's a wonderful idea. And it will be a fitting way to crown our achievement. There are a few politicians I want to invite and some of my old pals in the construction industry. I'll give you the list when I get a chance."

Marco got to work designing the menu which he insisted would have to be printed up in a special presentation package while Maddy and Annie bent their energies to the guest list. The restaurant was capable of seating a hundred and twenty diners but once they started considering guests, they soon realised they would have no difficulty filling it several times over.

"There are some people we really must have," Annie said, mentioning the names of several well-known actors and performers. "These people will draw the paparazzi and at the end of the day, this is partly what it's about."

Maddy was happy to bow to Annie's superior knowledge in this area. Annie knew who was in and out in the world of entertainment and fashion. But Maddy also wanted the property writers invited, particularly Paula Matthews.

"These people have stood by us through thick and thin," she said. "It would be unforgivable if we left them out."

"I agree. Just give me their names and I'll make sure they get on the list."

At their first attempt, the list came to over two hundred names and more were being added every day. Mick McCann's list alone included thirty people and Marco had added another forty.

"We're going to have to reduce this," Annie said. "There's no way we can cater for so many. And besides, we don't want the restaurant looking like Croke Park on All-Ireland Sunday. Let's begin again."

At the second attempt they got the list down to one hundred and forty which was still too many but might be manageable. The people who were excluded were then added to a reserve list in case anyone dropped out.

The invitations were duly printed up and despatched but even Annie was surprised at the take-up. Every day, news came in of celebrity acceptances and these were carefully leaked to the media so that there was a constant trickle of favourable publicity which quickly grew into a flood. Within a week, it became obvious that the restaurant opening had become the hottest ticket in town. And that's when the trouble began.

One morning, Maddy got a call at work from a suave male voice she didn't recognise.

"Miss Pritchard?"

"Yes," Maddy replied.

"I was told you were the person I should speak to. My invitation to the opening of Mr O'Malley's restaurant doesn't appear to have arrived."

"Oh," Maddy said. "Who am I speaking to?"

The man gave his name. He was a well-known politician, famous for his publicity-grabbing activities. The joke around town was that he would turn up for the opening of a Christmas card.

"I'm not actually handling the invitations," she explained.

"I was told you were. You see, I don't wish to offend Marco. He's a dear friend. I wouldn't want him to think I had snubbed him on his big occasion."

"Can you leave it with me?" she said. "I'll look into it."

But when she inquired of Marco she was surprised at the vehemence of his response.

"If that bollocks turns up, I'll personally run him off the premises!" he exploded with ire. "He's the biggest freeloader in town. I had to bar him from the Chalet d'Or for cadging free grub."

"Right," Maddy said. "So you don't expect to see him at the opening?"

"Not unless he wants to get a meat cleaver imbedded in his skull."

"I don't think that's the kind of publicity we're aiming for," she said and put down the phone.

Suddenly, everyone wanted an invitation to the opening and both Maddy and Annie were inundated with requests. But by now, the guest list was vastly oversubscribed and the reserve list was overflowing. Short of the President seeking an invite, there was no possibility of accommodating any more people.

Of course, Marco was delirious at the publicity. He was in constant demand for television and radio interviews. Newspaper reporters and gossip columnists were falling over themselves to get quotes so that Maddy wondered how he found the time to put the finishing touches to his restaurant *and* prepare his gala dinner. But he seemed to thrive on it.

So did Mick McCann. The razzmatazz had succeeded in shifting the remaining apartments which meant The Wharf had managed to sell all the units right off the plans. Paula Matthews duly marked this unprecedented achievement in a large half-page interview with McCann, complete with photograph, and proceeded to dub him Developer of the Year, a title that greatly pleased him.

A few days later, he invited Maddy and Annie to dinner to celebrate.

"I'm absolutely delighted with you guys," he said, as they sipped champagne in the corner of a fashionable bistro in Baggot Street. "You handled the PR like a dream. Imagine selling all the units before the development is even finished. Nobody has ever done that before. It's an unprecedented record."

"It would have to be if it's unprecedented," Maddy replied with a grin.

The developer scowled.

"You know what I mean," he said. "It's never been done before."

"You should give yourself a pat on the back," she said.

"But it was *your* idea to include the commercial development. And it was a stroke of genius to get Marco involved. I've taken the liberty of writing to Tim Lyons to tell him how pleased I am with your work."

At the mention of Tim Lyons' name, Maddy's face clouded over.

"Oh?" Mick said. "Did I do the wrong thing?"

"Not at all. A good word never goes astray."

"And I'll let you guys into a secret. Now that The Wharf is almost finished I'm thinking about another project. Even bigger and more ambitious, three hundred apartments, this time. And I'm going to appoint Carroll and Shanley sole marketing agents."

"When do you expect to start work?" Maddy asked.

"In six to nine months' time. It's all supposed to be hush-hush so I'm trusting you to keep it to yourselves. But after the success of The Wharf, I expect big things."

Maddy left the dinner with a warm feeling. Since their bust-up, Mick and her had been getting along together like a house on fire. He was a handsome man *and* he was single. She let the thought play around in her head as she drove home to Ranelagh with a smile on her face and a cosy feeling tugging at her heart-strings.

As the evening of Marco's restaurant launch approached, the atmosphere came to resemble the awards ceremony at the Oscars. The story had now taken on a life of its own. Every day brought fresh reports about whom was supposed to be attending, who would be accompanying who and what sort of dress they'd be wearing. One gossip columnist even printed what he claimed was an exclusive scoop of the menu which later turned out to be a hoax planted by a rival columnist.

The day before the event Maddy spent a hectic afternoon at the restaurant with Marco and Mick as they tried to reach agreement on the seating plan. But what had the potential to turn into a screaming match eventually went off very smoothly and Marco rounded off the occasion by pouring McCann a bumper glass of a rare brandy while the two men clasped each other and toasted the success of the venture.

Maddy eventually arrived home with thoughts of the gala dinner foremost in her mind. Unlike many functions she had to attend in the line of duty, this was one event she was really looking forward to. She had her outfit selected – an off-the-shoulder white silk evening dress which she had purchased in the January sales. She would wear it with a silver lamé stole.

And tomorrow afternoon at three she had an appointment with her hairdresser. The dinner would be a fitting climax to months of hard work that had occasionally caused her blood pressure to soar and sometimes threatened to sever her professional relationship with Mick McCann. But now she had an overwhelming feeling that it had all been worthwhile.

Little did she now realise as she ran her bath and looked forward to a relaxing evening, that when tomorrow came she would *not* be attending the gala dinner.

Chapter Thirty-eight

Maddy had never forgotten Jane Morton's warning that Tim Lyons would be a bitter enemy. She had forced herself to bite her tongue and congratulate him on his success and he had looked through her as if he didn't believe a word she was saying while he automatically shook her hand and thanked her.

Meanwhile, he left her largely to her own devices. Occasionally he would inquire about the progress of The Wharf and Maddy would give him a printout of sales and commissions earned and keep him up to date with any developments. But the bulk of his time seemed to be taken up with reorganising the firm.

A number of appointments had already been made. A lettings division had been established and a new branch opened in Dublin city centre. But what caused surprise and much resentment was that both positions went to men – one of them a twenty-three-year-old who had only been with the firm a couple of months – while more senior women were passed over. Maddy couldn't help thinking that if Tim Lyons wanted to antagonise the entire female staff, he was going the right way about it.

She had hopes of her own from the reorganisation. She had been doing her present job for almost four years. It was time for a change and she had set her sights on developing a new commercial and office division. This was a lucrative market and she had already gained a foothold for the company in her dealings with Mick McCann. But she was totally unprepared for what was about to occur when she came into work the following morning.

She had barely opened her post and checked her messages when Tim Lyons's secretary approached and said he wanted to see her. Maddy got up immediately and followed her into his office where she found him seated at his desk with a pile of documents before him.

"Take a seat," he said, pointing to a vacant chair. "As you know, I've been reassessing the situation. We have to strengthen our position and open up new opportunities. I think the time has come to move you."

"What did you have in mind?" Maddy asked, not daring to hope that she would get the commercial division.

"I've decided to open a new branch in Bray. It's a large town with a growing population and at present it's only served by two small local auctioneers. I think it provides a big opportunity for us. I want you to run it."

Maddy was taken aback. A few years ago such an appointment would have been a promotion but now with her expertise and experience, it was a sideways move. Besides, Bray was miles away from Ranelagh and would entail a lengthy journey.

"You seem surprised," Tim Lyons said.

"I am," Maddy replied. "I was expecting to be moved. But I was hoping you might have asked me to develop a commercial division. I already have some experience from my involvement with The Wharf."

Lyons cut her short.

"I've asked Conor Casey to do that."

Maddy swallowed hard. Conor Casey was another fresh-faced young man barely out of college, with only limited experience in residential property and none at all in the commercial market. It was an amazing appointment.

"Are you sure?" she asked.

His eyes sliced through her. "Are you questioning my judgment?"

"No. I just thought . . ."

"I want you to start next week. First thing is to go out there and locate suitable premises. We will want somewhere in the centre of the town, preferably on the main street with a good big window for display. You don't need me to tell you what to do. When you're up and running, we'll allocate a secretary."

"No other staff?"

"Not for the time being. I think you'll be more than competent on your own. Once you have the branch fully functioning we'll reassess the situation."

"May I ask who will be getting my present job?"

"Sue Donovan. She'll take over from you on Monday."

This was another setback. Jane Morton had been her deputy for the past two years and was widely regarded as her natural successor. She was going to be furious at the news.

But a further blow was still to come.

As she excused herself and made for the door, Lyons called after her.

"One more thing."

"Yes?"

"This gala dinner tonight at The Wharf – I've decided to go."

She stopped and turned around.

"But all the places are allocated," she replied. "You were sent an invitation and didn't reply."

"I was too busy. Now I've changed my mind. I've decided as Chief Executive I ought to be there. We have a close relationship with the developer."

"It's going to cause some disruption."

"No, it won't," Tim Lyons replied with a dismissive wave of his hand. "I'll simply go in your place."

Maddy was trembling with rage as she left the office. She had been passed over and humiliated. And the cruellest cut had been the way

Tim Lyons had taken her place at the gala dinner. She had been eagerly looking forward to the event which would crown her successful partnership with Mick McCann. And now even this had been snatched away from her.

Immediately, she ran into Jane Morton. She grabbed her by the arm. "You and I have got to talk. See you in the Bean Bag coffee shop in five minutes."

As soon as they were seated, Maddy recounted her interview with Lyons.

"This is not good news for either of us," she began, her eyes ablaze with fury.

"You better tell me," Jane said.

"I'm being moved and Sue is going to replace me."

She watched as Jane's face collapsed in shock.

"Where are you going?"

"Bray, to open a new branch."

Jane took a deep breath.

"I was afraid something like this was going to happen," she said, after a pause. "Of course, you can see what he's doing, can't you? He's moving you as far away as possible because he sees you as a threat. He doesn't want you in the office. He knows how popular you are with the staff. As for me, I'm being punished for supporting you."

"I'm sorry," Maddy said.

"I don't mind Sue," Jane continued. "I can work fine with her. But I'm senior to her and I've been your deputy for two years. If there was any justice, I should have been promoted." She struggled to hide her disappointment. "It all goes to show how bloody insecure he is. These young male models he's been promoting are just the type of people he wants around him. Yes-men, who will agree with everything he says and pose absolutely no threat to him. Only problem is, they're barely toilet-trained."

"He's about to appoint another one."

"Who?"

"Conor Casey. He's getting the commercial division instead of me."

Jane sank back in her seat. "I don't believe it. At this rate, Tim Lyons will have destroyed the company before the year is out."

Maddy went back to the office and rang Mick McCann to explain that she wouldn't be able to attend the dinner after all.

"But that's ridiculous," McCann protested. "You *have* to be here. The restaurant was your idea. You've been involved from the very start."

"Tim Lyons will be representing the company. He's the Chief Executive. We felt the occasion demanded the most senior person."

"Nonsense, you have to come! You can join my table. We'll just squeeze in another place."

But by now, Maddy had had enough. She just wanted to avoid any more controversy. If she accepted Mick McCann's generous offer, it might antagonise Tim Lyons even further.

"That's very kind of you, Mick, but I really can't come. Besides, I won't be working with you any more. I'm being transferred to Bray."

There was a shocked silence.

"Tell me I'm hearing things."

"I'm afraid it's true."

"Are they nuts? Do they know what they're doing?"

"It's not my decision, Mick."

The developer gave a weary sigh.

"Well, I'm really sorry to hear that, Maddy. I'd been looking forward to collaborating with you on my new development. But if that's what Carroll and Shanley want, there's nothing I can do. Promise me you'll keep in touch."

"Sure I will," Maddy said. "Enjoy the evening."

But the fuss about the dinner wasn't over yet. Half an hour later, she got another call, this one from an apoplectic Marco O'Malley.

"What's this I hear from Mick that you won't be attending tonight?"

Maddy explained what had happened.

"But you must come," the chef continued. "I insist."

"I can't, Marco, really."

356

"Who is this upstart who has taken your place?"

"My boss."

"Well, he sounds to me like a very nasty piece of work. I have a good mind to spit in his soup. And I can tell you this is the last meal he will ever eat in my establishment. If he ever attempts to darken my doorstep again I'll personally spray him with cockroach repellent."

Despite her crushing disappointment, Maddy found herself smiling.

"And one other thing, you shall be the first guest when we open for business. I'm giving you a personal invitation. And bring a friend. This will be on the house."

"Thank you, Marco. You're very kind."

"Kind? It will be my pleasure. I've always liked you. You're my sort of woman and I hope to see more of you in the future."

To cheer herself up, Maddy kept her hairdressing appointment and afterwards she rang Rosie. What she needed now was a good old chat with someone she could trust.

"What are you doing tonight?" she asked when her friend answered the phone.

"Watching television. Adam is attending some conference in Galway so I'm on my own."

"Do you fancy a drink and maybe a bite to eat?"

"Has the Pope got a balcony? But look, why don't you come over here and I'll rustle up something?"

"Okay. That sounds good. What time?"

"Seven o'clock."

"I'll be there."

She went home to Auburn Grove, showered and got changed. As she opened her wardrobe she saw her evening dress still in its plastic wrapper from the dry cleaner's. All over town, people would be excitedly preparing for Marco's gala dinner, hoping to be snapped by the hordes of paparazzi who would doubtless be clamouring for pictures.

Oh, damn Tim Lyons, she thought. He had gone from being Mr

Nice Guy to Mr Slimeball in a matter of weeks. And now he had placed a huge question mark over her entire future. Once he had banished her to Bray, he would keep her there forever, far removed from the centre of influence, reduced to being a mere spectator as younger, less experienced colleagues advanced in their careers.

No matter how hard she worked, she knew she would never be promoted any further. Jane Morton was right. Tim Lyons saw her as a threat and would do everything to restrict her progress. Eventually, she would become a figure of pity whispered about by sympathetic colleagues as an example of what happened to someone who got too big for their boots. Was that what she wanted?

She thought of the offer she had received a few years ago from Peter O'Leary to come and reorganise his sales team. She had been a fool not to take it. By now, she would have her seat on the board, directing the affairs of the company and be highly regarded in the property world. But she had placed her loyalty to Carroll and Shanley before her own career and this was how she had been rewarded. She couldn't help feeling bitter as she thought of the injustice of it all.

She rang for a taxi and while she waited, she hunted out an expensive bottle of Bordeaux wine that someone had given her as a Christmas present. By the time she arrived at Rosie's house in Clontarf, she was starving and was pleased to be met with an appetising smell from the kitchen.

"It's only shepherd's pie," Rosie apologised. "But it's a fresh shepherd. The butcher swore he was caught this morning. Come in and sit down. But, hey, I only thought of it after I put down the phone earlier – why aren't you at this restaurant thingy this evening?"

Maddy explained what had happened.

"What a miserable sod," Rosie said in horror. "Why would he do that to you?"

"Because he can. He's the Boss. He can do what he likes."

"But there's such a thing as basic human decency."

"I challenged him for the top job. There was a time when I might have had my head chopped off. I suppose I should be grateful that things have moved on."

"Well, he doesn't sound like a very nice person to me."

"He isn't," Maddy said, "and I completely misjudged him. But look, I'm not here to complain about work. What's the latest news from Sophie?"

"I had a call from her yesterday. She's settling into her new job and she seems to find London very much to her liking. She asked me to pass on her regards and to tell you she'll phone over the weekend. Now where do you want to eat? It's getting a bit chilly to sit in the garden."

"Then we'll eat in the kitchen if that's okay. And I brought you a little pressie."

She fished the bottle of wine from its bag.

"Bordeaux?" Rosie said in surprise. "But this is much too good."

Maddy smiled and kissed her friend on the cheek. "Not too good for someone as special as you, Rose. Why don't you save it for a romantic evening with Adam?"

"No, we'll drink it," Rosie replied. "If he wants wine, he can buy it himself."

"But we'll get pickled."

"So what? You're not driving. You can stay overnight if you like."

"Are you sure?"

"Of course. It'll be like old times in Auburn Grove. I'll make you scrambled eggs for breakfast. Which reminds me, have you managed to get tenants for Munster Road yet?"

"I think so. I've got a young couple coming to view tomorrow. They're from Boston. He works for a multinational company that makes mobile phones. They sound ideal."

"It won't be too big for them?"

"They've got two children as well."

"And you don't mind having kids in the house?"

"Why should I? We were all children at one time, Rosie."

After they had eaten, they sat in the living-room and watched the shadows fall across the lawn. Despite her earlier resolution, Maddy found herself telling Rosie all about her problems at work.

"What an absolute bastard," Rosie said. "He sounds like he's really got it in for you."

"I'm afraid you might be right. I think it will only be a matter of time before he drives me out of the job altogether."

Rosie put down her glass and turned suddenly to Maddy.

"So why are you waiting?"

"How do you mean?"

"Why wait till he fires you? With your experience you could walk into another job in the morning."

"And have to start all over again? I'm not sure I'd want to do that."

"But you can't continue in a situation that's only going to make you unhappy. And from what you have told me, things aren't likely to improve."

Maddy sank her head in her hands.

"I can see that. But the trouble is, Rosie, I just don't know what to do."

She woke the following morning feeling slightly hung-over and with the same question hanging over her mind. What was she going to do? She was thirty years of age and had no academic qualifications. The only thing she knew was the property business. But she had been good at that and she knew she had drive and imagination and buckets of energy. Yet the thought of going to work for another agency left her cold.

While she was using the bathroom, she could hear Rosie busy in the kitchen. She emerged to find the table set with a big pot of tea, a pile of toast, butter, marmalade and honey and Rosie in her apron scooping scrambled eggs and ham onto plates.

"Are you hungry?" she inquired as she turned to smile at Maddy.

"I am now."

"Well, tuck in. And whenever you're ready I'll phone for a cab. Did you sleep all right?"

"Like a baby. I was out cold two minutes after my head hit the pillow."

"It must have been the wine."

Maddy took the cab directly to Munster Road and arrived at two o'clock, half an hour before her prospective tenants. The house had already been thoroughly cleaned after Sophie's departure so all she had to do was go around and open the windows to air the rooms.

Just before half past two she heard the sound of a car pulling up outside and glanced out to see a couple in their mid-thirties emerge and scoop two young children from the car. She hurried to open the hall door.

"Hi, I'm Maddy. You must be Corrine and Bob?"

"That's us. And these guys are Angie and Bob Junior."

Maddy shook hands with the two polite children who stared at her with inquisitive eyes.

"So you want to see the house? Come in. I'll show you around."

She led them through the ground floor and out to the garden where the children's faces immediately brightened.

"A garden is one of the features we're looking for," Corrine remarked. "It's a safe place for the kids to play. We're staying in a hotel at the moment and they're bored to tears."

Twenty minutes later they had finished their inspection.

"If you want to view it again, just ring me," Maddy said.

"No need," Corinne said with a glance at her husband. "I think we'll take it. What do you say, Bob?"

"Sure. We won't do better than this. This place has got everything we're looking for."

Maddy couldn't help smiling to herself. She had got new tenants and it had been as easy as falling off a log. They agreed on the rent and Bob undertook to contact her on Monday with references and a month's deposit. In the meantime, she would prepare a twelve-month lease. They all shook hands again and the tenants drove away.

The following day, she went over to St Margaret's Lane for Sunday lunch.

"What's the matter with you?" her mother inquired. "You look as if your mind is miles away."

"I'm just thinking about work."

"You should forget about work at weekends," Mr Pritchard said. "It's not a good idea to bring problems home with you."

"You're right," Maddy said, straightening up and attacking her mother's roast beef.

But she couldn't get the thought of work out of her mind. It hung about her neck like a ball and chain. When she got home, she poured a glass of wine and went to sit on the patio to catch the dying rays of the sun.

She knew she had reached the end of her career with Carroll and Shanley. Rosie had been right. Better to go now while she still retained some dignity. Better to cut her losses and start afresh. But what was she going to do?

She thought of the young American couple who had agreed to rent Munster Road. They would be in Dublin for four years which meant a steady stream of income. And the rent more than covered the mortgage, so she was making a profit. And all the time the value of the house was appreciating. She remembered what people had been telling her over the years – that she had a genius for spotting good properties for investment. What was to stop her doing it again?

The more she thought about it, the more attractive the proposition became. She had equity built up in two good houses. The banks would lend her the money. She had contacts in the industry. And best of all, she would be her own mistress. She would be free of interference and petty vindictiveness. She could do exactly as she pleased.

She went to bed that evening feeling far better than she had for a long time. She knew now exactly what she was going to do. The following morning she sat down at her desk and wrote out her resignation letter from Carroll and Shanley.

Chapter Thirty-nine

When she gave her letter to Tim Lyons, he read it quickly then looked at her without the slightest hint of surprise or emotion.

"You don't have to work out your notice," he said. "You can go immediately."

"Really?"

"Yes. You're anxious to go, so go."

"What about my salary?"

"You'll get everything you're entitled to."

Maddy barely had time to say goodbye to Marina and Jane and her numerous friends before she found herself on the street clutching a plastic bag containing her possessions. In her wallet was a cheque for her salary and commissions plus her P45. After twelve years working for the company it was a sad and lonely way to leave.

But her departure set off of a minor chain reaction. Within weeks, Jane Morton and three senior female sales staff had followed her example and found jobs with rival estate agencies after deciding they had no future at the firm. And more was to come.

A month later, she heard on the grapevine that Mick McCann had transferred the leasing contract for his new development to the firm of O'Leary and Partners after coming to the conclusion that

Conor Casey wasn't up to the task. Maddy wasn't surprised. It was beginning to look as if Jane Morton's prediction about Tim Lyons destroying the company before the end of the year might actually be coming true.

One of the very first things Maddy did after leaving was to take Paula Matthews to lunch.

"It seems like the end of an era," Paula said when they were comfortably ensconced at an alcove table of The Blue Parasol restaurant off Grafton Street. "You seem to have been doing that job forever. You've become an institution."

"Oh, for God's sake, I'm only thirty," Maddy said. "You make it sound like I'm Mrs Thatcher."

"You've certainly got some of her characteristics – an iron determination for one thing and an appetite for hard work. You know your departure was like a bomb going off. What is that guy doing with that company?"

"I could be nasty and tell you he's running it into the ground but I won't. Let's just say that he doesn't seem to have a very high opinion of women."

"Well then, he's a fool. Women are taking over the property business. They're everywhere."

"Not in Carroll and Shanley, they aren't. You know I was asked at my interview if my nerves would be able for the stress of the Chief Executive job. Another old buffer asked if men would find it difficult to take instructions from me. I was waiting for somebody to ask me how I would handle an attack of the vapours."

They collapsed in a gale of laughter.

"I hear one or two rival companies are looking at you," Paula said, wiping her eyes.

"I've already had offers," Maddy admitted. "Quite attractive ones too."

"Are you interested?"

She shook her head. "I'm going to work for myself."

"Doing what?"

"I have a plan to renovate old houses and sell them on. I already have some experience. I thought it might be something I would enjoy. And I would be my own boss, Paula. That's the wonderful thing. I'd be working for myself."

"Well, if I can help in any way."

"You can," Maddy said. "You can keep your ears open. If you hear of any properties that might suit, I'd appreciate it if you would let me know."

"*You've got a friend*," Paula began to hum as she refreshed their glasses.

But she wasn't just relying on Paula. In the coming weeks, Maddy recruited a network of contacts in the estate agencies around town. Now that she had left Carroll and Shanley, she was no longer regarded as a rival. Maddy had a good reputation in the industry and people were anxious to help her.

She had already told them what she wanted – properties that were in bad repair and had become stuck on the market and which she could pick up cheaply. A few weeks later, she got a call from Paula to tell her she had heard of something that might interest her.

"It's a large six-bed house in Harold's Cross. Practically derelict from what I hear. It's with Kelly and Anderson. They've had it on their books for the last six months and can't shift it. I hear they're desperate."

"What price are they looking?"

"Seventy grand."

"Thank you, Paula. I'll look into it."

She rang the firm of Kelly and Anderson and made an appointment to view that afternoon. When she approached the house at the end of a leafy road, her immediate reaction was that it wasn't suitable. It was far too big for one thing and it really was in a dreadful state of repair. It would need an awful lot of work. Nevertheless, she waited for the young negotiator to arrive to show her over the property.

She promptly turned up at three o'clock.

"Hi, I'm Jill Crawford," the young woman in the grey trouser suit said with a pleasant professional smile that Maddy remembered from her own days on the beat. "Been here long?"

"I've just arrived."

"Good." She handed Maddy a brochure. "That will give you the dimensions of the rooms and other information. So, if you're ready, I'll show you over."

She opened the front door and they proceeded through the house. It was in even worse repair inside. Indeed, Maddy's first thought was that whoever bought it would have to knock it down and rebuild. Nevertheless, she followed Jill through the rooms and up the rickety stairs to the top of the building where there was a view out of the window over the vast overgrown garden.

"How much land is there?" Maddy asked.

"Almost half an acre."

"And what's its history?"

"It was originally built by some bigwig in the brewing business over a hundred years ago as a family residence. Eventually, it passed out of the family to a private landlord who converted it into flats. He died last year and now his executors want to sell."

Maddy could understand the executors' point of view. Nobody could possibly live in this house without carrying out extensive and costly repairs.

"It needs a lot of work," Jill Crawford admitted, as if reading Maddy's mind. "But this is a good area and it's going to get even better. A lot of young married couples are moving in. It's very close to town and there are plenty of good schools. It's really a bargain at the price."

Maddy said nothing and they conducted the rest of the viewing in silence.

On her way home, she turned the matter over in her mind. The house was totally unsuitable but there was an additional factor that she hadn't been aware of until she viewed. It sat on half an acre of land. And there was no disguising the desperation in Jill Crawford's voice. Maddy had heard it before. She was in no doubt that she could buy the property for much less than the asking price.

When she got home, she rang Paddy Behan.

"Maddy!" he said. "Where the hell have you been? I thought you were dead, I haven't heard from you for so long."

"I'm very much alive, Paddy, and I might have a job for you."

"Shoot."

"I'd like you to look over a property for me and give me your professional assessment."

They agreed on six o'clock that evening. Paddy turned up ten minutes late which for a builder like him was good timekeeping. He took one look at the house and turned to Maddy.

"You want my honest opinion? If you're thinking of restoring it, forget it."

"Come with me," she said and led him round to the back of the house where the garden stretched on all sides.

"There's about half an acre here," she said. "If I knocked down the main house and built smaller three-beds, how many could I fit?"

Paddy's practised eye surveyed the land.

"You want to give them all some garden?"

"Yes."

"And separate entrances?"

"Of course."

He stroked his chin. "I reckon you'd manage four without too much bother. But this is really a job for a qualified architect."

"Last question, could you do the work if necessary?"

"I'd have to hire in some extra crew but the answer is yes."

"Okay, Paddy. Leave it with me."

For the next few days, she pored over figures and calculations. What she had in mind was very risky. She would have to persuade the bank to lend her the money and then negotiate her way through the planning laws to get building permission. And there was always the possibility that some neighbour might object, which could mean lengthy legal delays. The next thing to do was to get a reliable architect who could take the matter a stage further. Once again, Paula Matthews came to the rescue.

"There's a young guy I know called Simon Rafferty. He's not long qualified but he's hot shit and he certainly knows the business."

Maddy took Simon Rafferty's number and left a message. An hour later her phone rang and she heard a deep, male voice come on the line.

"Madeleine Pritchard?"

"That's me," Maddy said. "I got your number from Paula Matthews. I might have a job for you."

Over the next five minutes, she explained what she had in mind while Simon listened attentively and asked an occasional question. They ended the conversation with an agreement to meet the following morning so that he could view the site.

He turned out to be a handsome, dark-haired young man in his late twenties dressed casually in slacks and sports shirt. They shook hands and Maddy took him round the back of the house to look at the extensive garden.

"There is more land here than you think," he said, after he had walked to the edge of the lawn and gazed along the garden where the overgrown grass impeded his path, "particularly when the house is knocked down."

"Would I be able to get four houses?"

"Comfortably. When this house was built, land was cheap so people could afford massive gardens like this one. You could easily develop four houses here and still allow for space."

"What about planning permission?"

"That's something of a lottery, I'm afraid. But I can't see why they should refuse if we come up with a design that fits in with the rest of the neighbourhood. I tell you what, why don't I bang out some rough drawings and you can tell me what you think."

"Okay," Maddy said.

But events were moving faster than she realised. No sooner had she returned home than the phone began to ring and she found Jill Crawford on the line.

"Had any more thoughts about that house?" she asked.

"I'm interested," Maddy said, "but not at the asking price. There's too much work involved to really make it viable."

"We can always negotiate."

"I don't want to insult you."

"Go ahead. I'm used to it."

"Thirty thousand is as high as I would be prepared to go."

"Okay," Jill said, without pausing for breath. "Let me put it to the executors and hear what they say."

Why did I just do that? Maddy thought as she put down the phone. She rarely acted on impulse and she hadn't intended to make an offer till she was sure of finance and planning approval. But if they accepted her bid she was getting the property at a bargain-basement price. The land alone was worth more than £30,000. Maybe she had done the right thing after all.

That afternoon, Jill rang back to say that her clients would accept her offer.

"It will be subject to the usual conditions?" Maddy said. "No complications with title and so on?"

"Of course."

"Okay. Go ahead and prepare a contract."

Next she had to contact Conor Black. He was every bit as surprised to hear from her as Paddy Behan had been. It was several years since they had last spoken.

"Maddy! What have you been up to? The last time we talked, you were setting out to become a property tycoon."

"I'm still working on it," she said with a chuckle. "But I have some way to go."

"I've no doubt with your determination it will only be a matter of time. Now, what can I do for you?"

Conor listened while she outlined the details concerning the property.

"It sounds like a bargain," he said when she had finished.

"The house itself is practically derelict. But it has half an acre of land. That's what I'm really interested in. I don't suppose we could make this purchase subject to planning permission?"

"We could try," he replied, "but I can't see the vendors agreeing to that. Besides, there's another angle you should consider."

"Which is?"

"You could be alerting them to its potential."

"Don't you think they can see that for themselves?"

"Not necessarily. The executors are likely to be relatives of the deceased owner. They probably just want the property sold so they can get their hands on the loot. They might never have seen the house."

"I hadn't thought of that."

"Well, it's something you should consider. My advice is to buy the property and seek planning permission afterwards. I know it's a gamble. But that's the same with most investments."

"You're right," she said. "I'm glad I talked to you."

"Nice to hear your voice again," Conor replied. "I'll be in touch when the contract comes through."

Meanwhile, Simon Rafferty had been busy with the plans. He called a few days later to say he had some rough sketches he'd like her to see.

She gave him her address.

"I'll drop them in on my way home," he said. "You can study them at your leisure."

He arrived shortly after six o'clock wearing a dark turtle-neck sweater and Levis and carrying a large rolled-up bundle of papers under his arm. Maddy brought him into the kitchen.

"I was just about to make some tea. Would you like some?"

"Sure."

While she busied herself with the kettle and tea things, Simon unrolled the papers and spread them out on the kitchen table. As she approached with the tea, she was able to study his profile. He was thin and fit and his jet-black hair tapered to a point at the nape of his neck. Maddy thought he looked quite dishy.

"These are only preliminary drawings, just to give you an idea of what's possible," he said, pointing to the neat row of houses he had drawn, each with its own driveway and small garden.

"They have three bedrooms like you asked for and two storeys. I've deliberately kept them subdued so as to blend in with the character of the road. What do you think?"

"I think they're fantastic."

His face broke into a smile. "Good. So, do you want me to proceed with proper drawings?"

"Yes. My offer has been accepted and we're waiting for the contract."

"Okay, and I'll also lodge a planning application."

"How confident are you that we'll get approval?"

"We'll have to wait and see. As soon as the sale is agreed, I want you to ring and tell me. In the meantime, I'll get to work."

He rolled up the drawings again and gave them to her. She wished they could talk longer. She was enjoying this conversation. But Simon was anxious to get away.

"Thanks for the tea, Maddy. Now, I'd better be off." He glanced at his watch. "I've got another appointment in fifteen minutes."

She went with him to the front door and waved him off.

"Keep me informed," she shouted as he climbed into his car and drove away.

She closed the door and walked back into the empty house. Simon Rafferty really was a very interesting man. They would be working closely together in the weeks ahead. Who knew where it might lead? But she didn't have long to dwell on Simon. The following morning, Rosie rang with some very exciting news.

Chapter Forty

"I'm pregnant!" she said, when she called Maddy shortly before eleven o'clock.

"Pregnant?"

"Yes, you know what it means. I'm going to have a baby."

"Oh Rosie, I'm so thrilled for you."

"I've just got confirmation from Dr McDonnell. Isn't it a hoot?"

"What has Adam got to say? He must be over the moon."

"He's delirious. Mind you, all that might change when he finds out he's got to wash the dirty nappies."

Rosie gave a loud chuckle and Maddy could sense the joy and satisfaction her friend was feeling.

"We'll have to celebrate. Where are you now?"

"I'm at home. I've got to ring my parents and tell them. I'm not sure how my mother is going to react to the news that she's about to become a grandmother."

"And then you're free?"

"Yes."

"Well then, I'm on my way. We're going to sit down and you're going to tell me everything."

Maddy put down the phone with a smile. She was truly delighted for her friend. It didn't seem so long ago that they had all been gadding around town together, three single, carefree young women. And now Rosie was about to become a mum. How quickly their lives were changing.

On her way across town, she called into a wine shop and bought a bottle of champagne. Rosie was waiting for her in the living-room with the fire banked up and bowls of nuts set out.

"I take it you're allowed to drink?" Maddy asked after she had smothered Rosie in kisses.

"I suppose a sip or two wouldn't do any harm. I'm only ten weeks."

"Now tell me, how did your mother react to the news?" Maddy asked popping the cork and pouring.

"She's ecstatic. I'm relieved. You know, she pretends to be forty-five when she's actually fifty-eight!"

"But that would mean she had you when she was only fifteen."

"I know. Everybody just goes along with it. But she was absolutely delighted. She says I have to give up my job immediately and take to my bed."

"She did not?"

"She did. And she's coming round this evening with special home-made chicken broth. I think this is going to be the longest pregnancy in medical history."

Maddy laughed. "No morning sickness?"

"No, nothing like that. The doctor said that could come later."

"No special cravings? You haven't started eating coal or anything?"

"I'm saving that for later."

Maddy smiled. "It must feel wonderful to be pregnant."

"It's a beautiful feeling. I can't believe it's true. And Maddy, I've got a special favour to ask. I'd like you to be godmother."

Maddy felt a lump rise in her throat. "Oh, Rose! I'd love to. It would be an honour."

A few days later she got a call from Conor Black to say that all the legal work on the purchase of the Harold's Cross house was now completed and the papers were ready for her signature. When would suit her to come in?

"What about tomorrow morning?"

"That's fine. Shall we say midday?"

"Okay."

"Good. I'll look forward to seeing you."

The following morning she rose at nine and went for her daily jog. Now that she was no longer working for Carroll and Shanley, her days had become more flexible and occasionally she allowed herself the luxury of a lie-on in bed. But in some ways she missed the routine of the office and hated this interminable waiting. Until Simon Rafferty made progress with the planning application there was nothing much for her to do.

And there was something else she missed – the company of other people. That aspect of her life had changed completely. Sophie had gone and Rosie was happily married and now she was expecting a child. Maddy no longer had the camaraderie of the office and the workaday relationships with Jane and Sue and Marina and her other friends and colleagues. She had always prided herself that she comfortable with her own company but now she began to realise that she was lonely. She needed someone she could rely on, someone she could talk to, someone to share life's little triumphs and tribulations.

She returned from her run. She could feel her heart still pumping as she stood under the hot shower. She wrapped herself in a towel and went into the kitchen and ate a breakfast of cereal and fruit, then started to get dressed. She thought of the ritual that awaited her: the handing over of the cheque, the signing of the papers, the acceptance of the keys, the handshake that sealed the agreement and confirmed she was now the owner of another property.

But now that she was about to sign the deal, she could feel her courage begin to waver. She was taking an enormous leap in the dark with this purchase. Everything hinged on her ability to get planning permission to build the new houses. Not for the first time, she wondered if she was doing the right thing. Nevertheless, she put on a brave face as she picked up her handbag and checked to make sure she had all her possessions before locking the front door and getting into her car.

Conor Black was waiting in his office. It had been some time since she had seen him but he hadn't changed much. He stood up as she came in.

"So, you're intent on building up your property empire?" he smiled.

"Slowly but surely," she replied, noticing the fine cut of his suit and the snowy white shirt and the way his carefully groomed hair rested lightly against his collar.

"Well, I'm happy to say that all the legal work is in order."

He began to hand over papers for her to sign. If she wanted, she could still back out. She could simply say that she had changed her mind and didn't want to proceed. But she put her fears aside and plunged ahead. She took the pen he offered and duly scribbled her signature. When she had finished, Conor gathered the papers together and tied them with a ribbon.

"You look nervous," he said.

"Just momentary doubts."

"You brought the cheque?"

She took the thin white envelope from her bag and gave it to him.

"How is the planning application coming along?" he asked.

"I haven't heard."

He nodded and gave her a bunch of keys on a silver ring. "These things take time."

He held out his hand for Maddy to shake.

"Congratulations," he said. "I don't suppose a busy woman like you would have time for lunch?"

Maddy hesitated for a split second and then she found herself smiling.

"Why not?" she said. "If you've got the time to accompany me."

Conor smiled.

"For someone like you, Maddy, everything else can wait."

They went to a small restaurant nearby where he was obviously well known as the waiter greeted him by name and led them to a table for two at the back. Now that he was away from the office, Conor seemed to expand.

Maddy sat and took the opportunity to glance around. The restaurant was Italian and already half-full. There were prints of Florence and Venice on the walls and red linen cloths on the tables.

"Are you hungry?" he asked as they settled down

"Let's say I'm peckish."

"The veal is very good. Would you like some wine?"

"I'm driving," Maddy said. "I'd better not."

The waiter was back and Conor gave their order.

"Something has always baffled me," he said. "Where do you find the time for all this activity?"

"I've plenty of time now," she said. "I'm no longer working for Carroll and Shanley."

He looked surprised.

"Oh! I didn't know. I thought you enjoyed your job?"

"I did. But it was time for a change."

"So who are you working for now?"

"Myself."

He smiled. "I admire you, Maddy. You've never been content to just sit and wait for things to happen. You've always looked for opportunities and you've taken risks."

"I'm taking a big risk now," she said. "If I don't get planning permission for this house, I'm going to be left with a large white elephant on my hands."

He reached out and gently placed his hand on top of hers. His touch felt warm and comforting.

"Don't think like that. There's an old saying. Nothing ventured, nothing gained. You can't even consider the possibility of failure."

She looked up to see his soft blue eyes encouraging her.

"You'll get your permission. You just have to be patient. Some day you'll look back on this and laugh."

"I'll tell you what," she said. "The day I get planning approval, I'll take *you* to lunch."

The time passed in a lively blur of chat and laughter but at last Conor glanced at his watch and announced that he had to return to the office.

"Thanks for everything," she said as they left the restaurant in the bright afternoon sunshine. "Your encouraging words were exactly what I needed to buck me up."

He kissed her lightly on the cheek.

"I'm always available," he said. "Just stop worrying. Everything will turn out fine."

She got home shortly after three o'clock. As she opened the front door, she could hear the phone ringing in the living-room. She hurried to pick it up.

It was Simon.

"I was about to call you," she said. "I've just signed the contract."

"Well, I have news for *you*. I've just discovered something interesting."

"What?" she said, hoping desperately that it wasn't something bad.

"There's already an existing planning permission on that house."

"What exactly does that mean?" Maddy asked. Despite years working in the property business, at times the intricacies of the planning legislation still baffled her.

"I've just got back from the Planning Office," Simon continued, "and I was checking the register. Two years ago, the owner, a Mr Copeland, applied to build a second house at the back of the existing property. And the permission was granted."

"So why didn't he build it?"

"Who knows? But the point is, the permission is still valid. The executors mustn't have checked or they would never have sold the house so cheaply."

"So this means I can build another house if I want?"

"Exactly. And it strengthens our hand with regard to your planning application. In fact, we might be able to do some horse trading."

"That's fantastic news, Simon. So what do we do now?"

"Just sit tight and wait. As soon as I hear anything, I'll let you know."

She put down the phone with a feeling of excitement. It was amazing how quickly the situation had turned around in the space of a single morning. Now, if she wished, she could sell the house without doing a single thing and walk away with a profit. She wondered why no one had known about the existing planning permission. It was probably as Conor had suggested – anxious relatives keen to get their inheritance who hadn't bothered to check. But it was surely a bright omen that her new career was getting off to a good start.

It was a week before she heard from Simon again. He called unexpectedly one evening on his way home from his office, just as Maddy was preparing dinner.

"I would have phoned but I thought it was simpler to drop in on my way by," he explained. "Besides, I haven't seen you for a while."

"Come in. Would you like a glass of wine?"

"That would be nice."

She seated him in the living-room and came back with a bottle of chilled Frascati from the fridge.

"Is this okay?"

"It's fine."

She poured two glasses and sat down across from him.

"So, tell me the worst."

"We've encountered a snag," Simon said, brushing a stray lock of hair from his handsome face.

She felt her stomach churn. "I knew it," she said, putting down her glass. "I knew it would only be a matter of time before something went belly-up."

He held up his hand. "At this stage it's only a potential problem. I've been talking to the Chief Planning Officer and and he's sympathetic to our application. But the existing permission was granted in the teeth of some serious objections from the neighbours, an elderly couple named Buckley. The Planning Officer is convinced they'll object again. And if they do, it's going to cause serious delays not to mention the possible danger that it might scupper the whole plan."

"So what do you propose we should do?"

"I think you should go and speak to them."

Maddy looked surprised.

"But I don't even know them."

"I'll come with you. We'll bring the drawings and explain exactly what we're hoping to do. If there is some way we can convince them, it's going to save an awful lot of hassle."

"Okay," she said. "Let's do it."

The following morning at ten o'clock, they were outside the Buckleys' house. In her hands Maddy carried a bunch of flowers and a box of chocolates she had bought in Ranelagh village.

"A bribe," she explained to Simon.

The door opened slightly and a small, grey head appeared to reveal an elderly lady in a fawn cardigan. She stared at them intently.

"Yes?" she said after a moment spent looking them up and down.

"Hello," Maddy replied in a cheerful voice. "Mrs Buckley?"

"Yes. Who are you?"

"I'm your new neighbour, Madeleine Pritchard. And this is my friend, Mr Rafferty."

Simon smiled politely.

"I thought I'd call and introduce myself," Maddy continued. "I brought you these."

She pressed the flowers and chocolates into Mrs Buckley's hands.

Just then, another figure appeared in the hallway, a plump bald-headed man in shirt and braces.

"Who is it, Florrie?" the man enquired, stopping to look at Maddy and Simon.

"It's Mrs Pritchard. She's just bought No 96."

"Oh," the man said.

"It's Miss Pritchard, actually. I just thought I'd call and say hello."

"She gave me these," Mrs Buckley said to her husband and showed the presents.

"That's very kind, Miss Pritchard."

Maddy had been hoping she would be invited in but, as the

elderly couple hesitated, she pressed on. "I wonder if I could talk to you for a few minutes? It's about what I plan to do with No 96."

Mr Buckley frowned. "Plan?" he said. "What sort of plan?"

"Well, that's what I'd like to discuss with you, if you could spare me some of your time."

There was more hesitation while the couple conferred in the hall and then Mrs Buckley opened the door wider.

"You'd better come in," she said.

Maddy and Simon followed them along the hall while a small cocker spaniel barked playfully at their feet.

"In here," Mr Buckley said, pushing open the door to a tidy sitting-room where a fire burned brightly in the grate.

"Take a seat," his wife said. "Would you like a cup of tea?"

"No, thank you," Maddy said. "We won't be staying long."

"It's nice of you to come and see us," Mr Buckley said, seating himself directly opposite while his wife sat beside him. "We appreciate that. At least it shows some regard for your neighbours. Now what is it you're planning to do?"

"I'm going to knock the house down."

"That's no harm. No 96 is an eyesore. So what are you putting in its place?"

"Four new houses."

Immediately, the Buckleys' faces fell.

"*Four*?" said Mr Buckley.

"Yes. But before you say anything, let me explain. The previous owner, Mr Copeland, had permission to build another house in the back."

"He was going to open more flats," Mrs Buckley said. "We objected to it. There was noise morning, noon and night. And cars coming and going all day long. We got no peace."

"I know you objected. And that's why I thought it would be better if we discussed this matter first. How many flats did Mr Copeland have in No 96?"

"Six," Mr Buckley said, "and he didn't care who his tenants were. He had all sorts of undesirable types. There were parties every weekend. We had to call the police God knows how many times."

"We're retired," his wife added. "We don't bother anybody. All we want is a quiet life."

"That must have been hell for you," Maddy said.

"It *was* hell," said Mrs Buckley. "And Mr Copeland didn't care. He didn't take the least bit of notice of our complaints. He wasn't a very nice man, was he, Peter?"

"That's putting it mildly," Mr Buckley said. "He was an absolute gouger."

"Look," Maddy said, "if I wanted I could go ahead and build that second house. I could put in more flats. I could have twelve if I wanted. I have the planning permission."

A frightened look came into Mrs Buckley's eyes.

"But I'm not going to do that. Instead, I'm going to build four houses just like this one. They'll be for young married couples, the sort of people who'll look after their property. These won't be the types who are going to cause a nuisance. Believe me, four houses is a much better option than twelve flats."

The Buckleys looked at each other again, carefully weighing up Maddy's words.

This was the cue for Simon to unroll his plans.

"Let me show you what we have in mind," he said, laying them out on a table. "As you can see, the houses will be roughly the same size as your own. And they will be two storeys so you won't be overlooked in any way. Each one will have a garden which will allow for privacy. And they will also have separate driveways."

He glanced at the couple and smiled.

"They'll be the same size as this house?" Mr Buckley asked.

"Exactly.

"How many bedrooms?"

"Three."

"Bathrooms?"

"Two. One of them en-suite."

"And what about downstairs?"

"Kitchen, dining-room and lounge, plus a utility room for the washing-machine and tumble-dryer."

"Hmmmh," Mr Buckley said and rubbed his chin. "When will they be ready?"

"Once we get approval I expect they will take about six months to build."

Mr and Mrs Buckley went into a huddle.

Then Mr Buckley asked, "How much do you expect to sell them for?"

"Around £80,000," Maddy said.

The Buckleys exchanged another glance and fell to whispering once more.

Maddy and Simon glanced at each other and Simon raised a quizzical eyebrow. Eventually the old couple sat back and Mr Buckley spoke again.

"We'll do a deal with you," he said. "We're prepared to let the development go ahead."

"Fantastic," Maddy said, scarcely daring to believe it could be this simple.

But Mr Buckley was raising a finger.

"On one condition."

"Yes?"

"You sell one of the houses to our daughter. We're both getting on a bit and we'd like to have her near us in case anything goes wrong."

"That's understandable," Maddy said. "But are you sure your daughter would want a house here?"

"Yes, she would," said Mrs Buckley firmly.

Mr Buckley nodded emphatically, then raised a finger again.

"There's another condition," he said.

"Yes?" said Maggie nervously.

"We'd like a discount of 20%."

She had a quick intake of breath. She should have known there would be a snag. Twenty per cent of £80,000 was £16,000. It was blackmail but it was still a small price to pay to get her planning permission.

"Okay," she said. "And do I have your word that you'll raise no objections to the planning application?"

"You have our word. We won't object."

"Then we've got a deal," Maddy said.

In the second week of December, the planning permission was approved. Maddy was jubilant. Now the construction work could begin after Christmas. But first she had something else to do.

She rang Conor Black.

"Maddy!" he said. "What's the reason for this pleasant interruption?"

"I'm inviting you to lunch."

"I'm flattered."

"I said I'd do it when my planning permission came through. Well, I just got it this morning."

Chapter Forty-one

She had been looking forward to this lunch for some time and she wanted it to be special. She had a lot to thank Conor for. He had conducted the legal work on three house purchases for her over the years and had given her sound advice. Besides, he had always been available to talk to her out-of-hours when the occasion demanded. So she rang the Chalet d'Or and got hold of Marco O'Malley.

"I know it's coming up to Christmas," she apologised, "and you're bound to be very busy. But I wondered if there was any chance of a table for two in the next few days? I'm taking someone important to lunch."

Marco was effusive. "For you, Maddy, there is always a table. What day would suit?"

"Tomorrow?"

"Tomorrow you shall have the best table in the restaurant."

"It doesn't have to be the best. Any table will do."

"It will be the *best*. Now, what time would you like?"

"Twelve thirty?"

"I shall await you with enormous pleasure. It will make my day. Till tomorrow, my friend."

He made a kissing sound before putting down the phone and

Maddy found herself smiling. The runaway success of his new restaurant hadn't changed Marco in the least. And she was glad. She liked him exactly as he was.

The approval of her planning application had taken an enormous weight off her mind. But she still had a lot of work to do. First she had to talk to Paddy Behan and arrange a schedule with him to commence building. Then she had to persuade the bank to lend her the finance. But it was with a cheerful heart that she rang the builder to tell him that the first obstacle in her path had been cleared away.

"Congratulations," Paddy said. "That's the fastest approval I've ever heard of."

"It involved some wheeling and dealing," she said.

"Tell me about it," the builder replied with a cynical tone in his voice.

"So when do you think you could begin work?"

"First week of January, we could start clearing the site."

"And if everything goes smoothly when would you finish?"

"We'll aim to have the first one completed for Easter."

Easter would be perfect. The weather would be lovely. It was the ideal time to put the houses on the market.

"We'll have to sit down and talk finance," Paddy continued. "I'll need some cash up front. And we still have to agree an overall price. I'll need to see the plans."

"Okay. When would suit you?"

"Day after tomorrow? Say two o'clock?"

"That's fine. Do you want to come here?"

"I can do that."

"So, I look forward to seeing you, Paddy."

She got out her file and went over the figures again. To be on the safe side, she would need to borrow £150,000. It was a lot of money and the bank might baulk at the idea but on the positive side, she now owned three properties which she could use as collateral. She was confident she could persuade them if she pitched her proposal properly. She put all the material back in the file and rang the bank and made an appointment to speak to someone later that afternoon.

For this interview, she had to dress soberly. She took a shower and got out a charcoal business suit and white blouse. She brushed her dark hair till it shone. She applied a little make-up and put on a pair of silver earrings. Then she put on her suit and blouse. She studied her profile in the wardrobe mirror. Did she look like the type of woman a bank would entrust with £150,000 of its cash? Yes, she decided. She did. Feeling upbeat, she took her file and the bundle of plans that Simon had left and set off for her appointment.

She was pleasantly surprised to find Alan Semple waiting for her. He was the manager who had given her the loan to buy Munster Road, several years before. He would know her track record. And she was also pleased to note that he had been promoted in the meantime and now boasted the title of Manager, Loans and Finance.

"Well, Ms Pritchard," he said, ushering her into his office and indicating a chair for her to sit on. "It's good to see you again. How have you been keeping?"

"Very well," Maddy replied.

He had a computer screen blinking before him and she guessed he had been trawling through her records in preparation for the meeting.

"I'm very happy to hear that. So, you want to borrow some money?"

"Yes, a short-term loan. I'm developing some houses."

"Oh," he glanced up from the computer. "This is a new departure for you."

"Yes, it is," she replied. "But I've done my homework and my costings. This is a property I've recently purchased. I have already secured planning permission."

This information seemed to impress him.

"See here," she said, unrolling Simon's plans and spreading them on the manager's desk. "As you can see, there will be four detached houses. I have engaged a builder. We hope to start work early in January and have them completed by the summer. I expect to sell them quite quickly. In fact, I already have one of them sold."

He raised his eyebrows in surprise. "You certainly don't waste any time," he remarked, and leant forward to study the drawings. "They look like fine houses."

"They are."

"And you're confident you can sell them all?"

"Easily," Maddy replied. "I hope to have your loan repaid by June."

The manager studied the document she had prepared on costings and prices and nodded his head in approval.

"Excellent," he said at last. "Do you mind if I hold onto this?"

"Not at all. That copy is for you."

"So," he said, resting his arms on the desk and looking at her directly, "how much do you want to borrow?"

"One hundred and fifty thousand pounds."

His face showed no reaction. "We would need security, collateral of some kind."

"I own three houses."

The manager checked the computer screen once more.

"Two of them are already mortgaged," he said.

"But only for a fraction of their value. There is more than £150,000 worth of equity tied up in them. You're really taking very little risk. The site alone is worth more than £100,000 now that it has planning permission."

Alan Semple drummed his fingers on the desk and his face broke into a smile. "You've come fully prepared, haven't you?"

"Yes," Maddy replied, "I told you I had done my homework."

"Well, I think we can lend you the money. I can advance you a six-month loan. Do you think that gives you sufficient time?"

"Plenty."

"If you need longer to repay, we can always extend the term."

"Six months should be sufficient."

"The interest will be nine per cent per annum. Are you comfortable with that?"

Maddy nodded her agreement.

"When do you want to draw it down?" he asked.

"As soon as possible. I'll have to pay the builder some cash in advance."

Alan Semple stood up.

"I'll forward your application immediately with my recommendation. I don't see any problem."

He extended his hand and Maddy shook it.

"It's been good doing business with you, Ms Pritchard. I wish you every success and look forward to continuing our relationship."

"Me too," Maddy said and made her way out of his office with a singing heart.

Marco had placed her at the window with a view of the water. There had been an exuberant welcome with hugs and kisses and a complimentary glass of champagne while she studied the menu. She had accepted the champagne gladly for she had travelled here by taxi and didn't have to worry about driving. Besides, this lunch was a celebration and she had been eagerly looking forward it.

As she sipped her champagne, she allowed her eye to travel around the room. It was filling up quickly, businessmen with colleagues, groups of middle-aged ladies with too much jewellery enjoying a gossipy Christmas lunch, here and there an occasional man in blazer and tie dining alone. In the short time since it had opened, Marco's restaurant had become the favourite haunt of the rich and famous and the restaurant of choice for entertainers. Just at the weekend, a visiting rock band had booked six tables for their entourage and hangers-on. And to think of the arguments she'd had to persuade him to open here.

She felt a smile play around her lips. Mick McCann had long since departed The Wharf for new ventures, all the units were sold, his money was made and his reputation was secure. And she had played a crucial role in that success. She felt a small pang of regret about the way she had been treated by Carroll and Shanley. If she had been given the Chief Executive post she was certain she could have built further successes like this one. And from the gossip she picked up, Tim Lyons was in serious trouble, his staff deserting the company like a sinking ship, clients fleeing to other agencies, profits dropping like a stone, newly opened branches closing for lack of business. She felt a wave of sadness engulf her. It could all have been so different.

She looked up when she heard Conor's cheerful voice. He was standing at her shoulder, smiling down at her, his eyes sparkling with merriment. It was strange that she had never noticed before just how handsome he was.

"Sorry I'm late," he apologised. "I got a last minute phone-call. I know it's the standard excuse but this time it happens to be true."

"You're not late," she replied as he bent to kiss her cheek. "It's just gone twelve thirty. I took a taxi so I got here early."

He pulled out the chair next to her and sat down. "You look lovely," he said, flapping out his freshly laundered napkin and spreading it across his knees.

"Thank you."

"And you've snagged an excellent table at the most fashionable restaurant in town. How did you manage that?"

"I'm a friend of the owner."

"Really?"

"Yes. I persuaded him to locate here. Carroll and Shanley had the sale of The Wharf. It was my idea to open a restaurant."

At that moment, the subject of their conversation came advancing in their direction like a great white sailing boat, his chef's apron billowing around him as he approached. He bowed to Maddy and then Conor and presented him with a menu.

"This is my friend, Conor Black," Maddy said by way of introduction.

"Your *important* friend," Marco said grasping Conor's hand and shaking it vigorously.

She felt a blush creep into her cheeks. "He's my solicitor," she explained.

"I'm very pleased to meet you," Marco continued. "If you're a friend of Maddy's, you're already a friend of mine."

He commenced to reel off the culinary specials of the day while Conor blinked in confusion. It was obvious he had never met anyone like Marco before.

"Some more champagne while you decide?" the chef said, snapping his fingers till a waiter materialised to top up their glasses. "Is everything to your satisfaction?"

"Perfectly," Maddy replied.

"Take your time," Marco said and went sailing off again to say hello to a bunch of enthralled matrons at a nearby table.

"Is he always like this?" Conor asked when Marco was out of earshot.

"Yes, but people love it and he *is* a wonderful chef as you're about to find out."

"You look so happy," Conor said when they had ordered and the first course had been served.

"I *am* happy. For once, everything seems to be going right. I've secured my planning permission and the bank has agreed to lend me the finance. In January we'll start building. "

Conor smiled. "And then what will you do?"

"Look around for something else to buy."

"You never told me why you left Carroll and Shanley."

"It's a long story."

"I'd like to hear it."

As they ate, she explained the circumstances that forced her to give up her job.

"I don't blame you," he said when she had finished. "I would have done exactly the same. It seems they left you no option."

"The sad thing is the company is suffering. They're losing business and staff. I think it's only a matter of time before they go bust. The best people are getting out but lots of others will be hurt."

"Maybe they did you a favour," Conor said, taking her hand and gently squeezing it. "Would you have started out on your own if it hadn't happened?"

"Probably not."

"Then you should look to the future. You're a young woman, Maddy. And you have lots of talent. You should put it to work now."

It was past three o'clock when they left the Chalet d'Or after a wonderful lunch for which Marco refused to accept any payment.

"I promised you it would be on the house," he said, "when that blackguard prevented you from attending the gala dinner."

Conor and Maddy thanked him profusely and made their way out onto the road.

"How are you getting home?" Conor asked.

"The same way I arrived, by taxi."

"No. I'll take you. I have the car."

She settled in beside him, her head feeling light after the wine and the champagne. She asked herself when she had last felt so happy. Not since Greg had left. When they arrived at Auburn Grove, she invited him in for coffee.

"You haven't seen my house, have you?"

"No, I haven't."

"And you helped me buy it. It was another wreck. They couldn't give it away," she laughed.

She opened the front door and walked into the hall, then turned to face him. Next moment, Conor had her in his arms and his lips were on hers and she could feel the blood singing in her veins. She closed her eyes as his hot mouth explored her neck and his strong arms enclosed her.

"I've wanted you for a long time," he whispered, as she pulled him closer and felt her body melt.

The following morning he sent her roses and at eleven o'clock he rang.

"How are you this morning?"

"Exuberant, uplifted. Pick any adjective that means deliriously happy."

"Ecstatic?"

"I don't think that even begins to capture how I feel," Maddy replied and they both laughed.

"What have you got planned for today?"

"I've got the builder coming at two to give me a price for the work he's going to do. After that, I'm free."

"I've got tickets for the theatre," Conor said. "Eight o'clock. We could have supper afterwards."

"Oh, Conor, that would be lovely."

"What time would you like me to pick you up?"

"Seven o'clock, okay?"

"Sounds fine. And, Maddy, thank you again for a memorable day."

"But I enjoyed it too, Conor."

"That's what makes it special."

She made a light lunch of mushroom omelette and salad and at two o'clock Paddy Behan arrived and they spent the next hour and a half going over prices.

"I'll need £50,000 up front," he said. "I have to hire machinery and materials plus I'll have wages to pay."

"When do you need it?"

"Yesterday," he replied with a grin.

"I'll have it for you next week."

They shook hands on the deal and Paddy went off in his van. Maddy watched him go, then poured a glass of wine and sat at the window looking out at the garden, dead now and withered with the approach of winter. After a period of calm, her life was suddenly becoming frenzied once more. But she realised that she didn't care; she was enjoying every hectic moment and the best thing of all was that Conor was now part of it. It was wonderful how he made her feel – relaxed and elated at the same time, and with no doubts at all about her feelings! And to think that for all these years, he had been waiting patiently and she hadn't even known.

The following week, the bank loan came through and she paid Paddy Behan his deposit. She drew up a contract for the sale of the house to the Buckleys and, before she knew, Christmas was upon her with all the rush and madness of buying and spending and giving.

On Christmas Eve she brought Conor out to Raheny to meet her parents and Mrs Pritchard was delighted at the revived prospect of a possible son-in-law.

On Christmas morning he rang to say he was thinking of her. They had agreed to spend the day with their families. But on St Stephen's Day they went down to Killarney for a short break in a country hotel and whiled away the time in energetic walks, leisurely dinners, Irish coffees in front of a roaring fire and passionate love between crisp white sheets in a large four-poster bed.

On the 2nd of January she drove over to Harold's Cross and found Paddy Behan's men already on the site demolishing the old house with the help of a large bulldozer. Quickly, the ground was levelled and cleared, the rubble was removed and the foundations were dug. Drains were laid and pipes installed. Electricity cables were fitted. Cement mixers appeared along with a posse of bricklayers. Gradually the walls began to rise and the window frames were installed. On March 16th, the roof went on the first house.

And then on the 17th, Rosie's baby was born.

Chapter Forty-two

It was a little boy with a red face and a mat of dark hair, and hearty lungs that announced his arrival into the world with a bout of screeching that threatened to shake the hospital walls. He weighed nine pounds and six ounces as Rosie proudly told the relays of visitors who gathered round her bed bearing cards and presents and endless cuddly toys.

"You'll have to call him Patrick," Maddy said as she took the baby from his mother and gently rocked him in her arms and cooed into his face while Adam watched with a satisfied grin on his happy features.

"Of course," Rosie replied. "What else could I possibly call him?"

"You could call him Adam," her husband reminded her.

"Patrick's a nice name," Conor put in. "I like it. But Adam does have a point," he added diplomatically. "First-born son and all that."

"Why don't you call him Patrick Adam?" Maddy said. "And then everyone will be happy."

"Or Adam Patrick," Adam said.

"Maybe he should have been a girl?" Rosie grinned. "Then it would have been simple. We could have called her Patricia."

But the disagreement over the child's name was nothing

compared to the rivalry between the two grandmothers at the christening party which was held a few weeks later. By now, Rosie had been discharged from hospital looking radiant and adapting successfully to motherhood.

Maddy acted as godmother. She watched while the priest poured water over the child's head and declared him a member of the Christian faith while he struggled and kicked in the family christening robes which had been specially resurrected from Mrs Blake's clothing chest for the occasion.

But back at the party in Clontarf there was intense jockeying between Rosie's mother and Mrs Gray over who should have the honour of holding him for the photographs. In the end, a compromise had to be brokered whereby each grandmother held the squawking infant for separate sets of pictures before an uneasy truce was restored.

"Where's Sophie?" Maddy asked when she finally got Rosie alone in the kitchen. "I thought you said she was coming?"

"She cried off at the last moment. I got a phone call last night to say she couldn't make it. There's been a problem at work, apparently. She sounded genuinely put out."

Maddy was disappointed. She had been looking forward to seeing her friend.

"Is she okay? I've sort of lost touch with her. I can't remember the last time we talked."

"She's fine. She's found a flat in Fulham and appears to have taken to the London social scene like a duck to water."

"Are there any developments on the romantic front?"

Rosie grinned and sipped her drink. Now that the baby was born she allowed herself the occasional glass of wine. "You know Sophie. She'll not be happy till she marries some rich stockbroker with acres of land in Surrey, preferably an earl or a viscount."

"Which reminds me, what's the news about Arthur Brady?"

"Arthur has disappeared. Adam used to run into him from time to time but not any more. Nobody seems to know where he is."

"I hope he's all right," Maddy said. "I had a soft spot for Arthur. He was making a tremendous effort."

Their conversation was interrupted by Conor who came into the kitchen looking for another bottle of wine.

"What are you two plotting?" he asked playfully.

Rosie winked at Maddy. "More babies," she said and they all laughed.

By the end of May the houses at Harold's Cross were completed. Paddy Behan had done an excellent job. Where the derelict hulk of No 96 had once stood like a blot on the landscape, four smart new houses, complete with freshly laid lawns and spreading cherry trees now proudly stood. The Buckleys' daughter had taken possession of the house next door and Maddy had a waiting list of prospective buyers for the remaining three. She had decided to dispense with the services of an estate agent and simply placed an advert in *The Irish Times*. By June all the houses had been sold and she had repaid the bank loan. When she had settled her remaining taxes and debts including Simon Rafferty's fee, she had made a profit of almost £150,000 on the venture.

But she wasn't about to rest on her laurels. Already she was building a name as someone to turn to as a last resort when awkward properties wouldn't sell. Auctioneers would ring her in desperation with houses they couldn't shift and Paula Matthews would tip her off about bargains that were begging for a purchaser. But she was careful about the properties she took on. They had to be in a good location and they had to have potential. By the end of the year, she had bought four more and Paddy Behan was working for her practically full-time.

As time went on, her reputation as a shrewd operator continued to grow. One day in the spring of the following year, she received an unexpected phone call from Mick McCann who asked to meet her. When she walked into his office, she scarcely recognised him. The man who once looked so sleek and handsome had turned into an overweight caricature of his former self. His once-fit body had given way to fat. His belly hung over his trousers and rolls of flesh drooped from his cheeks like the wattles on a turkey-cock.

"Good to see you, Maddy," he said, raising himself with difficulty from his chair and giving her a friendly peck on the cheek. "You're looking as elegant as ever and scarcely a day older. How do you do it?"

"Healthy living," she replied with a smile.

"I could take a lesson from you," he said, patting his substantial paunch. "In fact I'm thinking of joining a health club. My doctor says I have to lose four stone."

"You should always listen to your doctor, Mick. This is what they call preventative medicine."

"It's my lifestyle," he said with a shrug. "Bad eating habits, too much gargle. No exercise. You wouldn't believe that I once played football for Mayo."

What Mick McCann had to tell her was that he was putting together a group of investors to buy an old hotel in Howth where he was planning to replicate his success with The Wharf. She listened attentively while he outlined the scheme.

"This place is right on the beach. Beautiful location only eight miles from the city yet you might as well be living in the countryside. It's got everything; bars, shops, rail links, schools, golf, sailing, you name it. There'll be gardens and fountains and I'm putting in a restaurant. Paul Le Brun is practically foaming at the mouth to get the concession after seeing the success that Marco made of The Wharf."

At the mention of her old adversary, Maddy frowned.

"These units will be aimed at high-net-worth individuals, people who want to trade down. I've done my research and believe me they are going to walk right off the site."

"How many are you building?"

"I'm limiting it to a hundred luxury apartments and a dozen penthouses, best of materials, no expense spared. The thing is, Maddy, I'm looking for someone to market them and I've come to you. You're the only person I would trust with this. Nobody else has your flair and vision."

"You're going to turn my head, Mick."

"Well, it's true. Carroll and Shanley have gone to the dogs since you left and I didn't find O'Leary and Partners a hell of a lot better. There's nobody else in town with your experience. You can name your price. What do you say?"

"These investors you're bringing together, who are they?"

McCann rattled off a list of wealthy individuals, most of whom Maddy knew by name or reputation.

"How much are they putting in?"

"Half a million each."

"Ummm," she said. "What about planning permission?"

"That won't be a problem. I've already spoken to the authorities. It's practically guaranteed."

"And what's the time scale?"

"I expect to complete the purchase of the land and the planning application in the next two months. Then we start building. I aim to have the whole development completed within eighteen months."

Maddy was thinking furiously. A new idea was beginning to take root in her head.

"So are you interested?" McCann asked.

"I might be, if the terms are right."

He immediately looked relieved. "That's the answer I was hoping for."

"I might also be interested in investing."

He drew back and observed her closely. "You would?"

"Yes. I'm assuming you can still take another punter?"

"Certainly. The more the merrier. It reduces my borrowings."

"Let me think about it. I'll get back to you."

That evening, she raised the matter with Conor as they were having a quiet drink in town after he had finished work.

"Have you any advice to give me?" she asked.

"Half a million pounds is an awful lot of money."

"But the potential rewards are great. I have a hunch that Mick McCann is right about this development. There's a whole new market emerging, people whose families are raised, who've retired from work, people who don't need a big house with half a dozen bedrooms and all the housework involved. Not to mention the gardening. Those are the people he's targeting and I think he's on to something."

"Can you trust him?"

"I think so. You could always draw up a contract for me that will safeguard my investment."

"But you realise you can't safeguard it completely?"

"I know that. There's always a risk involved. But remember who told me 'Nothing ventured, nothing gained'?"

"Remind me."

"It was you."

Conor smiled. "I think you've already made up your mind."

When she got home, she sat down at her desk and took out her calculator. When she had finished her projections, she reckoned she would have to borrow £100,000. But this was a major leap forward – the biggest thing she had done so far. She would be investing all her assets in one venture and if it went wrong she would be right back where she started. In fact she would be worse off, because she would still owe the bank £100,000 and would probably have to sell the house in Munster Road to repay the debt.

She turned the matter over in her mind. Was this something she wanted to do? Was she going too fast, rushing ahead of herself, becoming greedy? But she remembered the fears that had originally gripped her when she contemplated buying the house in Munster Road and the feeling that she would never forgive herself if she passed up the opportunity and someone else got it instead.

She felt her old confidence return. Her instinct had never betrayed her in the past. All her ventures had turned out well. Why should this one be any different? She had a feel for this development. She could tell that Mick McCann was right and that it would be an outstanding triumph. And Maddy wanted to be part of it.

The following morning she arranged an interview with Alan Semple and half an hour later she had reached agreement to draw down a loan of £100,000. She rang McCann and told him she was joining the scheme and was also taking up his offer to market the development. He didn't baulk at her demand for a £70,000 fee. She got Conor to draw up a contract and the following week paid the first tranche of her investment. Two weeks after that, the purchase of the hotel went ahead, quickly followed by the granting of the planning permission as McCann had predicted. Maddy rolled up her sleeves and prepared to go back to work. She was eagerly looking forward to it.

The first thing was a name. Mick McCann wanted something with connotations of the sea and made various suggestions such as The Moorings and The Cove, none of which got Maddy wildly excited. And then by accident she discovered that years before there had been an old harbour near the site owned by a man called Bell. She knew at once she had found what she was looking for.

"Bell's Harbour," she said, when she reached McCann on the phone. "It's got the sea and the local angle and a bit of history. But above all, it's got class."

"You think so?"

"Positive, trust me. This is the name we want."

"Okay. Go with it."

So while Mick was busy with his architects and planners, she got to work creating some publicity. First call was to her old contact Paula Matthews who was surprised to find her picking up the marketing reins once more.

"I thought you had left all that behind," she said.

"That was the idea but Mick McCann persuaded me otherwise. You might say he made me an offer I couldn't refuse. I'm letting you have first bite of this, Paula."

"Tell me. I'm all ears."

"It's a new development in Howth on the site of the old Sutton Hotel. We're calling it Bell's Harbour. One hundred luxury apartments overlooking the ocean, a dozen penthouses, gardens, terraces and a top-of-the-range restaurant."

"Sounds fabulous. Who'll be running the restaurant?"

"That hasn't been finalised yet but I can tell you it will be an award-winning chef."

"Not Marco again?"

"Afraid not. He's not a magician. Unfortunately he cannot be in two places at once."

"Thanks for the tip, Maddy. Keep me in the loop."

"Will do."

A few days later, Paula ran a large news story in her supplement which was quickly picked up by the other property editors. It was exactly how Maddy wanted to play the publicity, releasing pieces of information gradually to whet the appetite and maintain momentum. It secured its objective for almost at once her phone began to ring with inquiries from possible purchasers.

The question of a selling agent had not yet been agreed so Maddy dealt with these queries herself, taking details and promising to keep the callers informed. And then a thought occurred to her. As well as handling the marketing, why shouldn't she look after the sales? After all, she had handled the sales of The Wharf when she was working for Carroll and Shanley. It would mean a vastly increased workload but she was certain she could manage it. Why allow the commission to go to someone else when she could collect it herself?

She put the thought to Mick McCann.

"Would you have the time to do it?" he asked.

"Why not? I did it before. I'm already handling the marketing. It makes sense to do both."

"I'd love you to do it, Maddy. I was simply concerned about the workload."

"Let me worry about that. Have we got a deal?"

"Sure we have."

"One other thing. Who's handling the legal side for you?"

"That hasn't been decided."

"I might have someone for you."

She put down the phone and smiled. The commission on the sales should net her another £100,000 after tax. And if Conor was able to take on the legal work, he would benefit handsomely too. Her business relationship with Mick McCann was already proving lucrative.

Conor snapped up the opportunity. It was a guaranteed source of work handling the conveyancing of the apartments and would raise his profile considerably.

A week later, after he had agreed terms with McCann, they went to dinner. Conor poured the wine and raised his glass.

"To Bell's Harbour and all who sail in her."

Maddy laughed. "Here's to a smooth journey and no squalls."

"I'd settle for a few squalls," Conor said with a grin. "It's the hurricanes I'd be worried about."

Maddy was in a good mood but under no illusion about the workload that lay ahead. And there was one source of potential trouble already looming on the horizon. Her next task was to negotiate the terms of his lease with the truculent Paul Le Brun. She braced herself for trouble.

But as it turned out, Le Brun was a different man to the one who had shut the door in her face four years earlier when she tried to interest him in the restaurant at The Wharf. Marco O'Malley's success had obviously taught him a lesson. This time when Maddy turned up, he was waiting with a large smile and a warm welcome to lead her to an office above the restaurant where he fussed over her and offered her a comfortable chair.

"Please sit down, Ms Pritchard," he said, as if he was meeting her for the very first time. "Can I get you something to drink?"

"Coffee," Maddy said and Le Brun immediately lifted a phone and rang the kitchen.

"Mick tells me you're interested in purchasing the lease on our restaurant," she began.

"Yes. I certainly am."

"What exactly do you have in mind?"

"Something to seat between eighty and a hundred people. Open plan. I take it the restaurant will have views of the sea?"

"Of course."

"I was thinking of a speciality fish restaurant. There's a need for a few more in Dublin, and Howth would be ideal."

Maddy was already warming to the idea. It would fit in perfectly with the marine theme of the entire development.

"I have my Michelin star. And I have built up a solid reputation here at Pigalle," Le Brun said.

Maddy knew what he said was true. Apart from Marco O'Malley, Paul Le Brun was the best-known chef in Dublin. His name would lend tremendous appeal to the development and greatly help with sales.

She outlined the terms which she had already agreed with Mick McCann. Le Brun didn't bat an eye. It was obvious that he was determined not to allow this second opportunity to slip through his hands.

"You accept the terms?"

"Yes."

"Then we have an agreement. I'll arrange for you to receive a contract in the next few days."

Le Brun's face was now wreathed in smiles. He opened a cupboard beside his desk and took out a bottle of twenty-year-old Napoleon brandy and two crystal glasses.

"Let's drink a toast," he said, handing one glass to Maddy. "To a long and fruitful partnership!"

She sipped her glass. The brandy tasted like elixir and it slipped effortlessly down her throat. It's true what they say, she thought. Nothing succeeds like success.

The news that Paul Le Brun was to open a new fish restaurant at Bell's Harbour was selectively leaked to the media. Maddy arranged for photographs to be taken with the sea lapping gently in the background while Le Brun delightedly gave interviews to a number of food writers and broadcasters. He seemed to relish the opportunity to compete with his arch-rival, Marco O'Malley, in the publicity stakes. Within a matter of weeks, she had secured deposits on four of the penthouses and a dozen apartments and so far not a single sod had been turned on the site.

But that was about to change. Now that he had secured planning permission and approved the designs, McCann moved swiftly to begin construction. The old hotel was demolished and the site cleared and the ground marked out. Large wooden hoardings went up and behind them a battery of cranes and mechanical diggers set to work. The scene was transformed into a hive of activity with a small army of bricklayers and labourers pouring foundations and building walls.

Meanwhile, Maddy got to work on the publicity brochure. After giving the matter much consideration, she decided on the slogan *Bell's Harbour, Gracious Living by the Sea*. The brochure extolled the virtues of the new development, gave prominent emphasis to the location, and was lavishly illustrated with photographs of Howth and artists' drawings of the planned complex. It was launched at a press party for the property writers who were sent home happy with a presentation pack of delicacies from Paul Le Brun's restaurant. The result was another rash of publicity and more inquiries and bookings.

Exactly six months after work began, the first phase was completed and the show apartment opened. At last, they had something to show the public and the serious business of marketing and selling the development commenced. Maddy rang a leading Dublin department store and arranged for an interior designer to furnish the apartment at a special rate in return for a prominent mention in the publicity material. When the young designer had finished, the apartment looked like something out of a Hollywood film set. To coincide with the launch, she took out half-page adverts in the property supplements accompanied by further editorial coverage.

There was a flood of visitors and a rash of inquiries. Even Maddy was surprised by the level of interest. It was a hectic period and both she and Conor were swamped with work. In the first three weeks, they took bookings on another fifty apartments and only two of the penthouses remained. It looked as if Mick McCann was about to repeat his success with The Wharf.

But Maddy and Conor did manage to get some time to themselves. In June, Conor announced that he had got the loan of a friend's cottage in West Cork. They decided to take Monday off and have a long weekend. They spent the time lazing around, exploring the beautiful countryside and relaxing in quaint little pubs and restaurants. Then it was back again to the hectic round of promoting and selling the apartments at Bell's Harbour and dealing with the myriad problems that entailed.

Maddy had never worked so hard in her life but it was satisfying work and she knew now that she had made the right decision. Her investment was secure and was on target to pay a handsome dividend. Twenty months after they had first discussed the venture, Mick McCann completed the last apartment and the development was complete. All but a handful of units had been sold.

Maddy was now thirty-three and already on her way to earning her first million pounds.

And to crown her happiness, Conor had asked her to marry him.

Chapter Forty-three

Years later, Maddy would look on that frenzied period and wonder where she had found the time and the energy to get married. It seemed that back then she had been working non-stop from the moment she woke in the morning till she crawled exhausted into bed at night. But somehow they managed to grab a half-hour here and another twenty minutes somewhere else to arrange the myriad details that were involved in becoming man and wife. And she was eagerly assisted by Rosie Blake who had been through the whole thing herself and felt like a veteran.

Just like Rosie's nuptials, this was a small wedding confined to close friends and family – not because they couldn't afford the expense of a grand occasion as Maddy now had the money to stage a wedding that would propel her into the social columns – but because she just couldn't handle all the fuss. So a few weeks after the celebration party to mark the completion of Bell's Harbour, Maddy and Conor walked up the aisle of her parish church watched by thirty of their friends and promised to love and honour each other in sickness and in health.

There was one disappointing note. She had planned to have three bridesmaids – her sister Helen, Rosie and Sophie Kennedy. But try as they did, no one could locate Sophie. Rosie, who did most of the searching, reported that she had last been heard of in Edinburgh where she had gone to live with a musician. But no one had an address or telephone number and all attempts at finding her came to nothing. It seemed that the bonds that held the three friends had at last been sundered and Maddy reluctantly had to make do with just two bridesmaids.

After the wedding, they flew out to New York for a two-week honeymoon. Neither of them had ever been in America before and the novelty was exciting. They wandered the streets of Manhattan like impressionable teenagers, staring at the towering office blocks and the swirling crowds and the honking yellow taxis. They took boat rides on the East River, visited the Bronx Zoo, climbed to the top of the Statue of Liberty and stared down from the dizzying heights of the Empire State Building.

They ate pancakes with maple syrup for breakfast and rib-eye steaks and crawfish for dinner. They drank Budweiser beer and exotic Tequila Sunrises. They visited Greenwich Village and Coney Island, went to the movies, browsed in bookshops and art galleries and strolled hand in hand in Central Park like the young lovers they were. And all the time, they let themselves unwind and relax while they dreamed about their future together.

Maddy never had a moment's hesitation when Conor proposed marriage. She had known from the first time he kissed her that she was in love with him. There was no uncertainty about it in her mind as there had been with Greg Delaney. And it was a different type of love to what she had known with Greg. Conor's was a steady, constant, undemanding love that never questioned, never was jealous and never was moody or suspicious. She knew that Conor loved her unreservedly as she loved him in return.

In the early months of their relationship, she sometimes asked herself if she had truly been in love with Greg. He had been handsome and charming. He was witty and made her laugh. But she was younger then and he was the first man she had ever been seriously involved with. He had made a big impression on her and she had given her heart to him. But was it love or simple infatuation? Had he swept her off her feet with his smart black BMW and his penthouse apartment and his dining in fine restaurants?

She knew one thing for certain. What she felt for Conor was deeper and infinitely superior to what she had known with Greg. Above all, she knew that he would always be faithful. With Conor, she would never have to doubt.

The honeymoon finally ended and they returned reluctantly to Dublin. But now that she was married, Maddy wanted a new house and she had the money to pay for it. Her involvement with Bell's Harbour had convinced her of the wild beauty of Howth and now she had fallen in love with the place. Besides, it would be closer to her parents in Raheny and to Conor's family in Malahide. She decided to take some time off from work while she searched for somewhere new to live.

She soon found it – a large five-bedroomed house with extensive gardens perched in a commanding position overlooking the Baily Lighthouse. Ironically, its owners were people she had already met through business, a retired couple whose family was raised and were now trading down to a penthouse apartment in Bell's Harbour. The house was called Islandbawn, the white island, and it was bright and airy and needed little work besides some minor alterations and a thorough redecorating job. Maddy had already chosen one of the bedrooms as an office. It looked down across the garden to Dublin Bay and the green peaks of the Wicklow Hills.

The asking price was £250,000 and Maddy was in such high spirits that she didn't even attempt to haggle with the agent, a bright, intelligent young woman called Carol Greene who showed them over the house not once but three times. Maddy knew it was a bargain and it was the house she wanted. She could picture her life here, the sun on the garden in the mornings, the sighing of the sea, the winking lights of Dalkey across the bay. Islandbawn had everything she wanted and particularly it had space – enough room for a child to wander and play – for by now, she was two months pregnant.

She was ecstatic at the prospect of a baby. She was godmother to Rosie's little boy and she could sense the joy and satisfaction that he brought into their home. She wanted the same thing for herself but she knew it was going to put a rein on her hectic work schedule. So when Mick McCann rang a few weeks later to say he wanted her to work for him again on another development, she declined.

"I'll take on the marketing and I'm sure Conor will be happy to handle the legal work but I can't deal with the sales."

He sounded disappointed. "I was relying on you, Maddy. We're a great team together. Who am I going to get to replace you?"

"I know the very person."

She gave him Jane Morton's number. Jane had recently set up on her own account and was looking for business.

"Is she any good?" he asked, cautiously.

"She'll be ideal. I trained her myself. And Mick, if you're looking for investors, talk to me."

"Okay, I'll get back to you."

With the move to Islandbawn, they now had three investment properties in their portfolio: Auburn Grove, Munster Road and Conor's apartment in Seapoint which he had vacated when they got married. They were let on long leases to corporate tenants and were bringing in a steady stream of rental income. And Maddy would earn another hefty fee for the marketing work she was about to undertake for Mick McCann. With Conor's legal practice now flourishing they were very well off. Maddy could afford to take her foot off the pedal and concentrate on the arrival of her first child. She was looking forward to it with unconcealed delight.

It was a little girl, with coal-black hair and dark eyes, and right from the beginning everyone said she was the image of her mother – even Conor who was squeezed out of things by all the fuss over Maddy but didn't seem to mind. They had decided to call her Emma which was Mrs Pritchard's name and one that they both liked and which Maddy said was in line for a revival.

To celebrate the christening, they decided to combine it with a belated house-warming party and invited the neighbours, several of whom came out of politeness and others because they were dying to get a good look over the house and see what sort of job the Blacks had made of it. But it was a good party with lashings of food and drink and the weather held up and everyone had a great time chatting and wandering round the garden and trying to identify landmarks across the bay.

Rosie returned the compliment and was godmother to the new baby and brought Adam and Patrick who was growing fast into a sturdy little boy and spent a good part of the afternoon trying to climb trees and chasing the kittens round the house. But eventually everyone said their goodbyes and Conor and Maddy were left to clear away the debris and put Emma into her cot before collapsing on the sofa to watch some silly quiz show on television.

She was busy again. But it was different to the work she had been engaged in before. Now, it was bathing Emma and changing her diaper and feeding her and putting her down for her nap and taking care of the dozens of little jobs that raising a baby entailed. And before long, she was pregnant again with their son, Jack, who was born thirteen months after his sister. It was exhausting work and Maddy insisted on doing most of it herself although she had got hold of a good assistant from the village – a woman called Betty Rickard who helped out on the occasions when she had to go shopping or into town.

But once the children were old enough to go to school, she found she had time on her hands once again and she began to think of going back to work. By now, the stirrings of a new property boom were starting to be felt. Everywhere you looked, building work was under way. Cranes dotted the city skyline. Old buildings were being torn down and new apartment blocks and shopping centres were shooting up. People with disposable income seemed to be rushing into property, buying apartments to let or as second homes. And this time it was happening not just in Dublin but in cities and towns all over the country.

One evening as they sat on the patio after dinner, she said: "I'm thinking of going back to work."

"Doing what?" Conor asked.

"What I've always done. What I'm good at it. Property."

"You don't have to," he said. "We're comfortably off. You don't ever have to work again."

"But I want to, Conor. I like to be busy."

"Have you anything particular in mind?"

"I've got one or two ideas. I think I'll make a few phone calls tomorrow."

When the children had been safely deposited at school, she sat down and rang Jane Morton.

"Hi, Jane," she said. "This is a voice from the past."

"My God, Maddy, how are you? You know, I was just talking about you the other day."

"All positive, I hope?"

"Of course, how could it be otherwise?"

"Well, the good news is, I'm fit and bursting with energy. The bad news is that I'm beginning to get bored and itching to get back to work."

She could hear Jane laughing.

"That doesn't surprise me. People were taking bets on how long you'd be able to stay away."

"Look, Jane, do you think we could meet? I've got some ideas I'd like to kick around with you."

"Sure. I could drop out to Howth if you like."

They agreed to meet at Islandbawn the following morning at eleven o'clock. Maddy set the tea table on the patio where they could watch the ships passing up and down the bay. At three minutes to eleven she heard Jane's car pull into the drive. She led her through the house and out to the back.

"What would you like to drink – tea, coffee, juice?"

"A nice cup of tea would be sheer bliss," Jane said, sinking back into the wicker settee and looking down the garden to the sea.

Maddy returned with a tray containing cups, saucers, plates and a large carrot cake.

"I thought we'd indulge ourselves," she said. "It's been so long since we talked like this. How is your business coming on?"

"Very well. That work you sent me from Mick McCann came in very handy."

"Would you say you're working at full capacity?"

"I'm only a small agency," Jane explained. "Just me and a secretary. I'm not complaining. I'm making far more money than I did with Carroll and Shanley. And I don't have to put up with all that bullshit."

"But you could be even busier?"

"Of course."

"Well, I have an idea that could work to our mutual advantage."

Over the next half hour, Maddy explained what she had in mind – an agency that would combine both sales and marketing in a way that had not been seen since she had worked with Mick McCann on Bell's Harbour.

"The economy is growing, interest rates are low, people have never been better off and you just have to look around to see the construction work that's going on. All the ingredients are there for a property boom like we've never seen before. These developers have to sell their apartments and to do that they've got to market them cleverly. An agency that can deliver both services could be very successful. And you and I have proven track records in these areas. Are you interested?"

"Does a bear go in the woods?" Jane said, putting down her teacup with a rattle. "Of course, I'm interested."

When they finally broke up at twelve thirty they had agreed to set up a new agency – Tara Properties. Jane would handle the sales and Maddy would deal with the marketing. They had also decided to hire some extra staff. Maddy had her eye fixed on Annie McNamara, the young media advisor who had worked with her on The Wharf. Jane said she was going to contact Sue Donovan who had taken Maddy's old job at Carroll and Shanley. She had heard that Sue was unhappy and was quietly looking around for an alternative.

Suddenly Maddy felt flushed with enthusiasm. She could feel the adrenalin flowing. It was just like the old days when she was racing around town arranging deals, fixing meetings, setting up publicity opportunities. By the time the children got home from school, she had contacted Annie McNamara who said she was definitely interested and would give a decision in the next few days. And she had drawn up a roster of things to be done in preparation for their launch.

Over the coming days, both Sue and Annie agreed to come on board. It was decided that the new company would work out of Jane's existing office in Clare Street in Dublin city centre. But the most important news was that they had secured their first client. Mick McCann was planning another large development at the north docks and was keen to engage their services.

It was in high spirits that Tara Properties was launched a month later at a party attended by Paula Matthews and the property editors, people from the newspaper and television world that Annie had recruited and several leading developers. And the launch itself became a focus of media attention when Marco O'Malley insisted on doing the catering and turned up in person, as eccentric as ever in his chef's outfit and white hat. The result was acres of positive publicity in the following day's papers.

As the party drew to a close, Maddy found herself alone at last with Conor and the children.

"That certainly went off with a bang," he said, putting his arm around her and kissing her cheek. "Are you happy now?"

"Oh, yes, Conor. I'm very happy."

"Then I am too. I knew the first time we did business that you were headed for big things. You had a vibe."

"Did I really?" she laughed.

"Yes. You wanted to buy Auburn Grove and nothing was going to stop you."

She smiled and lowered her eyes.

"Congratulations, Maddy. You deserve all the success that Tara Properties will bring."

Conor was right. Tara Properties was a huge success. Within three years, they had a turnover of five million pounds and had hired more staff to handle the huge volume of apartment sales alone. Maddy had read the mood perfectly. A property boom was under way and builders were putting up apartment blocks as fast as they could get planning permissions. It made sense for them to give the promotion and sales to a single company that could provide both services. Conor's legal practice also benefited as Maddy channelled much of the conveyancing work to him. And the beauty of the arrangement was that she could work at her own pace and devote time to the children. Now she had a team around her, people she could rely on and trust.

But the past had not entirely gone away. One morning, she was in her office when the receptionist announced that a man had arrived to see her. She was surprised because she wasn't expecting anyone.

"Oh," she said. "Did he give a name?"

"Yes. Mr Lyons. He said you know him."

She felt a jolt. Tim Lyons, after all these years! She asked the secretary to show him in.

She barely recognised him. He looked frail. His face was lined and his back bent and stooped like a much older man.

"Tim," she said, barely able to conceal her shock. "Please take a seat."

"Thanks for seeing me, Maddy," he began, as he lowered himself into a chair. His eyes darted quickly round the bright office with its smart furniture, fax machines and gleaming new laptop computers. "I hear things are going well for you."

"Yes. What about you?"

"Not good. Did you know I've been let go by Carroll and Shanley?"

"No," she said. She had not heard this news and it dismayed her.

"Business has been doing badly. We weren't prepared. We didn't keep abreast of the trends."

"I'm really sorry to hear that, Tim."

He shrugged. "Well, I was the boss and I had to pay the price. I've come to ask a favour."

"Yes?"

"Would you have a job for me?"

Before she could reply he rushed on, nervously wringing his hands.

"I'm really on my uppers. I've four children to get through school. Two of them are at college. I'm desperate."

She was aghast. To watch her former boss sit before her and beg for work gave her no satisfaction despite the harm he had done to her in the past.

"We have no vacancies, Tim."

"Please. I'd do anything. I was good at sales once. And I'd work hard."

She looked at him. There had been a time when she would have gladly wrung Tim Lyons's neck but not now. The sight of him pleading with her only filled her with immense sadness.

"Let me think about it," she said at last.

But when she spoke later to Jane and Sue, their reaction was hostile.

"I hope you ran him off the premises," Jane said. "Imagine the cheek of him coming to us after what he did."

"He's a broken man," Maddy said. "I felt sorry for him."

"It's his own fault. He shouldn't have promoted all those idiots."

"I know he did us wrong. But we can't live in the past. If we continue to harbour resentment we're only hurting ourselves. We're doing well. Can't we afford to be generous? And he has a young family to support."

Sue bit her lip and Jane frowned.

"I suppose we could always use another sales person," Jane said at last. "But how is he going to fit in?"

"Let him worry about that. I think he'll be so grateful to get a break that he'll work his butt off."

"All right," Jane said at last. "I've no objection. Take him on."

Other developments were under way. Maddy was discovering that nothing in life stays still. Rosie came to visit one Saturday afternoon with important news.

"Adam has been offered the chance of a big promotion," she said, breathlessly, after Conor had taken the children for a drive and the two women were alone together on the patio.

"Congratulations. You must be thrilled."

"Well, yes and no," Rosie said, lowering her head. "It will mean going to live in Cornwall."

"Cornwall?"

"Yes. And I'm not sure I want to leave Ireland."

The news was upsetting. Rosie was Maddy's best and oldest friend. They had known each other since childhood and in recent years, they had grown even closer. If she left, Maddy was going to miss her terribly.

"Does he have to go?"

"If he wants the promotion. It's the firm's headquarters, you see."

Rosie mulled it over for a week and in the end she decided to go.

"I don't really see this as permanent," she said tearfully when the time came for them to leave. "We'll come back again in a few years and, of course, we'll keep in touch. I'll write to you and I'll ring every week."

"Go and build a new life," Maddy said, as she bit her lip. "You'll make fresh friends and Cornwall is beautiful. You'll love it there."

She watched as her friend drove away and the tears welled up in her eyes. She was barely able to contain her grief. The three friends had often sworn enduring loyalty to each other. Now they were scattered, Rosie to Cornwall and Sophie to God knew where. It was as if she was letting go of part of her life – those bright years when they had been young and everything had seemed possible and the world had been filled with golden promise.

Epilogue

Time passed quickly and the children grew up. Emma finished school and went to work with Paula Matthews, training to be a journalist. She was turning into a beautiful young woman, tall and slim and dark like her mother. Already she was beginning to turn heads. But Jack was the clever child and fond of sports. He played rugby for his school and wanted to be an architect.

The business grew and prospered. Tim Lyons showed his gratitude by working hard. Eventually he was put in charge of the sales team – the job he had with Carroll and Shanley when Maddy first met him. Over time, he became a valuable member of the staff. Conor's practice expanded in conjunction with Tara Properties till he had more work than he could handle.

Maddy remained extremely active. She jogged every morning before work. She played golf. She immersed herself in professional bodies and charity work. She led a busy social life – keeping in touch with her many friends and throwing regular dinner parties at Islandbawn. So it was with something of a shock that she realised her fiftieth birthday was approaching.

She wanted to keep it secret, to let it slip by unannounced but she hadn't counted on Emma and Rosie. Emma had organised a surprise party and Maddy could have killed her when she walked into the ballroom of the Ambassador Hotel and found all those people waiting to greet her. But she had enjoyed it despite her loathing of fuss.

And now Rosie had located Sophie in Paris of all places and had arranged for them all to meet in London. She glanced once more at the email that had arrived that morning. *A reunion of the three friends*, was the heading. A line of an old song popped into her head. *We'll meet again.* Here it was coming true after all these years.

She would have to go, of course. She couldn't miss this for the world. To see her friends once more, to discuss the old days together, to hear what life had done to them in the intervening years. And so much had happened. There would be some merry tales to tell.

She logged off her laptop and reached for the phone. She would begin to arrange the trip right away.

Maddy stepped out of the opulent foyer of the Savoy Hotel and into the bright sunshine of a London afternoon. It was three o'clock. In an hour's time, she was meeting Sophie and Rosie at Claridges for afternoon tea and later they were going for drinks and dinner at a cosy little restaurant in Soho. She couldn't wait to see them both again. She could feel the excitement tingling along her spine and right down to her fingertips. But first she had a small job to do.

There was a boutique she had spotted in the Strand yesterday after she had arrived on the mid day flight from Dublin and settled into her room at the Savoy. She walked there now and pushed open the door. A young sales assistant immediately came to attend her.

"I'd like to see some handbags, please."

"Yes, madam. What exactly did you have in mind?"

"Something smart, something that will look fashionable and attractive."

"We have a very extensive range."

"Could I look at some of them, please?"

The assistant hurried away and came back with an armful of bags. She laid them on the counter for Maddy's inspection. They came in all shapes and sizes. But one immediately caught her attention. It was a brown Louis Vuitton. It would be perfect. She glanced at the price tag. It wasn't cheap but it didn't matter. This was a very special occasion.

"I'll have two."

"Yes, madam." The assistant didn't blink. She turned and went off again.

While she was gone, Maddy examined some silk scarves that hung on a rack nearby. She selected two and laid them on the counter to be wrapped along with the bags and the birthday cards she had written this morning. The assistant put them into separate carrier bags and Maddy produced her credit card. Now all that remained was to get to Claridges and await the arrival of her friends.

She was early so she selected a seat in the lounge where she could watch the door. A waiter came to serve her but she told him she was expecting some company and would order later. While she waited, she looked around. It was a rich, opulent room filled with comfortable furniture and the clientele were mainly ladies like herself chatting animatedly over the bone-china teacups. Her mind went once again to the meeting that lay ahead. She had thought of practically nothing else since she received Rosie's email.

What would they look like now? How would they have aged? And what stories would they have to tell? It had been five years since she had last seen Rosie on a flying visit to Dublin to see her parents. But Sophie had vanished completely. Twenty years had passed since she had set eyes on her. She had gone to London and then Edinburgh and now she had turned up in Paris – living with a young painter of all things. Maddy felt a smile pass her lips. Sophie had always been a bohemian at heart despite those frantic efforts to find a solid professional man who would settle down and marry her. She was going to enjoy listening to her adventures.

Her reverie was interrupted by the sight of a small, flame-haired woman in black jacket and white linen trousers come tentatively into the room and gaze around. Maddy looked closely. It was Rosie! But my God, she barely recognised her. She had lost a couple of stone in weight and what had she done with her hair? She stood up and waved. Rosie saw her and came rushing across the room and straight into Maddy's arms.

"Let me look at you!" Maddy said, as they had hugged and embraced like survivors from a sinking liner. "You've changed completely. You're thinner. And you've taken to dyeing your hair again!"

Rosie fingered her hair and smiled. "Do you like it?"

"It's fantastic. It makes you look so much younger."

"I got it done specially for this trip. I wanted to surprise you."

"And how did you get so thin? Did you go on a diet or something?"

"That's all down to healthy eating," Rosie said. "I'm taking very good care of myself now. Do you know, I grow my own vegetables and make my own wine?"

"Yes, you told me in your mail."

"Well, between exercise and watching my diet, that excess weight just fell away. And I feel an awful lot better. But look at *you*, Maddy. You've barely changed at all. Still jogging?"

"Most mornings."

"How are Conor and the children?"

"Prospering. What about Adam and Patrick?"

"Adam is talking about early retirement once we've got Patrick safely through university. He's at Durham studying Dentistry."

"Smart boy," Maddy said. "There's money to be made in pulling teeth."

The waiter was back, hovering in the wings.

"What would you like?" Maddy asked.

"I'd really love a gin and tonic."

She gave their order and the waiter went off again.

"We've got so much to talk about," Maddy said. "But first I want to hear about Sophie. How did you manage to track her down?"

"You'll not believe it. It was through Arthur Brady of all people."

"Arthur?"

"Yes. He's working in London and totally reformed. He hasn't touched the booze in years. He's a pillar of Alcoholics Anonymous, apparently."

"Well, I'm delighted to hear that. I always liked Arthur."

"Adam managed to get a phone number from someone and I rang him. It turns out he ran into Sophie last year in Paris and they kept in touch. So he was able to give me her address."

"And how is she?"

"From what I can gather, she's fine. She runs a small marketing business and lives in Belleville with a young painter called Pierre Dumont. She'll tell you all about it when she arrives. I spoke to her this morning. She'll be here by four."

Maddy glanced at her watch. It was now five to four. At that moment, the waiter arrived with the drinks.

Rosie lifted her glass and took a sip.

"You don't know how good it is to see you again, Maddy. It feels just like old times."

At four o'clock on the dot, Sophie came striding in, looking elegant in a knee-length cream designer dress and with her blond hair in a bob. She had aged somewhat but Maddy recognised her instantly.

"Hi, strangers," she said with a smile as they all stood and embraced.

"Look at you!" Rosie said, standing back to admire her. "You still look like that giddy young thing that used to turn heads in the Pink Parrot when we were only fresh out of school."

"A lot of water has flowed under the bridge since then, Rose. How are you both?"

"We're fine," Maddy said. "And I needn't ask how you are. You seem to be thriving. Is it this young lover you've snagged?"

"Could be," Sophie replied with a lascivious grin. "Remember what Mae West once said. It's not the man in your life but the life in your man."

They laughed so loudly that some heads turned to stare.

The waiter returned and Sophie ordered a glass of wine.

"Before we begin," she said. "I've got some apologies to make. I didn't get back for the christening of your children, Rose and I feel ashamed. And worst of all, Maddy, I didn't get to your wedding."

"It's okay. We missed you. But these things happen. Now you're back again."

Sophie fingered her glass and her face suddenly became grave. "The truth is, I just couldn't face it. I was going through an awful time. I had so much trouble in my life that I just wanted to hide as far away as possible."

"Oh, Sophie," Rosie said, stretching out a hand to stroke her arm.

"Most of all, I was consumed with guilt."

"Guilt?" Rosie laughed. "What are you talking about?"

Sophie was now staring directly into Maddy's face.

"I have wrestled with this for most of my adult life. And when Rosie contacted me about this reunion, I finally decided I had to confront it."

"What is it?" Maddy asked, softly.

Sophie paused as if gathering her courage.

"I have a confession to make. That row between you and Greg Delaney. The trouble over the letter?"

"Yes?" Maddy said in a quiet voice.

"It was me."

The shock struck Maddy like a blow. Beside her, she heard Rosie gasp. She felt a jolt as the pain came surging back, the memory of the lies, the denials and most of all, the betrayal. And it had not been Lorna Hamilton after all. It had been her best friend, Sophie Kennedy!

"But how could it be you? The letter was signed L?"

"It was his name for me. He called me the Lynx."

She reached out and grasped Maddy's hand.

"Please forgive me, Maddy. I have tortured myself over this. There is not a day that has passed that it hasn't haunted me. Why do you think I left Dublin? Why do you think I broke off contact? Because I couldn't face you and I couldn't live with the guilt."

She was weeping now, the tears streaming down her cheeks.

"How did it happen?" Maddy asked, her mind numb with the shock.

"It happened when Arthur broke out drinking the second time. I was very upset, very vulnerable. And Greg used to drive me each night to the clinic to visit. You know I had always admired him. On those journeys he would talk about the difficulties you were having, the fact that you didn't like his family and you had cancelled the holiday in Marbella. One night after visiting Arthur, it happened. We began an affair. I knew from the start it was wrong but I was besotted with him. It was as if I had no free will. And then you found the letter and everything fell apart. I hated myself for what had I done. And I have hated myself ever since."

She was weeping copiously now, her chest heaving with sobs. Her hand tightened on Maddy's arm.

"Can you forgive me?"

Maddy sat in stunned silence. She felt terrible emotions warring in her breast – shock and anger and pain at what Sophie had said. It was almost impossible to forgive. Yet deep down, she knew she must. Otherwise, she too would carry the burden that Sophie was now trying to shed.

Slowly, she stood up. Slowly, she reached out and took her friend in her arms and hugged her close. She felt her own eyes fill up with tears. After all these years, Sophie was finally seeking freedom from the guilt that had tortured her. Maddy had no option but to release her.

"Of course, I forgive you."

"Really? You can do that?"

"Forever friends, remember? When we said that we didn't put any conditions on it."

The two women stared into each other's eyes as the tears rolled down their faces. Years of guilt and remorse and hurt were being washed away. Maddy felt a tug at her shoulder and Rosie's small frame squeezed in beside them. They stood in the middle of the floor, three fifty-year-old women hugging each other and weeping while, around them, fashionable London society stared in amazement but was too polite to ask what was going on.

The End

If you enjoyed *Forever Friends*, don't miss out on
The Book Club, also published by Poolbeg.

Here is a sneak preview of Chapter one . . .

THE

Book

CLUB

KATE McCABE

The Book CLUB

Chapter one

Whenever people asked Marion Hunt why she started the book club in the first place, she would always say it was because of the weather. It was the first week in January, the worst time of the year as far as she was concerned, with cold, wet, miserable days and long dark nights and nothing to look forward to till Easter which seemed so far away that she couldn't even summon the energy to think about it.

Every year she swore that she was not going to spend another January in Dublin if she could possibly help it. Come hell or high water, she was getting out. She would save up her annual leave and take herself off to somewhere nice and warm where she would spend the entire month lazing on a sandy beach, sipping ice-cold Pina Coladas and watching the handsome lifeguards playing volleyball. And she would text her friends back at home about the clear blue skies and the golden sun and drive them mad with envy while they shivered in the cold.

But each year, January came around again and Marion was still stuck in Ireland. With all the crazy spending at Christmas and her credit-card limit just a distant memory and bills arriving with every post so that she began to suspect that the postman was conducting a personal vendetta against her, she just didn't have the money to spend a whole month in the sun. She didn't even have the money for a weekend break. So each January she gritted her teeth and solemnly promised herself that the following year she would definitely manage things differently. But of course, she never did.

And that was how she came to be sitting at the window of her apartment in Smithfield in Dublin on a grey Saturday afternoon staring out at the rain instead of sipping a *cerveza* at a sidewalk café in Los Cristianos – which was what she had promised herself twelve months before. The rain had been falling like a grey sheet since early morning and one glance at the menacing sky told Marion that it was likely to continue for the remainder of the day and probably tomorrow as well.

Oh well, she thought, trying to make the best of things, at least I'm nice and cosy in here and I don't have to venture out for anything. She had done her weekly shop the evening before after returning from her job at the Department of Education where she worked as an Executive Officer in the School Buildings division. So she had all the provisions she required to feed and sustain herself even if the rain didn't stop till Monday.

Marion's apartment was her pride and joy. It was a smart two-bed in a bright new building called The Cloisters which was just a stone's throw from the river and ten minutes' walk from the centre of town. She felt so proud of her new home and the fact that she owned a piece of Dublin property, particularly since prices kept spiralling upwards as if there was no tomorrow. She had bought it the previous September after months of heart-searching and further months traipsing all over the city to view properties till she felt she had become an expert on the apartment scene and could probably write a book about it.

But once she saw the plans for The Cloisters, she knew her searching was over. The apartment had everything she was looking for. It had two large bedrooms – the main one with a smart en-suite bathroom and a smaller one which she sometimes considered turning into a study. In addition, it had a second bathroom, a large sitting-room with an adjoining kitchen and the *pièce de résistance* – a beautiful timber-decked terrace from where you could see the whole city skyline on a fine day.

This was the place for her and she just had to have it even though the asking price was a staggering €350,000. It was at the very outer limit of what she could afford. To buy it, she had to take out a hefty mortgage that gobbled up a large chunk of her salary every month and was another reason why she couldn't spend January in the Canaries. Purchasing in The Cloisters left Marion broke but at least she owned something and she kept telling herself that the repayments were chipping away at her loan – which was much better than paying rent that went straight into the pocket of some greedy landlord.

And by buying off the plans, she was able to save some money and managed to secure one of the best units in the development which pleased her no end. She also congratulated herself that she had the foresight to fix her loan at 3 per cent before the interest rates had started to go up. Some of her colleagues had advised her to go for a variable rate so that she would benefit if interest rates fell. Where would she be now if she had taken their advice? Probably in the Debtors Court, she thought, ruefully.

To help pay the mortgage she had briefly considered taking a lodger for the spare bedroom instead of converting it to a study. But she didn't think about it for long. What held her back was the thought of sharing her home with a stranger, maybe someone she might not like who would leave wine stains on the carpet or block the sink with tea leaves or horror of horrors, leave underwear drying on the radiators. Besides, she had already had one bad experience with a flatmate years before and she had never forgotten it.

So, despite the crippling mortgage, she took comfort from the thought that in ten years' time, her salary would have risen and the monthly repayments might not seem so much. And if she ever decided to sell, she was sure to make a profit. Not that she had any intention of selling. As far as Marion was concerned, she was here to stay. The Cloisters was her home. She was happy here. She often joked with friends that the only way she would ever leave was if she won the lottery when she might consider buying a mansion in

Wicklow – and the chances of that happening were about the same as the odds on Brad Pitt asking her to marry him.

Marion was twenty-nine, although she kept reassuring herself that she was a *youthful* twenty-nine with all the vigour and energy of someone five years younger. The Big Three O might be drawing closer but it held no terrors for her. Marion was a firm believer in positive attitude and in her mind she was still twenty-four with the idealism and enthusiasm of youth but tempered with the life experience of someone older. She told herself it was a good combination and she was lucky to have it.

Her family were hard-working farming folk from County Offaly so owning property was in her blood. Her father, who had a good eye for a bargain, had succeeded over the years in buying up small parcels of land and adding them to the family farm so that it now stood at a respectable 200 acres. He was fond of saying that land was one thing that God was making no more of. And he impressed on all his children that once you had the title deeds to a property in your fist no one could ever put you out on the street. Provided you kept up the mortgage repayments, Marion thought ruefully.

She had come up to Dublin ten years earlier filled with wild excitement after successfully completing the Executive Officer exams for the Civil Service. Marion was too laid-back to be an academic high-flyer so she was never destined to become a vet or a barrister or a heart surgeon. But she was bright and she always managed to study just hard enough to pass her various exams. So her family were proud of her success in securing a good well-paid Government job with a pension. Her father was particularly pleased. He said a pension would provide her with a guaranteed income when she came to retire and went about telling all the neighbours about her great achievement and the fancy job she had landed in Dublin.

For a while, Marion was proud too until the reality began to sink in. She quickly discovered that the work was routine and repetitive and she soon got bored with it. She was just a small cog in a vast administrative machine. And worst of all, she never got out of the office to meet people. As for the pension, it seemed so far away that she couldn't even contemplate it. For all she knew she could be dead by the time retirement came around – probably found suffocated under the weight of paper that descended on her head every day.

She watched with envy as some of her friends secured glamorous jobs in advertising and journalism and publishing. They seemed to spend most of their time at drinks parties and receptions and product launches meeting exciting people and attractive men. They were out and about having a gay old time while she was stuck at her desk reading letters from school principals complaining about leaking toilets and broken windows which she duly initialled and stamped before passing them on to her supervisor, Mr McDonald.

But despite the drawbacks, she never once thought of giving up her job. She knew she had found a good safe berth even if the work had become so mechanical that she could do it in her sleep and with one hand tied behind her back. The world outside the Civil Service might appear more exciting but it had its price. There were frequent casualties. Some of the companies her friends worked for eventually went bust and they were let go. Marion knew that would never happen to her. The Department of Education would never go bust. She had a job for life.

In those early days in Dublin, she shared a large flat with three other girls in Ranelagh. It was the top floor of an old Edwardian building with big bay windows that looked out onto a quiet tree-lined street. There was a large kitchen and one bathroom, which meant there was always a clamour in the morning to use the loo as people tried to get ready for work. And in the evening, somebody was always fussing over the stove in the kitchen cooking up a meal. But she loved it there.

After her sheltered life on a farm, she found the experience exhilarating. It was like living in a hippy commune. People were always coming and going and it was never dull. Her flatmates were forever bringing home friends so very quickly she got to know a wide network of people. And most weekends there was a party. People would arrive from the pub with bundles of tapes and bottles of wine and they would dance and sing and have a wild time till the old lady in the flat above banged on the ceiling with a broom to get them to quieten down.

Marion had grown up to be a very attractive young woman. She was five feet eight inches tall, slim but with a good figure. She had dark skin and ebony hair which she wore to her shoulders. But it was her eyes that most people remarked upon. They were a delicate shade of green and for some reason men seemed to find them fascinating. As a result, she was never short of boyfriends.

It was at one of these parties that she first met Alan McMillan. Later, she was often to ask herself what she ever saw in him for Alan McMillan was not her type at all. He was from Belfast and was training to be a solicitor. He was pale and slightly built and of average height. He had the type of undistinguished features that would never cause anyone to give him a second glance. But he had excellent manners and was very attentive. He seemed to fasten onto Marion. He asked her to dance and then stayed by her side for the remainder of the evening. When the party was over, he wrote down her telephone number in a little notebook he kept in his breast pocket and asked if she would like to go out with him some evening. Marion, who didn't have a regular boyfriend at the time, felt sorry for him so she agreed.

For their first date, he took her to the Savoy cinema to see Nicholas Cage in *Leaving Las Vegas* and afterwards they went to an Indian restaurant on O'Connell St where Alan treated them to a bottle of house wine to accompany their chicken korma. It was a very pleasant evening and Marion enjoyed it. At least it was better than sitting at home in the flat watching soaps on television. After the meal, they shared a taxi to her flat and Alan deposited her safely on the doorstep where he kissed her goodnight and asked if he could see her again. Marion agreed and a few days later he rang her at work and took her to see a play at the Peacock Theatre.

Before long, she was seeing quite a lot of Alan. She found him interesting company and a change from the wild young men who usually frequented the Ranelagh flat. And she enjoyed the attention he lavished on her. In those days, neither of them had very much money but Alan always managed to buy her little presents. As the weather turned warmer, they sometimes went for walks in Stephen's Green or took the train out to Dalkey and strolled over Killiney Hill. Since they were both from outside Dublin, there was a sense of adventure in discovering the delights of the city. Occasionally, instead of going to the cinema, they went to a pub and spent the evening chatting over half pints of beer which was all they could afford.

As time passed, she got to learn all about Alan. She discovered that he was an only child whose father had died when he was young leaving him and his mother in very poor circumstances. But he was a clever student and did well at school. He proceeded to study Law at Queen's University and was now in his final year of apprenticeship with a firm of solicitors in Drury St.

But perhaps his most outstanding characteristic was his obsessive personality. Once he got his teeth into something, Alan refused to let go. This was something she would regret later. But when she first met him, she found it attractive. Alan was *driven* and the thing that most obsessed him was his career. His early experiences had left their mark on him and he was determined to get on in the world.

"I'm going to be rich some day," he would boast. "Money gives you the freedom to do what you want."

"Oh, and how are you going to do that?"

"By specialising in employment law," he told her. "That's a growing area. There's a whole raft of EU legislation coming down the tracks and there aren't too many lawyers who know anything about it. I'll become an expert and make lots of money. You just wait and see."

Marion would listen attentively while he outlined his plans till suddenly he would stop and sit up straight.

"I'm boring you," he would say. "You don't want to listen to all this stuff."

But Marion would gently press his hand and urge him to continue. She found a strange fascination listening to Alan confide his dreams and ambitions. And he seemed so dogged and convincing that she believed him.

"Please go on. I find it interesting."

"Are you sure?"

"Yes. I always thought the Law was stuffy, you know, old dusty books and things like that. I didn't know it could be so fascinating."

His eyes would light up. "Oh, it's far from stuffy, Marion. It's certainly a lot more exciting than most people realise. And when I'm rich, maybe you will share it with me. That would make me very happy."

But Marion wasn't so sure. Sometimes, she would ask herself where this situation with Alan was going. She liked his company but that was all it was – company. She was forced to admit that there was something cold and calculating about him. Underneath his dull exterior she could sense a streak of ruthlessness. And he lacked romantic passion. He wasn't the kind of man she read about in novels who would sweep her off her feet and take her breath away. Their relationship was more like a friendship than a romance. Never in a million years could she imagine herself falling in love with Alan McMillan.

One by one, her original flatmates left and the Ranelagh flat became much too big and the rent too costly for just one person. Marion moved into a smaller apartment in Harold's Cross with a girl called Julie who she met through an ad in the *Evening Herald*. Julie was from Arklow and worked in a restaurant in South George's St. She wasn't exactly Marion's ideal flatmate. By now, she was beginning to outgrow her earlier bohemian phase and was starting to prize stability and order in her life. So she found Julie a bit on the wild side with her tendency to stay out all night at parties and bring strange men home in the wee small hours of the morning. But she was clean and tidy and paid her share of the household expenses on time, so Marion put up with her. It was easier than trying to find another flat.

Then came her sister's twenty-first birthday and a big party was organised to celebrate the event. Marion planned to go down to Offaly on Friday evening after work and return on Sunday night. So when Alan rang on Thursday afternoon to inquire about her plans for the weekend, she explained that she had to go home for the party and wouldn't be able to see him again till Monday. She thought he sounded disappointed that she hadn't invited him to join her but there was no way she was bringing him down to Offaly. It might give him ideas that this relationship was heading somewhere that it wasn't.

The party was held on Saturday night in the local hotel and was a mad success. Marion dressed up in her best gear and met lots of her old school friends who were dying to hear stories about her exciting life up in Dublin which she happily provided. What with all the chatting and the dancing and the flirting, it was after four when she finally fell into bed and the following day she was exhausted. The return train left at six and got into Dublin around eight-thirty. But on this particular Sunday there was an accident on the line outside Tullamore and the train was cancelled. Marion's mother heard about it on the radio after lunch and immediately flew into a panic.

"You'll have to take the bus," she said, fussing round her daughter. "Otherwise you'll be stranded here till Monday. C'mon, you'd better get moving. The bus leaves the depot at three o'clock."

Marion hated the bus. It was usually packed and the passengers were stuck in their seats like sardines without the freedom to move around that you enjoyed on a train. But this was an emergency and she had no choice. Reluctantly, she packed her bag and her father drove her to the depot, kissed her goodbye and instructed her to ring her mother as soon as she got home to say she had arrived safely.

The bus was even more cramped than usual because of the cancelled train and she had to endure three hours of misery till they finally pulled into their destination. She was so worn out by the journey that she just collapsed into the first available taxi and asked to be driven directly to her flat.

It was half past six when she arrived. As she turned the key in the lock, she thought she heard laughter coming out of Julie's room. She gave a weary sigh. She was in no mood to meet another of Julie's stray men. She just wanted to take a hot bath and settle down in front of the television with a nice glass of wine while she recovered from her bus ordeal.

But just as she put her bag down, the door of Julie's bedroom opened and a figure came out.

Marion couldn't believe her eyes.

Alan McMillan emerged, dressed only in his underpants. It was the first time she had seen him in this state and her stomach immediately threatened to disgorge her mother's Sunday lunch. His pale skin and scrawny legs made him look like a freshly plucked chicken while his bulging eyes reminded her of a rabbit caught in the headlights of a car.

For a moment, they stared at each other in shocked silence. Then, Marion quickly averted her gaze.

"Excuse me," Alan said remembering his good manners, as he hurried past her into the sitting room where she could see his shirt and trousers draped over the back of the settee.

The incident shattered her faith in Alan McMillan. He rang the following day to explain.

"Nothing happened," he began, nervously. "It's not what you think."

"What do I think?" she asked, coldly.

"That we were up to hanky-panky. All we were doing was discussing music."

"Oh?" Marion said, with such ice in her voice that she could feel the handset freeze. "And you normally discuss music in your underwear, do you?"

"Of course not. I got wine on my trousers. I was drying them, that's all."

"Why is it that I don't believe you?" she said with as much sarcasm as she could muster. "Why is it that I think you are lying through your teeth?"

"At least let me explain," he pleaded.

"No," Marion said, flatly. "I don't want to hear any more lies."

"You're emotional," he said. "I can understand that. But you'll think differently when you calm down. You should never do anything when you're angry, Marion. You might regret it."

She gasped at his bloated arrogance. Regret packing in Alan McMillan? Her real regret was that she hadn't done it sooner.

"Listen carefully, Alan. I don't want to see you ever again. I don't want you trying to contact me. You and I are finished. Goodbye."

She put the phone down as firmly as she could without smashing it to pieces. She *was* emotional, that much was true. But who wouldn't be under the circumstances? What a selfish prick Alan McMillan had turned out to be. But what really hurt her was the betrayal, the fact that someone she had trusted could behave so callously. And in *her* home! Marion's pride was hurt but in a strange way she was glad because the incident had brought matters to a head and gave her a good excuse to get rid of him.

Of course, Julie had to go. There was no possible way the two of them could share the same small living space after what had happened. She didn't argue, just packed her bags and left the following day. Marion cancelled the lease and moved out of the apartment and stayed with a colleague from work till she decided what to do next.

By now, she'd had enough of flat sharing. It was time to settle down. Her career lay in Dublin so it made sense to have a permanent home in the city. She decided to buy an apartment and began to save, setting herself a target each month and lodging the money in a deposit account with her bank. She knew the account would stand her in good stead when the time came to look for a mortgage.

But trying to save had a severe impact on her social life. She was forced to cut back on clothes, she stopped eating in restaurants and limited her outings to pubs and clubs to Friday nights. She told herself that the deprivation was worth it. In no time at all – two years at the most – she would have the money saved for a deposit and then she would get her own place. But something else was beginning to happen too. Her circle of acquaintances was starting to shrink as people settled into relationships or got married. In the end, she was left with only two or three people she could call real friends. Of these, Trish Moran was by far the closest.

She had known Trish since her schooldays. She had started off as a clerk in a bank in Dame Street and now she had risen to be a personnel officer in the Human Resources department. She was a large, chubby woman who seemed to have a permanent sunny disposition. In any situation, she could always be relied upon to see the positive side. It was Trish who had counselled her after the incident with Alan.

"The first thing to bear in mind is that this is not the end of the world."

"Are you kidding? I feel like I've just got out of jail," Marion replied.

"Good. But you realise you can't possibly take him back," Trish said, firmly. "If you do, he'll know he can get away with this sort of thing again. And then you'll really have a problem on your hands."

"I've no intention of taking him back."

"Excellent. You weren't in love with him, were you?"

"Are you mad?" Marion exploded. "I'm surprised I went out with him for so long. He's not even my type."

"Well then, nothing is lost. Just forget about him. It won't take you long to meet some other nice man. You're an attractive woman and you'll find lots of admirers. Now what are you drinking?"

On Friday nights after work, Marion and Trish would meet in a city-centre pub and have a few drinks and then go for a meal and end up in a club. But Marion was beginning to find the clubs too noisy and a lot of the men were either drunk or so high on drugs that you couldn't hold a sensible conversation with them.

And then, Trish met a young policeman from Cork called Seán and before long she was seeing him all the time. Marion contacted some of her other friends and discovered that they too had steady boyfriends. Suddenly, she woke up to the fact that all her friends had settled down and she was now more or less on her own.

But Trish was right about one thing. Marion had no trouble attracting men. It was the men who were the trouble. After dumping Alan, she went out with a handsome young administrative officer called Brendan who worked in her department. He was six foot tall, dark, thirty-one years old and played rugby for Old Belvedere. Marion had spotted him one day talking to her supervisor Mr McDonald and thought he looked quite dishy.

For their first date, he took her to a nice restaurant on the quays where they held hands and looked into each other's eyes while Brendan told her funny stories about his flatmates and his family and the people he worked with. He seemed to have a laid-back, relaxed attitude to life which made a nice change after Alan McMillan's intense obsession with his career. It was on the second date that Marion sensed something was going wrong.

This time, Brendan was morose and depressed.

"What's the matter?" she asked, gently stroking his hand and looking into his intense brown eyes which seemed like deep wells of sorrow.

"Nothing," he said with a shrug and tried to look away. "It's just, well, my girlfriend rang this afternoon. Sorry," he said, correcting himself, "I should have said my ex-girlfriend."

For the remainder of the meal, Marion had to endure a lengthy tale about some woman called Sinéad whom Brendan had been seeing for the past eighteen months and who had recently left him for another man and how his heart was broken as a result. By the time the desserts were served, she was ready to scream for help. It was obvious that Brendan was still in love with this Sinéad person. Marion made up her mind. There was no way she was going to nurse this guy through his broken romance. Life was just too short. When the bill came, she suddenly remembered an urgent phone call she was expecting, ordered a taxi and beat a hasty retreat.

Next, she took up with a young rock journalist called Phil whom she met one Friday night at a club in Temple Bar. Phil was like a breath of fresh air. He was an inveterate partygoer and seemed to know all the movers and shakers in the music business. And he got free tickets to all the big concerts. For a while, Marion's life was an exciting round of gigs and promotions and champagne-swilling sessions in Lillie's Bordello. All her colleagues envied her glamorous lifestyle till one evening she found Phil snorting a line of cocaine in the bathroom of her flat. That was it. She quickly got rid of him. She didn't see her future tied up with a man who had to face the rigours of life with the help of Colombian marching powder.

After that she had a string of relationships but none of them worked out. The men were all too weak or clingy or pompous and arrogant and immature. She longed for a sensible, handsome reliable man. Someone she could put her faith in, someone she could look up to, someone she could share her life with. But she was finding that men like that were thin on the ground in Dublin.

Meanwhile, Trish kept telling her she had to find a boyfriend.

"You're not a youngster any more," she said, "and if you leave it too late all the best men will be gone."

"Don't say it," Marion warned. "Don't tell me I'll end up on the shelf like a special offer in Tesco's."

"I didn't mention Tesco's," Trish said, looking offended. "But just bear in mind that while you're getting older, the competition is getting younger every day."

But after her recent experiences, Marion had become quite choosy and she wasn't going to throw herself away on just anyone. She knew she was attractive because people kept telling her. But she was also a romantic. The man she would settle for didn't have to be rich like Alan McMillan planned to be. And he didn't have to so breathtakingly good-looking that women would fall at his feet. But there was one vital qualification and she wasn't going to compromise on it. He had to be a man she could fall in love with.

However, all this debate about men was quickly forgotten with the purchase of the apartment and the attendant excitement of decorating it and buying furniture and choosing floor coverings and drapes and decking out the kitchen. Trish, who had a good eye for décor offered to help and together they had a dizzy time visiting department stores and warehouses and looking at settees and kitchen appliances and fabrics.

In the end, they opted for light pastel shades for the walls and Scandinavian minimalist furniture for the sitting room and some smart pictures and cosy rugs for the pine floors. When they were finished the apartment looked absolutely stunning and Marion was bursting to show it off so she gave a housewarming party and invited all the people she knew.

About sixty guests turned up and it was just like the old days when she lived in the flat in Ranelagh. People brought little presents of tea-towels and toast-racks and egg-timers and someone even gave her a fancy juicer. She served wine and canapés while her guests admired the apartment and made wowing sounds and complimented her exquisite taste and told her how much they envied her good fortune to have such a lovely home of her own like this and her not even thirty yet. It made her feel warm and grateful and smart.

When they had all finally left, she took her glass of wine and sat on her terrace in the warm night air and admired the lights of the city twinkling before her like a canopy of stars. She had been in Dublin for almost ten years. She had a good steady job and she was independent and now she had her own place. She *was* a lucky woman. She told herself she was happy.

Now she sat at her window and looked out at the rain. It fell in a steady downpour, gusting against the pane in a familiar dreary rhythm. She sadly shook her head. Come next January, she *would* go to the Canaries no matter what happened. But now, there was nothing for it but to make a nice cup of tea and finish the book she had been reading. It had been a Christmas present from Trish, a wonderful tale of love and intrigue that had Marion totally absorbed. She had about two chapters left to read and couldn't wait to get to the end.

Twenty minutes later, she put the book down and gave a contented sigh. The novel had finished beautifully with an ingenious twist that had taken her completely by surprise and left her feeling good. She would have to ring Trish at once to tell her and offer to lend her the book so that she could read it for herself.

But when she rang her number, there was no response. She was probably out somewhere with her boyfriend, Seán. Who else could she call? She was so excited that she had to talk to someone. But the next half dozen numbers she rang were either engaged or didn't answer. Marion put down the phone with a feeling of disappointment. Part of the joy of reading a good book was being able to talk about it with other people. But what did you do when there was no one available? She could hardly run out onto the street and stop the first passer-by.

Maybe Trish is right, she thought. Maybe I should make more effort to find myself a man. At least if I had a steady boyfriend, I wouldn't be sitting all on my own like this on a wet miserable Saturday afternoon with no one to talk to. And then a thought struck her. There was one sure way she could discuss books with people. She would join a book club!

She had heard about the idea on a radio chat show recently. The plan was that everyone in the club would read a selected book and then they would meet a few weeks later and discuss it. It was a brilliant concept. It would provide an opportunity to meet new friends and would help to while away these long, dreary winter nights. And she would also be doing something that she thoroughly enjoyed.

But Marion didn't have any luck. After spending another half hour on the phone, she came away with the information that the nearest book club was in Sandymount, several miles away across the river and it had a waiting list to join.

"Dammit!" she said to herself. "I'm not giving up. There's only one thing for it. I'll start my own club."

She reached for a notepad.

Now, she thought. The first thing to do is put up some notices.